"Hello," the caller said. "I'm ringing to report the imminent collapse of Western civilisation as we know it."

Lucy stifled a sigh. "Sorry," she said. "You've come through to the out-of-hours helpline, and we only deal with urgent emergencies, whereas Western civilisation has been in irreversible but gradual decline ever since the fall of Constantinople in 1453. Our regular helplines open at eight-thirty a.m. Mondays to Fridays, and one of my colleagues will be happy to assist you. Thank you ever so much for calling. Bye."

"Hold on a minute," the caller said. "It may have *started* in 1453, though personally I consider that a rather arbitrary choice, and if asked I'd probably plump for the early stages of the Counter-Reformation. Be that as it may. The point is, Western civilisation is in *imminent* danger of collapse, and I want something done about it *now*."

The
Management
Style
of the
Supreme
Beings

Tom Holt

www.orbitbooks.net

Copyright © 2017 by One Reluctant Lemming Company Ltd.
Excerpt from *Kings of the Wyld* copyright © 2017 by Nicholas Eames

Cover design by Lauren Panepinto
Cover images by Shutterstock
Cover copyright © 2017 by Hachette Book Group, Inc.

Orbit
Hachette Book Group
1290 Avenue of the Americas
New York, NY 10104
orbitbooks.net

Simultaneously published in Great Britain and in the U.S. by Orbit in 2017
First Edition: June 2017

Orbit is an imprint of Hachette Book Group.
The Orbit name and logo are trademarks of Little, Brown Book Group Limited.

The publisher is not responsible for websites (or their content) that are not owned by the publisher.

The Hachette Speakers Bureau provides a wide range of authors for speaking events. To find out more, go to www.hachettespeakersbureau.com or call (866) 376-6591.

Library of Congress Control Number: 2017937882

ISBNs: 978-0-316-27082-3 (trade paperback), 978-0-316-27081-6 (ebook)

Printed in the United States of America

LSC-C

10 9 8 7 6 5 4 3 2 1

For Ian Prometheus Yule,
The Iron Treasurer

Three strands for the French hens, under the sky,
Seven for the swimming swans, my true love gave
    to me.
Nine for the gracious ladies dancing by,
A partridge for the Red Lord, in a pear tree.
Tinsel ensnares them all, tinsel entwines them,
Tinsel confounds them all and in the ice-floes
    binds them,
In the land of Kringôl, where the reindeer fly.

1

Dad, as is tolerably well known, is omnipotent and can do anything. Some things, however, are more difficult than others, even for him; most notably, finding windows in his busy schedule for a little quality time with his dearly beloved son, with whom he is well pleased. On the rare occasions when they can fit it in, they like to go fishing together on Sinderaan, a small yellowy-red planet in the Argolis cluster. The problem, of course, is who they leave behind to mind the store.

In front of Dad the rainbow bridge sparkled with all the glory of light being ripped apart into its constituent themes. For the third time he stopped and turned back. "Don't forget," he said. "*One* rotation every twenty-four hours."

"Yes, Dad."

"Six hours of rain in Lithuania, Monday and Thursday morning."

"Yes, Dad."

"The keys to the thunderbolt cabinet are on the hook behind the bathroom door; *don't* use them unless you absolutely have to."

Kevin, the younger son of God, marginally less well

beloved and with whom his father was not always quite so well pleased, stifled a yawn and pulled the collar of his dressing gown tight around his neck, because of the cold. "*Yes*, Dad," he said. "You told me already, about a zillion times. It's cool. I can handle it."

His father winced. "If there's a problem, you've got my number."

"Yes, Dad."

"Just be careful, that's all. Think about what you're doing. And no parties."

"Goodbye, Dad."

With a shrug, Dad turned, shouldered his backpack and rods and walked slowly up the rainbow to where Jay was waiting. If he was tempted to turn back one last time, he thought better of it. Before long, they were two tiny specks against the multicoloured curve, and then they were gone. Kevin sighed, pulled a face, wriggled his toes as deep into his slippers as they'd go and wandered back to the house. A light in an upstairs window of the east wing (the house had many mansions) told him that Uncle Ghost was awake, though the chances were that he wouldn't transubstantiate into anything fit to talk to until much later, after he'd had his coffee and read the papers.

Six-thirty a.m., a ghastly time to be awake. Kevin sat down on the rocking chair on the stoop, stretched out his feet and turned on his LoganBerry. He was playing *War in Heaven 3* (he was being Dad for a change; usually he was Uncle Nick) when a sharp cough behind him broke his concentration and made him jam the tablet in his dressing-gown pocket. "Hi, Uncle Mike."

He'd been quick, but not quick enough to deceive an archangel. Uncle Mike didn't approve of *War in Heaven 3* for some reason. "Kevin. Have you got a moment?"

Irony, except he was pretty sure Uncle Mike wasn't

capable of it. "All the time in the world. Something up?"

Mike was frowning. "Cusp in the causality flow. We need a policy decision."

"What, from me?"

Mike nodded sadly. "Looks like it, doesn't it?"

"But Dad said it was all sorted out for the next three days. He said nothing was likely to come up."

"Well, it's no big deal," Uncle Mike said. "Not a *very* big deal, anyhow. You'd better come inside and sort it out."

"Dad said I wouldn't have to do any policy decisions."

"Ah well." Mike shrugged. "Mysterious ways, Kevin, mysterious ways. Come on if you're coming."

The interface console, where the individual case inputs were coordinated into the predestination stream, was a dingy shade of concrete-coloured plastic, and the lettering was starting to wear off the keyboard. Kevin had been on at Dad to upgrade to a higher-spec system for as long as he could remember; these old Kawaguchiya XP7740s belonged in a museum, he'd said over and over again, what this outfit needs is the new Axio 347D StreamLine. He punched in the laughably archaic 3 ½-inch floppy that held the startup codes and waited for the shameful green letters to appear on the antiquated black screen. Pointless explaining to Dad that he had over ten times as much computing power on his phone than this entire system. Oh no. It had been good enough for dividing the waters which were under the firmament from the waters that were above the firmament, it worked just fine and he was used to it. A fan whirred. Kevin tapped his fingers on the desktop and stifled a yawn.

A few minutes later he strolled back out onto the stoop, where Uncle Mike was refuelling his flaming sword from a butane cylinder. "Uncle Mike."

"Kevin."

"You know how it's the house rule that as long as they honestly and sincerely believe, trivial differences of doctrine aren't important?"

"Sure."

"Well." Kevin sat down, his hands folded in his lap. "There's one sect that believes the entire Trinity is female."

Uncle Mike nodded. "I've heard of them, yes."

"So, according to them, and bearing in mind that in view of their irreproachable faith their interpretation is held to be equally valid, that would make me female too, right?"

Uncle Mike frowned. "I guess so."

"You wouldn't hit a girl, would you?"

Sigh. "What've you done?"

"It's that stupid computer. I keep telling them, we're so behind the times it's unreal. It's amazing stuff like this doesn't happen every single day."

"Stuff like what?"

"I think it's the keyboard. Someone must've spilt coffee on it or something, because the springs don't work properly. I told Dad a thousand times, that system is a disaster waiting to happen."

Uncle Mike knew him too well. He frowned. "Kevin?"

"I guess it got tired of waiting."

A long sigh. Uncle Mike turned down his flaming sword to the bare flicker of the pilot light and put it carefully on the table. "What have you done?"

"It wasn't me. It's all the fault of the system."

For some reason Uncle Mike sort of smiled. "Sure," he said. "You'd better show me."

An hour later (linear time doesn't pass in Heaven, but never mind) Uncle Mike leaned back in his chair, finished his now-cold coffee in three mammoth gulps and massaged his forehead between thumb and middle finger. Kevin stepped up and peered over his shoulder. "All done?"

Uncle Mike nodded. "Kevin."

"Yes, Uncle Mike?"

"Where's that list of stuff he left for you to do while he's away?"

Kevin scrabbled in his pocket, found and uncrumpled it. "Here. Why?"

Mike took the list and tucked it away in the sleeve of his robe. "It's OK, Kevin," he said. "You leave all that to me. No need for you to bother. Just go and do whatever it is you do all day."

For a moment or so Kevin stood perfectly still. Then he said, "Uncle Mike."

"Yes, Kevin?"

"That's not fair."

Mike looked away. "Sorry, kid."

"But it's *not*. It says in the rules, doesn't it? You've got to forgive. Not just seven times but seventy times seven. I think—"

Mike sighed. "Seventy times seven is four hundred and ninety," he said. "Personally, I stopped counting back in the low thousands. It's fine," he added, and Kevin guessed he was genuinely trying to be kind. "Some people just aren't cut out for this kind of work. That doesn't make them bad people. I'm sure there's all sorts of things you'd be good at, in an infinite Universe."

On the other hand, Uncle Mike being kind made Vlad the Impaler look cissy. "Uncle Mike," Kevin said, "I know I can do this stuff. I know I can."

Mike pursed his lips. "No," he said. "Sorry."

There are times when you just can't speak. This was one of them. Kevin turned away and walked out onto the stoop, sat down and poured himself a glass of orange juice. In the near distance a new galaxy hatched like a fiery egg. He threw a pretzel at it. He missed.

The family business.

Not everybody wants to follow in their daddy's footsteps, as witness the considerable number of people called Smith who don't spend their days pounding hot iron. Traditions fade. Teenage Amish dream of working for Google, and young Clark Kent leaves the farm and heads for Metropolis. But Kevin had always believed, always assumed . . .

Unlike so many kids his age, Kevin was pretty sure he knew who he was. If he'd had blood, the family business would've been in it. That was what made him so mad, sometimes. Take the computers. Why couldn't Dad see that the whole system needed replacing? It was obvious that was why mistakes happened. True, they only seemed to happen when Kevin was at the keyboard, but that was simply because Dad and Jay had got used to the stupid, obsolete old machines and could anticipate their ridiculous quirks. That was what it came down to, basically. Which did Dad think more highly of, his own son or a beat-up old Kawaguchiya XP7740? And that was one of those questions you just don't ask, for fear of the answer.

He picked up his LoganBerry. *War in Heaven 3*—a ridiculous game because the good guys always win, inevitably, no matter what you do. A thought crossed his mind, and he grinned. He switched the LoganBerry to phone mode and tapped in a number.

It rang six hundred and sixty-six times. Then an angry voice snapped, "What?"

"Uncle Nick?"

Sigh. "Oh, hi, Kevin. Look, can it wait? I'm a bit tied up right now."

He could believe it. Uncle Nick's department was chronically overworked and understaffed. Nevertheless, he hardened his heart and said, "Uncle Nick, you know how Dad's always going on about me getting work experience in all the departments?"

Another sigh. "No, Kevin."

"Uncle Nick—"

"Forget it. Not after the last time."

Kevin scowled. He'd explained. It hadn't been his fault that Hell had frozen over. "Uncle Nick—"

"It's not up to me, kid," the voice said. "I got strict instructions from your old man. Not allowed to set foot Flipside ever again. Not exactly a grey area."

"He said that?"

"Gospel truth, son. Sorry. So, if you don't like it, you'll have to take it up with him. Gotta fly, I've got someone on the stove. Bye now."

The line went dead. Kevin scowled horribly at the screen and switched off. Fine, he thought. No problem. If Dad and Jay want me to slob around the house all day, I can do that, you bet. Who needs the stupid business anyway? It was enough to make him turn atheist. (Except he'd tried that once, and it hadn't been a conspicuous success. Dad had argued, plausibly enough, that if he didn't exist, neither did the fridge, the sofa, the TV or Kevin's bedroom. After twenty-four hours shivering in the existential void, Kevin had solemnly burned the collected works of Richard Dawkins and been allowed back into the kitchen. Never again.)

Ungrateful, he thought. Wicked, ungrateful. Right now there were countless millions of ex-humans (lawyers, politicians, investment bankers) who'd give the charred stumps of their right arms to be where he was now rather than down there in Uncle Nick's gloomy jurisdiction. But that was the point. Countless millions of other ex-humans had striven all their lives to be virtuous and good, and had thereby achieved Heaven; he'd grown up there, never been anywhere else. So, if Uncle Mike and Uncle Nick were right and he wasn't cut out for the business, if he didn't belong here, if he didn't belong in his own *home* . . .

The door opened, and Uncle Ghost wandered out onto the stoop. In one hand was a coffee cup, in the other yesterday's *Herald*. "Kevin. You seen my glasses anywhere?"

"You're wearing them."

"My other glasses."

Kevin stood up and made a show of searching. "What do you need to read the paper for, Uncle? You know everything that's going on."

"Passes the time."

Time, that old thing. There had been a time when Uncle Ghost had been the driving force of the business: its energy, its spark, its dancing breath of fire. Hard to imagine that these days. He's done his fair share, Dad would say, he's earned the right to take it a bit easier. Trouble was, Uncle Ghost didn't seem to be taking it easy at all. If anything, he was taking it very hard.

"Damn glasses," Uncle muttered, lifting a tablecloth and putting it back crooked. "Can't see a thing without 'em these days."

Was Uncle Ghost *old*? Well, he'd existed before Existence itself, but sequential linear time didn't apply to the family, in the same way that fish can't drown. The mortals say you're as old as you feel. So how do you feel when you've been everywhere and seen everything? The official answer to that was wise, compassionate and understanding.

The glasses turned out to be hiding under the cushion of the chair Kevin had just been sitting on. "It's all right," he said. "I'll straighten them out for you."

"Don't you dare." Uncle snatched them away and stuffed them down the front of his shirt. "I'll have Mike or Gabe fix them. You break everything."

"Thanks, Uncle. That's just exactly what I wanted to hear right now."

"Was it? Why?"

"Forget it."

Uncle Ghost sighed. "Why not?" he said. "These days, forgetting's what I'm best at."

More than just trace elements of truth in that assertion, which was why Uncle Ghost didn't do any actual work any more. Overdue sunrises, March winds and April showers in July ... *He's a menace*, Dad had told Jay one dark midnight as they hurriedly dragged clouds in front of a crescent moon that should have been full. Kevin hadn't been meant to hear that, of course. It was also significant that celestial mechanics had been added to Jay's chore list. It was the easiest part of the business; a child could do it, or a fool. But not a burned-out old man. And not, apparently, Kevin.

He yawned. Through the open door he could hear the mechanised voice of the answering service: *Sorry, there's no one here to hear your prayer right now, please leave your name and we'll get right back to you.* He felt ashamed. Of course he didn't begrudge Dad—or even Jay—a little time off now and again; they worked so hard, they deserved it. But there should always be someone on call to hear the prayers, it was in the Covenant. (Or was it? Offhand he couldn't remember. But if it wasn't, it should be). Nominally, Uncle Ghost was the duty Trinitarian, which was good enough for the Compliance people but cold comfort for the poor saps down there who actually believed.

Face it, bro, you just aren't cut out for this line of work. Jay had this unfortunate streak of honesty. He claimed it came with the territory, though why he couldn't sometimes be content with just being the Way and the Light, Kevin couldn't say. The truth can be unkind, and surely kindness was more in line with the essence of the mission statement than mere factual accuracy. But if he was right . . . Well, was he? So far, Kevin's record wasn't impressive, he'd be the first to admit that. But maybe that was because they'd never given him a chance, never explained to him how things should be done. *And besides*, Jay would add at this point, *we're so rushed off our feet we simply haven't got the time to show you. Quicker to do it ourselves.* Quite.

The soft buzzing noise was Uncle Ghost snoring. Kevin got up, went inside and fixed himself a coffee—just instant because when he'd tried to use the cappuccino machine something had gone wrong with it, and Dad hadn't had time to mend it. He flicked on the TV, but it was just reruns of *Touched by an Angel*. I'd pray, Kevin said to himself, but who to?

2

Here's a tricky one. How many drops of nitroglycerine, delivered by way of a standard laboratory pipette from a drop of sixteen feet, does it take to blow a three-foot-square hole in a four-thousand-year-old Egyptian basalt slab carved with bas-reliefs of Pharaoh doing obeisance to the Reinvigorated Sun, while doing as little collateral damage as possible?

The answer, Jersey devoutly hoped, was four. That was all the nitro he had left, having used the rest of the bottle getting this far, and it'd be a confounded shame to have gone to so much trouble, and done so much irreversible damage to a designated World Heritage Site, only to wind up one drop short. In the event, he was proved right. At which he was so mightily relieved that he actually smiled.

The echoes died away, gradually and with disconcerting echo effects. The acoustics in the basement of a pyramid are distinctly weird. Sound lingers, and just when you think you've heard the last of it, back it comes again, like audible stomach acid. Creepy like you wouldn't believe, not to mention the risk of somebody outside hearing. That would be very bad. Naughty echo.

His timetable allowed three minutes for the dust to

settle. Over-optimistic. He couldn't really see worth a damn and had his handkerchief tied over his nose as he dropped his rope ladder through the newly blasted hole in the floor, checked one last time that it was securely anchored and slowly began to climb down into the darkness.

It had been a long day. To get this far, quite apart from the discomforts associated with setting off multiple explosions in a very confined space, he'd had to put up with a tiresome sequence of booby traps—walls that shifted and slabs that fell away when you trod on them, flights of poisoned arrows, razor-sharp pendulums and all manner of similar nonsense; how come, if ancient engineers could devise stuff like that, nobody had managed to come up with a functional flush toilet until 1778?—and his reserves of patience and energy were getting dangerously low. At this point he should be trembling with feverish anticipation, not fatigue. Somewhere in the gloom below him, if he'd got it right, was the secret he'd been searching for all his adult life, the greatest discovery in human history, the key to the last and greatest mystery of all. He should be feeling *something*, apart from a splitting headache and a dull pain in his chest which he unrealistically hoped wasn't a cracked rib.

After what felt like a lifetime his feet touched down on something level and solid. Taking one hand nervously off the rope ladder, he fished out his flashlight and flicked it on. Floor. Thank God for that. He shone the beam up. The hole in the roof was a very, very long way above him, and he was glad he'd taken the trouble to secure the ladder with four molybdenum steel crampons hammered into the living rock (twenty-nine dollars and ninety-nine cents from eBay; he was on a budget, but the Chinese make good stuff these days).

Well, he was here now; might as well get on with it. He shone the torch around the walls. An Egyptologist, or anyone whose aesthetic sense hadn't been blunted down to nothing by a really miserable day blowing holes in walls and dodging sudden death, would've been stunned by the beauty of the frescoes, their colours as fresh and vibrant as the day they'd been painted, two thousand years before a bunch of shepherds gazed across an Italian hillside and one of them said, "I know, let's call it Rome." He yawned and muffled a sneeze. He knew what he was looking for, and it had to be here somewhere. Now then. If I was the most carefully hidden secret in the Universe, where would I be?

"Dr. Thorpe."

He spun round so fast he nearly stumbled, just in time to see his rope ladder drop to the floor in a heap at his feet. He swung the flashlight up and picked out a face peering down at him through the hole in the roof. The face had a big moustache and was grinning.

"Well done, Dr. Thorpe. We tried to warn you, but you just kept going."

"I might have guessed," Jersey said bitterly. "You're one of them. You've been on their side all along."

The man with the moustache grinned at him. "Of course," he said. "You know me as Yusuf, a humble porter, but know that I am Constantine, two hundred and seventh Grand Master of the Guardians of the Secret. For a hundred and thirty-six generations my forefathers have striven to guard that which must never be revealed. Console yourself with the thought that nobody has ever come this close before, Dr. Thorpe. Be proud of it. Revel in that satisfaction until your dying day, which," he added, "by my calculations will be Thursday. Or early Saturday morning if you remembered to bring sandwiches.

Goodbye, Dr. Thorpe. I'd just like to say that I've enjoyed our little game of chess."

"Thank you."

"But I won't because my order values the truth above all things. Farewell."

Jersey stooped for something to throw. His hand closed around some small, heavy thing, but by the time he'd straightened up, the face had gone. He glanced at the object in his hand, recognised it as a priceless Eleventh Dynasty ushabti figurine, and threw it at the wall. "Constantine," he roared, "your feet smell and your moustache looks ridiculous." Echoes, then silence. Buggeration, he said to himself.

Still, *if* he was right about the secret, it wouldn't really matter terribly much. Everything now depended on how long the batteries in his flashlight lasted. He set about examining the walls inch by inch, his practised eye effortlessly translating the columns of hieroglyphs at sight. All sorts of guff about the imperishable glory of His late Majesty, and a load of gloomy though probably accurate predictions about what would happen to any unauthorised person who reached this spot; all well and good, but not what he was looking for. Boast, threat, boast, boast, threat, boast . . . Hello, what's this?

Suddenly the weariness and the ennui evaporated like spit on a griddle, and his heart started to pound. His hand shook as he fumbled for his notebook and pencil. Numbers, a string of hieroglyphic numerals. He leaned forward. The glow from his torch was yellowing as the batteries faded. Zero. Dear God, the first number was a *zero*.

His hand was shaking so much, he broke his pencil. It took an agonising forty seconds to sharpen it. Zero. Followed by an eight. Then zero, zero.

He could hardly breathe. An 0800 number. Could it really be true?

He wrote down the remaining six digits like a man in a dream. By the time he'd finished, the torchlight was the dying glimmer of a faint amber sunset. He squinted at the numbers scrawled on the page, then slowly drew out his cellphone and keyed them in.

The dialling tone. One ring. Two.

Hello. All our lines are busy right now. Your call is being held in a queue until an operator is available. Your call is important to us. Please hold.

He could hear music. It might have been a chorus of angels inside his head, but it was probably the phone playing Vivaldi. It didn't matter. He was through.

Please hold, the voice repeated. Like a man with his fingertips hooked over the threshold of Heaven, he held.

3

When Kevin spoke to him on the phone, he'd assumed Uncle Nick was in his office. In fact, thanks to the miracle of cellular telephony, Uncle Nick, or Mr. Lucifer to his many subordinates, had taken the call on the thirteenth hole at Velvet Lawns, where he now spent a large proportion of his time. In his absence, the department was mostly run by Bernie Lachuk, his deputy assistant private secretary.

Bernie—he hated Bernard, with the stress on the second syllable—was a civilian, a fact he was painfully aware of and rarely allowed to forget. He'd joined Flipside as part of a major rationalisation and downsizing exercise about thirty years ago (Bernie was still only twenty-six; we don't need no steenkin' sequential linear time), when a considerable number of the straightforward administrative functions had been outsourced to private contractors. That hadn't worked out for a number of reasons, but Bernie and quite a few other civilians had stayed in post nevertheless. A lot of the older team members were still uncomfortable about working alongside mortals, but most of the logistical difficulties—toilets, temperature controls, doors, floors, etc.—had long since been ironed out, and even the diehards couldn't deny that the Squishies (you weren't supposed to call them that, but everybody did, including the mortals themselves) got the work done in half the time and at a fraction of the cost. As for the Squishies, by and large they found the working environment congenial, the work itself challenging but rewarding, and the pay a whisker on the lowish side of acceptable. Bernie, for example, had been a trainee supermarket manager before he came to work Flipside. *It's like I'd died and gone to Heaven*, he told his mother at the end of his first week. *Or something like that*, he added quickly.

Maybe he wasn't quite so enthusiastic now. Mr. Lucifer, he suspected, tended to take advantage of him, and since he'd advanced as far up the hierarchy as a Squishy could get, the incentive to go the extra mile to accommodate his boss wasn't quite as strong as it had been. Take this morning, for instance. *Just mind the store for me*, Mr. L. had said to him as he swept up his golf bag and stuck his brightly coloured cap on his head, *I've got to go and shmooze a supplier. See you later, bye.* Bernie wasn't so sure about that. Mr. L. spent a lot of time shmoozing suppliers at the links or in restaurants and nightclubs, but the prices they paid for everyday consumables never seemed to go down; the opposite, in fact, and ten minutes research on the Net convinced Bernie that they could get an awful lot of the stuff considerably cheaper elsewhere, and without the need for a single golf ball to be inconvenienced or a single margarita consumed. He'd mentioned that, of course. Mr. L. had smiled at him and told him he didn't understand How Things Worked. Fair enough. It was Mr. L.'s train set, after all.

Another concept Mr. L. seemed to have trouble with, probably because of the sequential linear time thing, was normal working hours and overtime. Minding the store, for example, seemed to Bernie to constitute days, weeks, sometimes months of frantic activity (but when you're rushed off your feet you don't notice the passage of time particularly, so that was all right), for which he received no additional payment and which didn't leave him much scope for a personal life. He understood, of course. He was mortal, Mr. L. wasn't. Naturally the boss had trouble seeing things from his perspective, just as a bird doesn't find it easy to understand a fish. And someone had to do keep the place ticking over, and yes, he did want to keep this job, so . . .

Quite. And yet.

One of the phones—the green one, which always meant trouble—rang, and he grabbed it without looking up from the figures on his screen. "Lachuk."

"This is Malephar." Oh dear. "Number Six furnace is down again. Get me Maintenance."

Malephar was a Duke of Hell, had been ever since the Fall. He didn't like Squishies very much. He was also terrible at his job, but it wasn't Bernie's place to criticise. "I'll get on to it straight away, Mr. Malephar, but they told me this morning they're running just a bit behind on non-essentials, so it might not be today. Sorry for any—"

"Don't give me that. I want them here, now. Got that?"

Or there'd be Hell to pay (acting senior payroll clerk, B. Lachuk). "Yes, Mr. Malephar, I'll see what I can do. Thank you for—"

The line went dead. He put the phone down, counted to ten under his breath and picked it up again. "Hello, this is Bernie Lachuk, front office. Could I possibly speak to—?"

"Wait."

You could never entirely forget where you were and who you were dealing with: a certain something in the way they spoke to you. "Sure," Bernie said. "I'll hold."

A long, long time later a voice said, "Now what?"

"I've just had a call from Duke Malephar. Apparently Number Six is playing up again. He wonders if you could possibly see your way to—"

"Impossible." He recognised the voice. Awkwardness lay ahead, because although Malephar was Head of Operations, which theoretically took precedence over Maintenance, Balam, the Clerk of the Works, was a King and outranked Malephar by two clear pay grades. In real terms, of course, Bernie was acting boss of them all and they had to do what he told them to; the skill, of course, lay in the telling. "I've got requisitions backed up to infinity and half my demons are off sick. Tell the old goat to fix it himself."

Strictly speaking, there was only one old goat in the Department, and he was off playing golf. "I can certainly pass your message along," Bernie said, "but you might care to consider—"

"What?"

"Well, I was just thinking," Bernie said meekly. "Naturally, if you've got other, more pressing jobs on the list, then that's absolutely fine. But it occurs to me, if the furnace is offline for very long, it'll cool down and the lining will crack, and obviously that wouldn't be *your* fault, but you know how unreasonable some people can be, naming no names, so maybe if you could see your way to—oh, I don't know . . ." He called up the maintenance duty rosters on his screen, took in all the relevant information at a single practised glance and did the mental juggle. "Hey, here's a thought. How'd it be if you reassigned Blue Team from repainting the lines on the tennis courts to plumbing that leak in the brimstone vats, which would free up Purple Team to handle the low gas pressure problem, which means you could have Red Team go take a look at

Furnace Six? Just a suggestion," he added quickly. "You know the maintenance business a heck of a lot better than I do, but—"

"Just a moment. Don't talk so damn fast. All right, Green Team to the brimstone vats."

"Um, Blue."

"Say what?"

"Blue Team to the vats," Bernie said patiently. "Purple on the gas, leaving Red free to deal with Furnace Six. Green, I'm sure I don't need to remind you, is currently mucking out the perjurors on Level Five, so maybe it wouldn't be the best possible idea to—"

"God, no. All right," the King growled, "we'll do it your way. Just tell that jackass he owes me, all right?"

"I'll pass the message on," Bernie lied. "Thank you, Mr. Balam. Have a nice day, now."

He replaced the phone, slumped back in his chair and took half a dozen deep breaths. Another crisis averted. Well, that was what he was there for, and they weren't such bad fellows really, once you got to know them. But wouldn't it be nice if, just once, he could get all the section heads singing from the same hymn sheet? Or something.

This time it was the red phone. He swapped back to the screen he'd been working on earlier and picked it up. "Lachuk."

"Hi, kid. Everything under control?"

"Yes, Mr. Lucifer. No problems at all."

"That's the boy. Sorry, looks like I won't be through here as early as I'd hoped. The supplier wants to go out to dinner after the game, maybe take in a show later. You can cope, can't you?"

"I'll do my best, Mr. Lucifer."

"Great stuff. Oh, and I might be in a tad late in the

morning. Got a few errands to run on my way to the office."

"No worries, Mr. Lucifer. Just leave everything to me."

"Good boy. Bye now."

His observations over the past thirty years had led him to conclude that they didn't do irony. Sarcasm, yes, they were very good at that, but the milder, more subtle isotope seemed to go right over their heads like a flock of migrating geese. Probably just as well. He sighed. In theory there was a night shift and a night duty manager he could hand over to at midnight, but the night duty manager was Prince Sitri, who had better things to do of an evening than sit around in an office taking flak from a bunch of bureaucrats, and since he was Mr. L.'s nephew, there wasn't an awful lot that could be done about it. He pressed the intercom. "Jenny? Get me catering."

He quite liked Jenny. If you didn't know better, you could take her for a Squishy. She wasn't, in fact; she was something Prince Sitri had conjured up about seven hundred years ago to tempt a particularly stern hermit who lived on top of a stone pillar in the desert. Her function fulfilled, the Prince had neglected to unconjure her, and she'd drifted about the place looking lost ever since, until Bernie had suggested she might like to try her hand at running the switchboard. It turned out she was good at that, not to mention pathetically grateful to have something to do. "Catering. Eligos speaking."

That was all right. Eligos was one of the good guys, figuratively speaking, a Duke of Hell who didn't mind rolling up his sleeves and getting his claws dirty. "Hi, this is Bernie Lachuk, front office. Do you suppose you could send a couple of cheese rolls and a flask of coffee up here some time?"

"Sure." The voice chuckled. "Let me guess. Working late again."

"Someone's got to do it, Mr. Eligos. Thank you ever so much."

"No bother. You want mayo on that?"

Catering's mayo had more calories in it per cubic centimetre than concentrated honey. Not for nothing was Eligos subtitled the Tempter. "Just straight, thanks."

"Cheesecake? Profiteroles? I happened to go through the kitchen just now, and Mario was whipping up a really great-looking *zuppa inglese.*"

"Just the rolls, please. But thank you for offering."

Gluttony, according to the map on his office wall, was the third ring out from the hub on Level Two. Never forget who you're working with and what they are, even the nice ones.

Back to the quarterly cost efficiency reports. They made depressing reading. In spite of the pretty unambiguous directive he'd sent out six months ago, section heads were still exceeding the per-capita torment delivery targets by a margin of 6 per cent, with the result that, on average, it was costing a completely unacceptable one dollar seventy-nine cents per day to keep a Class D sinner in unbearable agony. The report he'd commissioned from a leading firm of efficiency experts clearly showed that an equivalent level of discomfort and despair could be sustainably provided for one dollar and seven cents, simply by shopping around for basic everyday supplies and utilising less highly qualified agency workers to supplement trained professionals where appropriate. The section heads took no notice. It made no sense, but they carried on doing it the old-fashioned way.

Up to a point, he could see where they were coming from. This is how we've always done it, they said, it's how it was in the beginning, is now and ever shall be, and we don't need some jumped-up Squishy—

Indeed. And the more he pushed, the more they pushed back. He knew that if he used all the strength of the front office, to which as Mr. L.'s authorised deputy he was fully entitled, he could run over them like a steamroller—which would, of course, be the worst possible thing he could do, and they knew it. Politics, always politics. Well, naturally. Remember where you are.

His screen flickered; the columns of numbers faded, and a message appeared in letters so fiery-bright they made him wince: *And I saw a new Heaven and a new Earth, for the first Heaven and the first Earth were passed away, and there was no more sea. And all at sensible prices. Coming soon!!!*

The message vanished as suddenly as it had come, and the efficiency figures stared back at him from the screen as though they'd never been away.

Huh?

Well, what else could you expect from clapped-out old Kawaguchiya XP7740 running Burning Bush 3.1 and DOSpel? He'd said it himself, in a strongly worded memo that Mr. L. assured him he'd glanced at: their system was the answer to a hacker's prayer, and sooner or later the pranksters would find a way in and make hay. He sighed. It really was a shame that nobody ever listened to him, because a lot of what he said actually did make sense, even if he was just a mortal who'd only been there five minutes and couldn't possibly understand the underlying ethos of the organisation. Still, he told himself, I only work here; it's not as though I *belong*. Heck, no. Perish the thought.

A new Heaven and a new Earth. A very special kind of word, *new*, like *change*. Inherent human optimism makes you instinctively assume something *new*—a *change*—must be better, in spite of a hundred thousand years of race memory telling you it usually isn't. Except that the vast majority of the personnel viewing these screens weren't human, and therefore had no such assumptions. Evidence, if any was needed, that the originators of the message were human mortals, or at the very least trying to pass as such. Fooling nobody. Of course, it was entirely possible that the attack was the work of a disgruntled Squishy—plenty of those, unfortunately—equally plausible that it was down to a resentful native Flipsider who wanted to make it look like the work of a disgruntled Squishy. Plenty of them too. Or it could be precisely what it appeared to be, an outside job. Or an inside job designed to look like an outside job, to demonstrate the manifest shortcomings of the IT system. Or—

The red phone rang.

"Lachuk. Yes, Your Grace, I saw it. No, we haven't traced it quite yet, we're working on it, should have something for you any moment now. As soon as I've got hard data I'll get straight back to you. Yes. Yes, I know. Though you might just care to consider that if we upgraded the hardware like the Resources Committee recommended back in 1476 . . . Yes, right away, I'll see to it personally. Yes, thank you, Your Grace, goodbye now. Yes, and you. Thank you."

Marvellous. Now he had the Archangel on his back. Wearily, he dialled a number. "Security? This is Bernie Lachuk. I— Yes, it's about that. No, I understand. No, I don't expect miracles. Just please do your best; I'm getting a certain amount of pressure from Topside. Yes, I told them, but you know what they're like, so if you could possibly— Yes, thank you. Have a good one, bye."

He put the phone down, closed his eyes, counted to ten and opened them again. Yes, absolutely, but do you really want to go back to working for Walmart? No, thought not. In that case get on with it and do your best.

And at sensible prices? Hm.

Security got back to him about four hours later. Yes, they could absolutely confirm that there had been an unauthorised message. They could also categorically assure him that it had come from either inside or outside the organisation, possibly from one of their own workstations Flipside, or from one of the Topside departments, or the mortal world, or it might be of extradimensional origin. That it might have been malicious in intent was quite definitely one of the hypotheses they were exploring with exceptional vigour, and they firmly anticipated making more enquiries in the short to medium term. They were being careful to rule nothing out at this stage, though of course it would be jumping the gun to make any premature assertions until all the relevant facts were available. They had good reason to suspect that the person who'd done it was very likely the perpetrator, though that wasn't to say that they'd dismissed the possibility of an accident or a freak random data discharge that just happened to look like a message. Yes, they stood four square behind everything they'd just told him, but maybe it'd be better if he didn't quote them. Just say, *an informed source moderately close to the Security Department* . . .

"Thanks," he said. "You've been a lot of help." The irony thing again.

No sooner had he put down the phone than Jenny told him she had Mr. Lucifer holding.

"This is awful," said Mr. L., raising his voice over background noises Bernie couldn't quite identify. "It's a disgrace. How could you let something like this happen?"

Definitely the clink of glasses, buzz of voices, soft background music, but something else too, a sort of whirring. "Sorry, Mr. Lucifer. I've got Security on it, they say—"

"Them? They're useless, you can't leave something like this to them, we'll be the laughing stock of the organisation. I don't know. I turn my back for five minutes and everything goes to Us in a handcart."

"Um, I'm sure the IT team will be able to—"

"Forget about the IT team," Mr. L. thundered, "this needs *action*. You've got to get on to it personally, right away. You got that? You know my watchword. If a thing's worth doing, you've got to do it yourself."

"Absolutely, Mr. Lucifer, I'll make sure I supervise every single thing myself. It's just that I'm not sure I've got the time—"

"Then make the time, for crying out loud. And you can forget about *supervising*. Get off your backside and deal with it yourself, instead of lounging around all day. We pay you enough, for crying out loud."

"Certainly, Mr. Lucifer, I hear what you say. Talking of which," he added, "just out of curiosity, are you in a sushi bar?"

"What?"

"A sushi bar. Only that swishing noise I can hear, is that the little belt thing that moves the dishes round?"

"Just deal with it, Bernie. When I get back, I'll want a full report."

"Of course, Mr. Lucifer. Thank you. Bye now."

It's the job, Bernie told himself; it's just part of the job. Duties include running the entire Flipside operation practically single-handed (the other hand being tied firmly behind his back), liaising with inefficient section chiefs afflicted with inverse brain/ego ratios, running interference for a boss who's never here and getting unfairly yelled at. It's not always a pleasant job—neither is sewer maintenance or sweeping up after the night shift at the slaughterhouse—but this one pays better and you get to sit down most of the time. As long as you *know* it's part of the job, you don't mind, you don't take it personally.

Do you?

Well?

Fortunately the phone rang again before he could go there. Like three quarters of his daily calls, it was somebody asking him why something hadn't been done yet; the answer, needless to say, being that people kept ringing him for progress reports, severely reducing the time available for making progress. He didn't say that. He said he'd look into it and get right back.

He'd taken the call with his eyes shut. It was a habit he'd got into, and it helped, a bit. When he opened them again, there was Jenny. He liked Jenny.

"If it's Moloch chasing the stationery requisitions," he said, "tell him he can't have so much as a paper clip until he fills in his green forms. Tactfully," he added.

Jenny shook her head, causing her long, straight hair to move in a ripple effect for which there was doubtless a perfectly mundane mathematical explanation. "I just wanted to tell you I'm off now."

"Goodness, is that the time already?" Bernie glanced at his watch. Force of habit. Flipside, the only watches that functioned at all came from the workshops of S. Dali & Sons. "OK, route the main switchboard through to here when you go."

"Sure."

She hadn't moved. He looked up at her. Something seemed to be expected of him, but he didn't know what it was. Small talk? He tried to remember the kind of things people said in normal offices, in real time. "Well, have a good evening. Anything planned?"

"No."

"Ah well. A nice relaxing evening in with your feet up. Sounds great."

"Is that what you do?"

He frowned. She had the knack of asking questions like that. "Sometimes," he said. "Not that often, in this job."

"Is it what normal people do?"

Would it have killed her to ask those two questions the other way round? "Yes. Definitely."

"Ah. So you're not normal."

He smiled. He found it helped. "Let's rewind and rephrase, shall we? Is that what most people do? Yes, it is. Is that what you do? Yes, but not as often as I'd like. All right?"

She nodded. "How do you do a nice relaxing evening with your feet up? Is it difficult?"

"Um, no. Not terribly. Most people seem to manage."

"Normal people." She had that blank look. "Is there a book about it?"

His fault. Whenever she'd quizzed him about life skills before, he'd short-circuited the enquiry by referring her to a book or Wikipedia. But it's so embarrassing, being asked by a grown woman how you brush your teeth. "I don't know. Probably."

"Could you show me?"

A small voice inside his head told him that there was nothing he'd like more. He ignored it, though with effort. Prince Sitri did good work, when he could be induced to do anything at all. "Maybe another time."

"All right. When?"

Her personnel file classified her as a succubus, Third Class. He'd googled it. A perfect illustration of the dangers of enquiring too deeply into the past lives of one's co-workers. He tried very hard indeed not to think about it every time he saw her or spoke to her on the intercom.

Fortunately he knew exactly what to say. "Leave it with me and I'll get back to you, OK?"

Trouble was, she'd heard him say that a lot. "Tomorrow?"

"Tell you what. Why don't you go to the movies?"

She shook her head. "I tried that. I didn't like it very much."

"Ah. What did you see?"

"*The Exorcist.*"

"Mphm. You really ought to give it another go. Try a nice Disney film. You'd like that."

"All right. Will you come with me?"

Programming, said a voice in his head, a different one this time; it's just programming. It's what she was built for, the poor, victimised creature, and you happen to be the only human mortal male on the block. "I don't like Disney films."

"But you think I will?"

Prince Sitri didn't build dumb blondes for the same reason Raphael didn't paint matchstick men. "Bowling? Have you ever tried that?"

"No. Is it something you do?"

"I don't do anything, I don't have the time. Excuse me," he added gratefully as the purple phone rang. It was Duke Malephar, bitching about Furnace Six again, and Bernie was really glad to hear his voice.

4

"Hello," the caller said. "I'm ringing to report the imminent collapse of Western civilisation as we know it."

Lucy stifled a sigh. "Sorry," she said. "You've come through to the out-of-hours helpline, and we only deal with urgent emergencies, whereas Western civilisation has been in irreversible but gradual decline ever since the fall of Constantinople in 1453. Our regular helplines open at eight-thirty a.m. Mondays to Fridays, and one of my colleagues will be happy to assist you. Thank you ever so much for calling. Bye."

"Hold on a minute," the caller said. "It may have *started* in 1453, though personally I consider that a rather arbitrary choice, and if asked I'd probably plump for the early stages of the Counter-Reformation. Be that as it may. The point is, Western civilisation is in *imminent* danger of collapse, and I want something done about it *now*."

Lucy breathed out through her nose. "Do you think it'll possibly last till the morning?"

"Say what?"

"Because if it can struggle on till half-past eight, which is—" she glanced at the clock on the wall "—three and a bit hours from now, I'm very sorry but I really can't help you."

Short pause. "Dunno. It'll be touch and go."

"What I can do is," Lucy said, "I can leave a note for the duty manager to call you back as soon as the lines open and a colleague is available. Will that do?"

"It'll have to, I guess."

Lucy reached for a yellow sticky and scribbled a few words. "All done," she said. "Have nice day now. Bye."

She pressed the sticky into the top left-hand corner of her screen, then logged the call on her worksheet; *West civ AWKI collapsing, no action; time taken 32 seconds.* A pity, really, because it was high time someone did something about Western civilisation, and it was no use leaving anything to the day shift, they were useless. Still, rules are rules.

Buzz buzz. "Hello, helpline." She sat up a bit straighter in her chair. "Lucy speaking. Can I help you?"

A slight delay. Then a voice said, "Is this the helpline?"

Oh for crying out loud. "Yes," she said. "You're through to Lucy. What can I do for you?"

"*The* helpline?"

"Yes. By the way, I'm Lucy. What do you want?"

"Oh my *God*," said the voice. "This is amazing. Do you realise, I've spent my entire adult life—and you really *exist*? You're not a myth?"

"Could I have your user authorisation code, please?"

"Yes, yes, I've got that. Hold on." She heard vague scrabbling noises. "I know I've got it because in order to get it I had to decode a fiendishly arcane riddle encrypted into the penultimate lines of the even-numbered sonnets of Shakespeare. Just a tick. It's 773 4790."

"I'm sorry," Lucy said, "that's not a valid—"

"No, hold on. My mistake, that's my mother's cellphone. Here it is: 4 946 8331."

Lucy raised an eyebrow. A very old authorisation code, but still valid. "And your name, please."

"What? Oh, right. I'm Jersey Thorpe."

"Sorry, we have nobody registered with that name."

"Try Dr. N. Jersey Thorpe."

"Ah yes, got you. I'm sorry," Lucy said, "but the authorisation code you just gave me is registered to King Solomon. Unless you have— Hello?"

The line had gone horribly crackly.

"Hello? You still there?"

"Yes," Lucy said.

"Thank God for that. Look, my battery's almost flat, I'm nearly out of credit and the signal isn't exactly wonderful, so could we—?"

"I'm sorry," Lucy said. "But I need evidence that you're authorised to use that authorisation code. Otherwise—"

"No, wait!" Definite panic in the voice. "I can do that. It tells you how in the seventy-third chapter of the Midianite Book of the Dead." Pause. "Except, I don't happen to have a copy with me. Look, you couldn't be really, really nice and just take my word for it, could you?"

"Unfortunately not," Lucy said. "However," she added, googling quickly as the tug on her heartstrings became too much to bear, "if I were to tell you that the first line of the seventy-third chapter is 'Behold, I am Solomon, king of kings, and my number is ninety-nine times nine—'"

"Eight hundred and ninety-three."

"You mean one."

"You what? Oh, right. Eight hundred and ninety-one."

"Code identified," Lucy said smoothly. "How can I help you?"

She knew a sigh of relief when she heard one. "Oh boy," said the voice, "where do I start? I mean, my whole *life*—"

"Sorry to interrupt, but this is the emergency helpline. Routine enquiries—"

"I'm trapped in the basement of a pyramid with no way out, no food or water and enough air for forty-eight hours."

"One moment, please." Lucy called up the GPS screen. "Would that be the pyramid of Uten-mep-re, Valley of the Kings, Egypt?"

"That's the one, yes."

"Well," Lucy said, "I'm sure you appreciate that I can't do teleportation or magic or anything like that, because this is just the out-of-hours helpline. I could call in one of our engineers, but by the sound of it you'd be long dead before he reached you."

"Ah."

"That said, I can point out that approximately two point three three seven metres left of where you're standing, there's a hidden trapdoor that leads to an access tunnel that'll have you out of there in about four minutes. It comes out just behind the kebabs-and-postcards stand twenty-one degrees three minutes west of the main entrance to the pyramid. Would that help, do you think?"

"Brilliant. Amazing. You're an angel."

"No," Lucy replied, "I'm the out-of-hours helpline. If you'd like to speak to an angel, I can take your name and number and ask one of my colleagues in Human Affairs to get back to you."

Pause—about the time it takes for a man to close a mouth that's suddenly dropped open. "Dear God," he said. "You really are the helpline. *The* helpline. That's just so—"

A caller-waiting light was flashing. "I'm sorry, but unless you have another urgent enquiry, I have to hang up now. Thank you for calling and have a nice day."

Dear God, he'd said. *Angel*. Lucy grinned and shook her head. Good guesses, she thought, but no. I only work here.

5

"Jay," said Dad, "there's something I need to talk to you about."

It had been a good day. The fish had been biting, and the suns (four of them; it was a Tuesday; Sinteraan is complicated) were just beginning to set. "Sure, Dad," Jay replied, not looking up from the fly he was tying. "What's on your mind?"

The smallest fish on Sinteraan are ninety feet long and weigh a quarter of a ton. Anything that size a conscientious angler would of course throw back. "It's about the business," Dad said.

"Come on, Dad, you know the rules. No talking shop when we're fishing."

Dad gazed for a moment at his float, bobbing gently in a pool of superheated helium. There are plenty of fish on Sinteraan, but no water. Overhead a giant bird spiralled slowly, its circles winding up a clockwork sun. "I got an offer," he said.

Jay put the half-finished fly carefully down where he wouldn't lose it, then turned round. "Oh," he said.

"From the Venturi people."

"I see."

The relationship between Dad and Jay is both simple and complex. They're father and son but also equal aspects of the One; it's therefore logically impossible for them to disagree. But the way Jay turned his head and looked out over the helium marshes spoke volumes. "You hate the idea," Dad said.

"I didn't say that."

Dad grinned. "Can't say I'm mad keen on it myself," he said. "But what the heck, it's an offer. We haven't exactly been inundated."

Jay shrugged. "Told you it wouldn't be easy finding a buyer. Not as a going concern."

There was a warning note in there somewhere, albeit buried eyebrow-deep in due respect. But Dad had promised, when he first mooted the suggestion, that they'd sell it as a going concern or not at all. No way were the asset-strippers going to get their nasty paws on the Firmament they'd spent seven long days building with their own hands. "If you don't want to sell, there's an end of it," Dad said. "It's your business as much as mine. I just thought . . ." He pulled a small, sad face. "Forget it. Forget I ever mentioned it."

Which was, of course, impossible. Jay sighed. "What's the deal?"

Dad mentioned a number. It couldn't possibly exist in human mathematics. They'd have to invent six new symbols and fell every tree that's ever grown on Earth just to write it down. Jay raised an eyebrow. "Cash?"

Dad shook his head. "Half in cash, the other half in stocks and bonds. But I checked them out. They're reputable people."

The float twitched, and Dad grabbed his rod and started to work the reel. Sinderaan fish exist in five dimensions; unless you play them just right, they can easily slip into the past and refuse to take the bait, or zoom forward into a future where your line snags on a submerged rock. For three minutes, local time, all their concentration was fixed on the task in hand. Then, with a deft flick of his wrist, Dad jerked a sparkling silver shape out of the helium froth and into the keepnet. "Way to go," Jay shouted, and Dad grinned. Jay loved to fish, always had.

The fish was a metempsychotic grayling, three hundred and seventy feet long, with iridescent red and purple scales. Over the centuries the species has produced seventeen of Sinteraan's greatest physicists and nine of its finest playwrights. They weighed it and threw it back. "So," Jay said, "what do you think?"

"What?"

"About the deal."

"Oh that." Dad frowned. "I don't know. Everybody seems to think the Venturi boys are a safe pair of hands."

Jay baited the hook, and Dad cast. The cunning fly blazed through the air like a shooting star and glowed back up at them through the banks of congealed vapour. "I guess it's as good an offer as any," Jay said. "Question is, do we really want to sell?

Dad took off his hat and looked at it. It was his special fishing hat: baggy, weatherbeaten, torn and frayed in places, utterly irreplaceable. It went without saying, Dad could have a better hat; he could have any hat he wanted. But this hat was his fishing hat, and it had been part of their joint lives for as long as Jay could remember, which was, of course, for ever. "That's the question, all right," Dad said. "Well? Do we, or not?"

Jay stood up. He was, needless to say, incapable of a violent or ungraceful gesture or movement of any sort. But. "Let's try a bit further downstream," he said. "I think the smaltfish might be biting."

They were. Sinteraan smaltfish had split the atom and proved the existence of the Higgs boson when Earth was still entirely inhabited by plankton, but they still hadn't figured out that bits of sparkly feather suddenly appearing out of nowhere right in front of their noses were very bad news indeed. "About selling," Dad said. "I guess I can take that as a no."

Jay sat perfectly still. "I want what's best for you, Dad," he said. "If you want to sell, we sell. That's all there is to it." He closed his eyes for a moment. "It's just, the Venturi boys, for crying out loud. You know what they'll do. The moment our backs are turned, they'll fire the staff, sell off the freeholds—"

Dad shook his head. "Absolutely not. We'll have a contract. Anything like that, *streng verboten*."

"Sure," Jay said. "Dad, the Venturis, they've got lawyers—"

"So have we got lawyers," Dad replied with a smile. "At any rate, your uncle Nick's got lawyers, any amount of 'em. Had to build a whole new wing out back of the perjurers. Son, I promise you, there'll be none of that. We keep a golden share, so we can veto any downsizing or restructuring, and if they do anything we don't like, we have the right to buy the whole lot back. Come on, Jay. You think I'd let them screw up everything we've built? You know me better than that, boy."

The eighth day, so legend has it, Dad, Jay and Uncle Ghost spent hiding from the product liability lawyers. As with every legend, a grain of truth sparkles in there somewhere. Even so. You build a business from the ground up, you care for it, worry about it, you take pride in its progress, you're there for it when things don't go so well. But there always comes a time when you have to let go. Or does there?

"Fact is," Dad said, looking out over the rippling purple bay, "I feel old."

"You're not—"

"No, but I *feel* that way. Maybe it's time to step aside. New ideas, new energy. Didn't I tell you once, every day in the job ought to feel like the first day—you know, bursting with energy, bubbling over with ideas? That's just not me any more, son. And you know I'd hand the whole thing over to you like a shot, I've got every confidence in you, of course I have. But I ask myself, would that be what you really want? Well? Be honest."

Jay was silent for a very long time. Dad went on, "I know you've always done your very best, never less than one hundred per cent, every second of every minute of every day. But what I'm asking is, did you do it for the business or did you do it for me?"

Jay looked at him. The float bobbed unregarded. Then Jay said, "Sure, Dad. But the Venturis, for crying out loud—"

"They wouldn't be prepared to pay so much money for it if they weren't planning on looking after it real well. They're not bad people, son. Maybe their approach is a little different, but who's to say that's a bad thing? A new approach. Fact is, son, I don't know that we've been doing the greatest possible job lately. Well? What do you think?"

Jay's head was still turned away. "They sure see things different," he said.

Dad laughed softly. "We were like them once," he said. "We used thunderbolts. We smote. I seem to remember a whole lot of smiting, at one time."

"Yes, but for their own good."

Dad shrugged. "Who's to say they weren't the good days? We expanded from a small tribe in a desert to half the population of the planet, back in the old smiting days.

The balance sheet never lies, Jay boy. They really wanted to believe, back then."

"They were *scared*—" Jay broke off sharply. "Maybe you're right," he said. "It's just, I never really took to the Venturis, you know?"

Dad shrugged again. "Mankind," he said. "You think they're happier now? Than they were back in the smiting times? Genuinely happier?"

Jay sighed. "What does Uncle Ghost think?"

"He's with me," Dad said firmly. "And that's another thing. Got to think about what's best for him. He's not as young as he was."

Jay, who'd always been as young as he was, made a vague gesture. "If he's happy with the deal, well, that makes it two to one, doesn't it?"

"Jay. You're my eldest begotten son, with whom I am well pleased. We won't do anything unless you're absolutely sure. But think about it, will you? Just think about it, that's all I'm asking."

Jay let out a long, deep sigh. "I guess you're right, Dad," he said. "I didn't do it for them, I did it for you. And if you want to call it a day . . ." Suddenly he smiled, like the sun bursting through clouds. "Sure," he said. "Let's go for it."

6

"Hello? Is that the helpline? Listen, you've got to get an engineer over here as quickly as possible. The sun's just gone out."

Another day in the office. "Let me just stop you there," Lucy said. "When you say gone out, what do you mean, exactly?"

"What I said, you idiotic girl. One moment it was there, riding proudly through the heavens, the next moment this ghastly black disc started sliding across it, and we were all cast into darkness unspeakable. And what I want to know is, what are you going to do about it?"

"It's all right," Lucy said. "It's just—"

"It is *not* all right," the caller yelled, making Lucy's head rattle. "It's eleven o'clock in the morning, and according to our Believers' Agreement, we're entitled to nine more hours of daylight. You're useless. Put me through to your superior."

"It does that sometimes," Lucy said mildly. "It's called an eclipse."

"A what?"

"It's a natural phenomenon," Lucy said. "It happens

from time to time when the Earth's orbit round the sun happens to coincide—"

"No, no, you stupid child, you've got it all wrong. The *sun* orbits round the *Earth*. Everybody knows that."

Lucy sighed, but not into the mouthpiece. "Silly me," she said. "Yes, of course it does. What you're experiencing is a minor exhibition of divine displeasure, caused by someone in your community committing one or more abominations unto the Lord. You can fix it yourself quite easily by sacrificing a goat and rooting out the evildoers among you. Thank—"

"Then why didn't you say so in the first place? I don't know, wasting my time with a lot of heretical mumbo-jumbo—"

"Thank you for calling the out-of-hours helpline," Lucy continued, soft and remorseless as the incoming tide. "Should the problem persist, please feel free to call the regular technical helpdesk during normal hours, when a colleague will be only too pleased to suffer you gladly. Goodbye."

She glanced at her watch. Three hours to go. She didn't know which she minded most, the idiotic calls or the long, dreary intervals between them. She picked up her book and tried to find her place.

The phone rang.

"Hello? Is that the helpline?"

She frowned. She knew that voice. "Yes, you're through. Lucy speaking. How can I—?"

"Was it you I was talking to the day before yesterday?"

Oh, she thought, him. Trapped-in-a-pyramid man. "Yes," she said. "And I have to tell you, I checked your authorisation code and strictly speaking it's no longer—"

"You really are the helpline? *The* helpline."

Actually he sounded rather sweet, but she'd had a long

day. "I think we've been through all that before," she said. "This is the *out-of-hours emergency* helpline. For *emergencies*. Confirmation of the existence of the Supreme Being is not an emergency. May I suggest that you call the regular helpdesk during normal office hours, when a colleague will be pleased to assist you."

Numb silence. Then, "All right. Could you give me the number?"

"Sure," Lucy said. "Got a pencil? Fine, here goes. Six seven thweep four sningy—"

"You what?"

Lucy breathed out through her nose. "I said, six seven thweep—"

"What the Hell is thweep?"

He was starting to sound like all the others. "It's an integer between nine and ten," she said. "I'll start again. Six seven—"

"What, you mean like, nine and a half?"

"No, I said an integer. That means a whole number. No fractions."

"But there aren't any whole numbers between nine and ten."

Oh dear. "You're a human mortal, aren't you?"

"Yes. So?"

"Certain mathematical entities are only available to authorised customers. Sorry. It's the rules. Strictly speaking, I shouldn't have—"

"Look," said the voice. "How the Hell can I call this other number if the numbers in the number don't exist?"

"Access to the regular helpdesk is restricted to authorised customers only, I'm afraid."

"So I can't ring them?"

"No. Sorry. Thank you for calling the—"

"What time do you get off work?"

Lucy blinked. "I beg your pardon?"

"Only," said the voice, and she could hear an undercurrent of desperation that tugged at her heartstrings, "I was wondering, maybe we could have dinner."

"Excuse me," Lucy said, "and bearing in mind that your call is being recorded for training and quality-control purposes, are you asking me for a *date*?"

"If that's what it takes, yes. Why? Are you seeing someone?"

"Not at the moment, no. But that's beside the—"

"Please?"

There was something about the voice, definitely something. She heard herself say, "Three hours," and then thought, *You what?* But by then she'd already said it.

"Fine. I'll be waiting outside, if you'll tell me where you are."

Oh no you don't, Mr. Clever. "In three hours and ten minutes I'll be standing at the bus stop in Chernychevsky Street, Yakutsk. That's in Siberia, if you're not familiar—"

"Is that where your office is?"

"No."

"I'll be there."

She frowned. "You can get to the remotest town in Siberia in three and a bit hours?"

"Sure. I'm near an airbase, I'll steal a jet fighter."

"Do you think that's—?"

She heard laughter. "Compared to the stuff I've had to do to get this far? Piece of cake. Dinner?"

"Yes, all right. But I want a starter and a pudding."

The line went dead. She took the headphones off, stared at them for a minute and a half, then put them back on again. Crazy as six ferrets in a blender. Still, why not? She'd been happy enough with Dennis until he went off with that tart, but the unexpected and surprising weren't really in his line. Perhaps the sort of man who got trapped in pyramids and stole jet fighters might make a pleasant change. She raised an eyebrow, then shrugged. It looked like defrosting the fridge was just going to have to wait another day.

7

The administrative section of Flipside had a strict, conservative dress code and Jenny did her best, but the programming hard-wired into her in the workshops of Prince Sitri was hard to overcome. Bernie had developed a knack of not quite looking at her. It made life a little bit easier. It didn't help that the admin offices were next door to Number Six furnace, and Duke Hastur, their nominal head of department, insisted on keeping the central heating full on.

"It's very hot in here," she said. "I think I'll take my jacket off."

"Sure," Bernie muttered, concentrating very hard on an energy efficiency report. A drop of sweat trickled down his nose and onto his lap. "Um, did Maintenance get back to you about the cracked gas pipe in Gluttony?"

"I'll chase them up about it right now, Mr. Lachuk."

"Bernie, please." She seemed incapable of calling him by his first name. "Yes, if you wouldn't mind, that'd be great, thanks."

He glanced back up at his screen, but the energy efficiency report had disappeared. In its place he saw, *Thou shalt have no other god but me, folks. Ho ho ho!*

He sighed. The merry prankster was at it again. Accidentally-on-purpose he nudged the green phone off its cradle with his elbow, then massaged his forehead with his fingertips. All the effort, energy and resources they'd put into tracking down the prankster had come to nothing. The Third Floor was livid about it, the techies were fed up and resentful at his mild reproofs concerning lack of progress, and where the energy efficiency report had gone nobody would ever know. Why do people do that stuff? he wondered. Then he remembered where he was, and that there doesn't necessarily have to be a reason for certain sorts of behaviour. Even so. Why couldn't they go away and hassle the Pentagon or a nice bank or something?

He opened his desk drawer, pulled out a crumpled sheet of paper and scribbled down the words on the screen. Then he leaned back in his chair (which stuck awkwardly at about fifteen degrees from the vertical; he'd asked Maintenance to do something about it; when we've got five minutes, they'd promised him faithfully) and contemplated what he'd recorded so far, the collected literary works of the merry prankster.

There was a theme to it all, he felt sure, if only he could figure out what it was. Not the obvious one, the religious-nut angle, which he felt sure was a pose or a front. No, the point of the messages lay in the subtext: what you see with your peripheral vision, not what you're focusing on. Certain turns of phrase in the bits that weren't direct quotes from the Procedures Manual—hints, nothing more. He sighed. It wasn't his job—they had security guys for this sort of thing—and he had plenty of work of his own to be getting on with. Even so, the tiny end of string poking up out of the vast roiling tangle intrigued him, and he couldn't help it. Ever since he was a boy, he'd been obsessive about knots and tangles. He even owned a Rubik's cube, buried in a cardboard box somewhere.

A new Heaven. No other god but me. Ho ho ho. Crazy.

Duty called. He restored the green phone to its cradle. Immediately it burst into raucous song. He picked it up, said, "Lachuk here," then held the receiver at arm's length for ten seconds.

8

"**I** caught a retrospective gudgeon this big," Jay said, throwing his arms wide, "and Dad got a record Schrodinger's catfish, and there's something he wants to tell you. Great to see you again, bro. We missed you. Bye."

Jay dashed past him, up the steps into the house. Kevin frowned. The Way, the Truth and the Life can't lie, obviously, but since linear time didn't apply within the boundaries of the compound, he was under no obligation to give you all the facts *right now*. I'm not going to like this, Kevin decided and advanced to meet his father.

Dad looked up. "Hi, son."

"Hi, Dad. Have a good trip?"

"Fantastic. You've got to try Sinteraan one of these days, son. You'd love it. It's so relaxing."

Kevin had often speculated that if he relaxed any more, he'd drift apart to the point where his molecules no longer collided, and he'd gently evaporate. "That's great, Dad. Jay said you caught a big Schrodinger's."

Dad grinned. "You should've seen the one that got away."

Kevin knew just enough about fishing on Sinteraan to

recognise that that was a joke, so he smiled dutifully. "He said there's something you want to talk about."

His father's face fell, just for a moment. "Later, son; we just got back. So, everything going OK? No disasters?"

"Everything's fine now," Kevin replied, which was perfectly true. Of course Dad would get the grisly details from Uncle Mike in due course. And besides, he wasn't responsible for the unscheduled earth tremors. Properly speaking, they were all Saint Andreas' fault. "Want me to carry your bags for you?"

Dad gave him one of his special smiles. "Thanks, son. I'd like that."

With Dad it was the little things that mattered. As Kevin hefted the three kitbags, he decided that whatever the bad news was, it couldn't be anything he'd done. A relief but at the same time rather more worrying. Anything he'd done, Dad would inevitably forgive, but from the way he'd been acting, Dad was the one who was feeling guilty about something.

Jay met him in the doorway. "I've got coffee brewing on the stove," he said. "Unless you'd prefer a Coke."

Ominouser and ominouser. "What's going on, Jay?"

"What? Oh, Dad'll tell you later. Looks like you kept everything ticking over nicely while we were gone."

"You haven't been talking to Uncle Nick, have you? Only, I wasn't really going behind Dad's back. I just thought—"

Jay smiled at him. Maybe the understanding and compassion was just force of habit, or maybe it was more case-specific. "We kept our phones turned off the whole time, bro. How about I fix you a vanilla latte? Your favourite."

Beyond ominous and nudging up against terrifying. "Sure, Jay. Thanks. I'll be in directly."

He paused on the threshold and looked back. The sun was setting—yes, he'd remembered to wind it up, admittedly because Uncle Mike had stuck a Post-it note on the switch of his bedside lamp, so it couldn't be that. He was so used to everything being his fault that it was hard to think outside the confines of that particular box. *But if it's not me, what is it?*

Only one way to find out. He slouched into the kitchen.

Jay was frothing the milk for his latte. Dad was in his usual place at the head of the table. "Sit down, son," he said. Jay handed him his coffee then left quickly. Kevin sat down.

"Got some news for you, son." Dad was looking past him, at a spot on the wall just above his head. "Your brother and I. We've had an offer for the business."

There had been that time, back in the Beginning, when they were wiring up the Firmament. Jay was seeing to the Earth, Dad was up a ladder fixing a loose connection in Heaven, Kevin holding the ladder steady for him. *Whatever you do, son, don't touch that cable—it's hot.* So, what had he done? He'd prodded the cable with the tip of his finger, just to see what would happen. What happened, ultimately, was leap years, but the immediate effect was Kevin sailing through the as-yet-undifferentiated void and bashing his head against a drifting shoal of dark matter. Déjà vu. The same sensation of stunned bewilderment.

"Dad?"

"We're selling up, son. Jay and I have given it a lot of thought, and we figure it'd be the best thing all round. We reckon we've done our fair share, and now it's time to take it easy and enjoy life."

The words *you can't* froze on his lips like a sneeze in Antarctica. Of course Dad could; the very phrase was tautologous. But ... Playing for time, he said, "Where will you go?"

Dad shrugged. "Well, Sinteraan is nice. Or Astrovegas. Or we could head over to the Lesser Magellanic Cloud for dove season. We figured we could just, you know, roam around for a bit. Get ourselves one of those big RVs and cruise the cosmos. It'll be fun. You'll enjoy it."

"Me?" It wasn't the word he'd expected to say, but it came out before he could even think about it. "You want me to leave Earth?"

"Well, yes. Naturally we'll stick together. We're a family."

"But this is my home."

Dad frowned. "Home is where the heart is, son. You know that."

"Exactly," Kevin said. There was something in his eye. He wiped it away and his finger got wet. "Really, that's fine. If you and Jay want to go trekking through the stars in a camper van, you go ahead. I'm staying here. I like it here. It's my home."

Dad was giving him what Kevin always thought of as his business look: profound, compassionate, infinitely wise. "Sorry you feel that way, son. Would you like to talk about it?"

"What's to talk about? You already made up your minds."

The faintest of sighs. "It's for the best, son. It's not just us, your brother and me. Those folks down there, they need someone up here who's firing on all cylinders, giving it 210 per cent, all day every day. Your brother and I feel ... well, that's not us any more. It's time we stood aside. New ideas, new categorical imperatives. Every day like the first day, remember?"

Kevin stared at him. "But you're *Dad*, Dad. I mean,

you're the greatest. By definition. Are you trying to say you're handing over to someone better than you?"

Maybe Dad winced a little. "Not better, maybe. Different. Fresh and new. Change, Kevin, that's what this world needs. Real, genuine change."

Kevin frowned. "Why?"

Dad opened his mouth and closed it again. He took a deep breath. "Sorry, son, but our minds are made up. We're leaving. And we'd really like for you to come with us."

"Really? And do what?"

Maybe just a slight hardening around the mouth. "What you always do, son. What you're best at."

It had been bad enough coming from Uncle Mike—just go and do whatever it is you do all day—from Dad it was unbearable. "No thanks," he said. "If you can make decisions, so can I. And I've decided. I'm through with just loafing around. I'm going to go out there and . . ."

"What?"

"Do something."

"Ah."

"And I'm going to do it here," Kevin said defiantly. "On Earth, where I belong. You can send me a postcard. Keep me updated about what you just caught."

Dad sighed. "The thing is," he said, "when we hand over to the new people, they're going to want, well, vacant possession. They may not want one of us hanging around."

Kevin looked at him. You're not supposed to, not without sunglasses, but he didn't care. "Since when was I one of you?"

He'd done it now. Sure, Dad would forgive him, in due course. But not straight away. "You do what you like, Kevin—it's up to you. But I want you out of this house by the time the sale goes through. Is that understood?"

Kevin knew better than to answer back when Dad was in one of his where-were-you-when-I-laid-the-foundations-of-the-Earth moods. He drained his latte, spilling a bit of froth down his chin, and left the kitchen, slamming the door behind him.

A moment or so later, Jay stepped in from the stoop. "How'd it go?"

Dad shrugged. "He's upset, naturally."

"He'll come round. He always does."

"I guess." Dad got up and dumped Kevin's empty cup in the sink. "He reckons he wants to stay on when we leave."

"What, here?"

"On Earth, yes."

"The Venturi boys aren't going to like that."

"It won't happen," Dad said. "He'll come round. He just needed to blow off steam, that's all. Even so." He ran the tap and rinsed the cup. "Jay, are you sure we're doing the right thing?"

"Sure, Dad. You convinced me." Jay laid an arm across his father's shoulders. "And don't worry about Kevin, all right? It'll be hard on him, for sure, but it's the best thing for all of us in the long run. You'll see."

Dad smiled. "You're right, of course. It's just I don't like to think of him being unhappy."

"He'll be fine," Jay said firmly. "Cruising the starways, seeing the sights, chilling on multidimensional beaches: what's not to like? He'll be fine. Trust me."

9

Ab and Snib Venturi started out among the harsh dunes of Mars. Theirs is a classic rags-to-riches story. Beginning with a few scattered adherents among the rock-pool-dwellers of Hostjj, they spread their unique brand of Word across the entire planet in less than seventy Martian years before selling the Red Planet to a local consortium and transferring their operations to the Andromeda galaxy. Now, although the Corporation reigns undisputed over a billion Andromedan suns, their origins are still proudly commemorated in the company logo: two sun-gold arches (representing the Founders, fraternally sharing the central pillar) set against a stark red background. It's the most universally recognisable symbol in the Multiverse. Wherever you go, there it is.

The unfortunate events that led to the total extinction of life on Mars were not the Venturis' fault. As Snib Venturi said in an interview for *Galactic Investors* magazine, "It was a going concern when we handed it over; we had no reason to believe those guys weren't properly funded and fully competent. It's a tragedy, but what can you do?" Nevertheless, the destruction of their first enterprise has always rankled with the Venturi twins, and it's highly probable that a desire to clear any hint of tarnish from their reputation in the Milky Way was one of the factors that made them so anxious to acquire Terra, Mars' undistinguished neighbour in the Sol system. "I guess you could say we're going home," Snib Venturi told a stock-holders' rally on Atrevati IV, shortly after the purchase was announced. "Sometimes you just gotta buy with your heart, you know?"

The Venturis arrived on Earth for the final round of negotiations in a sleek black helicopter full of lawyers. Dad hadn't been happy about that. Supposing someone sees you? he objected, whereupon Snib Venturi grinned. So they see us, so what? They'll be seeing an awful lot of us in the near future. It's the way we do things. Dad nodded glumly and cut the Skype link. Different approaches. Change. Well, too late now.

The helicopter was the size of Sumatra and did nasty things to the weather on the way to the meeting. "What do you need one of those things for?" Dad asked as soon as they'd landed.

"What does God need with a starship, as one of your great Earth philosophers put it?"* Snib Venturi shrugged. "We're not like you. We like to put on a show. It's kind of a trademark. Say, is there anywhere here we can get warm? I'm frozen."

"This way," Dad said. "There's coffee on the stove."

The Venturis' lawyers filled the kitchen. Five of them had to stand out in the porch with the door open, which vexed the warmth-craving Venturis. "There's just a couple of loose ends we want to tie up," Snib Venturi said, pulling his collar around his necks. "Then we can all sign on the dotted line, and we're done."

* William Shatner; *Star Trek V: The Final Frontier*

Dad and Jay exchanged glances. "Shoot," said Jay.

Ab Venturi pulled a thick legal pad from his briefcase. "Point one," he said. "I see you've got a number of key administrative functions contracted out to indigenous labour."

Jay nodded. "We had to," he said. "With the fall-off in attendances, we had to rationalise. They're doing a good job, actually. Efficiency is up seven point six three . . ."

Snib shook his heads. "Not the way we do things," he said. "They'll have to go. Full severance pay, naturally. OK, moving on—"

"Just a moment," Dad said. "You're going to fire all those people, even though they're doing a good job?"

Ab grinned at him. "Don't worry about them," he said. "Soon there'll be great new employment opportunities for everybody, you'll see. Meanwhile, they've got to go. Time for the saints to go marching out. If you'd let Greb and the boys have copies of all the relevant contracts."

Dad scowled, but Jay said, "Sure, I'll see to it. What else?"

The Venturi twins exchanged a glance. "This Flipside facility of yours," he said. "Now that could be a real problem."

Dad took a deep breath. "I'm sorry," he said. "I know it's not how you do things, but Flipside's what you might call fundamental. It's at the very root of our moral code."

Snib Venturi smiled that smile that always put Dad in mind of a fraught encounter in a garden, long ago, under an apple tree. "Look, we're not here to argue about our different takes on ethical systems. You've always been Good/Evil, we respect that, and we know you've made binding commitments that you have to honour. Kinda like God making a rock so heavy he can't lift it, but hey, that's your choice, you had every right. On the other hand, we have no use for anything of that kind, and quite frankly we don't do Eternity. It's not our way."

Jay said, "You can't close down Flipside. That's a deal-breaker."

A moment of silence, broken only by a few of the lawyers rattling their wings. "I don't think anybody suggested closing it down," Ab said. "We didn't, that's for sure. What we're proposing is, all new admissions are to cease from midnight tonight, Greenwich time. After that Flipside is effectively sealed off. We allow it an adequate budget to keep it running, build a wall round it, leave your guys there to get on with it. For ever and ever, world without end. It'll be a separate jurisdiction. We leave them alone; they don't bother us. It's not an ideal solution, but it's practical."

Jay turned to his father. "Uncle Nick's not going to like that."

Dad made a vague gesture with his hands. "I don't know," he said. "It all seems a bit arbitrary to me. How are we going to explain to the mortals that if you commit a deadly sin before twelve midnight tonight, you're going to burn in fire and brimstone for all eternity, while if you wait an extra minute . . ."

Snib gave him a cold look. "With respect, we've never done Good/Evil, so we've never had to deal with this kind of issue. I'm afraid you're going to have to sort that out; it's outside our area of expertise." He softened his voice just a little. "Guys, it'd be an awful shame if this whole deal fell through on account of a few no-goods among the livestock. We think we've been pretty damn accommodating. We've promised open-ended funding and complete autonomy for your people running the show down there. What more could you reasonably expect?"

Jay's lips were set in a tight, thin line. Dad sighed. "Fair enough," he said. "You've got a deal." He turned to his son and added, "You leave your uncle Nick to me. I'll talk to him. It'll be fine."

"Splendid," Ab said. "Right, so that just leaves one small issue. I couldn't help noticing, there's this box in the Requisitions on Title form you left blank. I take it that was just an oversight."

He pushed a sheet of paper across the table. Dad didn't need to look at it. "Actually, no," he said. "I was meaning to talk to you about that. Sort of a grey area."

"Really?" Ab rested a foreclaw on the wording just above the empty box. "Please certify that your chosen people have no other gods but you. Looks pretty open and shut to me."

Dad and Jay looked at each other. "It's like this," he said.

He told them all about the Old Gods, and the thousand years they'd spent rounding them up and persuading them to retire to Sunnyvoid, a comfortable and well-appointed retirement home with magnificent views out over the Portals of the Sunset, where they could spend the autumn of their everlasting lives enjoying a wide range of properly structured leisure activities—

"Sure," Ab interrupted. "You boys did a fine job; I remember reading about it at the time in the trade papers. So what? You got them all, and they're safely kettled up in this Sunnyvoid joint. No problem, surely."

Dad lowered his head. Jay said, "Actually, there was one who got away."

The Venturis looked at each other. "That's not good," Snib said. "It's a fundamental term of the agreement. Vacant possession."

"He's no bother to anyone," Dad said quickly. "Just let him be, and he won't cause you any trouble."

The laywers hissed. Ab held up his hand and they fell silent. "You're telling me," he said, "you're omnipotent supreme beings and you couldn't catch this one renegade and bring him in. I find that hard to accept."

Dad waved his hand. "I guess we could've, if we'd set our minds to it. It's more a case of collateral damage, if you know what I mean. Really, trust me. He's no bother. Nobody believes in him anyhow."

Jay glanced down and noted that under the table Dad had the fingers of his right hand crossed.

The Venturis whispered to their chief lawyers in Martian for a while, then Ab said, "Well, if nobody believes in him, he doesn't count, so that's not a problem." He peered at Dad and added, "You're sure about that. Nobody believes."

Dad nodded. "For legal purposes, yes. I can give you an absolute assurance on that."

If the Venturis noticed the slightly odd form of words, they didn't comment. Instead, Snib Venturi reached his hand out across the table. "In that case," he said, "we got ourselves a deal."

After the helicopter had gone, scattering dead leaves and wisps of cloud in its slipstream, Dad and Jay didn't say anything to each other for a long time. They washed up the coffee cups and put them away, straightened the kitchen. Dad gazed sadly at the deep scratch-marks left by some lawyer's claws in the polished top of a cherished table, then reflected that it no longer mattered. They'd resolved to leave with nothing more than they could fit comfortably into the RV—no thought for the morrow, consider the lilies of the field, all that. As one of humanity's great philosophers nearly said, what does God want with a Louis Quinze coffee table, anyway?

"You didn't tell them," Jay said.

"What?"

"About Kevin."

"What about him?"

"You didn't tell them about him staying on."

Dad made a slightly impatient gesture. "Won't happen," he said. "Kevin's coming with us. Got to let the boy do his bit of melodrama, and then he'll see sense. He's not a bad kid, really."

"All right then," Jay said doubtfully. "But if he does stay behind, they won't be happy."

"Like I said, it won't happen. Besides, Kevin wouldn't be a problem for them. Even if he did stay, he'd just mooch around. There'd be nothing for him here."

"OK, Dad. I'd better look in on him, don't you think? He's been acting awful depressed."

Jay climbed the stairs, knocked on Kevin's door and waited. Knocked again, waited some more. Then he tried the handle.

The room was empty. The drawers of the bedside table were open, certain key things missing. A lighter patch on the wall showed where Kevin's Map of Middle Earth poster should have been but wasn't. Some of his clothes were gone too. And, on the pillow, a yellow Post-it note.

Jay read it and frowned. Then he went back downstairs.

"Read this," he said.

Dear Dad and Jay
I thought it'd be best if I just went.
Don't worry about me, I'll be fine. Have a
great time. Hope you catch lots of fish.
Love, Kevin.

"He can't have got far," Jay said. "I'll find him."

"No." Dad looked away. "No, it's OK. He's a big boy now."

"But you said he—"

"I know." Dad carefully folded the note and put it in his glasses case. "He can look after himself. He'll be just fine."

10

"**S**orry I'm late, I got held up. Now, I know this great little place on Pushkin Street where they do a wicked asparagus *goluptsi*."

He was shorter than she'd expected, maybe a year older, considerably better-looking. He was wearing dark trousers and a black parka, and his hands were covered in engine grease.

"Have you got any money?" she asked.

"Um."

"My treat."

He smiled. Nice smile. "I'll pay you back," he said, "as soon as I can find an all-night jeweller's."

She frowned. Then: "Let me guess. You only carry uncut diamonds."

He nodded, pulled a grubby handkerchief from his pocket, unfolded it to reveal a cluster of what looked for all the world like upmarket coffee sugar, but which wasn't. "Long story."

"Let's eat. I'm starving."

Goluptsi turned out to be mostly cabbage leaves, and he kept looking over her shoulder towards the door. "Expecting someone?" she asked.

"Expecting isn't quite the word. Dreading, maybe."

"Did you really steal a jet fighter?"

"Didn't want to keep you waiting. Trouble is, it was an American jet fighter. Sort of a tactless place to leave it lying about, if you follow me. Still, I'm here and you're here, and that's all that matters. Have some more *smetana*."

"Is that the rancid cream?"

"Yup."

"No, thanks. Look, Mr ... I'm sorry, I didn't catch your name."

"Jersey. Jersey Thorpe."

"Interesting. You don't strike me as one of Nature's Jerseys."

He raised an eyebrow. "You're very perceptive," he said. "It's not what my parents chose for me. I changed it."

"Ah."

"Originally I was called New Jersey. My mother's an Egyptologist, my dad's a film critic."

"Parents have a lot to answer for."

He grinned. He'd got a blob of *smetana* on his chin. She mentioned it.

"Thank you."

"You're welcome. Look, Jersey Thorpe, I know perfectly well that you only asked me out because I worked for the helpli—"

He frowned. "Excuse me. Worked?"

She nodded. "I got fired this evening."

"For talking to me?"

"Sweet of you to be concerned, but no. Everyone in my department—well, all the ..."

He looked at her. "All the humans?"

"Yes. No warning, nothing. Just a round-robin email and three weeks' pay in lieu. So, if you were paying for this, you'd be wasting your money. Not to mention the F-16 and all that expensive fuel."

"You got sacked? Just like that?"

"Yes. Bit of a surprise, actually. I thought, you know, working for the Big Guy ..."

"You'd anticipated something a bit more ethical."

She shrugged. "Bosses are bosses," she said. "Presumably they found a cheaper deal somewhere. They were always on about increased efficiency, keeping costs down. What do you expect, working on a public-sector contract?"

"What's outsource for the goose, and all that. Quite." He was peering over her shoulder again. "That's a shame, it really is."

"Absolutely. You go to all this trouble, and your only lead goes cold."

"I didn't mean that; I meant—"

He broke off and dived under the table. She sighed. "Would it be better," she said to the empty space where he'd been sitting, "if we went somewhere else?"

"Mphm."

"Right. It just so happens, my travel warrant is valid till midnight. Can I drop you off somewhere?"

"Yes, please."

"Where?"

"Anywhere but here?"

Two men in fur hats with machine guns were standing in the doorway. A waitress was directing their attention to the specials board. "How about Amsterdam? They really do have all-night jewellers' there."

Her last chance to use the travel warrant. Ah well. She reached under the table and connected with his outstretched hand, then closed her eyes and made a wish. When she opened them again—

"What happened?"

She smiled. Early evening on Middenweg. "I know this great little place where you can get a wicked *rookworst*," she said. "After we've cashed in a diamond."

"You know," he said, some time later, with his mouth full, "this has turned out better than I expected."

"Really?"

"Mphm. I guessed *rookworst* was sausage made from rooks. Do you live here?"

She smiled. "No."

"But your travel warrant—"

"Is valid till midnight. Local time."

He nodded. "So," he said, "there really is a Big Guy."

"Yup."

"Excuse me a moment." He put down his knife and fork, clasped his hands together and gazed at the ceiling. "I'm sorry," he said, "really, really sorry. And I promise not to do it again. I mean it too," he added, picking up his fork and spearing a strand of pickled cabbage. "I mean, it's just common sense, isn't it? If you know there genuinely is Someone up there, and he doesn't take kindly to certain sorts of behaviour."

"Indeed." She considered him for a moment. He looked like a rather short Greek god, but if she had to sum him up in one adjective, it would probably be 'businesslike.' "So that's it, is it? Mission accomplished."

"I guess so." He grinned. "All my adult life I've spent chasing round investigating cryptic clues, figuring out abstruse codes embedded in centuries-old manuscripts, getting chased by bad guys and damaging scheduled monuments, and where's it got me? Yes, there's Someone up there. So, I've made my peace, and I now know more than all the rest of the human race. Nearly all," he amended. "That's great. Fantastic. This is the point at which the camera pans out and the credits start to roll. Only, that doesn't seem to be happening. Ah well."

She crumbled a bread roll. "So," she said. "What are you going to do with your amazing newly won secret knowledge?"

He shrugged. "Get a job, work hard, retire and die. While taking great pains to be very, very good. Not much else I can do, really. I mean, it's the ultimate secret, for which Mankind has been searching ever since they figured out that mountains with holes in them made for good shelter. But it's not actually very . . ."

"Useful?"

He pointed his fork at her. "Exactly. Like a first-class honours degree in literature."

She nodded. "I've got one of those."

"Plus you share in the ultimate secret." He drummed his fingers on the tablecloth. "So, what will you do next?"

"I have considerable experience working in call centres. I might go and work for Amazon. They pay slightly better than my last job, and they only *think* they rule the planet. How about you?"

"Good question. I have a lot of very specialised skills, but my CV would get me locked up for a very long time. I might open a health-food shop somewhere."

"With all those diamonds?"

He pulled a sad face. "They're not strictly speaking mine," he said. "And knowing what I do, I guess I really ought to give them back."

"Pity."

"For a substantial finder's fee. The labourer is worthy of his hire—1 Timothy 5.18," he said to the ceiling. "My mother's father was a lawyer," he explained. "I inherited a flair for memorising section numbers."

She glanced at her watch. "So where do you live?"

"The last twelve years? Here and there. Wherever the trail took me. I have American, British, French, Swiss and Guatemalan passports, some of which I'm entitled to. My net assets are what I'm wearing and a hanky full of coal derivatives. You?"

"Saffron Walden. It's a small town in East Anglia. That's in—"

"There's a coincidence. My grandmother lives in Bishop's Stortford."

She raised an eyebrow. "Really?"

"Cross my heart. From now on, the truth and nothing but the truth. For obvious reasons."

She hesitated for a moment, then scribbled a number in the margin of the menu card. "Next time you're visiting Grandma, give me a call. If you want to, that is. Sorry, but I've really got to go. I'm glad it worked out for you."

He smiled. She stood up. Then she sat down again, buffeted into her seat by a mighty rushing wind.

In the middle of the room a patch of empty air began to sparkle and then coalesced into a shining silver screen. A deafening voice said, "People of Earth, your attention, please."

11

Kevin Godson looked up from his hamburger at the flickering image and frowned. He knew why it was flickering: the idiots hadn't allowed for signal decay when calculating the Heisenberg variables. But then, if they were struggling to come to terms with the hardware they'd inherited from the previous management, they had his sincere sympathy.

"People of Earth, your attention, please."

He shovelled a few fries into his mouth. The Venturis didn't muck about. One minute past twelve, by his watch.

He recognised the speaker as Snib Venturi, whom he'd never met but whose face was a familiar sight to anyone who lit the kitchen stove with back numbers of the trade papers. All around Kevin, people (my fellow humans, he thought, and winced) were staring, struck dumb, transfixed. He dipped a fry in the little paper pot of ketchup and nibbled the end off.

"There is no cause for alarm. This is not, I repeat not, an alien invasion. You are in no danger. On the contrary. Those who have dwelt in darkness are about to see a great light."

Kevin frowned. Steady on, he thought, and besides,

isn't that breach of copyright? Or was the intellectual property included in the deal?

"For thousands of years Mankind has tortured itself with the fundamental, unanswered question, is there a god? People of Earth, the doubt and the darkness are over. Here is the answer. The answer is yes."

At the next table a fat man made that uniquely rude noise that happens when you try and suck up the last quarter-inch of a milk shake through a straw. His neighbours glared at him angrily, but Kevin thought, fair comment.

"Yes, people of Earth, there is a Supreme Being. Allow me to introduce myself. My name is Snib Venturi, and this is my twin brother Ab."

Big smile from Ab Venturi. A few tables away a thin man with a beard stood up and said, "Hey, what's all this shit?" then vanished in a puff of smoke.

Dead silence. Then Snib Venturi said, "Quite possibly you've just witnessed someone in your local area expressing doubt. Please don't be concerned, especially if the person in question was a friend or loved one. That was just a demonstration to prove the truth of what we're telling you. Be assured, no harm will come to them; they'll be back, good as new, around about ... now."

The thin man reappeared. He was wearing a dunce's cap, and he had an apple wedged in his mouth. He sat down, looking confused.

"The Venturi Corporation of Andromeda, which we have the honour to represent, has taken over the running of your world from the previous administration. We are now your Supreme Beings. Now, the question you're all longing to ask is, how does this affect me?"

The other customers were starting to mutter. One had fallen to her knees and was saying her rosary. Another one had taken off his shoe and was hefting it, ready to throw. Kevin slid off his stool, went quietly across and caught his wrist. "I wouldn't," he whispered. "I know these people." The man gave him a horrified look and dropped the shoe on the floor.

"The answer is, it's going to affect you a lot, in a whole load of wonderful, exciting ways. First—no disrespect for the previous regime, they meant well and they sincerely believed they had your best interests at heart; fair play to them—but we see things differently. They reckoned that in order to be saved, you had to believe—but on the flimsiest of evidence, it has to be said. The way we do things, you'd have to be crazy not to believe, because—hey, here we are. You can see us, plain as day, and you'll be seeing a whole lot more of us in the years to come. Doubt is at an end. The age of total certainty has arrived."

Show-off, Kevin thought. Even so, he'd often wondered why Dad and Jay made it so difficult for people. The occasional manifestation, from time to time a well-publicised miracle costs next to nothing and does wonders for getting bums on pews. But Dad didn't see it that way.

And neither, apparently, did the Venturi Corporation. "Next," said the sparkling apparition, "there's the whole question of morality. And this is another area where we have to agree to differ from the previous administration . . ."

12

"**T**urn it off, for crying out loud. It's giving me a headache."

Duke Ashtaroth shot the Father of Lies a sheepish grin and stabbed a claw at the remote. The voice fell silent and the hologram floating in mid-air shrank to the size of a playing card: two tiny Venturi twins, smiling and waving their arms. "Best I can do, I'm afraid," Ashtaroth said. "The signal's just too strong."

"That's not fair," said Kevin's Uncle Nick. "We're supposed to be entirely autonomous. Surely that means we can keep those two—" he used a rude word in the Infernal dialect which literally translated means *lawyer specialising in divorce settlements* "—out of here."

"Apparently not."

"Marvellous." Uncle Nick frowned then pulled the neatly folded handkerchief from his top pocket and looped it over the hologram, obscuring it completely. It fluttered a bit whenever Snib Venturi made a sweeping gesture, but otherwise it was fine.

"End of an era," Ashtaroth said.

Nick sighed, opened a desk drawer, pulled out a bottle and two glasses. "Toast?"

"Sure." Ashtaroth raised his glass. "To the last customer we'll ever get."

They each took a sip and pulled a face. "Out of interest," Nick said, "who was he?"

"She," Ashtaroth amended. "Susan Velikovski, retired, forty-six years with the Revenue. Died at one minute to midnight, poor cow."

Nick shook his head. "Save your sympathy," he said. "I figure she'll be better off with us. Don't know about you, but I'd rather have a nice cosy berth in Number Six than spend my next forty incarnations as a rat."

"Or a spider." Ashtaroth shivered. "I can't abide spiders."

"Is that a fact?" Nick said and scribbled a note on his jotter. Then he shrugged. "Sorry," he said. "Force of habit. I forgot." He crumpled up the sheet of paper and lobbed it into Number Four. "We don't do that stuff any more."

A single drop of sweat had formed in the middle of Ashtaroth's forehead. He borrowed the floating handkerchief to dab it away, then put it back. "Right," he said. "We don't."

Nick sighed. "That's right," he said. "We aren't bad guys any more. We're just—" he made a vague gesture "—curators, I guess. Caretakers. A team of dedicated specialists standing guard over something that no longer has any relevance at all." He picked up his glass and looked at it. "I never knew you had a thing about spiders."

"Well," Ashtaroth said. "Not something you mention, is it?"

Nick acknowledged a fair point. "Must've been tough. Explains why you and Duke Nimloth never saw eye to eye."

"Eyes," Ashtaroth corrected with a shudder. "Talking

of which, now that we're all morally neutral and buddy-buddy, I'd like to make a formal request. Kindly keep that bug-eyed freak the heck away from me."

Nick grinned. "I'll see what I can do. Though really she's not so bad once you get to know her."

"Take your word for it."

"No, really. Kind-hearted. She spun me a lovely scarf Christmas before last."

Ashtaroth picked up the bottle; Nick nodded.

"You know, Ash," he said as the Duke refilled their glasses, "it's going to take a while to sink in. I mean, it's a big change. No more Good and Evil."

"We're going to miss them, that's for sure."

"And this new place they're going to build, the Marshalsea. What sort of name is that for a correctional facility?"

"Not our concern any more," Ashtaroth said.

"True, true," said the Father of Lies. "Meanwhile, we've got our job to do, bearing in mind our customary high standards and the noble traditions of the Service." He shook his head. "This place is going to go to heck in a handcart, I can see it, clear as day. Stagnation, Ash boy, that's what we're looking at. We'll be a backwater. A footnote, an anomaly. I don't know. For two pins I'd quit. Cash in my pension, head out to the stars, start taking it easy for a change."

Ashtaroth pulled a face and Nick realised he'd been tactless. Ash and the guys didn't have that option. "It's all right," Nick said. "I'm just kidding. We'll see it through together, same as we always have. When I first saw this place, it was nothing but a bitumen lake and a few deposits of low-grade sulphur. And now look at it."

Ashtaroth smiled. "Two thousand and seventy-six consecutive Mephistos for Best Negative Afterlife," he said softly. "They can't take that away from us."

Nick flashed him a rare smile. He was proud of his Mephistos. He'd built a vast suite of lavatories behind the Gluttons especially to display them. "This reincarnation thing," he said. "They're not actually serious about it, are they?"

"Apparently. I checked out the Venturi Corp website, and they reckon they've introduced it successfully on over a hundred million worlds."

"Introduced." Nick scowled. "Means they set it up, then buggered off and left some poor sod of an assistant deputy manager to try and get it to work. I mean, second-hand souls, how cheap can you get?"

"Recycled," Ashtaroth amended. "Very green. I gather their carbon clawprint is practically nil."

Nick pointed at the bobbing handkerchief. "Would you buy a used soul from this man? Ah, the heck with it. Screw 'em." He drained his glass and poured them both another. "I know, I know," he said as Ashtaroth frowned slightly. "I want to go easy on this stuff, before it stops being the answer and starts being the problem."

"I didn't say a word."

"We know each other too well, that's our problem. Here's health."

"*Prosit.*"

The handkerchief quivered, then dropped to the floor.

"Looks like he's ground to a halt," Ashtaroth said.

"About time." Nick scooped up the handkerchief, screwed it into a ball and lobbed it into Number Three. The hot air rising from the vents reduced it to floating ash. "Let's forget about all that stuff for now and talk about something else, shall we? How goes the hunt for the merry prankster?"

"Oh that." Ashtaroth frowned. "Hardly seems important now."

"I despise loose ends."

"Funny you should say that."

"Ah."

Ashtaroth drew his chair a bit closer to the desk. "So we have this cluster of cryptic messages," he said, "apparently predicting—accurately—the regime change that's just happened. That's fine," he went on, "until you take a closer look at the timings."

"Ash, you know sequential linear time isn't worth a hill of beans around here."

"Internally." Ashtaroth gave him an owlish look. "But these messages came from outside."

"Ah."

"They entered our timeless continuum at a given point that can be triangulated with reference to external—"

"Yes, all right. I get the idea. So what?"

"We checked with Topside," Ashtaroth said. "The first message—the new-Heaven-and-new-Earth one—came in *before* His Nibs got the first offer from the Venturi boys."

Nick leaned back so far in his chair that the springs creaked. "You don't say."

"Checked and double-checked."

"That's . . ." Nick scratched his head, showering orange sparks like dandruff. "So whoever's been hacking our system knew about the deal before—"

"It looks like it. Now, think about that. Say what you like about the Venturis, their security is cast-iron. No way sensitive information like that is going to leak out where some hooligan in a backwater like this can hear about it. Wherever the prankster found out about it, I'll bet you anything you like it wasn't from the Venturis."

"That makes no—"

"And there's this." Ashtaroth took a folded scrap of paper from his top pocket. He spread it out on the table and scratched a line under three short words with the tip of his claw. Nick read it, and his eyes grew big and round.

"You're joshing me," he said.

"Cross my heart."

Nick flopped back in his chair as though he had a rubber backbone. "You know what this means."

"It's only a theory. Based on pretty thin evidence."

Nick shook his head. "Ho, ho, ho?" Then he grinned, ear to ear. "He's back," he said.

13

"**W**hat the Hell," Jersey asked, "was all that about?"
Before Lucy could answer, a window appeared
in thin air next to him and a man in a suit climbed out
of it and gave him a friendly smile. "Hi there," he said.
"Swearing in public, the H word. Here's your invoice."
He handed Jersey a sheet of pink paper. "You'll find a
choice of easy ways to pay on the back, or you may want
to consider our Pay-As-You-Sin cellphone app. Have a
nice day."

He vanished. Jersey glanced down at the pink invoice.
He owed the Venturi Corporation five hundred dollars.

"My . . . gosh," he said. "They mean it."

She'd gone white as a sheet. "Looks like it," she said.

"I thought it was just—"

"Apparently not."

They were alone in the deserted restaurant, the other
customers having fled during or shortly after the Venturis'
infomercial. "You know what this means," Lucy said.

"What?"

"My travel warrant is presumably no longer valid. How
the—?" She paused and swallowed, just in time. "How on
Earth am I supposed to get home?"

Jersey shrugged. "Plane? I'll stand you the fare. There's plenty of change out of that diamond."

"I haven't got a passport with me, have I?" She sat down, and they both knew exactly what she was thinking and not saying. If she hadn't agreed to dinner, none of this would have happened.

"I'm sorry."

"Not your fault."

"That was sympathy rather than remorse. I guess you'll have to go to the British consulate first thing in the morning. They get you home, don't they?"

"I believe so, yes."

That look in his eye was back. "In that case," he said, "you're not in any tearing hurry to be off anywhere, and this is a city that notoriously never sleeps."

"You want to go clubbing? After what we've just—"

"No." He fished in his pocket for what he hoped was enough to cover the bill, which had never arrived, and put it on a plate. "What I'm suggesting is, we find somewhere warm and quiet where we can get a coffee, and you can tell me everything you know about these Venturi people."

14

How long do you think it would take to convene a meeting of all the heads of state of the one hundred and ninety-six autonomous nation states that make up the political world? Answer: if you're the Venturi boys, less than a second.

It wasn't a mass kidnap because they'd been given due notice. In one hundred and ninety-six handsomely appointed offices across the globe a window had opened in thin air, a man in a suit had climbed out and told each of the kings, shahs, presidents and prime ministers that they were required to attend. Each of the leaders thus addressed had got as far as "You must be out of your—" when they found themselves seated at a long table in what they later found out was the Muscat Sheraton, the only hotel on Earth with appropriate facilities. Each leader was standing in front of a place setting with his or her name on it, a bottle of Perrier water, a plastic flower and an after-dinner mint.

"Please sit down," said Snib Venturi. "Thank you so much for coming."

Each mint had the Venturi logo embossed on its gold foil wrapping, and each leader heard Snib's words in his or her own language or dialect. There were guards on all the doors holding what had to be weapons, though the way in which they functioned wasn't apparent, which was probably just as well. A hundred and ninety-six hitherto very important people looked at each other, then sat down.

"I know how busy you are," Snib said, "so I won't detain you longer than necessary. I just thought it'd be great to have a chance to get to know you all, answer any questions and explain how all of this is going to work in practice."

The President of the United States shot to her feet. "I want to protest in the strongest possible terms," she said, "about this disgraceful tweet tweet tweet." She then flew three times around the room, spat the sprig of olive out of her beak and perched on the head of the Prime Minister of Tonga.

"She gets that one for free," Snib said, "as a token of goodwill, but the next interruption will count as blasphemy and will cost your taxpayers ten billion U.S. dollars. If you'd care to resume your place, Madam President, we can get on."

The white dove fluttered back to her seat. Someone placed a long ruler across the arms so she could perch more comfortably.

"That, ladies and gentlemen," Snib continued, "was a small demonstration, unplanned but timely. If you had any doubts at all, dismiss them. We—my brother Ab and I—are *it*. We *rule*."

A moment of deep silence. Nobody moved. Then Snib grinned and went on: "Now then. If you were paying attention to our inaugural broadcast, you'll have gathered that there are some mighty big changes in the offing. Let me take a moment to explain them to you.

"The Venturi Corporation started in the shadow of a

sand dune on Mars and now rules a billion worlds. We got big by developing a system of ... let's call it morality, because your languages are hopelessly underdeveloped, that gives the customers what they want. I'll cut to the chase. Traditionally, your planet, and millions like it, have lumbered along through the Dark Ages on basically dualistic moral systems. You think in binary terms. Mostly it's Good versus Evil, though in the past—credit where it's due—some of you went for the more rational and commonsensical Honour/Shame dichotomy—which you guys currently regard as quaintly primitive. But let's not dwell on that because everything's about to change. From now on, there is no more Right or Wrong, Good or Evil. We're doing away with all of that. It's holding you back: it leads to war, unhappiness and grossly inefficient distribution of valuable resources. It's gone. Don't give it a second thought."

The assembled leaders of the planet stared at him as though he'd just jumped out of a cake brandishing a flamethrower. He ignored them, smiled and continued.

"Welcome to the brave new world of Venturi morality. There is no more nasty and nice. There's just behaviour, and how you behave is entirely up to you. Nobody is entitled to look down their noses at you for what you choose to do or not do. The key word here is *choose*. It's all about choice. Feed the starving poor, though you'd better get a move on, because pretty soon there won't be any—your choice. Burn down an orphanage? If that's what you want, then fine. There is no more guilt, there is no more conscience. You can do whatever you like, and that's official. Always provided—" he stopped and grinned, and sipped from a glass of murky orange liquid "—always provided ..." he repeated. "Pin your ears back, people, because this is the fun bit.

"Under Venturi morality, every sentient being is master of his fate and captain of his soul. You can do what you want, when you want, how you want, provided you pay for it. And we're not talking some vague metaphysical, allegorical, wishy-washy philosophical price here. We're talking about a fixed tariff of charges, payable in your local currency, fourteen of your Earth days from date of invoice, no excuses, no credit. If you don't pay, you go to jail. We're currently building—" he glanced at his watch "—no, scratch that, we've just completed a magnificent new purpose-built facility in the heart of your delightfully arid Kalahari Desert to house payment defaulters. As a token of respect to your wonderful literary genius Dickens Charles, we've called it the Marshalsea. If you don't pay, that's where you go and that's where you stay until you or someone on your behalf settles the bill, plus interest and administration and handling fees. Let me stress, the Marshalsea isn't Hell. There's no punishment, no fire and brimstone, it's just very, very boring and absolutely one-hundred-per-cent secure.

"Now, you're dying to ask me, what counts as a sin and how much will it cost me? Well, full details are available for download from our website, www.venturi-bros.div, but let me give you the basics.

"We don't actually care what you people like or don't like. It's none of our business. We don't want to intrude, or offend deeply held cultural sensibilities. And you don't want to have to learn a whole new rota of dos and don'ts; it'd be confusing and you wouldn't know where you stand. So we're staying with the basic sins you people have been brought up on for generations, your Big Seven and their various offshoots. Feel free to change these at any time, as and when you feel comfortable doing so. Like I said, it's none of our business.

"So, your basic murder will cost you ten million U.S. dollars. Blasphemy is a flat-rate five hundred. Theft is a hundred times the value of the item stolen, same for fraud and embezzlement, only double that if the victims are widows and orphans. Pride is calculated as a multiple of your average yearly income, and we're doing an introductory special offer on coveting your neighbour's ox, one thousand dollars. And so on. If you want to sin and you can afford it, please go ahead. We value your custom. Bear in mind though that detection and invoicing will be immediate and unconditional, and we don't take excuses, justifications or American Express. Within ten seconds of committing your sin, you will be greeted by one of our accredited collection agents and handed a statement. Failure to pay within the specified time will land you in the Marshalsea, as I just explained, and interest on overdue bills will be 20 per cent per annum compound. Right now, all across the planet, people are finding out how the system works in practice, but I expect you'd like a demonstration. So, if I could have a volunteer? You, madam? Thank you. If you'd care to steal the pencil of the gentleman on your left."

The German Chancellor reached out and slipped the pencil into her bag. At once a window opened in thin air and a man in a suit climbed out of it and gave her a friendly smile. "Hi there," he said. "Theft of a pencil valued at forty-five cents U.S. Here's your invoice." He handed her a sheet of pink paper. "You'll find a choice of easy ways to pay on the back, or you may want to consider opening an account with us, entitling you to use our online One-Crime-One-Click option. Have a nice day." He vanished. The Chancellor stared at the pink slip, then scrabbled in her bag for her chequebook.

"There you have it," Snib said. "Divine justice. Quick,

efficient, infallible, incorruptible. You people came somewhere close to it back in your Middle Ages, with your system of indulgences, but for some reason you turned against it. Never mind. Now, I'd like you all to go back to your various nation states and think very carefully about what this is going to mean for your citizens and society in general. I think you'll find, as billions have before you, that the Venturi way is so much better than anything that's gone before. Thank you so much for your time."

The world leaders vanished. Snib Venturi pulled out a big red silk handkerchief and mopped his forehead. Then he drained his glass, strolled down the table to where the Chancellor had been sitting, picked up her cheque, folded it precisely in half, kissed it and slipped it in his top pocket.

15

Far over the misty mountains cold, in dungeons deep and caverns old and hopelessly unhygienic, bathed in the steel-grey light that filters through a half-mile-thick ceiling of frozen ocean, they live, work and occasionally eat each other. Their claws are hooked and needle-sharp, but they long ago learned to adapt, to make the most of what little they have, to turn handicaps into advantages. Because of, not in spite of, the claws they do the most amazing work in microcircuitry, each talon a precise pincer capable of gripping and manipulating the tiniest component. They're experts in other fields as well. They're blacksmiths and textile workers, carpenters, upholsterers, carvers, embroiderers, software engineers, machinists, specialists in plastic extrusion and precision injection moulding. The points of their ears are hard and sharp as blackthorn spines, they have teeth like sharks and their eyes are ruby red.

How long have they been there? They themselves don't know, or care. They still wear the colours that camouflaged them when they cowered in the underbrush of the greenwood, just as you still have vestigial claws on your fingers and toes. They've come a long way from the savage, terrified forest-floor creatures they once were, but there are some traditions they won't give up, even if they no longer remember what they once meant. You might call them stubborn or set in their ways. In matters of diet and cuisine, for example ...

A window opened in thin air and a smiling human in a suit stepped out of it. "Hey, guys," he said. "I notice that you're operating dangerous machinery without a guard or appropriate safety precautions, thereby endangering yourselves and others and contravening health and safety regulations. Here's your invoice, with details of convenient ways to pay on the back."

They looked at him, then at each other. Then one of them said, "Get him."

The smiling human didn't move. "In case you were thinking of eating me," he said, "may I point out that this would be impossible, since I am (a) an angel and (b) not strictly speaking present in a corporeal sense. It'd also be a Class A sin carrying a tariff of twenty million dollars. Theoretically even considering assaulting an officer of the Authorities is a Class B sin, so I would strongly recommend ..."

He tailed off. They were grinning at him. Even though he was immortal, immune and not there, he felt a tiny quiver of panic and stepped back into his shimmering window. It wouldn't open.

They took a step closer, their eyes red as a sniper's laser sight. "Guys," he said, "this is no way to behave, trust me. I don't care how rich you are, you can't afford it."

He'd said the wrong thing. "Money doesn't matter," one of them hissed through gritted fangs. "It's the thought that counts. Right, lads, on three. One, two ..."

He was immortal and immune, and according to the laws of physics prevailing in 99.67 per cent of the Multiverse, he wasn't there; he was somewhere else. But they ate him anyway.

16

" **A** nd that's the position," Mr. Lucifer said. "It's not exactly what I'd have liked, but it wasn't up to me, was it?"

Mr. Lucifer had just spent an hour telling Bernie everything he'd already found out about the new regime. Bernie felt sorry for him. He looked desperately tired, and his face was a pale shade of pink instead of its usual fire-apple red. Too long spent cooped up indoors when he could've been out on the golf course. "No, Mr. Lucifer. I guess not."

Mr. Lucifer poured himself a glass of water. It hissed slightly as he drank it, and wisps of steam drifted out of his ears. "What it comes down to," he said, "is money."

"Yes, Mr. Lucifer."

"We're going to need a lot of it."

"Yes, Mr. Lucifer."

"And what they're giving us won't be nearly enough."

"No, Mr. Lucifer."

A sigh that seemed to come from the centre of the Earth. "I tried telling them, but they just wouldn't listen. They kept talking about bottom lines. What's that supposed to mean? I said. They just looked at me."

It had come as a bit of shock to find out that, where

finance and commerce were concerned, the Father of Lies was hopelessly naïve and a bit of an idealist. It shouldn't have been a surprise, of course; he'd spent his entire working life in the public sector, so naturally what did he know about the harsh realities of the marketplace? To him, bottom lines were what you got if you sunbathed in a bikini. Bernie had been at Walmart before he got this job. If he lost it, he'd have to go back there, or somewhere very much like it. The thought of that had been concentrating his mind like nothing else.

"So," Mr. Lucifer went on, "if they won't give us enough money to keep this place ticking over, well, I don't know what we're supposed to do. It's *unreasonable*."

So much bewilderment, such a world of abused innocence squashed into five little syllables. "Yes, Mr. Lucifer. Mr. Lucifer . . ."

"Hm?"

"I've been thinking."

The Great Enemy looked at him, like someone who's just realised that the scruffy old painting that had been hanging on the lavatory wall since he was a boy might in fact be a priceless Old Master. "Say what?"

"I've been thinking, Mr. Lucifer. About the money."

"But I've only just told you—"

"Yes, well, I did a bit of, um, creative extrapolation."

Mr. Lucifer frowned. "You mean, you'd already got it all figured out before I told you."

"Um, not all of it. But I did have a few ideas."

The look on the Prince of Darkness's face was a picture. It was how Pooh and Piglet might have looked as Christopher Robin strode up to rescue them from some tiny but insuperable crisis. "You're a smart boy, Bernie. I probably haven't told you that often enough, but you're a really smart boy. What ideas?"

"Well." Bernie had written a list on a piece of paper, but he found he didn't need it. "The way I see it, we've got a lot of stuff we aren't going to need any more, right?"

Mr. Lucifer nodded sadly. "Redundant capacity," he said. "All of which has got to be maintained, and eating up valuable income."

"Yes and no, Mr. Lucifer. I prefer to look at it as resources."

He knew that Mr. Lucifer was on the cusp of one of his headaches. He took a couple of tablets from his pocket, dropped them in Mr. L.'s glass of water, and nodded at it.

"You're a lifesaver, Bernie. Don't know what I'd do without you."

Properly speaking, aspirin was utterly forbidden in Flipside, which was probably why Mr. Lucifer had never tried it until Bernie introduced him to it. Probably it was very wrong, but who was ever going to know? "Resources," Bernie repeated firmly. "Like, take Purgatory."

Mr. Lucifer rolled his eyes. "Please," he said, "be my guest. You know I had the builders' estimates a couple of weeks ago? They're saying the whole of the east wall is structurally unsound. You just won't believe what it's going to cost."

Bernie cleared his throat. "Am I right in thinking," he said, "that under the new system we won't be using that part of the facility any more?"

Mr. Lucifer nodded. "Still got to keep it maintained, though," he said savagely. "I told them, it's just not enough. What they're giving us is barely going to keep the furnaces lit."

"In which case," Bernie persevered, "we've got a large structure standing empty, with accommodation, assembly and activity areas and a large purpose-built lecture hall."

Mr. Lucifer frowned. "You could say that," he said.

"Ideal," Bernie went on, "for conferences, trade exhibitions, conventions—"

"Just a moment." The coal-red eyes had narrowed. "Are you suggesting—?"

"We hire it out." Bernie nodded. "We'll have to spend a bit to get it into shape," he added quickly. "Carpets, en-suite bedrooms, toilets, etcetera. But I've done a few projections." He handed Mr. Lucifer a sheet of paper. "I think you'll find that even on a quite conservative business model . . ."

Mr. Lucifer looked up from the paper and gazed at him. "That much?"

"I don't see why not. And yes, there's some initial outlay but, like you said, we'd have had to spend most of that just to keep it from falling down. And the potential returns—"

"And your lot—I'm, sorry, *humans*—they'd really pay money to come and stay in . . . ?"

"Oh yes." Bernie nodded confidently. "There'd be a lot of interest, I can guarantee it. You see, Mr. Lucifer, what we've got here is a brand."

"I know. Lots of them. And red-hot pokers and—"

"A brand," Bernie said, "which is instantly recognised. Everybody's heard of it. You have no idea how valuable that could be."

Mr. Lucifer sucked his teeth. "You sure about that? I mean, you people . . ."

Bernie shook his head. "You're thinking humans won't want anything to do with us because we're nasty."

"Well, yes. I mean, it stands to reason."

"With respect, Mr. Lucifer. Humans *love* nasty."

Mr. Lucifer blinked. "You do?"

"*They* do, yes. I mean, if you don't believe me, look at their literature, their entertainment, their popular culture."

Mr. Lucifer gave him a wry grin. "Have I got to?"

"My point exactly. Look at human make-believe, the stuff we invent in our heads for fun. We love murder and violence. We make heroes out of criminals; we get a thrill out of seeing people on a larger-than-life screen getting beaten up, robbed, hurt, made unhappy. As children we swoon over characters we'd run away from screaming if we met them in real life. But it's *not* real life. That's the difference, you see. As nasty as possible, as long as it's just pretend."

Mr. Lucifer blinked. "And your point is?"

"They'll be crazy about Flipside," Bernie said. "They'll come here in droves, just so long as they can leave when they're done. Theme parks, adventure weekends, things for the kiddies to do in the school holidays—and we don't even have to worry about the weather, cos it's all indoors. And the merchandising." He stopped and caught his breath. "The merchandising will be *huge*. Trust me."

"What's merchandising?"

Bernie closed his eyes just for a moment. Then he explained about merchandising. When he'd finished, Mr. Lucifer used his thumb to close his mouth, which had fallen open. "Really?"

"Really and truly."

"T-shirts with *me* on them?"

Bernie hesitated. "Maybe not," he said. "No offence, but I think we may have to get an actor or a model or something."

"Huh?"

During his time Flipside, Bernie had learned tact the way a man falling off a building learns to fly. "People have a mental picture of how they think you ought to look. It's not quite you, if you see what I mean. But that's not a problem. Like I said, we can hire someone. It's all about giving them what they think they want, you see."

"Not really, no."

Bernie pursed his lips. "The thing is," he said, "ever since they were kids, my lot—Squishies—have always believed they know what you look like. And that picture in their heads, to them it's the real you. So if they met the *real* real you, they wouldn't believe in it. So, we have to give them what they can believe in. You can't go messing about with that, or your whole brand becomes worthless. You've got to preserve that idea in their heads, intact, untarnished. What you might call the doctrine of the immaculate preconception."

Mr. Lucifer gazed at him for a moment, then shrugged. "Fine," he said. "I think I'll leave the whole thing up to you, if you're OK with that." He started to get up, then stopped as though an unseen hand was pressing him down into his chair. "You're sure about this?"

"Yes, Mr. Lucifer."

"Really, really sure?"

"Yes, Mr. Lucifer. I know people. All due respect, you don't. Trust me." He hesitated, then unfolded a scrap of paper and slid it across the desk. "Just an idea I had," he said. "It'll need work, but it ought to give you the general idea."

Mr. Lucifer glanced at it, and his eyebrows rose like gold prices in a financial crisis. "You're kidding."

Bernie shook his head. "Mr. Lucifer," he said, "there's an outfit Middleside called the Disney Corporation; they've got several of these places, bringing in billions of dollars a year, and I promise you, we could get ten times the throughput."

"This thing here." Mr. Lucifer jabbed a claw at Bernie's sketch. "That's one of those carrier things you people use to transport shopping."

"That's right, Mr. Lucifer."

"But it's huge. And it's got wheels on."

Bernie nodded. "Actually, it's a bus," he said. "The idea is, you sit in the bus and it drives around the theme park, and you can see all the sights without having to walk. The people who go to this sort of place don't like walking much. So you've got to have a bus."

Mr. Lucifer shrugged. "If you say so. But why make it look like a shopping thing?"

"For the slogan," Bernie said. "It's the slogan that does it. That's the principle on which all commercial activity Middleside is founded. Doesn't matter if the goods are no good and the services ain't serviceable, if you've got a few snappy words that catch the public imagination, you've won."

Mr. Lucifer massaged the roots of his left horn. "Fine," he said. "And what did you have in mind?"

Bernie felt himself blush, but he couldn't help that. As far as he was concerned, this was his moment; he had the right. *"Go to Hell in a handcart,"* he said. "We'll need to get it trademarked, of course, but that shouldn't be a problem."

A sad look spread over Mr. Lucifer's face. "You know what, Bernie?" he said. "Maybe all this has come at just the right time. Maybe it's a good thing, getting out of the business. It's at moments like this, I realise, everything's got so . . ."

Bernie shot him a look of genuine compassion. "Yes, Mr. Lucifer."

17

"It's ghastly," said the pink-faced man at the British consulate. "Absolutely appalling. It's getting so that I can't do my job."

"Oh?"

"We can't tell lies any more. Every time we do, some loathsome little man pops up out of thin air and charges us fifty thousand dollars. We're *diplomats*. How can we be expected to function under those conditions?"

Lucy nodded slowly. "Awkward," she said. "Still, in other respects it must make life a little bit easier. Like, for instance, you know without any possibility of doubt that when I say I'm stuck here with no passport, no money and no plane ticket I'm telling the truth. Which means you can fly me home without all the tedious business of checking up on me."

The pink-faced man frowned at her. "Ah yes," he said. "Now I've considered the circumstances of your case and I have to say, I'm not sure that you qualify for—"

Lucy held up her hand, then pointed to a space in thin air just over the pink-faced man's right shoulder. It would be just about where a window would form, and a Sin Guidance Adviser would materialise. "Fifty thousand dollars," she said. "Taxpayers' money."

The pink-faced man scowled at her. "Yes, all right. You see my point? There'll be hordes of feckless idiots rolling up here and we'll have to send them home again, just because they've got stupid *rights*. It's not the way we do things."

Lucy beamed at him. "Now then," she said. "About my friend."

The pink-faced man relaxed slightly. "Can't help you there. He's not a British citizen."

"He will be if he and I get married."

The pink-faced man winced. When it came to marriage, Venturi brothers morality was refreshingly cut-to-the-chase: if you say you're married, you are; if you say you aren't, you aren't. In due course, no doubt, nationality laws would adapt and catch up, once they'd been through committee and three times round the Upper and Lower Houses. Until then, however, you could marry in the departure lounge and divorce while waiting to pick your suitcases up off the carousel, and it'd all be perfectly legal. "Congratulations," the pink-faced man snarled. "I hope you'll be very happy."

"We will be once we're on the plane. Thank you so much."

*

But they weren't. "Keep it down, will you?" Jersey hissed as the slight kick of take-off nudged his spine into the seat cushions. "People are staring."

He might just have said the wrong thing. "Screw them."

"It's perfectly all right. We're airborne."

"That's a contradiction in terms. Don't contradict yourself, it's rude."

"There's absolutely nothing to be scared of." He lowered his voice slightly. "Come on," he said. "You're the one who used to go everywhere by magical zapping. Now that was scary."

"It was not," she snapped. "By definition."

"Excuse me?"

"God was doing the zapping; I was cradled in the arms of the Almighty—how safe can you get? This thing only stays up because of chemically induced flatulence."

Jersey shrugged. "Relax. I've flown hundreds of times— helicopters, microlights, jet fighters, once on the back of a very large eagle. There's absolutely nothing to be concerned about."

A slight gust of wind rocked the plane a tiny bit. Lucy screamed and scrabbled at the window with her fingernails. "I'm sorry," she said. "No, actually I'm not sorry at all. Make them turn this thing round and go back. I'm going to walk home."

Jersey closed his eyes. "Are you always like this?"

"Well, no."

"Just when you're with me. I see."

She shrugged helplessly. "Usually I cope by praying," she confessed. "I say Hail Marys under my breath all the way. Well, it worked, didn't it?" she added before he could say anything.

"Fine. Carry on, don't mind me."

She scowled at him. "I can't, not now."

He gave her a puzzled look. "Why not? I don't think they've made it illegal, have they?"

"No, but it won't do any good. Not now I know for a fact there's nobody there to listen."

"Yes, there is. Are. Two of them, in expensive suits. Beyond a shadow of a doubt."

"Yes, but not the sort you pray to. All they do is take your money. They're not going to intervene if this useless contraption decides to fall out of the sky."

"Um," Jersey said, "to be honest with you, I'm not convinced the previous administration was any better."

"Maybe not, but we didn't *know* that. You could hope. You could have faith. It worked for me," she added in a tone of voice that suggested reasoned arguments wouldn't be welcome. "And now it doesn't work any more, and I'm a million miles up in the sky riding in a machine that keeps itself from nosediving into the sea by farting fire, and we're almost certainly going to die, and all you can do is—"

"Excuse me."

The passenger in the seat in front had got up and turned round and was perching his elbows uncomfortably on the headrest. He looked about seventeen, but he had kind eyes.

"What?"

"Sorry," said the kid, "but I couldn't help overhearing. Are you nervous about flying?"

"Yes."

"Don't be." He smiled. "It'll be fine." He had curly white-blond hair and baby-blue eyes, peach fuzz on his top lip.

"What did you just say?"

"It'll be fine," the kid repeated. "We'll have a quiet, peaceful, very boring flight, and then we'll make a safe landing, and everything'll be all right. Trust me."

And for some reason she did. It made no sense. He was just a kid. She couldn't even be sure where he was from. He looked American, but his voice had no discernible accent of any kind, which was weird if you thought about it, which she didn't because she trusted him implicitly. "Sorry," she said. "I hope I wasn't disturbing you."

"Not a bit," the kid said, and he smiled again. It wasn't a movie-star smile, acting on the glands and knee joints, it was your big brother, who's just looked under the bed and declared it guaranteed free of monsters. Lucy didn't have a brother, and she'd always wanted to find a monster under her bed so she could bash it senseless with her slipper and take it in to school to show her friends. The only thing in the whole world she was scared of was flying. Only, apparently, not any more. "Sit back and enjoy the ride. It's good fun once you get used to it. And perfectly safe."

The kid turned and sat down, the back of his head invisible behind the headrest. Lucy took a long, deep breath, folded her hands in her lap and sat perfectly still for a while.

"You're grinning."

"You what?"

"Correction. Not grinning, beaming."

She made no effort to change her expression. "So what if I am?"

"A moment ago—"

"I'm better now. Let's not talk about it. I made a scene, big deal. I think I might just close my eyes for five minutes."

No sooner said than zonked. She snored, but only quietly. It was a sound you could get used to, like rain falling on the roof. Jersey folded his arms behind his head and tried to relax, but he realised he was wound up like a clock spring.

No surprise there, when you thought about it. A man spends his entire life fixating on the tantalising possibility that there may be a way to talk to God. After five years of non-stop action adventure, in the course of which he'd suffered a broken arm, four cracked ribs, multiple concussions, lacerations, burns, gunshot wounds, all manner of fun stuff, not to mention breaking countless laws, stealing aircraft, burgling top-secret government buildings, fighting mano-a-mano with violent men, giving no thought whatsoever to his CV or his pension arrangements and having absolutely no social life—all that, and finally he'd got what he wanted.

A wise man once said that he who attains his ideal by that very act transcends it. Put another way, if the sole purpose of your existence is getting a date with the prettiest girl in the class and she turns out to have bad breath and a laugh like a lemming in a blender, you run the risk of finding yourself in a place where you ask, "What now?" and no answer springs to mind. He'd done it—dreamed the impossible dream, fought the unbeatable foe, made the call and been put through—only to find the very next day that God had sold out to the Venturi boys and everything was suddenly completely different, rendering his colossal achievement meaningless. Oh, and he'd met someone who might well prove to be the girl of his dreams, except he'd been too preoccupied to give the matter proper attention. Which said it all, really. When true love comes bursting in on you like the radiant dawn, and you more or less tell it, *Please hold, your call is important to us*, it's a fair bet that something is wrong with this picture.

Well, yes. For example, what did the spotty American kid have that he didn't? One word from him and she stopped climbing the curtains, curled up in a little ball and went to sleep. Symptomatic, you might say, of a world gone mad. He realised that his hands had clenched into fists, which was silly. For the first time in years, the chances of his having to punch somebody out in the next ten minutes were practically zero, and clenching your fists is practically begging for carpal tunnel issues at some point down the line. Even so. He peered over and ascertained that there was an empty seat next to the irritating kid. He got up and went and sat in it.

The kid smiled at him. "She's nice, isn't she?"

"Yes, and just you—"

"She likes you."

Jersey blinked. "You think so?"

The kid nodded. "A lot. But right now she's confused and she's got a lot of other things on her mind. Well, you all do. We all do, I mean. With the change in management and everything. I guess coping with that and dealing with romantic feelings at the same time is a bit too much to ask, even though women are proverbially good at multi-tasking. I expect you're a bit mixed up too."

"Just a bit."

The kid nodded. "It's going to take some getting used to."

"You bet it is."

"The Venturi brothers—" the kid paused and frowned "—they aren't bad people, fundamentally. Just very focused."

"On making a lot of money."

The kid inclined his head. "Yes," he said, "to the exclusion of every other factor, but that's not necessarily a bad thing. After all, it's a business, and they're ultimately answerable to the stockholders."

"Is that right?"

"Oh yes. Of course, they own most of the stock. But you know what they say: if a thing's worth doing . . ." The kid sighed. "And who's to say the new system won't be better than the old one? I mean, it's worked all right on a billion other worlds across three galaxies. The old firm who used to run this place only had the one world. There's advantages to being part of a big organisation. I guess." The kid shook his head like a wet dog, then stuck out his hand. "I'm Kevin, by the way."

His grip was surprisingly strong. "Hi. And I'm—"

"Jersey. Pleased to meet you."

Must've seen his name on a luggage tag or something. It didn't matter. "Where are you headed?"

Kevin shrugged. "Just sort of drifting aimlessly about," he said. "How about you? Got any plans for the future?"

An odd way of putting it, if you didn't know someone's backstory. "No," Jersey said. "I've, um, I've just finished something I was working on for a long time, and now I'm, well, not quite sure, really."

"Drifting aimlessly?"

"Pretty much."

Kevin nodded. "It's not something I'd recommend long term, but now and again it does no harm to go with the flow. Also—" he paused, frowned then went on "—I had a bit of a falling-out with my old man. No big deal. I don't suppose you want to hear about it."

"No, please, if it'd help to talk . . ."

"Yes." Kevin flashed him a smile you could have toasted muffins over. "Yes, I'd like that a lot. You see, my father and my brother used to run the family business. Old-established firm, proud traditions, all that."

"Got you, yes."

"Now, all I ever wanted to do was work in it with them, but . . . well, the fact is, I couldn't make the grade."

"Surely not."

Kevin shook his head sadly. "No, they were quite right. They gave me a lot of chances, but I kept screwing up. You can't blame them. I mean, it's not like it was just the three of us to consider. There were a lot of people depending on us. Couldn't afford the sort of boo-boo I was forever making. They were very nice about it, but they had to draw the line."

"I'm sorry."

"Thank you." Another warm smile. "Anyhow, a short while ago Dad got this really great offer for the business.

And he thought about it very carefully and talked it over with my brother, and they decided to sell out and move away. And I . . ."

"Yes?"

Kevin closed his eyes, just for a moment. "I could've gone with them. Of course they wanted me to. But somehow . . . I guess, basically, I've done nothing all my life, just hung out and chilled, and the prospect of hanging out and chilling for ever and ever and never doing *anything* . . . We're not like that in my family, you see. We're doers. Always busy. Improving the shining hour sort of thing. We live for the job."

Jersey grinned. "That old Protestant work ethic, you mean."

For some reason Kevin had difficulty with that. He frowned and took a moment to choose his words. "Something like that. So anyway, that's not how I was brought up. I feel I ought to get out there and do something too."

"Fair enough. So, why don't you?"

Kevin smiled. "It's easy for you to say that. You're a genuine man of action, anyone can see that just looking at you. I'll bet that for as long as you can remember, you've had a definite goal ahead of you—difficult, maybe, perhaps practically impossible, but that never stopped you. In your vocabulary, *can't* is the name of a German philosopher as spelt by a greengrocer. No, you gritted your teeth, clenched your fists, got down and did it. And once you'd climbed one mountain, there was the next one facing you. Am I right?"

"Yes. That's amazing. How did you—?"

"Whereas," Kevin went on, "I've never had a goal in my whole life, except working with Dad and Jay, and that was out of the question. And so here I am. I can have anything

I want, and I don't want anything. Except something to want, if that makes any sense." He laughed. "Sounds pretty pathetic, doesn't it? I mean, there's so many people out there in desperate need, so what have I got to complain about? Nothing."

Jersey frowned. "No, I know just how you feel," he said. "Only in my case . . . Well, I'll spare you the sob story, but I just got what I'd always wanted and then—"

"It was taken away from you?"

Jersey shook his head. "It all just changed, that's all. It's really hard to explain, actually, but—"

"That's OK. I get the general idea. But at least in your case you can look back and say, I did what I set out to do, I prevailed, even though the Universe cheated by changing the rules at the last minute. That doesn't stop you feeling good about yourself. You can look in the mirror and see a winner. Meanwhile, you're a hero who's between adventures. Something else'll come along, and you'll snap back into action, no trouble. Right now you're feeling a bit low because you've found your Lost Ark. What you don't realise is that you've got your Temple of Doom and your Last Crusade still to come."

Suddenly Jersey felt like grinning. "And my Crystal Skull."

Kevin frowned. "On the other hand, there's lot to be said for knowing when to stop. But you get the idea."

Jersey laughed. "Well, there you go, then," he said. "The same goes for you, surely. You'll find your trilogy, same as I'll find mine."

"You think so?"

"I'm sure of it," Jersey said. "I mean, you're smart, you're understanding. You really know people, you know?"

"I haven't actually met very many," Kevin said. "But those I've met I've liked."

"Really?"

"Oh yes. When you get to know them, everybody's worth knowing. I mean, look at you and me. You came over here to smash my face in for talking to your girl, and now we're the best of friends. Honestly, there's no such thing as an entirely bad person. The way I see it, the good in people is like the meat in a supermarket lasagne. You've just got to keep on and on, searching and searching, until eventually you find it."

18

There are three dawns every day on Sinderaan. The first dawn comes up like thunder, drenching the canyons and the towering basalt pillars with red so deep you can practically feel it running down your face. The second dawn, two hours later, is a mellow flood of butter yellow. The third, around primary noon, is a searing, bleaching white heat, spooling threads of white mist off the lakes and rivers. You don't need to light a campfire on Sinderaan to boil water for your midday coffee.

Because the dry land is too hot to sustain life for so much of the day, it's no wonder that most of the serious evolutionary action took place in the ocean. Only the topmost six fathoms or so actually boils, except in midsummer; below that it ranges from tepid to luxuriously warm. Daylight for twenty hours out of the twenty-nine means deep-level photosynthesis is a given. Abundant underwater vegetation comfortably supports an incalculable quantity of fish, all of whom are smart, some very smart indeed. It's an open secret that when Snib Venturi's nephew Gred chose Fernwater College for young Ade, a substantial donation changed hands, although some of the hands were fins, which helped with the rather fussy entrance requirements, and everyone was a winner. In short, you have to get up pretty early in the morning to catch a Sinderaan fish.

Today, as on every other day since they'd arrived, the keepnet was full to bursting and third dawn was still several hours away. Jay was frying up a mess of snarg-fish (including four Snobel laureates and a professor of advanced particle physics—a waste, you might say, but on Sinderaan there are plenty more fish in the sea) while Dad sat behind a motionless float, reading the trade papers.

"It says here," he announced, "that Earth's been nom-inated for a Divvy."

Jay was concentrating on the pan and didn't look round. "Is that right?"

"That's what it says in the comic," Dad said. "In the Most Improved World category."

Jay frowned. There hadn't been any award nominations when they were running the place, and he knew that Dad had always felt a bit hard done-by on that score. "Well, you know what that's all about," he said. "If the Venturi boys ever have kids, they ought to name them Graft and Shmooze."

"The guy in the paper says there's been dramatic improvements in the first six weeks. He says—"

"Look out, Dad, you've got a bite."

Dad peered over the top of his paper, saw the bobbing float, put the paper down and effortlessly reeled in a forty-six-ton *szxnarpp* with brick-red horns and fluorescent pink wattles on each of its four necks. He scowled at it and threw it back. "Here's what it says," he said. " 'Apart from the occasional *crime passionel*, all crimes are committed by the rich. To do murder on Earth these days, you need to be pretty high up in the Forbes List. This is great for the poor, who are no longer slaughtered by the untouchable privileged elite, as well as being rewarded with a wonderful sense of moral superiority, and the actual crime rate is negligible. This is great for government, who no longer need to pay out for police, prisons, justice systems etcetera and can therefore afford proper healthcare for the mentally ill, who therefore no longer commit the proportion of crimes traditionally committed by maniacs and loons. Also, the cost of sinning is a wonderful spur to wealthy entrepreneurs, movers and shakers, who need to generate vast incomes—honestly and ethically; they can't steal, cheat or grind the faces of the poor, which would cost them more money than they make—in order to indulge even slightly antisocial whims and hobbies. Thus the free-market economy booms and everybody benefits. Once again the Venturi system proves beyond doubt that a happy, caring, prosperous society and a healthy bottom line aren't just not mutually exclusive, but inseparable cause and effect.'" He put the paper down and scowled. "Well, son, that's you and me told."

Jay shrugged. "It's nice to know the old place is doing so well. After all, we were never in it for the glory."

Dad sighed. "Sure," he said. "If they're better off without us, that's just fine. At least we did one thing right. We sold up and got out of there."

The trade papers, Jay had recognised from the outset, were a mistake. Whenever the old man read them, he got broody. "We did our best, Dad," he said, "and that's all anyone can do. And we didn't do so bad. After all, if the place was such a disaster, how come the Venturis wanted to buy it?"

Dad baited his hook with a glistening multi-faceted algorithm—bits of feather and coloured string just don't cut it on Sinderaan—and cast far out into the shimmering blue. There was a soft plop. He sat down and tilted his hat over his eyes. "How long till chow's ready? I'm starting to feel a bit peckish."

"Give it another two minutes."

"I wonder how Kevin's getting on. You heard from him at all?"

"No, Dad."

"I worry about that boy."

"He'll be fine," Jay said, as he did every day about this time. For some reason the smell of cooking always got Dad worrying about his younger son. Association of ideas, presumably; they'd only tended to meet at mealtimes. "He's not a bad kid really. He's immortal and invulnerable and immune from any form of illness, and he's got Raffa and Gabe looking after him. What harm can he possibly come to?"

"You're right, of course. I just worry, that's all."

"Course you do. You're his father. Come and get it while it's hot."

Jay was a good cook—he could work miracles with a couple of loaves of bread and a few fish—but Dad didn't seem to taste what he was eating. Understandable, but they'd been through all that. "Tell you what," Jay said. "Tomorrow, let's get up early and go try that place out beyond the electromagnetic reefs. They reckon there's *grllp* out there thick as your wrist."

"If you like, son."

"Or we could hire a comet and go out after *zbnsnorpak* in the Oort cloud."

"Sure. Why not?"

And that, Jay decided, was the problem with leisure. In order to enjoy a day off, there has to be something for it to be off from. But endless free time—free in this case meaning without charge, without price, therefore without value. Nothing to do, and for ever to do it in. Still, it had been Dad's idea and his decision. His free will, in fact. "Anything else in the papers?"

Dad shook his head. "That Venturi Corporation stock we took as part of the deal," he said, "just went up another three thousand and seventy-five points."

Jay's eyebrows rose. "In a week?"

"I guess that means we're rich."

"That's nice."

"Isn't it?"

Dad took off his old fishing hat and looked at it. Not a rich man's hat. It had been shabby right from the Beginning, and you could clearly see the marks where Dad had carelessly left it lying in the path of an advancing glacier. But money couldn't buy that hat. It was a companion, more than that, a witness. "He could at least call," Dad said sadly. "Or write."

"Never much of a one for letters, our kid."

"But he could call, just once in a while. Let us know how he's getting on."

Jay could smell danger. "If you want," he said, "I'll get on to Gabe, see if there's any news."

Dad shook his head. "They'd have let us know if anything had happened. No, it'd just be nice to hear from him, that's all."

"He's just fine, Dad. Trust me."

Dad shrugged. "Maybe that's what's bugging me," he said. "The thought that Kevin's there, and he's doing fine without us. Maybe he was only too glad to see the back of me, same as the rest of them."

Jay gave him a sad smile. "You know you don't mean that."

"No, I don't suppose I do. Still, it wouldn't kill him to pick up a phone."

"You could call him."

Dad frowned. "He made his choice," he said. "He wanted to stay on."

"Free will."

"Exactly."

Jay turned away and started scouring out the pan with a handful of dry grass. On Earth, under the Venturis, the phrase *free will* no longer had much meaning, unless followed by something like *with every divorce when you instruct Wheeler, Moresby & Shark*. Assuming they still had lawyers, or were they redundant too, along with the police and the jailers? Quite possibly. If so, he'd miss them, if only for the splash of colour they lent the world with their outrageous ingenuity. Who could forget the outfit who'd built the mile-long needle just opposite the gates of the Kingdom of Heaven? The eye on that thing was so big you could get an oil tanker through it, let alone a camel. You had to admire someone who could think like that.

"Haven't heard from Nicky, either."

"I guess he's busy."

"Sure." Dad scowled at his float. There had been a time when his slightest frown would have parted the waters in a flash, cleaving a channel through water and rock right down to the magma, but not now, not here. Here and now he was just another expat, filling in time and hassling the fish. "Never thought I'd live to see the day when I'm jealous of the Prince of Darkness because he's busy. Doesn't seem right, does it?"

Jay grinned. "Bet you anything you like he'd swap places in a heartbeat."

"Don't tempt me."

Jay pursed his lips. It was worse than he'd thought. By now, surely, the withdrawal pains should be easing off, not getting worse. But how would he know? He'd never been retired before. True, it was easier for him. His role in the organisation had been mostly in toxic waste disposal, taking away the sins of the world (sins of the world to take away; you want fries with that?) and, truth to tell, he'd never really cared for it much. A necessary job, no doubt about it, and someone had to do it, and he'd done it with all his might because he believed in what they were doing, in the organisation, in Dad ... But did he miss it on a day-to-day basis, the actual stuff he used to do, the scape-goating, the everything turning out to be his fault? No, to be brutally honest, he didn't. Nice to start off a bright new day without having to take responsibility for the twelve thousand murders committed the previous night; nice to see something less than optimal go down and be able to say, *Hey, nothing to do with me.* Nice, even, to burn the toast or spill the coffee and be able to feel guilty for something he actually had done, for a change. Simple pleasures, but none the less valid for that.

"Why do I get the impression," he said, "that something's bugging you?"

Dad grinned at him. "Because something is."

"Ah. That'd do it every time."

Dad heaved a long sigh. "You know what, son," he said. "I think I may just possibly have made a mistake."

"Surely not."

"Nice of you to say so, but—"

"I mean," Jay repeated, "surely not. Because of, you know, the infallibility thing? You, make a mistake. Not possible."

Dad laughed. "It's that old chestnut, isn't it? Can I create a rock so heavy I can't lift it?"

"Oh, I remember that one." Jay smiled fondly. "Took you a whole afternoon, and then we realised we couldn't get the darned thing out of the living room, so it had to stay there, and Mikey and Gabe had a go at it with cold chisels and turned it into a fireplace." He frowned. "It's still there, presumably. Unless the Venturis—"

He didn't complete the sentence, but the harm was done. "Yes, well," Dad said. "This is the same sort of thing, isn't it? Can someone who's infallible make a mistake? And if he can't, how can he be omnipotent at the same time? Only, I think I did."

A thought struck Jay. He tried to pretend it hadn't, but he was dealing with someone to whom all secrets are known. "Go on," Dad said. "Spit it out."

"When you first got the idea of retiring," Jay said.

A look of dreadful clarity slowly spread over Dad's face. "I remember now. It was here. That fishing trip. The one before last."

Jay nodded. "So when you thought it'd be a good idea to retire, you weren't on Earth; you were here."

"Out of my jurisdiction. On Sinderaan, where I'm just an ordinary Joe." Dad shook his head. "Figures. Well, I guess that settles it. I made a mistake."

For a long time neither of them spoke. Overhead, clouds masked two of the three suns. A *bzyggwazhk* nibbled at the bait on Dad's hook, saw the fallacy in the underlying premise just in time, and swam away unscathed.

Old habits die hard. "Drat," said Dad.

Jay nodded. "Still. Nothing we can do about it now."

"I guess not."

"I mean, if we were back home and you hadn't sold the business, we could, because we could do *anything*. But we aren't and you did, so . . ."

"Quite."

"Feels funny, doesn't it, not being able to do something."

"Yup. Not sure I like it much."

"Me neither. Doesn't seem right somehow."

"No."

Jay stood up. "Well," he said, "no use crying over spilt milk. I guess we'll just have to make the best of it. Come on, let's pack up here and try that place over by the Bottomless Lake."

"I'm sick of fishing."

Jay sighed and sat down again. "Me too. But what can we do?"

"Pray?"

"Yeah, right. Who to, Snib Venturi? I don't think so. Look, it's no good beating yourself up about it. These things happen."

"And I'm sick of this place too. I never want to see it again as long as I live."

Absolution, Jay thought, absolution and forgiveness is what he needs, so he can move on and make a new life. I should be able to do that for him—if not me, who else?—but I'm not sure I can. "I know," Jay said. "Let's fire up the Winnebago, head out to the stars and travel. Go places. Third star to the left and straight on till morning. Well? What about it?"

Dad frowned. Suddenly he looked old. "I don't know," he said.

"Sure you do. Dad, there's a whole infinite Multiverse out there, just waiting to be explored. All sorts of really crazy stuff. Dad, I never told you this before, but all my life I've wanted to travel, only I never could because of the business. There's so much out there I want to see, and—"

"And I've been holding you back."

Jay shook his head furiously. "I never saw it like that. But let's you and me go together, all right? Let's get out there, see the Infinite and have ourselves some *fun*."

Dad looked at him and thought, *Greater love hath no man than this.* He swallowed and turned away.

"Sure, son," he said. "Whatever you say."

19

Freedom of movement is a fundamental part of the Venturi way. Borders, they maintain, are just artificial conventions. If a person wants to leave one land mass and move to another, why not? The place he moves to ought to take it as a compliment—immigration is the sincerest form of flattery—and as long as he settles down, plays nice and pays his taxes regularly once he's there, what about it?

So Jersey moved to England. He went there because that was where Lucy was headed, and under the old regime the only way he could get out of Holland was to go with her, since he had no papers of any description and could no longer steal military aircraft without incurring severe financial penalties. Shortly after his arrival, the Venturis abolished borders, countries and citizenships, so he could go wherever he liked, if only he could afford the fare, which he couldn't. So he stayed. That's the cockeyed way in which things tend to come about, and even the Venturi boys haven't come up with an answer to it.

Bearing in mind the cause to which he'd devoted his entire adult life, there was a certain irony to the fact that the only job he could get was in a call centre set up by the new regime to answer those frequently asked questions that have always tended to interfere with the smooth passage of everyday life on this planet. These include the following. Is there a God? (Yes, there are two; follow this link to see their portraits and like their Facebook page.) What's the purpose of existence? (Work hard, earn a good living and be sure to get your self-assessment forms into the revenue in good time to avoid the rush.) Why did the chicken cross the road? (To take advantage of better employment opportunities suited to its skills and experience on the other side.) Is there a Santa Claus . . . ?

He scratched his head. Most of the answers he knew by heart, but for the more abstruse or rarely asked enquiries there was a handy booklet, arranged in alphabetical order. He thumbed through to S.

"No," he said.

"You what?" said the little girl at the other end of the line.

"No, Virginia, there is no Santa Claus. He's—" he squinted to read the small print "—he's an atavistic survival of primitive folk-belief; doesn't exist, and never has. Sorry," he added entirely off his own bat, though improvisation was not encouraged.

"My mummy says there is," said the little girl.

"Then your mummy's wrong, isn't she? Silly old mummy."

"My mummy says there is a Santa, and if I'm very good he'll bring me lots of nice presents."

Jersey closed the booklet. "That's because your mummy is still clinging to the outdated dualist fallacy of Right and Wrong," he said, "which is basically just obsolete Judaeo-Christian morality stripped of the Jehovah delusion, operating in the interests of the old regime to keep people from developing their true potential as vibrant economic entities. You might want to take a look at a great new colouring book just published by Venturi Press, *Janet and John Go Beyond Good and Evil,* which explains it all much better than I can be bothered to do, and for only six pounds ninety-nine. By the way, does Mummy know you're using her phone at one pound twenty a minute on top of her usual tariff?"

"There is a Santa," the little girl said. "I know, because I saw him."

Jersey frowned. There was something in her voice, a note of utter, unshakable conviction, but so what? Kids can believe anything, even, in extreme cases, election manifestos. "No," he said as kindly as he could manage, "that was just some grown-up pretending. However, don't be downhearted or disillusioned, because there are loads of wonderful things in the world that are really real, without having to make believe. For instance, right now you could be investing your pocket money in a Venturicorp Triple-Bonus Tontine Annuity Cash Bonus Bond, which means that when you're a little old lady, all grey and wrinkly, you could be getting a return of— Not interested? Ah well. Thank you so much for calling."

Santa Claus. As he answered the next call (Is there any point going on or should I end it all? What, and risk missing out on the Venturicorp Pacific Growth Derivatives Venture Capital Bond? You must be out of your tiny mind.) he found his thoughts straying back to a moment long ago, in the catacombs of San Callisto ...

"We meet again, Dr. Thorpe."

He could barely hear the rasping voice above the squeaking of the rats, the hissing of the snakes and the soft plop of the gorged leeches dropping off his legs into the oily floodwater around his knees. "Hello, Dmitri," he sighed. "Short time no see. Look, is this going to take long, because I'm on a schedule."

"Just long enough for you to die, Dr. Thorpe."

It had been one of those days. He'd been scorched in the lake of fire, bruised by the hurtling, tunnel-filling stone ball, stabbed in the bum by the portcullis of steel spikes; he'd lost a contact lens while dangling by one hand over the bottomless pit and quite possibly eaten a bad oyster the previous evening at the hotel. If his interpretation of the secret cabbalistic code woven into the first two stanzas of "O sole mio" proved to be correct, he also still had three nasties to overcome before he reached the hidden chamber. On top of all that, Dmitri was a bit much. "Whatever," he said. "Look, you wouldn't consider lowering me a rope, would you?"

"No, Dr. Thorpe."

"Ah well."

"Instead, I shall press this lever here, which will release a half-starved eight-hundred-pound alligator into the tunnel, which is blocked at both ends, so there's no possibility of escape. Goodbye, Dr. Thorpe."

"Alligator?"

"Yes, Dr. Thorpe."

"Why an alligator, for crying out loud?"

Brief silence. "Why not an alligator?"

"Dmitri," Jersey said, "this is me you're talking to. Why would anyone in his right mind go to all the trouble and expense of shipping a live alligator all the way from Florida to Italy, diddling customs, filling out false shipping manifests, feeding the bloody thing four times a day, building some sort of cage for it in the bowels of a scheduled ancient monument, just to do a job that a simple hand grenade could do just as well or probably better? An alligator, for God's sake. Whatever possessed you?"

Longer pause. "You don't like it."

His torch guttered and went out. Somewhere in the inky blackness, uncomfortably close, something splashed softly.

"I didn't say that," Jersey replied. "In a way I'm flattered. It's just such a screwy way of going about things, that's all."

"We wanted to do something special. After all, it's your—"

"My birthday. You remembered."

"Many happy returns, Dr. Thorpe." In the darkness a party squeaker sounded mournfully. "A vain hope in the circumstances, but heartfelt nonetheless."

The splashing grew louder. "Thank you."

"You're welcome."

"Next you'll be wanting to know what I want for Christmas."

A loud hiss. At first he thought it was the snakes, but no snake ever sounded quite so venomous. Interesting, and somewhat out of character for Dmitri, who he'd always found to be a pretty equable, easy-going sort, apart from the fact that every time they met Dmitri tried to kill him.

"Sorry," he therefore ventured. "Was it something I said?"

A pause, then, "I forgive you. After all, you'll be dead in a minute or so."

"Fine, so it was something I said. What did I say? Just out of interest."

"The C word." Dmitri spat it out so savagely that Jersey's cheek was fanned by the slipstream. "Don't ever let me hear you say the C word again. Well, you won't, obviously, because you're about to get eaten, but—"

"What, you mean Christmas?"

A shot rang out, followed by another. A few inches away

to his left something convulsed in the water, then became still. "Dmitri."

"Die, verminous infidel."

"I think you just shot your alligator."

"Oh, snot." Four more blasts echoed off the tunnel walls, followed by a loud splash. Then muttering, from which Jersey deduced that Dmitri, trying to reload his revolver in the pitch dark, had dropped it in the water. "Next time, Dr. Thorpe. The next time we meet, you won't be so lucky."

"What's so very bad about Christmas?" Jersey called out, but there was no reply. He counted to twenty under his breath, just in case, then took a few tentative steps forward. He bumped into something which moved away—the dead alligator, presumably—stopped and listened. No hissing or squeaking, which suggested that before it met its untimely end, the alligator had eaten the snakes and the rats, bless it. You wouldn't read about it, Jersey said to himself, and waded on until he barked his shin on a sharp ledge which proved to be the bottom step of a winding stone staircase that led him directly to the secret chamber. Piece of cake.

He spent a couple of minutes groping around in the dark for something—the tibia of a long-dead monk, by the feel of it—to push the door open with, just in case Dmitri had balanced a bag of flour or something on the top. As it turned out, he hadn't, so that was all right, and the remaining three nasties of the ancient defence system proved to have rusted solid, and it was all a bit of an anti-climax, not that he was in any mood to complain.

The chamber—five thousand years old, quite possibly older—was lit by a single shaft of light, neon-bright after half an hour in pitch darkness, lancing down from a slit in the roof a hundred feet overhead. That slit in the roof was his only way out, and soon he'd have all the fun and games of scaling the sheer wall without climbing gear, but he'd done that kind of thing so often in the past few years that the thought of it made him stifle a yawn. Meanwhile, ahead of him on the back wall of the secret chamber was an inscription in arcane cabbalistic symbols. Just as well he could speak arcane cabbalistic like a native.

Actually, a lot of it was irrelevant, and a whole lot more was stuff he already knew or had worked out for himself from first principles, so the net gain of actual useful information was pretty negligible and really not enough to justify all the aggravation. There was just one bit he didn't understand. A cluster of hieroglyphs in a far corner of the chamber, where the light from the roof was dim so that he could barely make them out, but one of them looked for all the world like a holly leaf. And the one next to it— well, you'd be forgiven for thinking it was a plum pudding, except of course it couldn't be, just as the one next to that one couldn't possibly be a reindeer, any more than the one next to it could be a sprig of mistletoe. In fact, the only bit he could make out was the writing directly underneath, which said quite clearly (in ancient Akkadian cuneiform), BEWARE, HE WILL RETURN TO THE CITY, unless what looked like a double dot over the final wedge was actually a natural flaw in the rock or a stonemason's typo, in which case it said, THIS WALL IS TEMPORARILY UNAVAILABLE.

He will return? Who, for crying out loud? In accordance with the ancient rule of textual analysis, *difficilior lectio*, he decided it had to be the second one, which made about as much sense as most things he'd read on walls in secret chambers lately, so stuff it.

*

All of which had been a long time ago in what was starting to feel increasingly like another life lived by someone else who'd had much more fun, and he hadn't given it a moment's thought since. After all, it had been pretty dark in the chamber, he'd been tired and wet and in a hurry, and there was no way that a five-thousand-year-old Akkadian inscription could have included pictograms of a holly leaf, a Christmas pud, a reindeer or a sprig of mistletoe, since none of the above were known in antediluvian Akkad, so they couldn't have had words for them, could they? And the alternative reading was so much more likely.

Except, now that he came to think of it . . .

The last thing he'd done before leaving the chamber was to take a few photographs. Force of habit, really, or the fanciful self-delusion that he was at heart a serious archaeologist. Probably they were still somewhere on his phone because he'd never quite managed to figure out how to delete stuff. So, as soon as his shift ended, he plonked himself down in a corner of the staffroom, fished out his phone and scrolled through until he found what he was looking for.

At the time he'd been primarily interested in all the other stuff, so the mysterious pictograms were right out on the edge of the frame, slightly blurred and none too bright, but a certain amount of zooming and digital jiggery-pokery worked wonders, and before long he was staring once again at those curious symbols, which still looked remarkably like a holly leaf, a Christmas pudding, a reindeer and a sprig of mistletoe. And from the angle the picture had been taken he could quite clearly see that the double dot was indeed a double dot, rather than a pimple in the stone or a bat dropping. Furthermore, directly underneath was a crude representation of a bearded thunder god driving a chariot drawn by horned beasts, and under that was a further line of Akkadian which he'd somehow overlooked: BEHOLD, HE COMPILES A CATALOGUE,

SCHEDULE OR REGISTER. TWICE HE PERUSES IT. SURELY HE WILL IN DUE COURSE ASCERTAIN THE VIRTUOUS ONE AND THE EVILDOER. And then, repeated, with the double dot unambiguously clear: BEWARE, HE WILL RETURN TO THE CITY.

Jersey sat and stared at the picture until the battery went flat, then he closed the phone and tucked it away in his inside pocket. *Oh come on*, he thought.

But, on the other hand, as far as traditional folk myths and quaint local customs were concerned, the Venturis were generally quite relaxed. They had no beef with deeply rooted indigenous superstitions as a rule, particularly ones with a proven track record of commercial exploitability. The only exception he'd come across so far, in fact, was Father Christmas, down on whom, however, they'd come like a ton of neutronium bricks. He flicked to the relevant page of the booklet and refreshed his memory. *An atavistic survival of primitive folk-belief; doesn't exist, and never has.* Pretty strong stuff from the sultans of laissez-faire. No, the Venturis really didn't hold with Christmas, not one little bit. In fact, the only person he'd ever come across who cared for it less was his old sparring-partner Dmitri.

He picked up the little wooden paddle and, in the sprinkle-flecked foam of his caramel latte, picked out in flawless Akkadian cuneiform, *Beware, he will return . . .*

Oh come on, he repeated to himself. Surely not.

20

"This time," said Mr. Lucifer, "I think you've gone too far."

Bernie's face fell. "You don't like it."

The banner headline was, HELL FREEZES OVER! The PowerPoint slides showed the Desolate Plains inches deep in synthetic snowflakes, the Lake of Burning Pitch covered with an inch-thick slab of ice, with happy Lycra-clad people skating up and down under the slogan, IT'S A HELL OF A WINTER WONDERLAND! Mr. L. shook his head. "It's not us," he said. "Really."

"I could work on it some more."

"You're a good boy, Bernie, and you've done well." Mr. Lucifer had that look on his face. It was all the worse because, just for once, he was trying not to cause pain and hurt, which of course made it far more painful and hurtful than if he'd been doing it on purpose. "In fact, you've done amazingly well. I can't believe some of the garbage humans will actually pay good money for. But demons dressed up as snowmen—"

"It's the incongruity factor," Bernie said quickly, "which lies at the base of all human humour. That, and one simple gag that catches the imagination. That's all there is to it, really."

He knew he had a point. So far, in the space of three weeks, over a hundred thousand human tourists had paid ten dollars a head to watch a not-particularly-inspired clown act performed by a scratch team of dog-headed fiends from Circle Five, almost entirely because they liked the name Cheeky Devils. It doesn't have to be good; in fact, you can be too good for your own good—too slick, too clever, off-puttingly excellent. It just needs to be a bit good, a bit quirky, a bit different, and have a catchy name or an earworm slogan. How else could anyone account for the amazing success of the improvised beach resort they'd thrown together on the shores of the Sea of Desolation, with a few skips of builders' sand, a dozen bird-headed fiends in penguin suits and the shout line *Between the Devil and the Deep Blue Sea?* Or, come to that, Google?

"Sorry," Mr. Lucifer said. "I'm not saying it's a bad idea; it's more about how much aggravation it's all going to make for the department heads. You know how much trouble they have with the temperature controls at the best of times." He sighed. "You'd think, with a bottomless pool of inflammable liquids and a box of matches, they ought to be able to keep a fire in, but . . ." He pulled a sad face. "Never mind," he said. "I bet your next idea will be a honey."

Bernie made an effort and masked his disappointment. He'd been living and breathing Hell-on-ice for the last week: all that work, all the attention to detail, right down to the colour scheme for the Snowflake's Chance slot-machine arcade. He'd been dreaming about it, which probably explained the bags under his eyes and the way he jumped at sudden noises. And to have it all arbitrarily dismissed with a shake of the head and some rigmarole about upsetting the deadheads in Engineering.

"Besides," Mr. Lucifer went on, "there's no need."

Made no sense. "Excuse me?"

Mr. Lucifer smiled at him. "No need," he repeated. "You've done so well with all those other ideas you had, we don't need any more money. We've got loads. We're lousy with the stuff. Our budget's twice what it was under the old management, in fact, I'm having a hard time thinking of anything to spend it on. Maintenance is bang up to date; we can replace Boiler Six with all new gear; carpets in the corridors; a brand new nail to hang the the executive washroom key on—everything we could possibly want. If we made any more money, it'd just lie around in the strongroom in big heaps, making the place look untidy."

Just when you think you've got them seeing the big picture. "With respect, Mr. Lucifer," Bernie said, "that's not how it works. You can't just make enough money and then stop."

"Can't you? Why?"

"Because it's not—" He stopped, calmed himself down. "We humans have a saying, expand or die. Either a business grows or it shrivels away. It's like driving on the freeway: you can't just stop dead in the middle of the traffic. You need momentum, you need dynamic energy, you need eager green shoots groping upwards towards the sun."

"No, actually, we don't." Mr. Lucifer was giving him that look again. "What we need is to keep the lights on and the roof from leaking. And we need to keep the department heads from throwing hissy fits and giving me a hard time. That's all, really. Sorry, I thought you knew that."

"Mr. Lucifer." He could hear the wobble in his voice. "With respect. You can never have too much money."

"Don't you believe it. Root of all evil, says so in the operating manual."

Bernie opened his mouth and then realised he didn't know what to say. What he didn't want to say—not if he knew what was good for him—was, *That's not how the Venturi brothers see things*, but he was having an awful job keeping those words the right side of his teeth. "Sure, Mr. L.," he mumbled. "Sorry to have bothered you."

Mr. Lucifer looked relieved. "Not at all," he said with genuine warmth. And that was the killer. Mr. Lucifer liked him, he knew; he was trying to be nice. "You're doing your best for the old place, I appreciate that, truly I do. And you've been a real help. I don't know how we'd have managed without you."

"Thank you, Mr. Lucifer. That means a lot to me."

"Sometimes I think you care more about this place than I do. Actually, I know you do. Which is so weird," he added with a frown, "but what the heck. That's what's so special about you humans. You can get fond of practically anything if you set your minds to it."

Sympathy from the Devil? Indeed. He thought about that last remark for the rest of the afternoon, as he wrote up the quarterly figures. Was it true? Did he care about, had he grown fond of ... well, Hell? Surely not. Hell was the place where bad people went and had bad things done to them for ever and ever. A bad place, a very bad place, the best that could be said for it was that it was a necessary evil—now, there was an idea for a brand name. Only you'd probably have to turn it round. Evil Necessities, EN swimwear, EN lingerie, the G-string from Hell, no, maybe not. A necessary evil, something you endure because there's no alternative, except that the Venturis had shown that simply wasn't true. You could get shot of good and evil, still have free will and make out like bandits while you were at it. In which case, the creaking relic of an outmoded ethical system to which he was devoting all his waking energies was an unnecessary evil, rightfully mothballed and quite properly obsolete, and here he was busting a gut to keep it going.

But it was true. He had grown fond of it. Or at least he'd grown fond of the people—some of them, a very few of them, because all the rest were arseholes, which was only right and proper, in context, and to be expected—and even the place itself, the gloomy shadows, the ominous red glow, the gaunt, semi-derelict buildings (not semi-derelict any more; I did that, he noted with pride). It wasn't much, in fact it was pretty ghastly when you looked at it object-ively, but it was his job, his responsibility, his baby. You can't help getting attached to something that depends on you for its very existence.

Just listen to yourself. He leaned back in his chair with his eyes wide open, and the calculator fell from his fingers onto the (newly carpeted) floor. In his mind he visualised a red carpet, lots of round tables crammed into a vast function room, tuxedos and shimmering designer gowns, a master of ceremonies beckoning him up to the podium to receive his Lifetime Award for Services to Treachery. *I would like to accept this award on behalf of all the tortured, agonised souls who made this possible, for the whole human race.*

"Necessary evil," he muttered under his breath, but that didn't compute. What's the function of divine retri-bution? To act as a deterrent, silly; everybody knows that. But the Venturis have abolished good and evil, therefore nobody needs to be deterred any more; this place is—his first thought was a *museum*, but it couldn't claim that distinction because museums preserve objects of great value. This place was a sump, a toxic waste depot, a silo for nastiness with a half-life of for ever and ever, and the poor creatures suffering in its pits and furnaces were only there because they'd had the misfortune to live and die before the Venturis came.

He shuddered right down to his socks. There but for the grace and capital investment of Ab and Snib, he thought. *Could easily have been me in there, and I wouldn't be enjoying it one little bit.* But they were very bad people, he told himself in a shaky little inner voice. *They deserved it.* That's what he'd told himself when he first took this job, traded his humanity for a regular wage and a health plan. But all the rules had changed, hadn't they?

Fond of the place, and the bitch of it was, it was true. Not just fond. Practically every waking thought he had was for the promotion and welfare of this abomination. He made himself pause and think about that. True or untrue? Was he on fire, pun intended, with passion for this institution and all it stood for, or was it because he'd just discovered he had a gift for management and marketing, and this place had given him the scope to use it? That and because there were a handful of people here who actually seemed to like him, and when someone likes you it's so very, very hard not to like them back, even when they're the Common Enemy of Man?

Um.

I need to get out more, he thought. Also, I should probably update my CV. Except . . .

You can hate the business and still love your job. Once, when running an errand to the Maintenance department, he'd got lost in the labyrinth of tunnels under the Despair building, opened the wrong door and found himself in the vast chamber where 99 per cent of the world's investment bankers had ended up over the decades. Naturally he got out of there as soon as he possibly could, but on the way he couldn't help but glance at the floor-to-ceiling screens that covered the walls, detailing the biographies of the inmates. Even a fleeting glimpse was enough to make it clear that there was a definite pattern. Take a bright young man, intelligent and keen to make the most of his all-too-short time on Earth. He goes to a good school and then to college. He soaks up ideas like a flower drinking sunlight; quite likely he marches to Stop the War or Ban the this or Save the that; he experiences the joy of friendship, the satisfaction of good company, the thrill of love. And then he gets a job. Part of him is ashamed because it's selling out, abandoning the possibility of the beautiful life of altruism and service to others, but not to worry, he says to himself; it won't change me; I'll still be me; I could never willingly hurt anybody. And then he starts doing the job, and he finds he's good at it. It's like being paid to play a wildly exciting game, and some of the people there like him, and winning is a great feeling, and he wins quite often. And the more you win, the more they want you to play, until the skill becomes the reason—the sensation of air in your wings, the dizzying splendour of the view from on high—and the money, as it rolls in in obscene waves and foam-crested breakers, the money really doesn't matter except, vitally, as the only really credible way of keeping score, of knowing how you're doing. Are you still as good as you were last year? Are you still up there bathing in the golden sunlight? Are you still *soaring*? And it's all right, because you know that what's keeping you up there is hot thin air. It's not real, it doesn't matter, and you don't stop to think what has to burn to generate that heat, until the wax melts, and you fall suddenly, and the next thing you see is a spotty kid who's lost his way in the tunnels, staring at you with unfathomable pity.

Those faces he'd seen in there had stayed with him ever since. They weren't bad people. They were thoughtless people who did bad things, because the system gave them scope to do so and didn't make it clear to them that what they were doing was wrong.

The W word. How quaint. How it dates you. I remember Right and Wrong, says the white-haired old man to his grandchildren, who don't really believe him, any more than they would if he told them he'd once seen a dragon. Because there can't really be dragons. A living creature can't generate fire inside its tummy, and a lizard that shape could never possibly fly. Likewise, the whole idea of Good and Evil is so ridiculously silly, looked at logically, that you can't bring yourself to accept that sensible, rational people ever *believed* in all that stuff.

"Sorry, I didn't mean to disturb you. I only wanted a stapler."

He opened his eyes, which had somehow closed, and saw Jenny standing in the doorway.

Could you pray to the Venturi brothers? There had been a certain amount of discussion about that over the past few weeks. Spokesmen for the Corporation tended to go a bit coy and mumble about the scientifically proven benefits of the placebo effect, so the answer was probably, yes, you could, but don't expect miracles. Unspoken prayers? Well, if that was what he'd just been unspeaking to himself, it looked rather like his prayer had been answered. Why do I stay here and knock my pipes out trying to keep this place going? Because of Mr. Lucifer, who likes me, and Jenny, who might just possibly . . .

"Stapler," he repeated. "In the desk drawer. I think."

She smiled. She was equipped with an ordnance-grade smile. Theoretically, since being withdrawn from front-line duty her offensive capabilities should have been decommissioned (offensive wasn't really the right word), but you know how it is: not everything that strictly speaking should be done actually gets done, not every minefield gets swept, not every smile gets toned down to within acceptably safe parameters. You shouldn't leave something like that lying around where it could hurt someone, but here, with just a handful of human staff who could possibly be affected, it was an easy corner to cut, and Duke Sitri had never liked him much anyway.

She was standing there, still smiling. After a long time (in context) she said, "If you moved a bit, I could get to the desk drawer."

He bounded out of the chair as though it had teeth, apologising like an idiot. Calm down, for pity's sake, he told himself; you're not usually like this, usually you can handle it. Maybe, but not today, apparently. Could be the yield on the smile was just that decimal point or two higher that makes all the difference, or his defences were unusually low for some reason, or maybe the effect is cumulative and he'd just passed the threshold. Didn't really matter what the reason was. He clamped his jaws together in the certain knowledge that if he opened them and spoke, the most appalling drivel was bound to come bubbling out.

"Got it," she said. "Thanks."

"No problem."

"Actually." She looked at him. All the skill and expertise of the Sentimental Warfare division had gone into designing that look, against which even blindness was an uncertain defence. "Have you got a minute?"

"Um."

"Only . . ." Pause to chew lip. He tried to look away but couldn't. "I was wondering if you could explain something for me."

Millions of light years away, on Sinderaan, a *gwlpp* fish with a doctorate in applied xenopsychology and another in advanced particle physics gazed at a steel U dangling incongruously a centimetre from its nose, shrugged its scintillating carapace and said to itself, *Go on, what harm could it do?* Which just goes to show: doesn't matter how smart you are; if it's got your number on it, there's no hiding place. Bernie swallowed hard and said, "Sure."

She looked over her shoulder at the closed door, then back at him. "I just got this on my screen and I don't know what it means."

From her sleeve she drew a torn-off scrap of printout, folded many times like a Chinese fan. "I don't want to get in trouble," she said. "But I thought, I can't just ignore it, in case it's important."

He stared at the piece of paper for quite some time before he realised he had it the wrong way up. He frowned. "Sorry," he said. "What's the problem?"

She gave him a blank look. "It's terrible. Ever since I got it, I've been so scared."

"Really?"

"I was sitting at my screen and then it suddenly went all red and this message appeared. And then it printed out, all by itself, and then everything went back to normal. It's horrible. What does it mean?"

"Um." Bernie read it again, just to make sure he wasn't mistaken. "It's just a poem. Well, a song, really. Human stuff."

"A song?"

Bernie nodded reassuringly. "People sing it at Chris— at a certain time of the year. It's traditional. Well, no, it isn't; it only goes back as far as the thirties. And people don't actually sing it; mostly they play it in stores. But it's harmless."

"It doesn't look harmless."

"But—"

She shot him an accusing stare. "It says there's some-one spying on me all the time, watching me, even—" she shuddered slightly "—when I'm in bed."

"It's just a bit of fun."

"It's creepy. And it says he knows if I'm good or evil, and if I'm not good . . ." She pulled herself together with an effort. "That's what I wanted to ask you, really. Am I evil?"

"Sorry. You what?"

"Am I evil?" She shot him an imploring glance. "Because this—this whoever-he-is is watching me all the time, he *knows*, and he says, if you're not good you'd better watch out, and I'm scared."

Her eyes were red and ominously watery. Bernie felt a wave of panic rising somewhere around his socks. "There's nothing to be afraid of. It's just a song, that's all."

"Why won't you answer the question? Am I evil?"

He opened his mouth, but nothing came out, so he paused and actually thought about the question. Well? On the one hand, she was the most wonderful person he'd ever met. On the other hand—make that claw—she was an artefact of a Duke of Hell, cunningly and skilfully designed to entrap men's souls and bring them to the everlasting (when there wasn't a problem in Engineering) bonfire. Put in those terms, it was actually a valid query. Just as well, really, that it didn't actually matter at all, because all she'd had was just some spam email.

Or maybe not. "This message," he said. "That's all it was?"

"Well, yes. Oh, and there was this terrible mocking laughter. It sent a shiver right down my spine."

"What, sort of, ho, ho, ho?"

"Exactly."

Oh boy, he thought. "Jenny, it's just a song. I've heard

it all my life. Usually it means somebody wants me to buy something. It really is no big deal."

She wasn't convinced, he could see that. "I don't know how you can say that. I mean, it's *awful*. And he says that if I tell anyone about it, he'll do something terrible to me."

"What it actually says is, you'd better not shout, cry or pull faces. It's not quite the same thing. Look, it's really quite a nice song. It's got ever such a jolly tune. Here. I'll whistle it for you."

If he'd been in a more rational frame of mind, he probably wouldn't have done that, bearing in mind how many of his family and close friends had asked him not to whistle over the years. But her anguished reaction couldn't be explained simply in aesthetic terms, not the way she screamed, clapped her hands over her ears and sank sobbing to her knees. Even his Bruce Springsteen impersonation had never affected anyone that badly.

"I'm sorry," he said desperately. "I won't do it again, I promise. *Please* stop crying. It's only a stupid song."

"It was *awful*."

"Yes, well—"

"It went through my head like a steel bolt. I could feel my brain starting to melt."

Yes. Well. His mother had said something to the same effect the last time he sang "Happy Birthday." Even so. "I know, I'm a hopeless whistler."

"No, you're not. I've heard you when you think no one's listening. No, it was that tune. It was so ..." She gulped like an ostrich swallowing a brick. "I didn't like it."

"I gathered."

"You still haven't answered my question."

Oh that. Well, he could try and explain. He could say that although yes, probably she was technically evil, on account of having been produced—manufactured?—by the Dark Powers for an unholy purpose, that didn't mean she was necessarily a bad person, that being evil in that sense was none of her doing, just as being French isn't anybody's *fault*, it's just an accident of geography; that in any event it really didn't signify anything now that the Venturi boys had effectively abolished Good and Evil, just as they'd abolished nationality and various other quite arbitrary and artificial divisions between people; he could say all that, provided he could get it all out without tying himself in knots, which wasn't very likely given how he was feeling and the way his heart was trying to kick the walls of his chest in. But, in her state of mind, she probably wouldn't believe him, and he could well make things a whole lot worse; whereas, if he went with Plan B and good old-fashioned non-verbal communication—

He leaned across the desk and kissed the tip of her nose. "There," he said. "That's how evil I think you are. Now, are you doing anything tomorrow evening after work?"

"Yes." Oh. "I'm going home, boiling an egg and defrosting the freezer."

He smiled at her. It took him more effort than lifting a hundredweight sack of potatoes, but somehow he managed to make it look like the easiest thing in the world. "Would you rather," he said, "go to the movies and then have dinner afterwards?"

She thought for a moment. "Yes," she said.

"Good, because by a strange coincidence that's what I'll be doing. Hey, here's a thought. Why don't we go together?"

"I'd like that."

"So would I."

"Would you?"

He nodded. "And that stupid song. You're not going to worry about it any more?"

"Yes."

"Oh. Oh well, never mind." The phone rang—the green one, which always meant trouble. For some reason, though, he didn't really give a damn. "Sorry," he said. "Yes, hello. Lachuk here. What? Not *again*. Yes, Mr. Malephar, I'll see to it personally, though you might just consider leaving the pilot light on when the furnace is down, because otherwise you get this big build-up of gas when you— Yes. Sure, Mr. Malephar, first thing in the morning, you have my word on that. Yes. Sure."

When he looked up she'd gone. Ah well. He turned his attention back to the accounts, but his eyes seemed to glance off the numbers like a file off hardened steel. At the back of his mind a tiny little query was jumping up and down clamouring for attention, but it simply couldn't compete with the firework displays and the loud, happy music booming out from the tannoys, so after a while it gave up and went back to sleep.

21

" **I** really hate my boss," the caller said. "I hate him so much I want to kill him."

Lucy stifled a yawn. When you come down to it, all call-centre jobs are the same. But some are more the same than others. "Fine," she said. "Now, if I can start off with a few personal details—name, date of birth, any capital savings or assets, your annual income net of tax for the last five years."

The customer profile came up on her screen. "I see you're a new customer," Lucy said. "How can I help you?"

"I just told you. I want to kill my boss."

"Of course you do. Any debts, county court judgements against you or unpaid credit card bills?"

"No."

"Well, for murdering your employer there's a fixed-rate tariff, fifty million dollars. Looking at what you've just told me about your finances, I don't think that's going to be possible. I'm very sorry."

Pause. "How about if I just smashed his face in?"

Lucy flicked to a different screen. "All right," she said. "That would be the sin of wrath, which is a variable rate depending on severity of provocation."

"It's the way he just looks at me and sneers when I bring him his coffee."

"Let's call that a Level Five," Lucy said. "Which means you're looking at forty thousand for the wrath, together with an actual bodily harm supplement which depends on how badly you damage him. Would a slapped face do?"

"I want to crush his skull like an eggshell."

Lucy did the sums in her head, faster than the calculator. "That's a seven-figure wish, I'm afraid. Would you settle for heavy bruising and some minor lacerations?"

"How much would that be?"

"You're still looking at ninety thousand plus. Of course," she went on, filling the sad silence that always seemed to follow the numbers, "there are other ways to pay. For instance, we offer a new endowment-backed earn-to-sin scheme. Basically, you pay into a unit-backed life policy, and when it matures you're free to transgress up to the assured amount, less management costs and administration fees and an early termination penalty if appropriate. In your case, how old did you say you were? Well, you should just about make it before you retire."

No sale. She thanked the caller anyway and moved on to the next in the queue.

"It's like this," the next caller said. "I've just inherited a nice little legacy from my aunt, and we were wondering what we could get for it."

"OK," Lucy said. "What did you have in mind?"

"Well," the caller said, "my wife and I, we've always quite fancied coveting our neighbour's ox—we live next door to a farm, you see. We've got a nice little bungalow on the south coast; we retired here from Birmingham about three years ago. You can see the sea from the bathroom window."

"That's nice."

"We like it. Well, it's either that or we could get the patio relaid and deck over the far end of the garden, and maybe have a rustic pergola with a nice teak bench and a couple of lavender bushes. We just can't make up our minds. What do you think?"

Lucy was doing complex mental arithmetic. "This bungalow," she said. "You own it outright? No mortgage?"

"No. What's that got to do—?"

"Only," Lucy said, "with the Venturi Personal Finance equity release scheme, you could have all that done and still afford the coveting. All it'd involve would be a simple charge-back on the property together with a fixed-rate premium with-profits life policy. Of course, you would have to bear in mind that the value of investments can go down as well as up. But, all being well, for a monthly premium of no more than . . ."

Five minutes later the caller thanked her, but he thought they'd probably go with the pergola and maybe a cruise. Lucy smiled as she replaced the receiver. The more you tried to sell, the less they wanted to buy. There had been calls where she could hear them actually whetting the knife in the background, but once she started to explain the Venturi Cash Sin-Now-Pay-Later variable interest loan account, it was amazing how quickly they calmed down. No bad thing, really. Good for the statistics, and one less pool of blood on the floor for some poor swine to clean up.

She wondered about that. The vast majority of the callers she advised decided not to sin after all, so she sold relatively few Venturicorp products, something the accountants at head office must have noticed by now. But the callers she spoke to were mostly ordinary folk from less favoured demographics. Wealthy individuals and big corporations tended to have their own Personal Transgression

Adviser, and get invited to special seminars on such topics as spreading the cost of fraud and tax-efficient corporate manslaughter. It was just a theory of hers, but maybe the brothers were only interested in the high rollers, with their carefully tailored portfolios of blue-chip offences and triple-A-rated guilts, and her job was to deter the man in the street from sinning beyond his means. What if the wealth of nations was like a vat of milk, and the best way to get the cream was to skim it off the top, rather than sieving through the dregs? Just the sort of metaphor the Venturis would use, and it worried her slightly that she might be beginning to think like them. Or would that really be such a bad thing?

Wash your brain out with soap and water. The longer she did this job—no, she couldn't put her finger on it, and probably it was quite illogical and irrational; but she knew she wasn't the only one, not by a long chalk. True, crime had fallen to negligible levels in a stunningly short space of time, the economy was booming and everybody could now afford at least one fifty-five-inch UHD flat-screen TV on which to watch the latest remake of *The Magic Roundabout*, which was one of the few things on the box you could afford to watch without being inspired to incur severe financial penalties. Fine. But were people happy? She wasn't sure about that. Definitely yes as far as the ones who would've been killed, beaten or robbed were concerned. Everyone else? A walk down the street and a look at all the long faces told its own story. Something about Venturi ethics wasn't working, but she was blowed if she could figure out what it was.

The next caller wanted to know how much it would cost to cheat on her husband. Only, she'd met this gorgeous man, there was definitely real chemistry between them, she knew it couldn't last, but a brief, wonderful fling—how much? Oh. Right. Sorry to have bothered you. Not at all, and thank you for calling.

Well, quite. Who really wants a fortnight of reckless passion if you've got to scrimp and save for thirty years to afford it? Not that the Venturis were total killjoys. You could still fool around for free, provided that you weren't in a long-term relationship with anyone and you didn't make any promises you didn't intend to keep. But it did rather polarise the field of interpersonal relationships into one-night stands and the death-do-us-part stuff, and it spoilt the mood rather if you were constantly on your guard not to say or do anything that might cost you the price of a four-door family saloon car. The Venturis had an answer to that: if in doubt, you can always call the helpline, and we'll be happy to let you know where you stand. No more anxiety, no more uncertainty—that's the Venturi way. Even so.

Maybe that was why she hadn't seen Jersey for a week. She thought about it; no, not really, though she did like him, a lot. It was just ... It was just those bloody Venturis—

She paused and waited, but no window opened in thin air, and she breathed a sigh of relief. At least you could still curse in your head without denting your bank balance.

—those confounded Venturis, and the whole attitude to life that came with the deal. There's that old chestnut, if there was no darkness, we couldn't see the light. If there's no evil, there can be no good. If there's no misery, there can be no joy. If nobody's unhappy, nobody's happy. Well, I'm not, that's for sure. Not unhappy either, just ... well, just quietly plodding along from day to day, and the thought of doing anything more exciting than work, basic cooking and laundry is just too much effort. Why bother? What's the point?

That was what the Venturis had done, drat them. They'd killed emotion. Once you'd got into the habit of stopping and thinking carefully and sensibly before you let your heart rule your head, it was hard to let go long enough to relish a beautiful sunset or the song of the nightingale or a haunting piece of music, or even a good-looking (though decidedly on the short side) man. Instead, you thought, well, we'd have to get married, and do I really want someone under my feet in the mornings when I'm getting ready to rush off to the office? And how would it affect my tax position, and as for the implications for personal pension planning . . .

One more caller, and then it was time for her break. Venturicorp was a good employer; you could choose your shifts to suit your circadian rhythms, and there was a nice staffroom with proper coffee and digestive biscuits, though nobody talked much. She sat down in the corner and took out her phone. *Dinner tomorrow?* She hesitated, then hit the send button. Yes, she thought, while I can still remember what it's like to be in love. Sort of in love. Whatever.

On the noticeboard there was a new sheet of paper from the management. It had come to their attention, it said, that several members of staff were under the misapprehension that the office would be closing for the day on 25 December, also that there would be unscheduled social activities immediately preceding that date and a bonus. This was just a foolish rumour. Staff will be expected to work their normal shifts, and any absenteeism will be treated severely. There are no exceptions. THIS MEANS YOU.

She frowned. That wasn't the Venturi style at all. They took the view that a contented workforce was a productive workforce, and if you wanted time off or a party, all you had to do was ask, hence the Venturi medical miracle: colds and flu down 36 per cent in a matter of months. Blanket prohibitions and block capitals were the old way of doing things and so last year. Clearly, therefore, the Venturis didn't hold with Christmas. Understandable, she thought, and then she thought, no, not really, because it's been decades since Christmas had any religious associations, so they can't feel threatened by it, surely.

Maybe they're fundamentally opposed to joy? That made her grin. If that was the reason, the Venturis didn't know much about it. Forget for a moment the grim office parties, the nauseating iconography ubiquitous from early September onwards, the griping terror that you might not have spent enough on your loved ones' gifts, leading to reckless escalation and mutually assured destitution; just consider the awful day itself, the dark heart of the bleak midwinter, trapped like a moth in amber, time standing still, marooned in a Sargasso Sea of scented soaps, bath salts, the literary works of Nigella Lawson, cold chestnut stuffing and torn wrapping paper, with nobody for company except your nearest and dearest. If the Venturis want to free us from all that, then bless them. Curious, though. Murder, domestic violence and divorce notoriously spike at Christmas, and for every one who strikes a blow or speaks the irretrievable word, there are a hundred thousand with mayhem in their hearts. A really great business opportunity, in other words, which the Venturis seemed determined to deny themselves. Why would anyone do that?

You know how a trivial anomaly can sometimes irritate the lining of your mind out of all proportion to its magnitude or relevance, like a tiny splinter lodged deep under the skin or the smallest wisp of sweetcorn skin wedged between the teeth. The Christmas thing was still bothering her when she met Jersey for dinner the next day. She'd been hoping for bright smiles, lively conversation, the human equivalent of the peacock fanning its tail to attract its mate. Instead, he seemed gloomy and preoccupied, just like she was. She decided to investigate with subtle, nuanced questioning.

"What's the matter with you?"

"Sorry?"

"Why are you so miserable? Work?"

He frowned. "Yes and no," he said. "The job's all right, I suppose."

She grinned. "Your first time in a call centre, isn't it?"

"First time in regular employment, actually."

"Really?"

He nodded. "It strikes me as a curious way to use up one's lifespan. Not actively unpleasant, but I wouldn't want to make a habit of it. And it cuts so badly into your free time, which is a nuisance."

"Didn't you even have a Saturday job when you were a kid?"

He shook his head. "We lived next door to an army firing range. I made my pocket money salvaging unexploded ordnance and selling it to collectors. Anyway, they said they were collectors. Saved enough to pay my way through college."

She looked at him. "So actually working for a living . . ."

"You know me, I'll try anything once. But trying it three hundred and forty days a year probably isn't my cup of tea. Trouble is, I'm not quite sure there's an alternative, the way things are now."

"The Venturis."

He shrugged. "I guess most people aren't like me. For most people this must be a sort of golden age."

"Hardly. Do you want your bread roll?"

"Not if you do."

"Good, I'm starving. This is not a golden age. Everybody you see is miserable. Like you."

"Actually, I'm more preoccupied."

He hadn't seen her for over a week and his mind was on something else. Fine. So, as it happened, was hers. "What's the problem?"

He looked at her, and he didn't need to preface his next words with, this is going to sound really strange but . . . "Why do the Venturis hate Christmas?"

Have you ever walked into a wall because what you thought was a doorway turned out to be a mirror? "You what?"

He shook his head. "Probably I've got it all wrong. But I get the impression—"

"Me too."

He looked up sharply. "Go on."

"It's true. They don't like it. One bit."

They shared a long, startled look. Then she said, "But it makes no sense."

"None whatsoever."

"You'd have thought the money-grubbing and crass commercialism would've touched them to the core."

"Yes, quite. Only . . ."

A man was hovering over them, but it was just a waiter with two plates of spaghetti. "Only what?"

He looked furtively round, then leaned forward. His shirtfront went in his Bolognese sauce, but she didn't mention it. She didn't want to break the flow. "Years ago," he said, "when I was in Rome, searching for the Eighth Seal of the Holy Blood, something weird happened."

"Quite probably."

"Something unexpectedly weird. There was this man called Dmitri."

He told her about it, and when he'd finished, she said, "That's so bizarre."

"Yes, isn't it? By the way, you've been winding your hair round your fork along with the spaghetti."

She looked down. He was quite right. "So what does it mean?"

"You were interested in the story?"

"The inscription. Compiling a catalogue, schedule or register."

"Checking it twice." Jersey nodded. "The thing about ancient myths is that they generally have some foundation in truth. In fact, pretty much always, in my experience. I spent five years navigating through tunnels and crypts using ancient myths like a satnav, and—"

He stopped. She knew what he was thinking, and it would be better if neither of them said it. All that effort, and some bastard changes the rules. "Behold, he will return to the city?"

Jersey nodded. " When you think about it, he shares most of the usual attributes of your traditional Eurasian thunder god. He rides through the air in a chariot drawn by magical horned beasts. He rewards the virtuous and smites the wrongdoer."

"Gives them bits of coal. That's hardly smiting."

"Coal. Cinders. What's left of you after a direct hit from a thunderbolt. Naturally you've got to allow for a little paradigm shift when you're dealing with four thousand years of oral tradition. He's heavily bearded, he dresses in rich robes coloured like blood, and the hat is strikingly similar to the headgear worn by storm deities in classic Babylonian iconography. Even the bobble. I think what we're dealing with here is a typical Indo-European weather god."

"The snow."

He nodded gravely. "The snow. His advent is heralded by a dramatic change in climate. Dark is his path on the wings of the storm."

She frowned. "But he's nice."

Jersey smiled grimly. "It ain't necessarily so," he said. "Consider the associated rituals. You hang up a sock. You leave out mulled wine and mince pies. You make burned offerings of plum pudding. Propitiatory sacrifices. Lord, take these gifts of food and clothing and spare the children. The mistletoe should've been a dead giveaway, but we were too blind to see it."

She felt a faint shiver run down her spine. "You think—"

"Oh yes. And there's no point barring the door and bolting the shutters, because he's so powerful he can come down the chimney. No hiding place, you see. And who else would you expect to come calling at the darkest, coldest time of the year? Nobody cheerful, that's for sure. Back then, before electric light and central heating, they must've been *terrified*. And he lives in the far north, the realms of perpetual ice. The Vikings believed that was the Land of the Dead. What would anybody *nice* be doing in a place like that?"

"Um."

"And the elves. You know what elves are, originally? Count yourself lucky. Take it from me, somebody who hangs around with elves is not the sort of person you'd want to have unrestricted access to your home at the dead of night, particularly if you have children. Tell me," he took a deep breath and gazed steadily into her eyes, "do you believe in Santa Claus?"

"Well, no. Maybe once, but—"

"I think the Venturi brothers do. And I think it's possible that they might know something that we don't. Or more accurately, something we've forgotten. I think he might just still be out there."

"Oh come on. That's—"

"Exactly what I said when the possibility first dawned on me. But—" he glanced around and leaned closer still "—what if I'm right? What if, when the previous management rounded up all the rest of the competition, he was the one who got away? Too strong or too crafty, or maybe he faked his own death or they underestimated him and reckoned he wouldn't be any trouble? And by the time they realised their mistake, it was too late. People knew. There is another. So they took the only course of action open to them. They whitewashed him. They hijacked his special time of year, distracted everyone's attention with presents and tinsel, confused the issue, got everybody thinking he's just some kindly old buffer with a merry laugh as opposed to a voice that splits rocks. What's the first thing your parents tell you about Father Christmas? You've got to be asleep when he calls, or he won't leave you anything. In other words, he *mustn't be seen*. Not, as the saying goes, someone you'd want to meet on a dark night."

Her spaghetti had gone stone cold. She didn't care.

"And the really insidious thing," Jersey went on, "where they've been so clever, is the way we believe in him. Which, left to ourselves, we would do, because he really exists and he's out there. So we're taught as kids, subtly and with nothing ever expressly said, that it's fine to believe if you're a child, but as soon as you start to grow up, you stop. We reach a certain age, and we're programmed to lose that deeply rooted inherent belief, something that's hard-wired into our DNA. When you stop and think about it, that's brilliant."

She gazed at him for a long time. Then she said, "You're barking, you know that?"

"Excuse me?"

"*Father Christmas.*" Heads turned and she lowered her voice. "Sorry, I didn't mean it to come out like that. But are you really serious?"

"Yes."

She pursed her lips. Time for a massive tact injection. "Isn't it possible," she said, "that because you spent all those years snooping round after some crazy cryptic-mystery-conspiracy theory—"

"Which turned out to be true."

"Yes, well, that's the typewriters-and-monkeys approach to philosophical enquiry: sooner or later one crackpot notion will prove to be the truth. That doesn't mean the other nine hundred and ninety-nine thousand aren't pure unadulterated dog poop. I think you miss the old days."

"Well, yes, I do."

"You yearn to be back chasing hooded villains down rat-infested sewers and battling deadly assassins on the roofs of moving trains. And fair play to you, why not? Much more fun than working in a call centre. I think that ever since you've been forced to settle down and actually earn a living—"

"Actually, it was more the intellectual challenge than the getting beaten up."

"—you've been casting around for some new hidden secret of the ancients to go rushing off after, and this is the best you've been able to come up with, and basically you're just afraid of growing up and committing to a serious relationship."

She stopped dead and turned pink. So did he. Five seconds passed, during which stalagmites grew and glaciers carved out valleys. "Basically," she said, "you're just afraid of growing up and facing boring, mundane everyday life. Hence all that garbage about Santa Claus."

He looked at her. "If I was going to go and look for him—"

"Which you shouldn't, because he doesn't exist."

"Maybe," Jersey said. "But if I *were* to go and look for him, I'd want you to come with me."

"Right," she said. "When do we leave?"

22

Kevin glanced down at his watch, frowned and shook it to see if it had stopped working. He was about as at home with sequential linear time as the average Anglo tourist is with speaking French: he could cope, just about, but deep down inside him was a little voice complaining that he shouldn't have to. To his mind there was something inherently silly about a system in which all the little seconds line up like a bus queue, and in order to get to the interesting bits you have to grind your way patiently through all the boring stuff, instead of skipping ahead. If all the seconds of all the minutes of all the hours in a week were laid end to end, eventually it would be Friday. For crying out loud. Where's the sense in that?

Still, when in Rome . . . No, bad example for a member of his family. When on Earth, do as the humans do. As we humans do. Time (on Earth, but decidedly not as it is in Heaven) is the water we humans swim in, it's the clay from which we are moulded, it's the cold congealed custard through which we wade . . . I'm never going to get used to all this, he told himself; it's just not going to work. To which his better self replied, patience. Stick at it. Give it, no pun intended, time.

People were looking at him as they walked by—not quite suspiciously, not exactly with disapproval, but it was clear that they were wondering why he was standing outside an Italian restaurant, in the dark and the rain, with no hat or umbrella. Fair enough, and yes, he ought to make more of an effort to blend in, not be conspicuous. But since rain didn't make him wet (sort of like diplomatic immunity), it was so easy to forget what a big deal the humans made of it. Well, he'd walked enough miles in their shoes recently to know that shoes gave him blisters and walking is an overrated pastime. So far he'd found being human was like moving from a mansion to a one-bedroom apartment on the thirty-second floor: it was cramped, inconvenient and rather disagreeable, but you could see a lot further, if that mattered to you.

None of this, he reminded himself, is my fault. I didn't decide what being human involves. I didn't boot them out of the Garden, force them to waste their time and energy on food and clothes and horrible tight shoes that grind down your heels. That was Dad and Jay, and, bless them, they had done what they thought was right; they only ever had the poor things' best interests at heart. Quite possibly they were misguided, or for some reason had never quite managed to figure out how to create the best of all possible worlds. Quite possibly they weren't as smart (he shuddered as he thought it) as the Venturi brothers. The fact remained: not my fault. I didn't do it, it's not up to me to do something about it, even if there was anything I could do, which there isn't. I wash my hands of the whole business.

Jay hadn't. Oh no, quite the reverse. Jay had gone the extra mile for these people, and though Kevin had never quite been able to see the logical connection between getting oneself lynched by a mob on a trumped-up charge and making things better for people, he was convinced there had been one, because Dad said so. But he'd felt at the time that it wasn't the way he'd have gone about it. Maybe a trifle too subtle for the human mind? Put yourself in their (toe-skinning) shoes for a moment. A guy comes along. He heals the sick, criticises the wealthy and suggests that we all be nice to each other, and so the Romans string him up. And the moral? Well, you didn't have to be a genius, did you? And that, judging by the results over the intervening centuries, had been the lesson they'd taken to heart. Screw the sick, suck up to the rich, stomp on your neighbour and you'll avoid the gallows. Just common sense, really.

Not what I'd have done—and that, presumably, was why they'd kept him out of the family business on the grounds of incompetence. Too dumb to see the subtle nuances of the grand design, which had led to ... Kevin frowned. To what? To a takeover by the Venturi corporation, a new Heaven and a new Earth. To everything getting better for everybody, as promised in the manifesto.

Some things are bred in the bone. No matter how hard you try, you can't run away from your heredity. If you're the son of the Big Guy, you can't help it: you're born with an overwhelming instinct to redeem, even if none of it's your fault and you had no say in the major policy decisions. The realisation hit him like a sock full of sand. I can't just walk by on the other side. I've got to do something. It's who I am.

Which—he guessed he'd known it all along—was why he was here, on the assumption that the two confused young people he'd met on the plane were the right ones to help him do what he had to do. Weird assumption, like saying that because the sun rises in the east we should all eat pimentos. One thing he'd learned from Dad, though: be decisive. Choose to do something and do it, even if it subsequently turns out to be incredibly stupid.

There's a knack to casually bumping into someone and making it look like a complete coincidence, one that Kevin had not yet mastered. The intended slight collision ended up with the young man in the gutter and the young woman rolling around on the pavement clutching her ankle. "I'm so sorry," Kevin said with feeling. "Did I hurt you?"

No need for supernatural mind-reading powers to figure out what the young man was thinking: *How much will it cost me to smash this clown's face in, and where can I raise the money?* Thank goodness for poverty. "Yes," the young man said. "And I think you just twisted her ankle."

Back in the old days Dad had attached a list to the fridge door with a magnet in the shape of a smiling sheep: THINGS KEVIN MUSTN'T DO. Number six on the list was HEAL THE SICK.

Mind you, it's hardly rocket science. All you do is picture in your mind a perfectly healthy, functional human body (which you can do really easily, since you designed it, every nerve, fibre and incredibly delicate blood vessel), then look at the deficient component and say, *Make it so.* All Kevin knew about the human ankle was that for the last few months he'd had two of them. Even so, how hard can it be? To which the answer, he knew, was, incredibly.

Still, everybody's got to start somewhere. "Make it better," he murmured under his breath, and either it was his imagination, or he heard a very soft, faint click.

The young woman stood up. She exhibited no obvious signs of discomfort. She said, "You idiot."

For a moment Kevin was stunned. A miracle.

The young man was on his feet too. "Why don't you look where you're . . . Hold on. I know you."

Kevin put on a weak smile. "You were on that plane."

"Yes. I liked you."

"That's right."

"I'm a lousy judge of character."

"He's said he's sorry," the young woman said. "And he didn't actually draw blood. Besides, you can't afford it."

"True."

"You could tread quite hard on his toe for only three hundred and ninety-nine pounds, because we're doing a special offer this month, but then you'd have to sell your bike."

"Oh, forget it." The young man smiled. "Anyway, I like him."

"That's all right, then," the young woman said. "Let's buy him a coffee instead."

It was a shame he couldn't tell her about the miracle, but then, if it was a miracle, it hadn't been for public adulation. "Thanks," he said. "I'd like that."

It was weird, Lucy thought, running into the nice kid from the plane again, almost providential. He was one of those incredibly rare people who you can really talk to, even though they're practically strangers, and right now that was exactly what she needed. And Jersey seemed to think so too, because when she caught his eye he nodded. Let's see what the kid thinks about this. So, as soon as they'd bought their drinks and found a table . . .

"Talking of which—" they'd been discussing the perfect cappuccino "—do you believe in Santa Claus?"

Kevin paused for a moment before answering. "You mean, does he exist? Yes, he does."

Jersey's eyes opened wide, but he didn't say anything. "You sound awfully sure," Lucy said. "That's, um, unusual in a grown-up."

"Well, yes. Do you believe in the internal combustion engine?"

"What? I mean, well, yes. It's not something you need to believe in. It's just *there*."

Kevin nodded. "They're both equally miraculous or equally mundane, depending on whether you happen to know for sure. Why do you ask?"

"Because we're looking for him."

"Why? Does he owe you money?"

"Excuse me?"

"What I mean is, if I tell you how to find him, will it get him in trouble? I wouldn't want that. I don't care what he's done."

What a curious thing to say. Still, Kevin seemed to make a habit of that kind of thing. "We just want to find him," Lucy said.

"He's not actually all that keen on being found," Kevin replied. "Especially these days, I would imagine."

Jersey's eyes lit up, and he glanced quickly at Lucy. "You mean, the Venturis—"

"I should imagine they'd be very keen to find him, yes."

"But they can't?"

Kevin nodded. "His location is a closely guarded secret," he said. "In the old days you'd have said, God knows where you'd go to start looking for him. Actually, that would've been incorrect."

A pause while Lucy translated that. "So nobody knows—"

"I do."

Kevin looked away. There are some things you don't talk about. He'd never told anybody—not Jay, not even Dad, who knew everything anyway. Did Dad know? Actually, he didn't think so. At least, he couldn't be sure.

He'd been something like six or seven at the time ('something like' being the operative words; see above, under *eternity* and *sequential linear time*). It was Jay's birthday, and they'd had a wonderful time. They'd all worn party haloes, and Uncle Mike and Uncle Gabe had sung funny songs, and Uncle Nick did the fireworks, and Dad did some of his conjuring tricks. The man swallowed by the whale was his favourite, followed by parting the Red Sea and one where he set a large rubber plant on fire and yet it was not consumed. And Jay walked up and down on the swimming pool and then pretended to fall in and get all wet, and Uncle Ghost flew around the table in the form of a white dove, and there was great food and all the fizzy orange he could drink. He'd gone to bed tired out and as happy as it's possible for anyone, even a child, to be.

How long he slept he had no idea, but at some point around the middle of the night a noise woke him up. Now in Dad's house there were no funny night-time sounds— many mansions, yes, but no clunking plumbing or creaky stairs; just dead silence until Dad's alarm went off and it was time to raise the sun.

Kevin wasn't scared because he knew there was nothing in Heaven and Earth for him to be scared of, but he was curious. He opened his eyes and raised a dim glow, so as not to wake up the rest of the house. "Hello," he said. "Anybody there?"

And then he saw a man, or something a man's size and shape, standing by the fireplace holding a sack almost as tall and wide as he was. "Shut up," the figure said. "Go to sleep."

"Who are you?"

"Nobody. I ain't here. You're having a dream. Go to sleep."

Kevin brightened the glow just a bit. "You're him, aren't you?"

He did fit the description, sort of. He was a big, burly man with long white hair and a big beard, white with streaks of black in it, like a badger, and curled into hundreds of tight ringlets. He looked old, the way Dad didn't. His robe was scarlet and he had a face like thunder.

Anyone else would probably have called it a cruel face, all pouchy cheeks and deep hollows under the eyes.

"You're him," Kevin repeated.

"Maybe." The intruder shrugged. "Everybody's somebody."

"Dad told me about you."

"I bet he did."

"He told me I'm not to talk to you."

"Better do as you're told, then."

"He told me you're bad."

The intruder grinned, showing teeth that weren't human. "Yeah, well," he said. "Your dad and I don't exactly see eye to eye. Mind, I got nothing against him. He's all right, your dad. He really understands weather and he can be pretty darn good company. Did he ever show you that one where he sets fire to a pot plant and yet it is not consumed?"

Kevin nodded. "I like that one too."

"Really broke me up, every time." He sighed. "Well, that was then and this ain't. Now go back to sleep before I smack your head."

An empty threat obviously. "Who are you?"

"You already know that."

"Yes, but who are you?"

The intruder looked thoughtful for a moment. "It's like this," he said. "You ask your old man that question, he'll tell you. I am what I am. Me, I am what I was, just about, give or take a few scratches in the paintwork. Will that do?"

"No."

"Tough." The intruder lifted his sack. It looked dreadfully heavy, so the intruder had to be very strong. "You know what I got in here?"

"No."

"Tigers," the intruder said. "And if I open it, they'll jump out and eat you."

"No, they won't."

The intruder rolled his eyes. "All right," he said. "If I ask you to close your eyes and look away, will you do it, just as a favour to me?"

"Sure."

"Cool. You're a good kid, Kevin. Do it. Now."

So Kevin closed his eyes and waited, and he waited and waited for a very long time. Then he opened them again, and the intruder had gone without saying goodbye or anything, which was a bit rude. Also, he'd left something behind, which was careless.

Still, if he was a friend of Dad's, Dad would know how to send it back to him. Kevin jumped out of bed and took a closer look. It was a package, all done up in fancy-coloured paper, with a big red bow. Some unaccountable and irresistible urge drove him to open it, even though he knew he shouldn't, because it wasn't his; it belonged to the intruder.

Kevin had never ever done anything deliberately wrong, and had never told a lie or made up an excuse. Nothing had ever just sort of slipped out of his hands, and no dog had ever eaten his homework. For obvious reasons. So if he opened the parcel, Dad would know, and he'd be so mad.

There was a label. It had a little picture of a robin, and his name: FOR KEVIN.

A present? But why? It wasn't his birthday. And why would someone he'd never seen before, someone *bad*, give him anything?

He looked at it. He really wanted to rip open the paper and see what was inside. But he shouldn't do that, should he? Well. Dad had never told him in so many words, if that red-robed man gives you a present, don't open it. He'd never do anything Dad had told him not to—only he had, because he'd been told not to talk to the man, but not talking would've been rude, so Dad couldn't have meant it literally. And he was burning up with curiosity, and . . . Aw, heck, what harm could it do?

It was a cowboy hat. More than that, it was the best cowboy hat anyone could possibly imagine, broad and swoopy and decorated round the brim with little silver conchos, and Kevin had yearned for one for as long as he could remember, but Jay had told him not to ask for one because Dad wouldn't approve. Just what he'd always wanted, and the red-robed man must've known that, unless it was the most amazing coincidence, and now he had one of his very own.

He shivered as though a cold wind had just blown under the door because he knew, deep in his heart, that he could never wear the cowboy hat, or mention it, or leave it anywhere Dad or Jay might come across it, and for the first time he knew what unhappiness is, and he wanted to cry, but he daren't. And later, looking back on that night over the years, he'd asked himself over and over again if that had been the reason, if the red-robed man had meant to upset him and make him unhappy out of spite or revenge on his father for some unknown slight, or simply because he really was bad. But he kept the hat, and nobody ever said anything about it.

And ever since, on the eve of Jay's birthday, he'd lit a roaring fire in the fireplace, then collected up all his socks from their various forgotten places on the floor of his room and locked them away in his big oak chest and piled heavy books on the lid. So yes, he believed. Nobody more so.

"Right," Jersey said. "So, where do we find him?"

"Not where. How."

The proprietor of the cafe was glowering at them. It was

well past chairs-on-tables time, and he wanted to go home. The only other customers in the place were a couple of old men in blue serge coats shiny with age and knitted hats, talking softly over big mugs of tea.

"Let's not get hung up on relative adverbs," Lucy said. "How do we go about finding him? That's what we want to know."

Kevin was perfectly still and quiet for a moment, as though he'd been switched off at the mains. Then he said, "Well, it's quite simple really. All you do is—"

At which point the door flew open, and a dozen men in yellow tracksuits burst in.

Why yellow? Well, the Venturi people had done a lot of research on that one. They wanted a colour for their security forces' uniforms that commanded respect without being unduly intimidating or antagonistic. Bright but not primary, their consultants recommended, and their first suggestion was pink (they weren't from Earth), later modified to primrose yellow, eye-catching and with positive associations of spring flowers, butter fresh from the churn and newly hatched chicks. It didn't actually matter all that much in the event, because the rest of the Venturi programme had gone so well that this was the first time that security forces had been deployed on the planet since the change of ownership. In fact, if they hadn't had AUTHORISED STORMTROOPER stencilled on their chests, it would have been easy to mistake them for a troupe of wandering mimes.

Their leader raised the visor of his helmet. "Freeze," he said.

Kevin turned his head, looked at him and smiled. "We will, if you don't close the door. You won't have noticed in all that gear, but it's bitter out."

"Nobody move."

"Oh, I see."

Kevin was still beaming amiably. Lucy was making up her mind whether this was trouble or rag week. Fair enough. But Jersey had seen that formation and heard that tone of voice many times before and knew exactly what they meant. Twelve to one was a bummer, but at least he could buy the others time to get away. "It's all right," he said quietly. "Go out the back way. I'll handle this."

"I wouldn't if I were—"

But Jersey wasn't listening. He picked up two teaspoons and bent them round the fingers of his right hand to form a rudimentary knuckleduster. "Just like old times," he said happily. "Right, who's first?"

A window opened in thin air and a man with a clipboard stepped out of it. "Hi," he said.

The yellow men fell back to give him room. "Hold on," Jersey said. "I haven't done anything yet."

The man with the clipboard beamed at him. "No, but you're about to, and usually we're quite happy to levy our charges in arrears, but where there's likely to be the sort of mayhem you've got in mind, we reserve the right to request a payment on account before you get started. Basically, I just need to take a swipe of a major credit card."

Jersey glared at him. "What about them? They're the ones who came barging in here."

The man with the clipboard kept smiling. "Yes, but they're properly accredited peace officers, whereas you're a private individual who's about to resist lawful arrest. By the way, can I interest you in a Venturicorp loyalty card? It means you can thump nine guards and get the tenth one free."

Jersey looked at him, then slowly unclamped the bent spoons from his fingers. As he did so, he heard a voice behind him saying, "Excuse me, will this do?"

It was one of the two old men in the corner, and he was holding out a slim rectangle of shining yellow metal. Not a Gold Card, a gold card. The man with the clipboard stared at it, then nodded quickly. "That'll do nicely," he said and vanished.

The old man gave Jersey a warm smile and a friendly clap on the shoulder. "Carry on, son," he said. "Go do that voodoo that you do so well."

"But—"

"All taken care of. Give 'em whatsisname."

And then he and his friend didn't seem to be there any more, and the yellow tracksuits were closing in, and it was just like riding a bicycle: you never forget how.

About ninety seconds later Jersey put down the chair leg he'd been using to such good effect and breathed a contented sigh. "Thanks, guys, that was fun," he said. Then he turned to Kevin, who'd been watching with a pained expression, and said, "Who was that? The old guy with the card."

"My Uncle Raffa."

"I think I may have cost him a lot of money."

"He can afford it."

One of the yellow tracksuits groaned softly. Jersey picked a stray cushion off the floor and tucked it under his head, so he wouldn't wake up with a cricked neck. Little acts of kindness. "I think we should go now."

"Probably just as well."

Lucy looked round for a waiter but there was nobody about, for some reason, so she put some money on the table to pay for the drinks. "Your uncle," she said.

"Not really my uncle, more a friend of the family. The other one was my Uncle Gabe."

"When you say family . . ."

Kevin grinned at her. "A bit like that," he said, "but not what you're thinking. I think we should leave. There may be more of them on the way, and your friend's had quite enough healthy exercise for one day."

There was a door at the back leading out through the kitchen. "You were just about to tell us," Lucy said, "how to find Santa."

Kevin swerved to avoid a projecting saucepan handle. "Yes, well, it's pretty straightforward, really. All you've got to do is—"

And then he vanished.

23

Snib Venturi closed the door, kicked off his shoes, loosened his tie, poured himself a stiff drink and sagged into his favourite armchair. It creaked slightly. He glugged a third of the drink and closed his eyes.

He wore the tie, the suit, the tight shoes and the corporeal body to remind himself of where he'd come from and how very far away, in all conceivable dimensions, that place was. Right now his feet ached and his arthritic hip was giving him grief. He savoured the sensations as though they were fine vintages and smiled. He thought about a pair of scared wide-eyed disembodied young water sprites without a nerve-ending or a scrap of skin, bone or sinew between them, cowering helplessly through the savage Martian sandstorms, remembering how they'd have given anything for bodies they could call their own—skin or fur or scales or carapace, who gives a damn, anything at all they could huddle up in and keep themselves together with, instead of being blown about by the slightest hint of breeze.

Now of course he and Ab could have any bodies they wanted, ten miles high, twenty-headed, fifty-armed, adamant or gold or burning plasma. But they'd stuck with the ones they'd started out with, even though they were hopelessly old-fashioned and starting to fall to bits. The way Snib saw it, a body is for life, not just for—

He frowned. Rephrase that. A body is for life; you don't just throw it away and get a new one as soon as the paint gets chipped or the ashtrays get full. You stick with it, patch it up and carry on, because the aches and pains are just as much a part of being corporeal as the strength and the mobility and the cohesion and all the really good stuff. All or nothing at all. Anyhow, that was how he saw it, and Ab always followed his lead, and that was just fine. And, heck, he *enjoyed* being tired. It let him know he was alive, and when you're immortal, that's very important.

Sleepy. It had been a long day. He snuggled back into the chair, relishing its support, and reached out into the friendly darkness, where he wouldn't have to be himself for twenty minutes or so. No such luck. A familiar voice hauled him back into the light, and he sat up.

"Snib," the voice repeated. "We got trouble."

That was Ab for you, always worried about something. Ab had had an anxious frown long before he'd had a face to wear it on. "What?"

"War's broken out," Ab said. "There's fighting in the streets."

Snib sighed. Ab tended to exaggerate; you needed climbing gear and oxygen to scale his molehills. "You sure about that?"

Ab nodded eagerly. "In a place called London, England. A whole regiment of our best guys wiped out to the last man."

Snib sighed, pulled his LoganBerry from his inside pocket and thumbed through to the latest sitrep. "That's not what it says here," he said. "According to this, some guy just beat up on a dozen yellowcoats."

"That's what I just said."

"Minor cuts and bruises, and all paid for in advance." His eyebrows rose when he saw the account number the charges had been debited to. "Who sent the yellowcoats?"

"I did. Sorry, I guess I must've forgotten to mention it."

Ab was a pretty hopeless liar. Also, he liked to do stuff on his own initiative once in a while, and the results were generally not helpful. "I guess so," Snib said. "Out of interest, why did you order them to arrest the son of the previous management? You know the deal. Cut him all possible slack."

"It wasn't him; he just happened to be there. It was the other two. They're dangerous."

Snib sighed. It was amazing what Ab could feel threatened by when he really set his mind to it. "Two humans."

"They're asking questions."

"They do that. Can't arrest every human who asks a question, we wouldn't have anywhere to put them."

"About—" here Ab lowered his voice, furrowed his brows and pulled a terrible face "—about the reindeer guy."

On the other hand, just once in a while (twice so far, in fact, since they'd left Mars) Ab got it right, and one of his hunches turned out to save the day and prevent a catastrophic disaster. "What sort of questions, Ab? Like, *Can you think of anything I could get my mother-in-law?* isn't a major issue."

"They want to know where he is."

Snib pursed his lips. "Just innocent speculation."

"They want to find him."

See above, under exaggeration. Also, over the years, the wrong end of the stick had been worn smooth by the touch of Ab's palms. "You sure about that?"

Ab gave him a pained look, as in *Why do you never*

believe anything I tell you? and played him a clip on his
LoganBerry. "Right?"

"OK, brother. This time you may have a point." Snib
frowned. "And Kevin G. picked up the tab for all this?"

"Not Kevin. A couple of his old man's button men.
They've been keeping an eye on him."

Snib could feel a mild headache coming on. "Fine," he
said. "Where is he now?"

Ab shrugged. "Disappeared."

"He can't have done, Ab. We got the whole planet on
CCTV. What you mean is, some fool on the desk—"

"Vanished. Into thin air."

The headaches made Snib Venturi feel real. But there
was no time for that now. "Impossible."

A reprise of the pained look, and Ab conjured a fistful of
stray photons into a holoscreen and played him the CCTV
clip. Sure enough, one moment Kevin was there, in the
restaurant kitchen, and the next moment he wasn't. Magic.

Snib Venturi prided himself on his easy-going nature—
any more laid-back and he'd be a spirit level. Some things,
though, even he couldn't tolerate, and being made a
monkey of (no offence to the dominant indigenous species)
was one of them. Fun is fun, he always said, but the Hell
with nonsense. "I want those two clowns arrested, *now*,
and locked up in the Marshalsea. Don't just stand there,
bro, see to it."

Ab quivered slightly, but he knew his place. "Sure," he
said. "How many troops should I send?"

Snib looked at him as if his brother had just asked the
time while standing underneath a clock. "All of them,"
he said.

24

To go from Hell to the movies, you take the Infernal Subway to Level 666 and then the escalator to the customs post at the Hub of Acheron (where you can reclaim any hope you may have deposited earlier, provided you've remembered to bring your claim check); you then proceed on the fast-track rolling walkway to the hellmouth of your choice. From the Hub, all the exits to the land of the living are equidistant, so your selection is guided simply by where you decide you want to go, the time zone, what's showing where, whose seat prices are cheapest and who's doing the best deal on nachos and popcorn.

Like 98 per cent of the human race, Bernie and Jenny had decided they wanted to see the latest Star Wars, because of the special effects and because the good guys always win. Hell runs on Greenwich time, naturally, and when they got to the Hub, Bernie's LoganBerry told him they were just right to catch the 6.15 showing at the Odeon, Leicester Square, London. As is or should be well known, there's a hellmouth on the Piccadilly line platform of the Leicester Square Tube during rush hour on weekdays, which was perfect. They mingled unobtrusively with the crowd, aced the ticket barrier with their

Brimstone cards and made their way up into the early-evening light.

"Here." Bernie had remembered to bring sunglasses for Jenny.

"Thanks," she said gratefully. "It's so *bright*."

"You get used to it." She looked sensational in sunglasses. "Come on, this way."

The square was crammed with brightly dressed humans out for a good time, though the atmosphere was curiously muted. It took Bernie a while to figure it out but then he realised. They were so preoccupied with not bumping into each other, which could provoke anger, harsh words and substantial expense, that having fun was the furthest thing from their minds. The pavement was scrupulously clean and litter-free, and the souvenir shops were all selling good-quality items at sensible prices which nobody was buying. Most of the bars and pubs had closed down since Bernie had last been there, though a few had reopened as organic food restaurants. It put Bernie in mind of Sunday in Switzerland, but without the raucous, carefree jollity.

"This is amazing," Jenny said. "All these people."

"It's a popular place to come for a night out."

Jenny frowned. "Reminds me a lot of work," she said. "They all look so miserable."

Yes, they did, didn't they? "Deep down they're having fun," Bernie said. "Come on. We've just got time for an ice cream."

Before they could cross the square, a window opened in thin air. No longer an unusual sight, but this one was *huge*. Out of it poured men in white plastic armour. The crowds, who'd initially stopped to stare, shrugged and carried on with that they were doing.

"You've got to hand it to their publicity guys," Bernie said. "They sure know how to inspire apathy."

The stormtroopers were forming up into a dense phalanx and marching across the square, the pavement quivering under the impact of their boots. Everyone drifted listlessly out of their way except for two people, a young man and a girl, who broke into a run. They weren't looking where they were going, and the man crashed into Bernie, nearly knocking him off his feet.

"It's all right," Bernie said quickly. "Accident. You didn't mean it. I'm fine."

And the curious thing was, no window opened, and no smiling clipboard-bearer stepped out of it. Instead, the white soldiers continued to march straight at them. And their toy guns looked even more realistic, the closer you got to them.

The young man was hobbling; he'd taken the worst of the damage by far. And the look on his face—he was terrified.

"It's all right," Bernie said. "It's just a stunt. For the movie."

The girl shook her head frantically. Bernie looked past her at the stormtroopers. They were still pouring out of the window, forming up, marching. There were thousands of them. *I've got a bad feeling about this*, he thought, appropriately.

"They aren't human," Jenny said.

No fear in her voice, just an observation, but Bernie knew in an instant that she was right, and therefore the picture in front of him was all wrong. But the young man and the girl were human all right, and they were scared stiff, and nobody had come to charge them for clumsiness, which was completely inexplicable. The stormtroopers were getting closer. Sometimes you only have a split second to decide.

"This way." He lifted the young man's arm over his shoulder and took his weight. "Follow me."

"Aren't we going to the movies, then?" Jenny asked.

"No, we're rescuing these people. Come *on*."

"All right. Where are we—?"

"This way."

Back the way they'd just come, across the square, into the station. The human girl had money for the ticket machine, luckily, and the stormtroopers got held up at the barrier—but not for long, because they quickly blasted it out of the way with their laser rifles, so either the Disney people had finally gone completely out of control, or it wasn't a publicity stunt after all. But they had all sorts of problems keeping step on the escalator, which just about gave Bernie the time he needed to get his untidy little party onto the platform and safely through the invisible barrier into the hellmouth.

"It's all right," he said, drawing a deep breath. "We're safe here."

The human girl was staring at him as the rush-hour commuters walked straight past or (apparently) right through them, oblivious to their presence in their transparent bubble of transdimensional Elsewhere field. "Where are we?"

"Hell," Bernie said cheerfully. "Well, sort of. It counts as Hell, like the U.S. embassy counts as a tiny bit of America. Like I said, you're safe here. They can't reach you."

Indeed they couldn't, though that wasn't stopping them from trying. Clearly they knew there was something there, a portal of some kind, though they couldn't see or feel it, prod and scrabble as they might. But, unlike Bernie and Jenny, they didn't have little plastic swipe cards; and no card, no access, them's the rules. "Who are those guys?" Bernie asked. "Any idea?"

"We think they may be Venturicorp security," the girl

said. "It's possible we may have annoyed the management just a bit, which would explain why they're after us." She hesitated. "Which means you could get in real trouble helping us, so if you'd rather we left . . ."

Bernie laughed. "It's all right," he said. "We're the bad guys."

A stormtrooper swung the butt of his blaster and hammered it against nothing at all an inch from Bernie's face. Nothing happened, but it was a bit unnerving. "Let's get out of here," he said. "We can go to my place."

"Are you sure?"

Good question, and yes, he was. "It's not far," he said. "You people look like you could use a drink."

Jenny shot him a dubious look, but he shook his head. "It's OK," he said. "Mr. L. likes me. Just for once, I'm going to take advantage of his good nature."

"Just a second," the young man said. "Did you say Hell?"

"Yup," Bernie replied happily, because for some reason he couldn't really explain he was enjoying this. Maybe an entire working life spent doing accounts and answering telephones had a tiny bit to do with it, maybe it was the warm glow of hero-worship coming from Jenny, on which he could have toasted bread if he'd had any and a fork. Who knows? "Come on. This way. Mind the step."

25

Kevin opened his eyes, blinked and looked around. Then he sighed. "Hi, Uncle Gabe."

He knew this place. It was basically a white box with white walls, white floor and white ceiling, no doors or windows, infinitely large but unmistakably confined. In his mind he associated it intimately with the words *Go to your room* spoken in a stern but not harsh tone of voice. I boobed, he thought. Ah well.

"Kevin, Kevin, Kevin." Uncle Gabe shook his head. He wasn't a scruffy old man any more, and Kevin shaded his human eyes against the glare of that transcendent brightness. "You just don't think, that's your trouble."

"The humans figure that to think is to be," Kevin offered hopefully, but Uncle Gabe wasn't having any. "All right," he said. "I'm sorry."

Uncle Gabe and Uncle Raffa looked at each other. "I don't think *sorry*'s going to cut it this time," Uncle Raffa said. "You just caused a severe theological incident."

The far wall of the box turned into a screen on which a vast army of white-armoured stormtroopers were prodding at something that wasn't there. Kevin winced. "That was me?"

"A direct consequence of your actions, kid. Let's just say you're not exactly popular right now."

Kevin nodded. "Which is why I'm here?"

"For your own good. We thought we'd better get you out while we still could," Raffa said gravely. "I'm not saying the Venturis would actually arrest you, but we reckoned, hey, let's not find out."

Kevin was shocked. "No way," he said. "I've got immunity. They can't do that."

The two angels gazed at him sadly, six pairs of shining eyes boring into him, and eight pairs of wings fluttering in disapproval. "It's not quite as clear-cut as that," Gabe said.

"Of course it is. I'm *his son*. They can't push me around like I'm some—"

Gabe clicked his tongue and shook his head. "If you'd been at the negotiations," he said, "you'd know there was a lot of difficulty about that. The old man said if you chose to stay behind you had to be free and clear, total immunity. The Venturis said no, sorry, we don't make exceptions for anybody. It came that close to being a deal-breaker."

Kevin caught his breath. It had never occurred to him that Dad would risk the whole deal just for him. "You're kidding."

Gabe smiled. "In the end, the old man and Snib Venturi went off somewhere and had a long private talk about it, and basically they agreed that, as far as the Venturis were concerned, you didn't exist."

Kevin opened his mouth and closed it again.

"An anomaly," Raffa said. "Like ... well, you know."

"Oh wow."

"Which was fine," Gabe said firmly, "and in real life, being practical about it, Snib Venturi reckoned he could turn a blind eye and simply not notice anything you got up to because the old man assured him, Kevin's not going to do anything dumb, he's a good boy, he won't cause no trouble. And on that basis Snib Venturi said, yeah, what the heck. On the understanding," he went on, frowning, "you keep your nose clean and your head under the radar, which the old man was sure you'd do because for all your faults you've got more common sense than a small piece of rock. He had faith in you, Kevin. You let him down."

"But you guys . . ."

Raffa scowled at him. "We saw you about to make an idiot of yourself with those two dissidents," he said angrily, "so we stepped in and did the only thing we could, just to get you out of there. Otherwise, those Venturi cops would've had to decide whether to arrest you or not, and we didn't exactly want a test case and a legal precedent."

Kevin was looking at the screen. "What about my friends?" he said.

"They're no friends of yours, Kevin," Raffa said. "They're just humans. None of our business now. And definitely none of yours."

"Where did they go?"

Gabe shrugged. "We don't know. And we don't care either. Sure, it's good fun to see Snib Venturi's goons made to look stupid once in a while, but I'm sorry, the fun comes at too high a price. Wherever they are, they're on their own now. Is that understood?"

On the far wall a window opened in thin air and all but four of the stormtroopers vanished. The quartet that stayed behind took up station on four sides of an imaginary box. They looked like they were planning to stay there for quite some time.

"That's a hellmouth," Kevin said, "isn't it?"

"No comment. And don't even think of hassling your Uncle Nick about it, because he's got some common sense, even if you haven't. He won't get involved, you can bet."

Kevin took a deep breath. "Listen," he said. "I'm really sorry I put you guys on the spot, and I'm really grateful to you for looking out for me, and I know you've got my best interests at heart, and I definitely hear what you say about the Venturi boys, and I really don't want to make trouble for anyone, believe me."

Gabe didn't look happy. "But?"

"Those humans," Kevin said. "They needed me. They were relying on me. They were practically, like, *disciples*."

"Stay out of the family business, son," Raffa said grimly. "You know what the old man said over and over again. You're just not cut out for it."

"Yeah? Says who?" Kevin pulled himself up short, appalled at what he'd allowed himself to say, even more appalled by the fact that he'd felt the need to say it. "I can't just walk out on them," he said quietly. "Think about it, fellas. That's not what Jay would've done, is it?"

"Sure." Gabe was looking at him particularly solemnly. "And I guess you remember what happened to him, don't you?"

"Yes. Well, then."

"The difference being," Gabe said, "that Jay was in sure and certain hope of the resurrection, so when push came to shove it really didn't matter a damn, did it? He knew it was just a matter of three days putting his feet up down at Nick's place, chilling out, drinking iced tea, watching a few old movies, then back to work and no harm done. But in your case, if they string you up . . ." He paused. "Different rules now, Kevin. And we're not in charge any more. Sure, Snib Venturi might be nice as a token of respect to your old man—professional courtesy. But then again, he might not, and in that case, there's not thing one we could do about it." He fixed Kevin with his bright golden eyes. "You want to take that chance, Kevin? For them? For *humans*?"

"Besides." Uncle Raffa was doing his still, small voice of calm. Bad angel, good angel. "What's all this about anyhow? It's not like those two want to do anything worthwhile. Quite the reverse. They want to get in contact with *him*. That lowlife. What good could possibly come of that, boy? So you see, it's not like Jay at all, so don't you go getting any ideas. You'd just be helping two troublemakers make trouble. Is that what you want to do? Is that worth pissing off the Venturis for? I don't think so."

Kevin had never heard one of his uncles swear before. "I guess not," he said.

"Good boy. So that's an end of it, right? You won't be helping those no-goods any more."

"No, Uncle."

Gabe smiled and ruffled Kevin's hair, which burst into flames. The two uncles burst out laughing, quenched it and grew the sizzled hair back. "It's weird to think you're human now," Raffa said. "It only seems yesterday you and me and Mikey were up there repainting the firmament."

Which was actually a pretty tactless thing to say, given on that occasion Kevin had proved he couldn't be trusted with even the simplest of tasks (and that, oh best beloved, is why your solar system now has only eight planets). Gabe hadn't meant it that way, of course. Hadn't he? Get real. Of course he had. "You remember that, huh?"

"What? You bet. How we all laughed. It's gonna take some getting used to, Kevin, you being technically, well, you know. But it was your choice and we respect you for it, don't we, Raffa?"

"Sure, Gabe. We respect you like anything."

The big grin didn't change, but the eyes suddenly went quite cold. "Just don't go doing any more dumb stuff, all right? Properly speaking, Raffa and me, we're retired now. It's time for us to fold our wings, put our feet up, take it easy. Which we can't do if we're forever having to chase after you cleaning up little messes. You copy that?"

"Yes, Uncle. I get that loud and clear."

"Of course you do." The eyes were warm again, and full of tenderness. "Right, so where do you want to be dropped off? Any place you want to go, kid—the world is your oyster."

"I take it you mean any place except London, England?"

"You don't want to go there, trust me." Gabe spread his hands cheerfully. "Crummy place. Rains all the time, the prices are a rip-off and the food is terrible."

"All right. Where would you recommend?"

"Goa," Gabe said firmly. "Long, golden beaches, hot sun, pleasant people and the most amazing fish. You'll love it. Nothing to do all day but soak up the rays and stuff your face."

"And there's a varied and exciting cultural life," Raffa added. "So they tell me."

"Yeah, all that stuff too. And the chicks—"

Raffa dug him in the ribs with his elbow. He blinked. "If you're into birdwatching, that is. They got brown shrikes there like you wouldn't believe."

Kevin kept his eyebrow unraised with an effort. In some of the older copies of the office manual in Dad's library there had been a bit about the *nephelim*, offspring of mortal women and angels, which didn't seem to appear in the more recent editions, and which had always puzzled him, till now. True, there is a special providence in the fall of a sparrow, or even a brown shrike, but Gabe had never struck him as a keen ornithologist. Even so. There's something profoundly upsetting about finding out that people you've looked up to all your life may not be as perfect as you once thought.

"And Blyth's warbler," Raffa said, "you can't spit

anywhere on Goa without a Blyth's warbler getting its head wet. Kind of an earthly Paradise."

Paradise, with his uncles standing guard out front with flaming swords. Kevin smiled slowly. "You think so?"

Gabe nodded. "Sure, kid," he said. "God's own country. Just stay well clear of the fruit trees."

26

What, apart from *that*, is the one thing everybody knows about the North Pole? That it's magnetic, of course. A compass needle will always point to it, no matter where you are. That's science, a fact, and not to be argued with. Why it should be so . . .

They'll tell you that it's because the North Pole is where the Earth's magnetic field points vertically down, and you accept that either because you can't be bothered to try and understand it, or because you genuinely believe that the Earth is a giant magnet, presumably anchored through all eternity to the invisible door of an enormous celestial fridge. Not so long ago they'd have told you a different story. There's a huge deposit of iron deep in the heart of some subglacial polar mountain, they'd have assured you on a stack of Bibles, and you'd most likely have fallen for that one too. It's people like you who make it easy for them to get away with telling us what they want us to believe.

Actually, the old version is a whole lot nearer to the truth than the new one, because there genuinely is a substantial quantity of iron stockpiled in echoing caverns deep under the ice, just off to one side of Pole Central. A lot of it is obsolete now, of course, though it could probably still give you a nasty nip, and its curators keep it polished and sharpened mostly from force of habit. It doesn't cause the magnetism, needless to say. In fact, the magnetism is a damn nuisance, because whenever he moves about in the adjoining chambers of the complex, everything in the stockpile wants to come too, which can be more than a little disconcerting for anyone working maintenance at the time.

Not that he gives a damn, or if he does (and of course he does; they're his people and he looks out for them) he takes pains to make sure they don't know it, because that's all part of his style, the image, the way he wants to be perceived. It's a good style for someone in his position. Old Blood-and-Guts, they call him. You'd better watch out, don't you dare cross him or get in his way or you'll get trodden on, and they admire him for it, because when every man's hand, angel's wing and demon's claw is against you, what you want most from your leader is invincibility combined with granite toughness. So, if you're pulling a double shift painting cosmolene on the throwing axes and the Old Bugger takes his morning trip to the john two minutes early, you don't resent the fact that the entire inventory flies up out of the racks and embeds itself in the wall while you're still working on it, even if it means you come off shift with rather less fingers than you're used to. Instead, you feel kind of proud that you follow a guy who's so hard and mean, iron longs to be near him.

For the same set of reasons, all the fittings in the executive bathroom are brass. Image is important, but it's good to be practical.

The magnetism thing causes problems in other areas too, for example when guests visit the complex. This doesn't happen often, but from time to time it's unavoidable. For example when Aiko Kawaguchiya succeeded her father as head of Kawaguchiya Integrated Circuits and demanded a personal one-to-one meeting to renegotiate all the licensing agreements for KIC's various computerised toy brands, one thing that somehow didn't get mentioned during the preliminary discussions was that Aiko had a steel pin in her leg because of a teenage cycling accident. The subsequent meeting was not a success, even though it was obvious that Aiko felt a strong, in fact an overpowering attraction to her new business partner. Likewise, the CEO of Guangdong Amalgamated Plastics was left tongue-tied and speechless for the duration of his visit simply because nobody thought to tell his hosts in advance about the wires in his dental plate.

The minor irritations are worth putting up with, however, when you consider the benefits, particularly in the area of perimeter security. Thus, when a sleek mile-wide silver saucer crash-landed among the ice floes and gouged a thirty-mile crevasse before coming gently to rest at precisely magnetic north, there was a contingent of suitably armed elves waiting to meet it.

A hatch popped and a being crawled out down the gleaming ramp. It was so profoundly cocooned in its environment suit that its shape was anyone's guess, but it had three pairs of gloves and six pairs of boots, and one goldfish-bowl helmet at one end and a slightly smaller one at the other.

It raised its front head and cleared its throat. "One small step for a Gryzon," it said, "a giant leap for— Hello, who are you?"

The elves looked at each other.

"We come in peace," said the Gryzon. "Take me to your— No, please be careful with that, I need it to breathe with."

The elves picked the alien up by its hands and feet

and carried it down some steps in the ice, while others slammed the ramp shut and nailed it down with six-inch nails.

"Our long-range scans," said the Gryzon, as its helmeted heads went bump-bump-bump down the ice-walled corridor, "said this planet was uninhabited. Do you folks live here or are you just visiting?"

"Shut up," said an elf. "Talking food gives me gas."

They emerged into a high-vaulted chamber hewn out of the permafrost. The pillars that supported the cathedral-high roof were shaped like pairs of rearing reindeer locked in combat, and boughs of holly hung from the architraves. In niches in the walls stood row upon row of shrunken heads, all crowned with floppy red hats. "I'd really like to talk to your head of state or foreign minister," squeaked the alien. "Or if they're busy, the secretary of state for agriculture will do fine."

A vast door at the end of the chamber swung open. It was made of three layers of material: steel and diamond with a dark-matter core, laminated in a herringbone pattern and clinched together with nails as thick as a man's leg. An even bigger, higher, gloomier chamber lay beyond it, in which the only light came from a single arrow slit a thousand feet up. In the darkness it glared like a searchlight, and it illuminated a monstrous throne made of reindeer bones heated and twisted together like wicker. A pale fire danced all around it, flashing and sparkling red, green, silver and gold in long strings that trailed across the floor and ran up the nearby pillars like scintillating ivy. If the alien had been able to get at its scanning device, it would have read the effect as anomalous electromagnetic discharges somehow related to the massive EM field that had literally pulled the Gryzon scoutship down from the sky. Behind the throne stood an ancient fir tree, from whose branches dangled what the alien recognised as super-enlarged isostreptic clusters, each tennis ball-sized particle glittering with silvery strepterons and snow-white metaquarks—enough energy, the alien calculated, to build a small sun or blow apart a very big one. That would account for the enormous build-up of ice on the outside at any rate, a simple refrigeration effect. What the alien couldn't begin to account for was the fact that the throne was occupied by something or someone who appeared to be alive instead of shrivelled to a crisp by so much unfiltered mythopoeic radiation.

Not just alive but bright-eyed, bushy-tailed and full of beans, a large, stout humanoid biped in loose-fitting red robes, its two arms resting on the splayed antlers that formed the armrests of the throne. It peered down at the alien through two small half-moon lenses supported by a wire frame and growled, "Now what?"

"Caught this one, boss, snooping around the north fence. It talks."

The Red Lord narrowed its eyes, and the alien felt a slight pricking sensation, as though it was being subjected to a high-resonance bleptyon scan. "Of course it talks, you halfwit. It's a Gryzon from Sigma Eridani Two. Highly advanced culture. Split the atom around about the time our lot realised that fire is hot. Let it go and bring it a nice cup of tea."

The Gryzon blinked. "You know about us?"

The Red Lord shrugged. "I've been around," he said. "You're a bit off the beaten track though, aren't you? What brings you out this far? Let me guess. You put the postcode for Sirius into your satnav and this is where it brought you."

The Gryzon shook its heads. "We're explorers," it said. "We seek a new home for our people."

"Is that right?"

Synchronised nod. "Millennia of war with our neighbours the Eee have left our planet barely habitable. Our scans suggested this world would be suitable."

"Mphm. And is it?"

"Geologically and ecologically speaking, it's just right. Of course, it also reads as uninhabited."

The Red Lord clicked his tongue. "I'd get a new scanner if I were you."

"It didn't register mammalian bipeds as sentient life," the Gryzon explained. "Back home, mammals are—"

The Red Lord smiled. "I know," he said. "Where you come from, you can buy little aerosols of mammal spray for keeping the little buggers off your roses. That's not the case here." He paused, then added, "But I don't suppose that'd bother your superiors very much."

The Gryzon made a complicated no-not-really gesture. "Our situation is desperate," it said. "Unless we can relocate immediately, we face extinction. Compared with that, wildlife conservation isn't an immediate priority."

The Red Lord steepled his fingers. "And of course your long struggle with the Eee has left you with overwhelmingly superior military technology and a huge fleet of warships. You think the indigenous life forms on this planet would be a pushover."

The alien hesitated, then nodded. "Of course, if it was up to me . . ."

"Quite," the Red Lord said. "But it isn't, is it? It's up to your superiors, who have their species to save and elections to win. I do understand." He reached under the throne and picked a long parcel off the floor. It was wrapped in red and silver paper decorated with jolly robins. He slit the paper with his fingernail and drew out a long zigzaggy thing.

"Got your scanner handy?"

"Yes."

"Scan that."

The device whirred, bleeped hysterically and blew a fuse. The insides of the Gryzon's helmets misted up.

"It's called a thunderbolt," the Red Lord said. "Let me point out that I'm a simple reindeer farmer, one of millions scattered across the planet, and we all have these. We use them for controlling agricultural pests—you know, bugs and creepy-crawlies. Of course, they're nothing like the kilotonnage of the big ones the military use."

"Um."

The Red Lord put the thunderbolt back under his chair. "You might care to mention that to your superiors," he said. "Quite possibly it could help them to make an informed decision."

"I'll do that," the Gryzon squeaked.

"Good lad. You might also suggest that they take a look at the third planet of 61 Cygni. I think you'll find it's much more suitable, and it really is uninhabited, not so much as an amoeba lurking in a rock pool anywhere. Ah, here's Grusmazhg with your tea. One magnesium chunk or two?"

A little later, when the elves had used their sleigh to pull the saucer out of the ice and the Gryzons had blasted off back to their distant home, the Red Lord leaned back in his throne, closed his eyes and breathed a long sigh of relief. A close call. He knew all about the Gryzons and their antisocial habits. Of course, he said to himself, it's not my job; properly speaking, I should've left it to . . . well, nowadays it'd be the Venturi, who'd have fought like tigers to protect their investment: injunctions and lawyers and space battles and huge clouds of mangled bits of starship orbiting the Earth like Saturn's rings, to achieve what I managed with a simple bluff. Or indeed a simple lie, which I couldn't have told if I was the official god around here, because gods don't, do they? Just as well I'm not the official god, then. Oh yes. Amen to that.

The Red Lord closed his eyes, letting his head slide forward on his chest, trying to clear the clutter out of his mind, trying to *think*. There had been times recently when he'd been sorely tempted to pack it all in, make some sort of a deal with the old fool and the young halfwit, retire, maybe even allow himself to dissolve back into the elements from which he'd been formed so very long ago. But then there was the change of management, and he didn't trust Snib Venturi as far as he could sneeze him out of one nostril, and also That Time of Year was coming up fast, and now this. There were times when he asked himself why he bothered with it all. He could ask questions like that, since he'd never pretended to be omniscient or even particularly clever; not clever, just a bit stubborn and very, very, very strong. And the answers he'd come up with over the years still rang as true as they always had: because it annoys Them—the bosses du jour, the Management—and for the Hell of it. And, of course, because sooner or later it was unavoidable that They would find him and come after him with lots and lots of celestial policemen, and he'd be intrigued to find out just how bloody a nose he could give them before They inevitably won. Meanwhile, just call it force of habit for want of a better phrase. And because *The Government doesn't want me to* is the best reason for doing anything, after all.

But maybe . . .

He sat bolt upright, catching a fold of his red gown on a projecting antler. Maybe there was a better way at that. Maybe there was one piece in the game that everybody had overlooked, and with a little subtle, dexterous wiggling it might just be possible to fix the Earth, get everything right for once and piss off the old fool *and* the Venturis into the bargain.

Memories, an ocean of them, flooded his mind, as they tended to do whenever he allowed it to wander. He could remember everything he'd ever seen or heard: the sudden blinding flare as a stray spark lit a giant gas cloud and it became the sun; the tentative flop-flop sound as the first upwardly mobile fish squirmed and wriggled out of the sea and up the beach; an enthusiastic caveman explaining to his sceptical wife that if you had four of them, you could nail them to a couple of planks and then you'd have a cart. He remembered umpiring wars, posing for Praxiteles, Raphael and Andy Warhol, choosing peoples, raising cities and smiting them down again because some fool had been eating shellfish, endless interminable sacrifices—roast goat *again*; just for once why couldn't someone slaughter him some nice fresh lettuce and a few spring onions? Out of the swirling mist, vague patterns loomed, the phases of human obsession, habit and apathy, the frenzy of belief and the long, slow decay of disillusionment. First it had been honour and shame, then right and wrong, and now the Venturis, with their wonderfully businesslike system that solved all the problems and left everybody miserable. To have seen it all was one thing. Scorn is easy, particularly when there's so much to be scornful about, and humans tended to cling to crucial institutions governing every aspect of their lives not because they were any good but because they perceived them as marginally less ghastly than the ones they'd tried before. Fine. The old fool and the young clown had put him out of business, chased him to the frozen end of the Earth and only left him alone because he was too much aggravation to catch: a fine excuse for washing his hands of the lot of them, and what satisfaction he'd had, watching the Venturis bulldozing everything they'd worked so hard and so ineffectually to achieve. Great fun, marvellous entertainment, but maybe he'd been missing the point all along.

Human politicians, when they're honest (and you can tell when that is by looking up at the sky and counting the passing pigs) will tell you that being in opposition is so much better than government. You can sneer and criticise and let everybody see how much more competent and clever you are, and you'll never be faced with the exquisite difficulties of getting something done or coping with the crisis du jour. For thousands of years he'd been the Earth's loyal opposition, and nothing had been his fault, and everybody loved him because of the tinsel and the presents and the cheerful red dressing gown and the faint illusion of distant sleigh bells. Was that the reason he'd got into this line of work in the first place? Come to think of it, no, it wasn't. And if there was a sudden revolution, and he found himself in charge, absolute power, lord of all he surveyed, would he be capable of making a better job of it? Of course not. Six weeks into the job and they'd all hate him to death, doubtless with good reason. A man ought to know his limitations. He'd had thousands of years to reflect on his, and there were ever so many of them.

But what if . . . ?

He laughed, and compass needles all over the world trembled and whizzed round like propeller blades. *What if?* It was a bloody stupid idea, but so what? Much better than all those good-ideas-at-the-time that had turned human history into a bizarre game of consequences, and it was so dumb, so profoundly silly that it might just stand a chance. And best of all, it could be boiled down into four little words, not ten commandments or five pillars, and no subsections, subordinate paragraphs or tendentiously phrased principles capable of differing interpretations. Just one rule, and not even a rule, because where you have rules, ten minutes later you have a buzzing cloud of lawyers, and every good intention is just another paving slab in the yellow brick road to the everlasting bonfire. Just one guideline, and make the buggers *think for themselves*.

And of course you'd need someone to announce the rule, to say the four little words—not something he wanted to do himself. He could do it, sure. Three thousand years ago he'd have relished the challenge. But now ... He yawned. Even the thought of expending that much energy made him feel tired, right down to the bone. No, he'd need someone else to front it, be the face on the poster, and if it worked and went well, to take charge and run things and make the sun rise and the plants grow and the atoms collide and the electrons orbit the protons and neutrons: all the endless admin. And who could he possibly think of who might— A thought struck him and he grinned. Yes, he thought. *Yes*. The perfect candidate. And wouldn't that be a laugh and a half?

And then he thought, well, yes, it might work, but can I really be bothered? And he waited for an answer to that one, but none came.

27

"**S**o this is Hell," Jersey said, looking round. "You know, it's not quite what I . . ." They found a table, and almost immediately a waitress came and took their order. "Just a coffee," Jersey said cautiously. "No milk or sugar. And no little cinnamon biscuit, either."

That made Bernie smile. "The other side of that door over there," he said, "you'd have made a wise choice. This side you can eat as much as you like and still leave. And they do fantastic cookies."

So they ordered some Sicilian biscotti and snickerdoodles. "I like these," Lucy said. "What are they called?"

"*Ossi dei morti,*" Bernie said. "It's Italian for—"

"Yes, quite. Those ones look nice too. Why don't I try one of them."

"This isn't Hell," Jersey said a bit later with his mouth full. "So where is it?"

Bernie made a vague gesture. "Well, it's not Topside. Sorry, that's our name for where you guys live. But it's not Flipside either." He lowered his voice slightly. "The thing is, when the old management signed the deal with the Venturis and we got kind of parcelled off as a separate entity, they marked out our designated turf on a plan with a thick red felt-tip pen. This space here is the thickness of the pen nib; neither one place nor the other. Which is handy," he added. "No-man's-land. More precisely, no-deity's-land. Doesn't actually belong to anyone, see. The guys with the franchise on this place don't pay rent; they just turned up here one day with a stove and two dozen plastic chairs, and now look at it. Reminds me a bit of those flowers that grow in cracks in the pavement."

Lucy was looking at the menu. "Actually, I fancy something a bit more substantial. What's the Thai green curry like?"

"Slightly too much chilli. Anyhow, it suits us, because there are . . . well, certain things we're not strictly speaking allowed to do under the terms of the charter, but we do them here and nobody can hassle us. Also, if you look over there, at that table in the corner . . . where those two big Asian guys are sitting?"

Jersey stole a glance over Bernie's shoulder. "Got you. What about it?"

"That's the new registered office of the Bank of the Dead. The man in the blue's Jackie Dao."

"Why's he playing the harp?"

"That's an abacus," Bernie explained. "He runs the whole of the bank's operations from that table. Amazing. The biggest financial institution this side of the Lesser Magellanic Cloud, and he does it all with a primitive adding machine and a piece of paper."

"I think I'll have the lemon sole," Lucy said.

Jersey's eyes were very wide. "So this place—"

"Doesn't legally exist," Bernie said "which means you're safe here, for as long as you can bear it and your money holds out. Though you could always talk to Jackie Dao about an overdraft. He's very approachable."

"The Venturis can't get at us here?"

Bernie grinned. "I'm not sure they've figured that out yet," he said, "but no, they can't."

Jersey frowned. "Best to make sure, though. Excuse me. Nothing personal."

He prodded the middle of Bernie's forehead sharply with his forefinger. A window appeared in thin air, flickered and faded out. "Ouch," Bernie said. "You could've taken my word for it."

"Sorry. But look, this is great. What's it called, by the way? Or hasn't it got a name?"

Bernie pointed at the name on the menu: THE HOLE IN THE WALL CAFE & GRILL.

Jersey nodded, then reached in his pocket, took out a pen and wrote above this, *The Free People's Republic of.* "There," he said. "Here, miss." He beckoned to the waitress. "I want to speak to the manager about holding free and fair elections."

She looked at him. "I'm the manager. Get lost."

Bernie frowned. "You know, they're fairly easy-going here, but if you're planning on founding a nation state, they'll probably throw you out. Just drink your coffee and behave yourself."

The manager walked away, and Jersey shrugged. "Probably just as well," he said. "I think it was Winston Churchill who said that democracy is the worst possible form of government, except for all the other ones. Let's just keep things informal."

A small movement in his peripheral vision caught Bernie's attention, and he realised it was Jenny, yawning. He'd actually forgotten about her, which was appalling. "Listen," he said. "I'd love to stay and chat, but you're now perfectly safe, and we were just on our way to the movies, so—"

Lucy looked up. "What are you going to see?"

"The new Star Wars. So, if you'll excuse us, we'll be making tracks."

"Ooh," Lucy said. "Can I come?"

Bernie glared at her, but Jenny smiled and said, "Yes, if you like. It'd be nice to have someone to talk to."

"Thanks. What did you think of the last one? If you ask me, the franchise has definitely lost its way since *Twilight of the Force.*"

"Well, it was much darker, but—"

"Hang on," Jersey interrupted. "We've just had a miraculous escape from the enemy goons; we've located a potential bridgehead from which to launch our counter-offensive and you're going to the pictures?"

Lucy shook her head. "*You* escaped," she said. "Which was only necessary because *you* beat up the guards, because *you* wanted to go looking for Father Christmas. I, on the other hand, have missed several meals and been chased across Leicester Square in unsuitable shoes. Also, I want to see the film. I like the talking robots. And," she added, before he could say anything, "I am not your side-kick. Got that?"

"Now you're just being unreasonable."

"I am *not* being unreasonable."

"Yes, you are."

"No, I'm *not*. Why is it every time I do something I want to do, it's being unreasonable? Whereas dodging Venturi death squads to hunt for Santa is clearly the quintessence of logic, I can see that."

"Would you mind keeping your voices down," Bernie muttered. "And if you could possibly see your way to not saying that name—"

"You agreed," Jersey said angrily. "When do we start, you said, so obviously you agreed that finding . . . um, the fat man is the only way—"

"I agreed because you'd obviously got your heart set on it, and equally obviously you wouldn't last five minutes without me along to keep you from getting in the most appalling trouble, which you've now done, thereby proving my point, and if you're going to persist in this ludicrous nonsense then I suppose I'll have to come too, since I appear to have taken responsibility for you, like a stray kitten in a hailstorm, my own stupid fault for being tender-hearted. But after I've been to the movies. And had something to eat. And changed my shoes. Got it?"

"See what I mean?" Jersey demanded in Bernie's general direction. "Completely unreasonable. Serves me right, I suppose, I should've known better than to expect an amateur—"

"Excuse me," Jenny said.

"No, you're wrong there," Lucy said bitterly, "because amateur means someone who does something for fun, and being around you and your idiotic theories is no fun at all, so you can forget all about that for a start. And just because I saved your life when you got yourself stuck inside a pyramid, a *pyramid* of all things, I ask you, that doesn't mean I'm going to throw up a perfectly good job and go scooting about the place getting shot at and arrested simply because you think the mince-pies-and-tinsel man is some kind of primeval thunder god."

"But he is."

This was Jenny. Everyone turned and looked at her, and she went all pink. "Sorry," she said. "I thought everybody knew."

Jersey crowed with delight, which made Lucy fold her arms and pull her oh-for-pity's-sake face. "Which changes nothing," she said. "All right, so he's a thunder god, so bloody what?" She paused and grinned. "You have no idea what a relief it is being able to swear again," she said. "I feel like I've been holding my breath underwater for the last six months."

"Are you two looking for, um, a man with reindeer?" Bernie asked.

"*He* is," Lucy said. "*I'm* going to see the new Star Wars. Anyone coming with me?" She stood up. Apparently not. She scowled at them all (but they weren't paying attention), sat down again and finished her caramel latte. Then she read the menu.

"I think," Jersey said, "that the fat jolly man is the only power left on Earth who could possibly stand up to the Venturis. Because they're scared of him, that's obvious, or why do I suddenly have a regiment of stormtroopers down the back of my neck? So it stands to reason—"

"Yes, but he's retired," Jenny said. "Well, he is; it's common knowledge. He just lurks somewhere up near the North Pole and makes toys for Squishy kiddies. It's no good trying to get him involved in anything, he's not interested."

"Can I just clarify?" Bernie put in. "You two were being chased by the Venturis because you want to find the fat man and get him to do something?"

"Which he won't," Lucy said with her head still in the menu. "Not interested. You heard her."

"Actually," Bernie said, and although he said it very gently and quietly he had their undivided attention. "Jenny, you remember those things that showed up on our computers? The virus stuff?"

"You mean the nasty scary threats. Yes, of course I do."

Jersey looked at her. Bernie smiled weakly. "She means," he said and hummed a few bars by way of illustration.

"That showed up on your computers? In Hell?"

Jenny nodded. "Like a kind of virus thing. Bernie says it's nothing to worry about, but I'm not so sure. I mean, if he really is watching everything we do—"

"I've changed my mind," Lucy said. "I think I'll go for the spinach and ricotta parcels with chickpea salad."

"What exactly did it say on your screens?"

So they told him, and he told them about the inscription in the secret chamber under the catacombs, and after that nobody spoke for a very long time.

"That's got to mean something," Bernie said at last, "but I have absolutely no idea what."

"Doesn't matter," Jersey said eagerly. "That's not how it works. You follow the clues, you get beaten up and dumped in scorpion pits and scrabble your way out and eventually you get there, and *then* you find out what it all means. If you knew before you started, what would be the point?"

"It only makes sense when you realise that all the horrible stuff is his idea of fun," Lucy said to nobody in particular. "Trust me. I know, I've been putting up with him for months now."

"It sounds," Bernie said, "like he's letting us know he's coming back. But when? And to do what? I mean, in the past he's never shown the slightest interest in, well, politics and stuff. Not his bag."

"Sack," Lucy grunted. They ignored her.

"Which is why," Bernie went on, "the old management gave up trying to catch him. More trouble than it was worth. Also, he was shrewd enough to think of the giving-every-kid-on-Earth-a-present thing, which meant he was so popular he was effectively untouchable. Well, think about it. What would your reaction have been if you found out that God had arrested Santa and locked him up in a dungeon twenty miles under the Himalayas? The smoke from burning cathedrals would've blotted out the sun."

"All right," Jersey said. "But that was the old regime. Everything's changed."

Bernie shook his head. "The fat man may be a bit eccentric but he's not crazy. I don't think you people realise who you're dealing with here. The old lot were ... well, if gods are shops, they were a street-corner convenience store, and the Venturis are Walmart. It was as much as he could do to keep out of the way under the old management. Do you really think he'd want to pick a fight with the largest theocratic corporation in the known Universe?" Bernie paused, then added, "And come to that, do you?"

"Hell, yes." No hesitation in Jersey's voice.

Lucy just shrugged and pulled a sad face.

"Look, you said it yourself," Jersey went on, his voice getting steadily louder and higher. "The Venturis are only interested in making a profit, right? So, if this planet turns out to cost more to keep subdued than it produces in revenue, what're they going to do? Pull out of course, just like Tesco had to do in the USA. Hit 'em in the back pocket, where it really hurts, and we can win this."

There was a long, awkward silence. Then Bernie stood up.

"Well," he said, "it's been nice meeting you, and I hope you manage to stay alive and free for as long as possible, but if you've set your heart on going to war with the Venturi corporation—"

"But we can win. I just told you."

"Mphm." He glanced at his watch. "Well, we've missed the film in London, but if we get a move on we can catch it in Geneva, Nairobi or Kuala Lumpur. I vote Geneva. There's a really great pizza place on the other side of the square and they accept U.S. dollars."

Both girls got up. Jersey glared at Lucy and said, "You're going, then."

She nodded. "The movies, followed by pizza. It's called real life, Jersey. You might care to give it a try some day."

"Fine." He'd gone as white as a sheet. "I don't need you. I managed perfectly well before you came along."

"Oh sure. You were trapped in a pyramid."

"Yes, but I got out again."

"Only because I rescued you."

Jersey made a wide, vague gesture that knocked over an empty cup. "Sure," he said. "I sweet-talked some dumb girl into helping me. Done it before, I expect I can do it again. There always seems to be one around when I need one."

"Goodbye, Jersey."

"Enjoy your movie."

He looked away, and when he turned back realised he was alone, not quite in Hell, with a collection of empty cups and a half-eaten snickerdoodle. He reached for it, and a shadow fell over him. He looked up and found himself gazing into the cold grey eyes of the manager.

"That'll be a hundred and sixty-four dollars and twenty-nine cents."

He blinked. "For four coffees and some snacks?"

"The prices are clearly marked on the menu."

"I don't have any U.S. dollars."

She nodded towards the far end. "Go see the bank guy. He does currency exchanges."

He considered refusing to comply, but something in her expression made him think that wouldn't be a good idea. "I'll be right back."

"I'll be here."

That he could believe. He stood up and walked over to the table where the man in the blue robe was sitting. It was bare except for a teapot and a small, exquisite porcelain cup. "Excuse me."

The elderly Chinese gentleman looked up and smiled at him. "Greetings," he said. "Would you care for some tea?"

"I'm more of a coffee person myself."

"Your loss. Sit down. How much?"

Jersey sat down. "Excuse me?"

"How much would you like to borrow?"

The Chinese gentleman had eyes that went straight through you, like a teredo beetle through a yacht's hull. "The waitress said you might be able to change my pounds into dollars."

"I can do that."

Jersey took out his wallet and sadly produced four twenty-pound notes. Sadly because now the only thing left in his wallet was the lining. The Chinese gentleman took them and laid them in a rectangle, the edges perfectly aligned and not quite touching. "I like doing this," he said. "It's fun." Then he closed his eyes and for a moment Jersey thought he was having some kind of a fit. The notes changed: they shrank a little and turned green, and there were six of them and they had a president on them rather than a monarch, and there was also a small column of shiny coins, stacked in ascending order. The Chinese gentleman opened his eyes, looked at the money and smiled. "Ain't that something," he said. "Well?"

Jersey blinked. "Thank you."

"No problem."

"How did you—?"

The Chinese gentleman put a finger to his lips. "Financial wizardry. Of course, I could tell you, but then . . ."

Bank of the Dead. Fine. "It's all right," Jersey said. "Please don't bother."

The Chinese gentleman held out his hand. "Dao Wei-qiang," he said. "For some reason people call me Jack. I wish they wouldn't."

"Oh, right. Jersey Thorpe."

"I wouldn't be the least surprised." Mr. Dao let go of

202 • TOM HOLT

his hand, then looked at him as though for the first time. "*The* Jersey Thorpe?"

"Excuse me?"

"Of course." Mr. Dao leaned back a little and closed one eye. "How stupid of me not to have recognised you at once," he said. "Mind you, your statue hardly does you justice."

"Uh?"

"The statue." Mr. Dao frowned. "Well, the statue of you in Tiananmen Square. I guess it's only a copy."

"Copy?"

"Of the original in Helsinki." Mr. Dao looked puzzled. Then he smiled. "Excuse me," he said, rolled up the sleeve of his gown and glanced at a handsome Rolex Oyster watch with no perceptible hands. "My bad," he said. "How careless of me, it's not that time yet. Please, forget I spoke."

"There's going to be a statue of me?"

Mr. Dao sighed. "There I go again," he said, "triggering temporal causality loops." From his other sleeve he pulled out a handkerchief. There was a knot in it. "To remind me," he said, "not to cause temporal causality loops. But it doesn't work, because I keep forgetting I've tied it. Or else I think I've decided to tie it but not got round to it yet. Are you sure you wouldn't like some tea?"

There was a second bowl on the table. It hadn't been there before. "Why not?" Jersey said. "Thank you."

"Now then." Mr. Dao beamed at him. "It's essential that you forget everything I just told you."

"About the statue?"

"About the statue. The one in Beijing and the original in Helsinki. Not to mention all the others."

"What others?"

Mr. Dao clicked his tongue. "Oops," he said. "Forget

about them too. The copies in every city and large town on Earth."

"Um."

"And especially the one in Thorpe City. I mean Washington. It's essential that you forget all about them because otherwise your foreknowledge of them might influence your future actions, which might in turn lead to you not actually doing the things that lead to you being famous enough to merit statues in every city on Earth. So blot them out of your mind. This instant."

"Um."

"I would strongly advise you to do so," Mr. Dao continued. "I would never forgive myself if my foolish mistake led to a pollution of the timelines." He smiled. "At least I wasn't idiotic enough to let slip what you become famous for."

"No, you didn't mention that."

"Indeed. Though I can tell you're smart enough to have formed a pretty shrewd idea without having to be told in so many words. I mean, a forty-foot-high solid-gold statue with the inscription SAVIOUR OF THE SPECIES. It's not the sort of accolade you get for inventing a better brand of soap powder."

"Saviour of—"

"Me and my big mouth." Mr. Dao shook his head. "I really should be more careful. Well, you'd better go and pay your tab or Arlene will have you thrown out. Take my advice, though."

"Hm?"

Mr. Dao leaned forward and lowered his voice. "Just hand the money over. Whatever you do, don't look at the back of the ten-dollar bill." He picked up his abacus and flicked a few beads along the strings. "And now, if you'll excuse me . . ."

Jersey stood up and walked slowly away. The ten-dollar

bill was certainly different. Instead of Alexander Hamilton (who he'd never liked much anyway) there was a picture of someone who might just conceivably be Jersey Thorpe, and instead of the U.S. Treasury building, there was a wide-angle view of Times Square dominated by a huge statue which might just possibly have been meant to be the same person as the portrait on the other side.

Oink, he thought.

Then the note was pulled from his hand, along with the five twenties and the small change, and the menacing glare of the manager made him take a step back. "Thank you," she growled.

"Excuse me," he said. "That ten-dollar bill. Is it, you know . . . ?"

"What?"

"Real money?"

She looked at it, held it up to the light, stroked the edge with a practised forefinger and licked one corner. "Lucky for you, yes, it is. Why?"

"Oh, no reason."

He started to move away, but a vice-like grip caught his arm and he stopped. "You ain't done it yet, golden boy, so don't get cocky. You hear me?"

He nodded stiffly. "Yes, thank you."

"That's all right, then." The grip relaxed very slightly, and blood stated to flow again. "Have a nice day."

She was even stronger than she looked. Without any perceptible effort, she propelled him backwards until he felt the distinctive shape of a doorknob pressing into the small of his back. "Just a moment," he said. "You can't throw me out."

She grinned. "Throw, no. Shove. Let's give it a try."

There had been no knob on the door he'd come in by. "Excuse me," he said. "This is the wrong door."

"Argumentative little thing, aren't you?"

"Yes, but—"

She shoved him hard. "Go to Hell," she said. And he went.

28

Back in the old days the TV reception in Kevin's house had been terrible, and they couldn't have cable because there wasn't enough silicon on the planet to make one that long. Accordingly, if Kevin wanted to watch something, he had to stream it on his laptop, which was an archaic Kawaguchiya XP970 with a cracked screen and only one functional speaker. Movies in a cinema, therefore, had come as a heart-stopping, though pleasant, revelation. Oh brave new world, and all that.

Above all, he adored the Star Wars films. He enjoyed the timeless archetypes, the strong dualistic morality, the world-building, the unique blend of mysticism and gritty realism and the talking robots, and above all the lightsaber duels, the last so much so that Uncle Gabe and Uncle Mike had tried to re-enact them for him using their flaming swords, but it wasn't quite the same, somehow.

So the chance of seeing the latest Star Wars in a cinema, on a wide screen with state-of-the-art sound and genuine organic popcorn was too good to miss. He selected his venue with care and opted for the newly opened megaplex in Geneva, which boasted the second-biggest screen in Europe and the cleanest seats anywhere. The last time he'd been to the terrestrial flicks, his seat had been sodden with semi-coagulated vanilla shake, and he'd found himself sitting behind two people who insisted on talking about foam-backed underlay all the way through *Spiderman 9*, which had ruined the film for him. Little chance of such distractions in Geneva.

He was queuing for popcorn and wondering what had become of the two hapless young people he'd been warned not to help any more when someone tapped him on the shoulder, and he found himself looking straight at one of them.

"Hello," Lucy said. "I thought it was you."

"Yes, it's me. You escaped then."

"Yup. Where did you suddenly vanish to?"

"What? Oh, right. I got scared and ran away. I'm not very brave."

To his surprise she smiled. "Very sensible," she said. "You know, reckless bravery is a bit overrated, in my opinion. In fact, most of the time it's hard to tell it apart from being really, really stupid. And pigheaded. And ignorant."

"Ah. Well, I'm glad you got away. Are they still after you?"

She shrugged. "Doesn't look like it."

"How did you—?"

She frowned. "You know, I'm not quite sure. We sort of bumped into some very nice people, and they took us to a sort of cafe place which apparently is some sort of no-man's-land between here and Hell. If you can believe that."

"Oh yes."

"Really? Gosh. Anyhow, we stayed there for a bit and then we decided to go to the movies. And here we are."

"Yes. Where's Jersey?"

He'd said the wrong thing. Her face froze. "Don't know."

"He's not with you?"

"Nope."

"He's not been captured or anything?"

"Not as far as I know."

"Ah."

He waited for her to expand on that, but she just stood there looking like the Tomb of the Unknown Popcorn-buyer, so he decided to change the subject. "You're a Star Wars fan, then."

"Oh yes." Considerably more animation in her voice than when discussing—declining to discuss—the possible doom of the young man he'd been sure she was in love with. "Though I thought the last one was a bit of a let-down."

"Well, it was certainly darker. These people you're with—"

She smiled. "They went on in. I sort of got the impression I was a bit surplus to requirements. I gather it's their first date. Very nice people, though. Very sensible."

As unobtrusively as possible, Kevin looked around. No sign of Venturi security, but then there wouldn't be; a window would just open in thin air and they'd come bounding out of it, all serried ranks and gleaming white plastic. The idea that the Venturi boys, having suffered a minor frustration, would just give up wasn't one he was comfortable with. He took a closer look at a couple of twelve-year-old boys eating ice cream on the other side of the foyer. One of them caught his eye and raised his spoon in a tiny salute. Hi, Uncle Gabe. Even so, he felt nervous.

"Do I take it," he said, "that you and Jersey have had some kind of falling-out?"

The frozen stare again. "Yes."

"Would you like to talk about it?"

"No."

"That's fine. What flavour of popcorn do you think I should get? I'm afraid I don't know much about it."

"Try the wasabi and sweet ginger, it's a riot."

"Noted." He looked away for a moment then added, "The people you came with. You sure they won't be missing you?"

"I hope not." She laughed. "I gatecrashed their first date. I'm amazed the Venturi haven't fined me a million pounds."

"If you get separated from them, how will you get home?"

She shrugged. "Not sure I want to go home," she said. "I might just put in for a transfer to the Geneva office and stay here permanently. I think a complete break and a new start might be just the thing for me right now. What do you think?"

Kevin gave her a serious look. "I think, if the Venturis sent stormtroopers to arrest you, they might be thinking they don't want you working for them any more anywhere. In which case . . ."

That shook her, he could tell. "Better still," she said. "I'll get a job doing something else. An even completer break, right?"

"That's a very courageous attitude."

"You mean, I'm being stupid."

Kevin pursed his lips. "My observations of human beings have led me to the conclusion that there's a higher form of sublime, almost transcendental courage that's very hard to tell apart from stupidity. I think you're being very brave."

"Thank you."

"Brave as two short planks."

"Indeed." She frowned. "I expect the film's about to start. Coming?"

He sighed. "Would you like me to?"

"You please yourself."

"I think it'll still be mobile phone adverts for another five minutes. I might just stay out here for a bit."

"Fine." She looked at him as though he was a Finnish verb in an English sentence. "Nice to have run into you again."

"Coincidence."

"Probably."

"I'm sure you'll find another job. You're very clever and efficient."

Her eyebrows went up like a close-run elevator race, but she nodded and turned away. Oh dear, Kevin thought, humans. The rebound effect? He'd been expected to go with her, keep her company for the rest of the evening, possibly with a view to replacing the unhappy Jersey, for whom, he felt sure, she still had feelings. I don't know, he thought. You give a species free will and self-determination and look want they do with it. Still . . .

"You could've been well in there, son."

It took Kevin a moment to identify the annoying old man with the missing front teeth and the salacious leer as uncle Gabe. "I beg your pardon?"

"Well, you're human now, aren't you?"

"So?"

"When in Rome, son."

Kevin frowned. "Not that human," he said firmly. "And besides, she's still in love with that hero person."

"You reckon?"

Kevin shrugged. "Give me some money," he said. "I'm going to buy some popcorn."

The old man pulled out a wad of banknotes as thick as *Anna Karenina*. "Try the wasabi and sweet ginger."

"I know. It's a riot, apparently."

"Water cannon and molotov cocktails?"

"Presumably. But in a good way, I imagine."

He sat with the two archangels, who didn't seem to care much for the film. Raffa slept noisily, and Gabe kept pointing out the plot holes and the bits where they'd got the science wrong, mostly with his mouth full of Kevin's popcorn. When the film was over, Kevin looked for Lucy in the crowd leaving the auditorium but couldn't see her. Maybe she'd got fed up and left early.

29

Lucy opened her eyes and screamed.

A word about the Venturi brothers. The species they'd belonged to, way back when they started out—no, that's misleading; they were always spirits of pure energy, immortal, indivisible, uncontainable, but like all of their kind they'd adopted the physical appearance of their worshippers (because it's only polite), and their earliest adherents had been the tough, wiry, no-nonsense *wplooplgrf* of the Martian sub-equatorial deserts. These are extinct now, apart from the half-dozen or so the Venturis took with them across the galaxy after they'd inadvertently obliterated all other forms of life from the surface of the planet. In due course, the Venturis carved out their new empire, predominantly among bipedal monocephalous smooth-skinned hairless humanoids, to whom they paid the compliment of refashioning themselves in their image. But the six invaluable Old Martians, who now headed up Venturicorp internal security, still looked pretty much the same as they had back in the old days in the Old Country. Rephrase that: very much the same. The word *pretty* has no place in the same sentence as Section Chief Fjopkhrdg Zrrn, even in a strictly adverbial capacity.

"Greetings," said the Section Chief. "Would you care for a glass of milk?"

Said is a gross oversimplification. The Section Chief had no vocal cords and communicated by rubbing his wing cases together, modulating the sound by varying the tension of the chitinous fabric. Consequently his English had a slight accent.

"In case you're wondering how you got here," he went on, "we teleported you out of the entertainment venue using a depolarised actyon beam. There should be no significant lasting effects, though you might care to redo your manicure at some point."

Instinctively, Lucy glanced down at her hands, which were clamped to the arms of a chair with centimetre-thick bands of clear plastic. The varnish, she noted, was peeling off her nails in fat spirals. Also, she appeared to have acquired a sixth finger on her left hand.

"Don't worry about that: it'll wear off," the Section Chief said. "Truth is, we never beamed one of your lot before. Closest thing in the database was a Snaktigern's lemur, so we used that as a pattern and sort of fiddled it a bit. But your original configuration will reassert itself in the next hour or so. The tail will probably just drop off of its own accord."

A window opened in thin air and a smiling young man in a Venturicorp baseball cap materialised in the usual way. He was holding a clear plastic tray on which rested a glass of milk. "Nutmeg sprinkles?" he asked.

Lucy ignored him. "Who are you? What have you done to me?"

The Section Chief contorted his lower mandible in a manner that somehow, in spite of the total lack of a shared frame of reference, still managed to indicate reassurance. "Now I've got to do the official bit, but don't worry; it's not nearly as bad as it sounds. Now, then. You have the right to remain silent, but anything you do say will be taken down in analog form and cynically twisted to mean what we want it to. You have a right to an attorney, but trust me, you're in enough trouble already without getting involved with one of those bloodsuckers. Now, please indicate that you understand what I've just told you by saying the word *guilty*."

"Huh?"

"Close enough." A semi-translucent membrane flicked to and fro across the lens of the Section Chief's lower middle eye, conveying sheepish regret. "You're in the Marshalsea," he said. "But don't worry; you're just being held here until you're tried and found guilty, which means you're allowed to have something to read." He scraped two claws together, and a Kindle appeared in mid-air, hovering six inches from the tip of Lucy's nose. "When you've finished a page just say *turn*. Ciao for now."

A window opened in nothing at all. The Section Chief scuttled through it and vanished. Lucy looked at the Kindle. *Clouds of Glory: The Authorised Biography of Ab and Snib Venturi.* Fantastic.

Taking care not to make any sound that the Kindle might mistake for a request, Lucy closed her eyes and tried to remember everything she'd picked up about the Marshalsea. She knew it was where you got sent if you didn't pay your sin bill. Time, she recalled, doesn't pass there; you don't get older because the Venturis reckon it's cruel and unusual for someone to rot in jail while their life drains away, and there's nothing to see or do, you don't need to eat, drink or use the lavatory, you're tied to a chair for your own personal safety and there you stay until your bill is paid. Because your metabolism is effectively frozen, you don't get tired and so you don't sleep. There are no days to cross off because there are no days. At the insistence of Venturicorp's insurers, your health and well-being are guaranteed, so you can't die. You can breathe or not, as you wish. You just sit there until enough money changes hands and you're at liberty to go, with your youth and health intact and a free bumper sticker, Marshalsea sweatshirt and souvenir pen. Or, if there's nobody to pay for you or they can't afford it, you just sit there.

Tried and found guilty. That didn't sound very Venturi. It suggested that what she'd done—hanging around with that imbecile Jersey, presumably—fell under a different jurisdiction than all the usual terrestrial sins, for which the penalty was an on-the-spot fine and no messing about with empty forms of justice. Treason? Blasphemy? Something that meant they couldn't just decide her fate and throw away the key without at least appearing to give her a chance to defend herself. Something in the contract, perhaps, from when the Venturis bought out the old management? Or some theological equivalent of international law? Not that it mattered terribly much. Tried and found guilty, the Thing had told her. And then?

This can't be happening to me. You meet someone who's mildly interesting and all-right-looking (for a short-arse); he starts blethering about going to find Father Christmas because he's really some ancient Mesopotamian thunder god, and you say you'll go too, to shut him up—well, other girls go to watch football or motor racing or pretend they like cycling or fishing, on the strict understanding that once matters are put on a more formal footing there'll be no more of that sort of nonsense, thank you very much— and then he starts getting in fights with the police and you decide that tagging along is maybe not such a good idea after all. And for that you spend the rest of eternity strapped to a chair in a sort of minimalist departure lounge? It can't actually work like that, can it?

Can it?

There are things you can do. You can close your eyes and try to remember the lyrics of half-forgotten songs, or take a mental tour through every house, school, college campus and office you've ever known. You can be the casting director for a film of your life and times, deciding who ought to play you and everybody you've ever met. You can analyse your past and attempt to isolate the precise moments when everything started to go wrong. You can think of the questions you'd ask if you got the chance to meet your top twenty fictional characters. You can compile lists of your fifty favourite cheeses. She did all that. It didn't seem to help very much, so she tried a different approach. She imagined that she'd somehow managed to get out of there, and then she'd found Jersey, and now she was telling him exactly what she thought of him. That must've worked because she'd only just got started when some fool popped out of a window in thin air and interrupted her.

Oh for pity's sake, she thought. "What?" she snapped.

It was a Thing. a different one but unmistakably the same species. "Aren't you the lucky one?" it said. "You're going to see the boss."

"What?"

"You've got an appointment. Amazing." The plastic bands fell off her wrists and ankles. "Come on, let's be having you. You've got forty-five seconds to vacate the cell and then we start charging you rent."

"See the . . . ?"

"Boss, yes. You're going to meet your supreme being, face to face. Oh for crying out loud. You people. You're supposed to be *pleased*."

30

It had been, they agreed, a definite falling-off from the last one, definitely darker and with fewer talking robots, but well worth seeing nonetheless. They agreed on these points many times on the way back to the hellmouth, mostly so that they wouldn't have to talk about other issues, such as where they went next. There came a moment, however, when they were standing at the hellgate turnstile, and either someone was going to say, "Would you like to come back to my place for a coffee?" or someone wasn't. There was a silence as profound as intergalactic space, and then Jenny said, "Do you think the Hole in the Wall's still open?"

Genius. "I guess so," Bernie replied. "Let's find out."

It was, and they sat there and talked for ever such a long time, and drank more caffeine than was good for them, and then they both realised they'd have to get a move on or they'd be late for the office. They arrived together, to find a familiar figure sitting on the wooden bench at the back of Reception.

Jersey lifted his head and looked blearily at them. "You two," he said.

"Sure," Bernie replied. "What are you doing here?"

Jersey gave him a pitiful look. "That crazy woman in the coffee-bar place pushed me in here," he said. "Apparently I can't leave because I need an exit visa, but I can't go any further than this because I'm not registered. I don't know. What kind of a place is this?"

"Um," Bernie said. "Look, don't worry about a thing, I'll get you a visa and then you can be on your way."

"You can do that?"

"Sure. I work here."

"But you're human."

Jenny muttered something about some filing she had to get on with and disappeared through the connecting door.

"Do you want to get out of here or not?"

"I guess so." Jersey frowned. "Actually, I'm not sure. If I go back up to the world, presumably the Venturis will have me arrested."

"Well, yes."

"And I can't stay in the coffee-shop place, because I don't think the manager likes me or she wouldn't have pushed me in here, so I'm not entirely sure where I'm meant to go." He scratched his head. "You know, this is all getting a bit much, frankly. I think I used to like it better when I was blowing up pyramids."

"Well, you can't stay here for ever," Bernie said briskly. "We're officially closed to new customers. So, unless your name's down on the books, which it can't be, because you didn't die before the handover, we can't take you." A thought struck him. "Not as a resident, anyhow."

"What do you mean?"

Bernie suppressed a sigh. He had no idea at what point he'd assumed responsibility for this idiot, or why he'd done so, but apparently he had, and there was no getting out of it now. "We employ civilian staff," he said. "Like me, for instance. If I can get you a job here, you can stay."

That bewildered look. "A job? Doing what?"

"I don't know. What can you do?"

"Um." Jersey gave him a blank look. "I don't know."

"Fine. What qualifications have you got?"

"A degree in Egyptology from Harvard. Postgraduate degrees in pre-Columbian languages, Assyrian archaeology, aeronautical engineering and the theory of explosions. Also diplomas in Sanskrit, Oceanic anthropology and quantum theology."

"Fine," Bernie said. "In that case, I've got just the job for you."

31

Rather less than an hour later, Jersey had a new job, complete with uniform, and was being trained in various essential new skills.

"You put the bun on the table," said his instructor. "You put the salad on the bun. You put the burger on the salad. You put the other half of the bun on the burger. There. Now let me see you do it."

"Like this?"

"Sorta. But the top half of the bun goes on the other way up."

"Oh I *see*. Like this?"

The instructor hit him between the shoulder blades so hard his teeth rattled. "You got it," he said cheerfully. "Finally you got it. You da man."

"Thank you."

"What's your name again?"

"Jersey."

"That's a really stupid name."

"Yes," Jersey said, "it is."

Which was fine, as far as it went. During the day he did his job, occasionally catching glimpses of the tourists (humans, mortals, from the real world) over the shoulders of the counter staff. At night, though ... He explained his predicament to the manager.

"You're on the run," she said, "from the Venturis."

"That's right, yes."

"Oh boy." She pointed at the floor. "Do *they* know?"

"Well, Bernie—he's the man who got me this job—"

"You're in with Bernie?"

"I guess so."

"Oh, in that case." She frowned, then smiled as inspiration struck. "There's a storage room at the back. It's where we dump the empty packaging."

"Yes. And?"

"But you didn't hear about it from me, OK?"

"Ah."

You can sleep quite well on squashed cardboard boxes if you're tired enough, and if you work back-to-back shifts, you're tired enough all right. And he found he didn't really mind very much. It had dawned on him that this time he'd probably gone too far. The Venturis weren't like the usual villains he'd been dodging for so many years. They wouldn't try and blow him up, dump him at the bottom of snake-filled pits, chain him to the wall of rooms slowly filling with water, all that jazz. Instead, they'd arrest him and put him in a cell in the Marshalsea and leave him there, and that was a different proposition entirely. Compared with that, working in a burger bar and sleeping in a storeroom wasn't so bad. In fact, he found himself wishing he'd given it a try, or maybe something even more exciting and fulfilling, before he'd got himself into trouble with the omnipotent, omniscient bunch who now ran his planet. If only. Ah well. The important thing was to count his blessings, of which there were one. But a good one nevertheless.

As for Santa Claus and freeing humanity from the

tyranny of the Venturi Corporation, he could vaguely remember the passion he'd felt, the urgent need to do something. But that all seemed like a very long time ago, and he was finding it increasingly hard to understand why anyone could possibly think it was worth the risk of annoying the Management and ending up in the Marshalsea, just to ... what? Bring an end to a sociological and economic miracle that had improved the lives of billions? How presumptuous could you get? True, people were a bit more miserable, a bit less inclined to joy. He saw it on the faces of customers in the burger bar, heard it in their voices—or rather didn't hear it because everybody spoke so quietly now. But from time to time they left behind copies of the *United World* newspaper, which was always packed cover to cover with encouraging statistics about soaring economic growth, increased disposable income, buoyant capital investment, plummeting crime figures. To begin with he hadn't believed them, because you don't always take what you read in the paper at face value, especially if there's only one paper and it's owned by the United World Government. So he asked his human fellow workers, who lived Topside and had families and lives there. Yes, they said gloomily, it's all perfectly true. Nobody bothers locking their doors any more and we've never had it so good. Then why, he asked, are you all so sad all the time? At which they just shrugged and got on with their work.

He wondered what had become of Lucy. Not that it was any of his business, since she'd made it pretty clear she wasn't interested, and why should she be? All he'd ever done for her was get her in bad with Venturi security, and why? Because he'd been so dead set on, well, the holly-and-reindeer thing. Stupid. He hoped, very much indeed, that she was OK and the stormtroopers weren't still after her, but facts had to be faced. She belonged to an earlier phase of his life, the swashbuckling-and-conspiracy-theories bit, which was now quite definitely over and had been replaced with the earning-a-living-and-keeping-his-nose-clean imperative. So be it.

*

Time passed in a place where time has no meaning. He became an expert at putting the bun on the table, putting the salad on the bun, putting the burger on the salad and putting the other half of the bun on the burger, so much so that he was given the extra responsibility of opening the outers of styrofoam boxes, work that required the skilful manipulation of a small knife. Money was gradually building up in his account at the Bank of the Dead. He was issued with a new baseball cap and narrowly missed out on being named Employee of the Month, but he didn't mind that because it meant that there was someone else even more dedicated, loyal and hard-working than he was, and that was great for the company, and whatever was great for the company was great for him too. And more time passed, and someone higher up decided he was ready. His dedication, loyalty and hard work were finally recognised and he was promoted to front of store, operating Till 5, coincidentally just when Jolene left to have a baby.

For someone who'd spent so long working exclusively with mince, polystyrene and salad, interacting with people on a regular basis came as something of a shock, but he coped remarkably well, as his high-ranking sponsors had no doubt anticipated. He smiled as he took each order, smiled again as he handed over each tray, and if nobody ever smiled back that wasn't necessarily a criticism to be taken personally. In fact, everything was shaping up pretty darn well and he was beginning to think his life might just possibly be getting back on course when . . .

"Have a nice day," he said to the customer.

But the customer didn't move. In fact, the customer was looking at him.

"Have a nice day," he repeated. He felt uncomfortable. He'd never had to say it twice.

"You Jersey Thorpe?"

You got all sorts in the burger bar. Most of them were human tourists, but sometimes you got staff who felt like a break from canteen food, so a customer with blood-red eyes, pointed ears, teeth like a wild boar and three-inch talons was no big deal. This one was short, squat, muscular, of indeterminate gender and wearing a Hell staff white cotton T-shirt, the one inscribed

I FOUGHT THE LORD
AND
THE LORD WON

"That's right," Jersey said. "Can I help you?"

"When does your shift finish?"

"In about half an hour. Is there something I can get for you? Sauces? A coffee stirrer?"

The customer grinned. It was like looking into a very old cave: stalagmites and stalactites. "The jolly man says hello."

"Excuse me?"

"He wants to see you."

"I beg your—" But the customer had gone, vanished, if such a thing were possible, into thin air. On the counter, where he'd briefly leaned his massive forearms, lay a small sprig of holly with one red berry.

Fine, Jersey thought, as he worked the rest of his shift.

The jolly man wants to see me, but do I want to see him? Come to think of it, no, not really. I don't do that sort of stuff any more because it gets you in trouble and what does it actually achieve? You find the Ark; they stick it in some warehouse. You beat the bad guys so the good guys can win, and next thing you know the good guys have morphed into the bad guys (see *Politics, passim*) and don't you ever feel silly for having helped them gain power? You find out the secret arcane truths, but you can't tell anyone because the truth is so wacky nobody sane would believe it. Do I really want to get involved? No, I don't think I do. Different, of course, when there was doubt; then all I wanted was to *know*. But there's no doubt any more, and if you want to see angels, all you have to do is drop chewing gum on the pavement and get out your credit card. Maybe that was why everybody was so miserable. When you know the truth, there can, by definition, be no hope. Not that hope is everybody's friend. Significant, Jersey had always thought, that hope had been in Pandora's box along with all the other plagues and evils of mankind, and the only thing distinguishing it from the rest was its slowness in climbing out. Hope makes you stumble an extra ten yards in the desert before collapsing; it binds the addict to his needle. It's the unkindest lie of all. But people seem to need it in order to be happy, and what's happiness, after all, but a certain penchant for self-deception?

He finished his shift, folded his whites neatly and put them in the laundry basket, and drifted down the corridor to the coffee room. He had it to himself, which was unusual at this time of day. He put a coin in the machine, which ate it and declared itself out of order. Hooray for Life.

He sat down. His back was aching and his hamstrings weren't anything special either. He stared at the opposite wall, which he'd come to know quite well. There was something different about it today. For some reason, and very quickly and efficiently, causing no mess and leaving no trace, the management had seen fit to install a fireplace.

Oh no, you don't, he thought and jumped to his feet. Too late. Out of the grate jumped half a dozen goblins, five with spears, one with a very big sack. They had ears like coat hooks and they moved very, very fast.

Over the years Jersey had coped with all manner of enemies: guards, heavies, goons, henchmen and any number of fanatical devotees of diabolical secret sects, and none of them had caused him any real difficulty. Later, thinking back on the encounter, he decided that what made this one different was that all his opponents were four feet tall or less. Their skulls must've been an inch thick, and it's really hard to fight effectively when you're stooped double. He didn't reproach himself for losing— there was no point—he respected competent opposition. Let's hear it for the little people.

He didn't go quietly. But he went.

32

Not many packaging and wrapping products manufacturers can afford, or have a use for, a nuclear-powered submarine. But the Acme Novelty Paper Company of Pascagoula, Miss. has one. It picked her up for a very sensible price shortly after the break-up of the old Soviet Union, renamed her the *Season's Greetings,* reflagged her in Panama and had her refitted in a specialist shipyard in South Korea. There they decommissioned the active weapons systems but retained the torpedo tubes (with some modifications) since they'd be useful for storing and handling long cylindrical objects. Since then she's been in use more or less constantly, shuttling backwards and forwards between the company's manufacturing plant and its one and only customer.

Captain Simonov, who trained on *Grusha*-class subs as a young midshipman before the Wall came tumbling down, was a lucky find for the Acme people. Twenty-five years later, he knew the course like the back of his hand: Pascagoula to Anchorage, then Nome, across the Chukchi Sea to Wrangel Island, then deep under the ice cap until he reached a spot directly below the North Pole. Then came the tricky bit, manoeuvering the submarine so that her torpedo tubes were pointing straight up into the artificially heated well shaft of warm water leading to the surface that forces beyond his comprehension had cut and kept clear for this one purpose. After he'd done that, it was just a matter of pressing the button, realigning the ship, collecting the empties and heading home for the next consignment.

Once fired, the cylindrical self-propelled amphibious freight containers (best not to call them torpedoes, to avoid unnecessary legal complications) speed up through the well shaft until they hit a stop net, whereupon they're fished out, hauled up onto the ice, broken open and emptied of their contents before being weighted down with bricks and sent back to be collected for re-use. The contents meanwhile are loaded onto a sleek antigrav-powered monorail and sent hurtling across to a massive shed cut into the side of a giant glacier.

The contents come in three standard patterns: jolly robins, holly wreaths and snowmen, and a cartoonish and wildly inaccurate representation of the boss, driving an artist's misimagining of a reindeer-drawn sleigh. Each roll is enough to wrap seventy-five thousand standard presents (large) or one hundred and six thousand standard presents (medium) or half a million pairs of socks. Before they had the sub, the Acme people used to have to cart the stuff across the ice from Ellesmere Island on snowmobiles. It was a real drag, and there were sovereignty issues with the Norwegians.

Until the Boeing people built their factory in Everett, Washington, the wrapping shed was the biggest enclosed space on the planet. Fully automated yet 100 per cent carbon neutral (the main power source is a treadmill, worn glassy smooth by the scaly soles of elven feet), it can handle up to three quarters of a million presents per six-hour shift at peak productivity levels, and the automatic bow-knotter was designed by Leonardo da Vinci. The Sellotape dispenser is only slightly smaller than the London Eye, and turns on synthetic diamond bearings a foot thick.

None of this hardware is strictly necessary. If he wanted to, the boss could do it all himself in about three minutes. But it keeps the elves occupied. A significant problem throughout history has been the demoralisation that sets in when a standing army becomes a standing-about-with-nothing-to-do army. Making and wrapping presents gives the Green Horde a sense of purpose and achievement.

The other notable structure on the site is the Sports and Social Club, where the elves are free to occupy their off-shift hours with a wide range of leisure pursuits, including armed and unarmed combat, simulated airborne assaults on major cities, the Explosives Bee and the twice-weekly Elves for the Ethical Treatment of People spit-roast, darts match and real polo tournament. A thousand-odd years ago the Red Lord made some sort of treaty with the old management, as part of which he promised faithfully to disband his armed forces, but naturally he has no control over what his people choose to do in their free time.

The late shift had been amusing themselves and improving their minds with a game of pin-the-tail-on-the-human when the horn went off. Dutifully they filed out and made their way across the ice (clawed feet are essential at the Pole, or at least that's what the Red Lord told the decommissioning inspectors) to the well head to collect an unscheduled delivery. Usually the *Season's Greetings* called once a fortnight, regular as clockwork, and its last visit had been five days ago. Today, however, it was back again, having detoured on its way home to collect a special consignment from Denmark or Belgium or England or one of those places. No bother; if the late shift weren't doing this, they'd be doing something else, and it was all automated anyway. All they had to do was haul the stop net into position and wait for the torpedoes to hit it, then run the winch and position the crane. Yawnsville.

Today there was just the one torpedo, hardly worth going to all that trouble for, not that it was any trouble really. It hit the net rather harder than usual, but the restraining bolts held. The reason for the excess velocity was that it was considerably lighter than normal, leading those elves who could be bothered to speculate to wonder whether there was anything inside it, or whether some clown had inadvertently sent them a blank. But they hauled it out anyway, loaded it onto the monorail carriage and sent it on its way to Unloading, where it would be someone else's fault.

The unloading crew hefted their wrenches and crowbars and popped the side panel off the tube. There was no roll of wrapping paper inside, just a human-sized cocoon of cotton wool and inside that a very unhappy human. Fortunately they'd been warned what to expect (and besides, they'd already eaten) so they helped him out, stood him on his tottery feet and tenderly frogmarched him to the disused coal cellar that served as guest quarters on the rare occasions they had a visitor. Nobody had seen fit to tell them whether the ropes, handcuffs and gag were supposed to come off or stay on. The human didn't seem to like them very much. They left them on, just to be on the safe side.

Some time later the iron door creaked open. Three goblins bustled in and loosened the gag. "Shut it," they warned before Jersey had a chance to say anything. Then they backed away respectfully and a long shadow fell across Jersey's face. He blinked, and a voice that made the solid rock walls shake said, "Hello."

Large parts of Jersey's face were numb after forty-eight hours inside a torpedo, but he managed a shaky grin. "You again."

"Excuse me?"

"You won't remember," Jersey said, "because it was a long time ago and you must meet millions of kids in your line of work."

"Ah," said the Red Lord. "A peeper."

Jersey nodded. "On Christmas Eve I sneaked into the kitchen and ate half a jar of coffee granules so I'd be sure to stay awake. I had to know, you see."

The Red Lord nodded gravely. "Blessed are those who have seen and yet have believed."

"You could say that. Actually, by the time I was nine I'd more or less convinced myself that you were a hallucination brought on by a near-fatal dose of caffeine. But no, you look just the same as you did then. A bit fatter, maybe. But we're none of us as young as we were."

"I am," the Red Lord said. "Though young isn't a word I'd ever associate with me." He sat down on the pile of builder's rubble that served, somewhat inefficiently, as a bed. "You wanted to see me."

"Yup. But I changed my mind."

"That's a pity," the Red Lord said. "I had to go to a lot of trouble to get you here."

"I gathered."

The Red Lord dipped his head in acknowledgement. "It's all about jurisdictions, you see. Hell's all right—it's a self-governing autonomous nation state—and strictly speaking the submarine counts as Polar sovereign territory when it's on business for me, though of course the Venturis don't recognise me."

"Must be the beard."

"Recognise me diplomatically. Mind you, there's sod all

they can do about it. No, the only awkward bit was getting you from the hellmouth to the sub. Nice bit of piloting by the reindeer crew. Turns out Prancer can outrun a Venturi snatch-squad skimmer quite nicely, which is good to know. I'd been wondering about that, and I really didn't want to find out for the first time on Christmas Night."

"Glad it wasn't an entirely wasted exercise."

"Be quiet," the Red Lord said, and Jersey's eyes opened wide and his jaw dropped. He felt as though all the air had been squeezed out of him, as sometimes happens when you're caught up in a big crowd or a packed rush-hour bus or, in Jersey's case, when the bad guys have caught you and try to execute you by crushing you to death under a lorryload of watermelons. He managed to find just enough air to whisper, "Sorry," whereupon he found he could breathe just fine.

"That's perfectly all right," the Red Lord said. "I expect you're feeling a bit snarky with me for snatching you away just when you thought you'd made sense of your life and accepted the fact that you're really only a very ordinary, insignificant little man and not a superhero after all."

"Something like that," Jersey said, after the slightest of pauses.

"Understandable. However, now you're here I imagine you'll want to claim ethical asylum."

"Will I?"

The Red Lord shrugged. "I'd have thought so. After all, where else can you go? Anywhere the Venturis can get at you is out of the question. That leaves Hell, or here. Did you enjoy Hell?"

Jersey thought for a moment. "Enjoy isn't quite the word. But I survived. Was surviving, until some pointy-eared git—"

"Funny. I got the impression you were pretty miserable there."

"Yes, but no more so than I'd have been if I'd . . . Just a moment," Jersey said. "You were watching?"

The Red Lord smiled faintly. "Of course. I watch everybody, all the time. I find out who's naughty and nice, remember?"

"I thought that was just kids."

The Red Lord nodded sadly. "It used to be," he said, "but what do they call it? Mission creep. Everybody expects to get presents at Christmas, or the economy of the industrialised world would come crashing down in ruins. Used to expect," he amended, "and would have come crashing down. The Venturis have fixed all that, presumably, and probably no bad thing. It used to turn my stomach, seeing the first tinsel hit the stores in August. Anyway, yes, these days I watch every potential present recipient on the planet." He shrugged. "It's a bit of a bind. It's lengthened my average working day by at least seventeen minutes, but there you go. I live only to serve. You can do stuff like that when you're me."

Jersey nodded slowly. "Like God."

"Like *a* god," the Red Lord said deliberately. "I've always firmly believed in freedom of conscience and nonexclusivity. All that no-other-gods-but-me stuff, I don't hold with it. I took the previous lot to the Tribunal over it—restraint of trade—but guess who could afford the best lawyers. So I battle on anyhow, and screw 'em."

"But you were watching me," Jersey said, "specifically."

The Red Lord smiled. "There came a point where you started to become mildly interesting," he said. "It was round about when you figured out who I really am—sorry, was. I thought, an extra little something in that kid's stocking, for being smart. Consider this that extra little something."

"Consider what?"

The Red Lord sighed. "Being rescued," he said patiently. "Snatched from the jaws of Hell. It's not something I'd do for just anyone."

"What tribunal?"

The smile broadened. "Oh, you wouldn't be interested. Once upon a time you'd have been interested, but not now. You're through with all that stuff, remember? The truth, and the truth behind the truth, and the foam-backed rubber underlay beneath the truth behind the truth. Once you'd have given anything to know, but now you'd rather flip burgers. A bit like the human race, really. A wise man once said that people tend to get the government they deserve, and I guess it's the same with religions. Your generation got absolute certainty, and serve them bloody well right."

"What tribunal?"

The Red Lord sighed and snapped his fingers. The pile of rubble metamorphosed into a huge red velvet cushion, and he snuggled his rear into it luxuriously. "There's a tribunal," he said, "where people like the Venturis, and me, go to have their disputes settled when they fall out among themselves. It's not a court of law exactly—it can't force anyone to do anything—it's more like . . ." He closed his eyes for a moment, hunting for the word. "Self-regulation, I think they call it. Like with banks and newspapers and other institutions which think they can do precisely what they want and sod everybody else. Self-regulation is where they do precisely what they want with the approval of their peers. It's a very slight difference, but in the circles I move in any difference is colossal."

"There's a tribunal?"

The Red Lord nodded gravely. "If you're a bona fide divine entity in good standing, and if you can afford the court fees and the lawyers' fees, and if you can find forty thousand other divine entities to countersign your application, you can take your case there and have it decided by a grand jury of independent gods from other jurisdictions, all of whom would rather eat their own thunderbolts with chilli sauce than offend the Venturis. After all, it stands to reason that the buck has to stop somewhere. Usually in a brown envelope in someone's back pocket, but at least there's an established procedure, which is a great comfort, don't you think?"

"That changes everything," Jersey said. "We can take the Venturis to court. We can appeal. We can get rid of them."

When the Red Lord sighs, it's like the bitter east wind howling across the icy wastes of Siberia, only wistful. "You poor sweet innocent child," he said. "First, I'm not exactly bona fide or in good standing. Second, I haven't got that sort of money. Third—"

"Have you got a bit of paper I could borrow?"

"What?"

"And you couldn't just free my hands for a moment. And could I borrow a pen?"

The piece of paper was a corner torn off page 6,778,023 of the List for 1964, but that was all right. On it, Jersey wrote

Dear Santa,
What I want for Christmas is for you to
sue the Venturis for me.
Love, Jersey (34)

"I don't know if it actually has to be mailed in a postbox to count," he said. "If so, could I please have an envelope and a stamp?"

The Red Lord gave him a look so sour you could've mixed it with tandoori paste and made chicken tikka masala. "You can't make me do this."

"Listen," Jersey said, and the strength of feeling in his voice surprised him greatly. "Every year when I was growing up, when the other kids all got computers and bikes and games consoles, I got socks. And vests and pants and books that were on the school reading list. You owe me."

The Red Lord had gone pale, either from shock or anger. "Not that much."

"When I was twelve I got three complete changes of underwear, a pair of sensible black shoes, a fountain pen and the works of Tolstoy. When I was thirteen—"

"All *right*." The Red Lord's face was white apart from tiny red dimples on his cheekbones. "Actually, I lied, a bit. I have got that sort of money and I'm on the Register, just about, and it wouldn't exactly be hard to find forty thousand others who love the Venturis almost as much as I do. And I suppose it'd be fun, just to see the look on their faces."

"Well, then. Let's go."

"Mphm." The Red Lord frowned. "Just one little thing. What exactly are we going to accuse the Venturis *of*? What did they do wrong?"

"Well, they— " Jersey stopped dead. "They're just not . . ."

"Quite. Trouble is, that probably isn't going to be enough. Give you a for instance. Quetzalcoatl, the Feathered Serpent of the Incas—nice enough in his way— made the maize grow on time, but he would insist on the still-beating hearts of prisoners captured in battle, and we sort of felt he was giving the industry as a whole a bad name. But would the Tribunal do anything about it?" He shook his head. "Not prepared to intervene in the internal affairs of a recognised jurisdiction. Pissing off mortals is no crime. It's only if they've done something to their fellow gods that the Tribunal slithers into action. And face it: I bet you anything you like the Venturis have done all sorts of bad stuff, but can *you* find out about it and offer conclusive proof? Uh-huh. I don't think so."

Jersey gave him a sort of crooked grin. "That's what they said when I wanted to find the lost Death Mask of Amenhotep, which turned out to be an alien artefact of indescribable power, only the batteries had gone flat. If it was easy, it wouldn't be worth doing."

The Red Lord shook his head sadly. "No, you're wrong there," he said. "If it was easy, it wouldn't be quite so damn difficult. But what the heck. Apart from Christmas shopping for four billion people, it's not like I've got anything to do." He smiled and stood up. "Relax, chill, have a rest, think things over. Excuse me, I have elves to overawe. I'll have you moved to the guest quarters. Correction, these are the guest quarters. Tell you what, I'll leave the door open. Just don't wander too far, or you might get eaten. Ciao."

Halfway up the corridor the Red Lord stopped and allowed the grin which had been building up for ever so long to break out and spread across his face like floodwater.

33

Summertime on Sinteraan, and the living was easy. Fish were jumping—hardly surprising, ever since a D'zigrethph's mullet discovered how to create a stable anti-verteron field, and would have gone on to break the faster-than-light barrier if some clown hadn't broken his concentration by hauling him out of the water on a bit of string—and the *xzx'vxxxi* grass was high. Under the spreading branches of an ancient tree Jay snoozed contentedly until a nearby beeping noise woke him up.

"Dad?"

"Just a minute, son."

His father was sitting on the riverbank, but he wasn't paying any attention to the rods and lines or the brightly coloured floats bobbing in the lazy current. He was bent over his LoganBerry, and he looked worried.

Jay yawned, stretched and got to his feet. "What's the matter?"

"Nothing."

"Dad."

His father sighed and handed him the tablet. "See for yourself."

Jay glanced down and pursed his lips. "Dad," he said. "You didn't."

Dad rested his chin on his hands. "It seemed like such a good idea at the time."

The news report concerned the sudden and unexpected collapse of the Andromedan Bank of Ultimate Truth, which had just gone down the tubes taking the capital reserves of three galaxies with it. "All our money?"

"Not all. Just some."

"But how could you have been so—?" Jay cut himself off short. "It's not your fault," he said. "You couldn't have known."

Somehow what he'd said had made it worse. "No," Dad said bitterly, "I couldn't, could I? Because I'm not omniscient any more. And why? Because I traded it away to the Venturi boys for a ridiculously large sum of money. Most of which is now—"

Jay looked startled. "Most?"

"All right, some. It's OK, we still have enough. But how could I have been so *stupid*?"

"Define enough."

Dad thought for a moment. "More than lots but a bit less than loads."

"Mphm." Jay moistened his lips with the tip of his tongue. "So I won't have to, you know, go out and get a job or anything?"

Dad patted him gently on the shoulder. "Relax, son," he said. "Truth is, it's my pride that's taken the real damage. Any fool could see the bank was hopelessly extended in contingent futures."

Jay took the tablet from him and read a bit more. "Only because someone went and discovered time travel."

"Should've anticipated that. I would have."

"It says here," Jay went on, "that the biggest single investor in Ultimate Truth was the Venturi Corporation."

"Does it? I missed that bit. Gimme."

Jay handed Dad the tablet and carried on reading over his shoulder. "Oh dear," he said. "Oh, what a dreadful shame."

"And *they* should've known. They had no excuse."

Jay grinned. "Goes to show, really. Omniscient is one thing, thick as a brick is another. Not that I take any pleasure in the downfall of a fellow entity."

"Nor me. Still."

"Quite."

There was a long silence, broken only by the soft plashing of liquid argon against the roots of the old tree and the faint distant warbling of hyperdimensional gryphons. Then Jay said, "If the Venturis have just lost a shedload of money—"

"In their core business area, don't forget."

"Indeed. So maybe, right now, cash flow could well be a bit of a problem."

"Right. So they might be considering selling off some of their more peripheral assets—"

"Especially ones they haven't owned very long."

"—for whatever they can get for them, in what will definitely be a buyer's market, given the dreadful state the universal economy's going to be in—"

"Oh, dreadful, dreadful."

"—because of Ultimate Truth going pear-shaped. In which case, they might just be open to—"

"Offers."

Father and son beamed at each other. Then Dad said, "Of course, we might have to borrow some money."

Jay's face fell. "Neither a borrower nor a lender be, Dad. You said it. Your own words."

Dad frowned. "You sure?"

"Course I'm sure."

"I thought that was Shakespeare. Could've been me, I suppose. I've said loads of things in my time."

"It's a big step, Dad. I mean, what if something went wrong? We'd have to mortgage the planet as security."

"We wouldn't be borrowing that much. It'll be fine, trust me."

That, from someone who'd just lost a fortune on a dodgy investment. "I don't know, Dad. Maybe this isn't such a good idea after all. We're happy enough as we are. Why risk it all now?"

"You're happy," Dad said. "I'm not."

There. It had been said and couldn't be unsaid. A question for all you theologians. Can God put a foot in his mouth so big he can't take it out again? "Fine," Jay said. "In that case, it's settled. We'll borrow the money and we'll get the planet back, and everything will be just like it was. Maybe—" He stopped, but too late. And he thought, so that's the reason.

Dad finished the sentence for him, though there was really no need. "If we get the planet back, Kevin will come home."

34

One man's meat, and so forth. Over the centuries thousands of men and women have yearned to come into the presence of the Almighty. They huddled in caves, perched on the tops of pillars, knelt on the cold stone floors of monastic cells, prayed, chanted, starved, grew haggard, unkempt and unwashed, all in the hope of a single fleeting glimpse of the Ineffable. Almost invariably without success. Jay once remarked, in a rare moment of flippancy, that they might have stood a better chance if they'd been cleaner, less smelly and a bit less wild-eyed and noisy; fanatical devotion is all very well, but you really wouldn't want to invite that sort of person into your home.

Lucy considered this paradox as they escorted her down endless plush corridors. Maybe the only ones who get the chance are those who really don't want it. But then, the Venturi weren't the sort of gods Earth was used to. Maybe on all the other planets in their empire this sort of thing was regarded as perfectly normal, and their idea of Heaven was a vast office building with fire doors and potted palms and millions and millions of miles of beige-coloured industrial-grade deep-pile carpet.

"Wait here," said the Thing, pointing to a chair. There didn't seem anything particularly special about this chair or its location. It was in one of those nondescript empty bits of space you tend to get in really huge office buildings, probably where the architect put his coffee mug down on the plans and the contractors took the brown lines literally. There were a couple of doors nearby. They looked just like all the others she'd seen on her long march. Her feet hurt from all the walking. She sat down.

The Thing went away, and she was alone. For a brief moment she considered making a run for it, but then she caught sight of the CCTV camera peering down at her from the corner of the ceiling, and figured she probably wouldn't get very far. And even if she did, a girl could easily starve to death before she stumbled across the way out, and she still clung to the belief that if only she could find someone sensible and explain . . .

One of the doors opened, and a short fat man peered out, caught sight of her and beckoned. She stood up; he nodded. Simple as that.

"Hi," the fat man said. "Come in. Please take a seat. Sorry to keep you waiting."

It was a small office, very plain: desk, two chairs, three phones, computer screen, filing cabinet. Just one picture on the walls, a photograph of a ghastly-looking red desert under a pale grey sky. She vaguely remembered something about the Venturis originally being from Mars. The fat man wore a plain but expensive-looking grey suit and a shirt with no tie. He looked like his shoes were a tiny bit too tight.

"I'm Ab Venturi," he said. "My brother Snib was going to have joined us, but he got held up on a call. Can I get you a cup of—" he glanced down at a yellow pad on his desk "—tea?"

"No, thank you."

There was a lot of paperwork on Mr. Venturi's desk, memos and reports and printouts of emails, and Lucy could read upside down. Under other circumstances there would've been much to interest her. As it was . . .

"All right then, to business. You know a man called Jersey Thorpe."

"Mphm."

"Are you fond of him?"

She gave him her best ice-dagger look, which seemed to have no effect at all. Actually, he had rather a jolly face. "You're omniscient," she said. "You tell me."

He nodded, which wasn't at all what she'd expected, and turned a page on his yellow pad. "Your pal beat up a platoon of security guys."

"They were going to arrest us. And it was all paid for. In advance."

"Oh, quite, quite. No beef with you on that score; just making sure I've got the facts straight. You and Mr. Thorpe are trying to get in touch with—"

"Father Christmas, yes. Well, he is. Or I assume he still is. I don't know. I haven't seen him in yonks."

"But you aren't?"

She sighed. "Mr. Venturi," she said, "do you have side-kicks on your planet?"

"Which one?"

"Any of them."

"Oh yes. It's an established trope in escapist adventure literature."

"Well," she said, "for a few fleeting moments I thought I was going to be Jersey Thorpe's sidekick. And yes, at the time it seemed like a good idea, because in our culture that's what girls do, and I thought I quite liked him, and I guess the stereotype just sort of opened up in front of me like a fissure in the earth and I stepped into it without looking. And then I thought—"

Mr. Venturi smiled at her. He had a nice smile. "Quite."

"—this just isn't me, I thought. Because, let's face it, what does it achieve? The hero gets all the fame and the glory and the satisfaction of having been right and winning, and what does the girl get?"

Mr. Venturi nodded. "The hero."

"Exactly."

"Hardly fair."

"That's what I think. And presumably, once the credits roll, they move in together and she gets to iron his shirts and darn his socks and clean the toilet while he's off doing lecture tours on How I Found the Lost Thingummy of Whatever. It all seems a lot of trouble to go to when you can achieve pretty much the same result by going to the movies and having dinner a few times. Assuming it's a result you genuinely wish to achieve, which I'm really not sure about."

"Mphm. Moving on," Mr. Venturi said, pushing his spectacles back up his nose, "your pal wants to overthrow the government and install a known criminal in its place."

"I guess you could say that, yes."

"That's not very nice."

She thought about that for a moment. "No, I guess not."

"Point one, we paid good money for this planet and it's now our property. Point two, in the short time we've been here, we've improved the lives of practically every sentient being who lives here. Point three, you've got to be really stupid or worried about getting re-elected to get rid of one regime without having something a whole lot better to put in its place."

She scratched the tip of her nose. "Not so sure about point one," she said, "but the other two are hard to argue with. Sorry, what are you getting at?"

"Do you want to overthrow us and hand the planet over to a Bronze Age thunder god with a chip on his shoulder?"

She didn't have to think too long about that one either. "Not really, no."

"So that's where you and Mr. Thorpe part company?"

"Actually it was in a coffee shop off Leicester Square. Yes, sorry. You're quite right. Mr. Thorpe and I don't see eye to eye on that issue."

Mr. Venturi smiled at her, and she felt ever such a lot better. You see, said her inner voice, I was right. All you had to do was meet the person in charge and explain, and everything's sorted out. "That's fine," he said. "Seems to me that you haven't done anything wrong. You were just tagging along with Mr. Thorpe because you thought you liked him, and as soon as he started getting all those weird, antisocial ideas you quickly came to your senses and left him. Is that about it?"

She nodded happily. "Exactly."

"That's all right then." He pressed the intercom on his phone. "Could someone come and take the prisoner back to her cell, please?"

It was one of those walking-into-a-plate-glass-door moments. "But you said—"

Mr. Venturi looked up, as though surprised to find she was still there. "Yes?"

"—I hadn't done anything wrong."

"You haven't. We've established that."

"So why aren't you letting me go?"

"You're a hostage," Mr. Venturi said, as though explaining to a very old person or a foreigner. "A bargaining counter. Give yourself up or the girl gets it. From what we've gathered about Mr. Thorpe, he'll be round here like a shot to rescue you, and then ..." He grinned. "Gotta love those tropes," he said. "So much easier than thinking."

"But that's not right."

Mr. Venturi sighed, and you could tell that deep down he was fundamentally not a bad person, just a good person who happened to do a lot of bad things. "No," he said, "it isn't. According to the outmoded and obsolete morality of Right and Wrong, it's a bummer, because you're completely innocent, and if your pal chickens out and won't play ball, we'll kill you. Probably we'll have to pay quite a hefty fine. To ourselves, naturally. But so what? There's over six billion people on this planet, and only one of you, and the other six billion have decent jobs and free healthcare. You really do need to keep things in proportion, you know."

The door opened, and three Things stood in the doorway. She stood up because being dragged down corridors by the hair is so undignified.

"Nice to have met you," Mr. Venturi said. He was reading a report. "Soon as your pal's safe in the Marshalsea, you'll be free to go. Have a nice day."

35

Mr. Dao, chairman and CEO of the Bank of the Dead, looked up from his abacus and scanned the room. The Hole in the Wall was a bit quieter than usual, just a solitary, forlorn figure slumped over a caramel latte in the far corner. He got up and took his tea bowl over.

"Hi, Bernie," he said.

Bernie Lachuk acknowledged him with a slight nod, which wasn't like him at all. "Hi, Mr. Dao."

"On your own today."

"Yup."

"Usually you come in here with that charming young lady."

"Yeah, well. She dumped me."

Mr. Dao, who'd seen that coming for a long time, expressed suitable pained surprise. "I'm sorry to hear that."

"She said all I care about is work, and I'm no fun."

Mr. Dao frowned. "She's right, of course."

"Yes, but—"

"And you've got to respect someone who tells the truth."

"Sure, but—"

"The truth is a beautiful thing, Bernie."

"Of course it, is, but—"

"Quite probably the most beautiful thing in the Universe."

"I'm not disputing that, Mr. Dao, but—"

"And without truth, can there really be true happiness?"

"Maybe not, but—"

"Would you really want to date a pathological liar?"

Bernie looked up at him. "Thanks, Mr. Dao. You've made me feel a whole lot better. And now I think I'll just sit here on my own for a bit and drink my coffee."

"Glad to have been of service."

Mr. Dao was right, Bernie reflected as the sprinkles ate into the foam of his untasted latte. There has to be absolute honesty in a relationship, and absolute trust. Without truth and honesty, what would I have? Well, a girlfriend for one thing. Still, there's more to life. Yes. Of course there is.

For a start, there's quarterly returns. He'd brought the file with him. (Not that he was boring or work-obsessed; it was just that it had been in his hand when he left the office and he must have forgotten to let go of it. A mistake anyone could have made.) He opened it and started to review the figures, and at some point a yellow highlighter pen must have found its way in between his fingers, and a calculator appeared on the table, probably by magic. Weird stuff like that seemed to happen to him all the time, and he had no idea why.

"Bernie. They said I might find you here."

He looked up, his mouth a perfect O. Mr. Lucifer never set foot in the Hole in the Wall.

"Sorry, I was just . . ." He pushed the file across the table for Mr. L. to see, but he didn't even glance at it.

"Just a quick word, if you've got a moment."

"Sure, Mr. L."

Mr. Lucifer smiled and clicked his fingers. Immediately,

the waitress was at his elbow. "Two caramel lattes, please. One with sprinkles."

"Thank you, Mr—"

"You know, Bernie, it's about time you started calling me Nick. I mean, we've been working together for . . . how long is it now? Really? And you know how much I rely on you. I don't think this place would last five minutes without you."

"Gee, Mr—"

"You single-handedly made up the budget shortfall; you've been running all the sideshows and money-spinners; you do all the admin; you keep the section heads from biting each others' ears off. Most of all, you keep them off my back, for which I am sincerely and profoundly grateful." He paused while the waitress put the coffees on the table, and dropped three saccharine tablets into the foam on top of his cup from a plastic dispenser, which he put back in his pocket. "You know," he went on, "when I was a young angel just starting out in this racket, I never for one moment thought I'd end up running this place."

"Is that right, Mr. L.?"

"Sure is. You know what Lucifer means, son? It's Latin for 'Bringer of Light.' I was a sun god originally. Did you know that? It's true."

"Wow."

"Straight up. I loved working with the sun and the stars. You get the most amazing view from up there."

"I'll bet you do. So how did you . . . ?"

Mr. L. shrugged. "They opened this place and needed someone to run it," he said. "I remember young Jay called me into his office. It's a big responsibility, he said to me; we need someone we can rely on absolutely. The thing about jobs, he said, is they're work that's got to be done, not ways for people to occupy their time doing what they like doing in a congenial environment. He said, we need you in Hell, Nick, so that's where we're sending you. Are you OK with that?" There was genuine sadness in Mr. L.'s small red eyes.

"What did you tell him?"

"I said, sure, boss, whatever you think is best." He sighed. "I didn't want to come down here, I didn't want to spend the rest of my career hip-deep in *bad* people; I'm an angel, for crying out loud, I hate evil. But someone had to take charge down here, and the boss was relying on me, so here I am. And you know what, Bernie? This place kind of grows on you. After you've been here a while, like I have, you start to *care*. I know that sounds crazy—"

Bernie shook his head. "I know just what you mean, Mr. L."

"I know you do, son. I think you're the only one who feels about this place the way I do. That's why, when eventually I call it a day and hang up my pitchfork, I want you to be the one to take my place."

For a moment Bernie forgot to breathe. Mr. L. had to slap him on the back to get him started again.

"Oh gee, Mr. L. I don't know what to say."

"No, I don't suppose you do."

"I never really thought of myself as, well, the Dev—" Bernie stopped short. "In charge," he amended. "Of all this. I'm not sure I'm up to the job."

"It wouldn't be for a while. Quite a while. By then . . ." Mr. L. smiled. "I'll take that as a yes, then."

"Gee, Mr. L."

"Good boy. Meanwhile, there's something else I wanted to talk to you about."

Bernie was *glowing*. In fact, it occurred to Mr. L. that they could turn off Furnace Three and heat the perjurers just by plugging him into the mains. "Sure, Mr. L. Anything."

"This friend of yours. Jersey something. He works in Catering."

"Oh, him. What about him?"

"It's awkward."

"I'm sorry. What's he done?"

"Vanished."

A cold hand closed around Bernie's heart. "Like, you mean . . . ?"

"Gone. And no record of him leaving the premises. One moment there he was on the CCTV, the next moment, there he wasn't." Mr. L. had a serious look on his face. "I was wondering. Do you think you could shed any light on that?"

Just a second or two ago Bernie had almost felt the cushions of the chair in the Big Office engulfing the base of his spine like a marshmallow sea; now he was about to lose it all, because of that hare-brained lunatic Thorpe. "I'm sorry, Mr. L. I'm so sorry. I should've told you everything, right from the off, but it all happened so fast, and once he was, like, my responsibility, I didn't know how to tell you. And I never thought he'd be a problem. You have my word of honour. I guess I felt sorry for him, and the Venturis—"

"He was looking for the—" A spasm twisted Mr. L.'s face. "For the Christmas person. Wasn't he?"

All Bernie could do was nod.

"He was trying to establish contact with a *dangerous subversive*, and you thought it'd be all right."

"I guess I didn't think at all, Mr. L."

It was the disappointment in Mr. L.'s eyes that hurt the most. Of course making sinners feel bad was his job, but Bernie had never realised until now just how good he was at it, when he really tried. "And now he's gone, almost certainly with the Christmas person's help. You do see what a difficult position this puts us in."

"Oh yes, Mr. L."

"Because he escaped from *here*," Mr. L. ground remorselessly on. "And I know and you know that you didn't really mean to help him—you were just being incredibly dumb—but that's not how it's going to look, is it?"

"No, Mr. L."

"It's going to look like this organisation, which is on pretty damn thin ice as it is, actively helped this *desperate fugitive* to escape Venturi security and join up with a *dangerous subversive* with a view to *overthrowing the planet's celestial authorities by force of arms*. Well, isn't it?"

"I guess so."

"Bernie." Mr: L. let out a sigh that carved a passage through his heart like a cheesewire. "Bernie, Bernie, Bernie. Ah well, it's done now. Question is, what are we going to do to put it right?"

It was as though he'd had his back to the wall, and the firing squad had raised their rifles, and the officer had given the order, and they'd pulled the triggers, and out of the muzzles of their guns had emerged little coloured flags saying JUST KIDDING. The choice of pronoun: we. Implying that, against all the odds and the demands of natural justice, he still had a future with the organisation.

"Gosh, Mr. L., I don't know. What do you think?"

Mr. L. frowned, his incredibly deep mind swimming through the undercurrents of probability and human nature. "How would it be," he said, "if you were to send this Thorpe person a message?"

"Mr. L.?"

"Saying you've had a chance to think it over and you've decided that he was right all along and you want to help and you've got valuable tactical information about a weakness in Venturi security which the Christmas person could exploit, but you need to see him face to face to tell him about it."

Bernie blinked twice. "You think that would work?"

"We can but try."

"Yes, but will he trust me?"

Mr. L. smiled sadly. "I'm sure he will. You're the most trust-inspiring person I know, Bernie. Which is why I trusted you."

"Oh, Mr. L.—"

"So. Agreed?"

"Sure, Mr. L. And thank you. Thank you for giving me another chance. I promise I won't let you down again."

"I know you won't. You're a good boy. And some day you'll make a great Father of Lies."

"You think so? Really?"

"Some day. Now then, how are we going to get this message to him?"

Bernie thought hard, trying to remember something, anything, that might help. "There was this girl with him."

"That angle's already being explored."

"Oh. Well, I can look up and see what shift he was on, ask around, find out if anyone saw anything."

"Good idea. You do that. If we could find out how he escaped with nobody seeing him, maybe we can figure out where he went. Maybe there's a trail we could follow, something like that."

"Absolutely, Mr. L. I'll get on to it straight away."

"I know you will, Bernie. I know you will."

He smiled, got up and walked away, and Bernie sat for a long time on his own, trying to come to terms with it all. The Big Office. Father of Lies. And to have come so close to losing it all, except that Mr. L. was wise, kind and incredibly understanding. Mr. L. had faith in him, when nobody else would give him a chance. In fact, if there was a nicer, better person in the whole of the Universe than Mr. L. . . .

The waitress was standing over him. He looked up. She gave him the tab for two coffees. He paid it with a broad, happy smile.

*

Picking up the trail was easier than he'd thought. Because of the incredibly delicate temperature control system, essential when you store so much inflammable material—the Fire Department had done an inspection once and been truly horrified. An accident waiting to happen, they'd said, one stray spark and—it was possible to track Jersey's last moments in great detail by his body heat signature, pinpointing the exact time he'd left and precisely where from. There was also another reading, highly anomalous. A very cold person had been with him when he vanished.

A very cold person from a very cold place. No need to speculate too deeply there. Rather more intriguing were the unusual energy signatures, with high-spectrum electromagnetic discharge residues, at the place where the two of them had left. Whatever they'd done had altered the molecular structure of a patch of brick wall roughly a metre square, right down to the subatomic level. There were also unaccountable traces of carbonised wood, creosote and tar.

"A fireplace," Mr. L. said. "The buggers conjured up a fireplace."

Bernie frowned. "They can do that?"

"Looks like it, doesn't it."

"Why would they do that?"

"Think. What goes with a fireplace?"

"Tiles? A fender? A Scandinavian wood-burning stove?"

"A chimney." Mr. L. looked away, deep in thought. "They got him out up a chimney. Bernie, contact Venturicorp, see if they've got any UFO sightings, anything like that."

They had. A routine skimmer patrol had detected and given chase to an unauthorised flying vehicle with no recorded flight plan, apparently powered by a number of large four-legged animals. It had been too fast for them, and vanished in the general direction of magnetic north.

"Reindeer," Bernie said weakly. "A sleigh. Oh what fun it is to ride, all that stuff."

Mr. L. breathed out through his nose. "Well," he said, "it's what we expected. Anyhow, it makes your job easier."

"It does?"

"Sure." Mr. L. opened a drawer, took out a sheet of paper, an envelope and a pen. "You know where he is. Write him a letter."

J. Thorpe Esq.,
c/o Santa Claus
The North Pole

"You really think that'll work?"

Mr. L. scratched his nose. "It'll get there, that's for sure," he said. "Now, either the Christmas person will pass it on unopened, in which case we've succeeded, or he'll open it and read it himself, in which case either he'll be fooled or he won't." He shrugged. "Don't forget to put a stamp on it."

"I won't, Mr. L."

"And remember, if this goes wrong, it was your idea; you never told me anything about it. You're completely on your own. Got that?"

"Of course, Mr. L. That goes without saying."

"Good boy. After all, this isn't about you or me. It's about the good name of the organisation. We wouldn't want anything to reflect badly on the organisation, would we?"

"Perish the thought, Mr. L."

Bernie left for the nearest postbox, and Mr. Lucifer opened a drawer of his desk, took out a bottle and poured himself a stiff drink. Strictly speaking, the kid had brought it on himself by breaking the rules. He looked at the glass, in whose side he could just make out a distorted reflection of himself. You believe that, glass? Of course you don't. You believe that I deliberately and callously manipulated that dumb but extremely well-meaning kid into betraying his friend and arguably his entire species just so I'm spared the unpleasantness of having to stand up to the Venturis. What was that, glass? A backbone? Sure, but it's a bit late now, and besides where would I put it? Probably ruin the line of all my suits. Anyway, I'm supposed to be bad, aren't I?

He took a sip. As he raised it, the glass looked at him with its round amber eye. It didn't say anything, but he knew it wasn't fooled.

36

"This can't be happening," the organiser groaned.

Ah, but it was. Five thousand people had turned up for the Ulan Bator Festival, seven days of great music and uninhibited fun amid the grandeur of the wind-scoured steppes. They'd come from five continents, bringing with them enthusiasm, boundless positive energy, goodwill to all Mankind and fleece-lined sleeping bags; no food, because the organisers had undertaken to see to all that. Which they had done. They'd paid a considerable sum of money to a contractor, who had promised to airlift in everything necessary to cater for the discerning multitude: sit-down dinners, finger food, burgers, vegetarian and vegan options. And all would have been well, if it hadn't been for a freak blizzard. As it was, the tents, stoves, gas bottles and food were sitting in the hold of an Antonov 124 buried under ten metres of snow on the runway at Darkhan. Precious little chance of the perishables going off, with all that free refrigeration, but none of it was going anywhere in a hurry, and meanwhile . . .

"We're going to get eaten," moaned the organiser's assistant. "Five thousand starving people, and the nearest food is three hundred miles away across the desert. They're going to rip us into shreds and eat us raw."

Fortunately, news of the commissariat snafu hadn't yet leaked out, and the festival-goers were relaxed and happy as "Goin' Straight" by the Lizard-Headed Women bounced off the flanks of the nearby mountains and reverberated across the empty steppe. In half an hour, though, when the Women finished their set and all the happy, hungry people came spilling out looking for eats, things could well take a turn for the worse.

"Stop whining," the organiser said. "We've still got the Jeep—"

"What's that got to do with—?"

"—and enough gas for four hundred miles."

"Good point."

There was just enough room in the Jeep for the organiser, the organiser's assistant, the marketing manager, the head of technical operations and the chief steward. The organiser turned the key in the ignition. Nothing. The battery was dead.

"And so," said the head of technical operations, "are we. In about five minutes."

"We could walk," the organiser's assistant suggested hopefully. "All right, we'll die of thirst and exposure, but that's got to be better than being eaten alive. Well, it has," he added defiantly as the others looked at him.

"Could we order in pizza?" the chief steward suggested. "There's got to be someone in town who delivers."

A roar of applause from the main auditorium told them that the Women had finished their act. "Ah well," the organiser said, "I just hope I choke them, that's all."

"Excuse me."

They looked round and saw a pale-faced young man

with a serious look on his face. He didn't appear to be armed, but they backed away instinctively.

"Excuse me," the young man repeated, "but would I be right in thinking that there's been some sort of hitch with the catering?"

"Of course not," the marketing manager snapped. "Everything's absolutely fine. There is no problem. Go *away*."

A window appeared in thin air and a man in a three-piece suit, baseball cap and thick woollen scarf stepped out of it. "That's one lie," he said, "and one outburst of anger, so if you'd just put your card in the machine and type in your PIN. Thank you so much. Will you be wanting a receipt?"

He vanished. There was a brief silence. Then the organiser said, "Well, there's a very slight problem with the food, but nothing that can't be sorted out, so if you'd like to go back and enjoy the show, we'll get on with sorting it *right now*. Um, thank you."

The young man frowned. "But your plane's snowed in a thousand miles south of here, and the nearest town's three hundred miles away, and even if you could get there and back before the riot starts, there isn't nearly enough food there for all these people, so—"

"Yes, thank you. We know. Everything's under control, so if you'd just go back to the—"

The young man smiled. "Maybe I can help."

You ought to get out more, Uncle Gabe had said. Go and have a good time, mix with people your own age, enjoy yourself. To which Kevin had replied that there weren't any people his own age apart from Dad and Jay and Uncle Ghost, and Uncle Gabe had looked at him, and he'd gone out and booked a ticket for Ulan Bator, mostly because it was a long way away from where he'd been at the time.

So far he'd quite enjoyed the music, which was different from what he'd been used to, and the scenery was quite nice and there were interesting people to talk to. Maybe not fun exactly, but better than having your teeth drilled.

Anyway, he'd been sitting on the grass listening to the music when a little voice had spoken in his head. It said, there's going to be an awful lot of trouble here in a minute or so, unless you do something about it. And then he'd seen a mental image of a snow-covered runway, with the tip of a tail fin poking up out of the deep, crisp and even, and he just *knew* that all the festival's food was on board that plane.

It never occurred to him to ask, why me? Instead, he got calmly to his feet and went to look for whoever was in charge.

"You?" The organiser was scowling at him. "What can you do?"

"Well." Kevin opened his flight bag. "I've got some food."

"Have you really."

"Yes." He investigated. "I've got two bread rolls and a tin of anchovies."

The organiser drew in a deep breath with a view to telling him what he could do with two bread rolls, a tin of anchovies and the flight bag, if there was room left for it, but he didn't get the chance. "I'll need a table," he said, "and lots and lots and lots of paper plates. If that's all right."

They stared at him for five seconds, which in context was long enough to grow champion stalagmites. Then the chief steward ran across to a nearby tent and came back with a folding trestle and a plastic outer of paper plates. "Will these do?"

"I expect so," Kevin said, and got to work.

There were complaints, needless to say. Most of them were along the lines of, a dollar twenty-five for a fish sandwich? You must be kidding. Also, haven't you got anything except bread and goddamn fish? To which the catering manager replied that fish sandwiches were a local speciality. People came from miles around to experience Mongolian *panini di peschi*, Gobi style, and it was that or nothing, unless they'd care to try the bread without the fish or the fish without the bread, which would be a dollar extra. A surprising number of people went for that one, which all helped butter up the takings, and best of all nobody got eaten. And on the seventh day Kevin laid down his breadknife and spatula, sat down on the flattened grass and listened for the little voice in his head, which said, *Told you.*

Is that it? he asked.

What did you expect, praise?

He didn't answer that. Instead, he went to say goodbye to the organiser, who acted unhappy and nervous until Kevin made it clear he didn't want paying, after which the organiser was very nice and promised to send him a ticket for next year's festival. It's the least I can do, the organiser said, and Kevin thought, well, yes, it is, absolutely the very least. Thank you, he said, and did his best to make it sound like he meant it.

From Ulan Bator he flew to Sydney (six people on the flight who'd been suffering from tiresome colds got off the plane completely catarrh-free), where the voice in his head prompted him to gatecrash a wedding where the beer had run out, thereby avoiding a bloodbath and landing the hotel management with a colossal bill for tap water. He left the wedding and found a cafe, where he ordered a coffee and a slice of walnut cake. The waiter who brought his order put them down, glared at him and said, "What do you think you're playing at?"

Kevin stared at him, then he said, "Hi, Uncle Raffa."

"Answer the question, young Kevin. What's got into you?"

Kevin shrugged. "I'm not sure," he said, "but I think it might be the Holy Spirit. Is that possible? Only, I keep hearing this little voice in my head."

A woman at the next table stared at him, then quickly looked away. "It can't be," Raffa said. "Your dad handed it over to the Venturis, along with the rest of the plant and equipment."

"Oh." Kevin frowned. "So what could it be?"

"Hypothesis one—" Raffa turned back into himself and sat down in the seat opposite "—you've gone off your rocker."

"Can I do that?"

"You're human, aren't you? Which means you're running software that the hardware was never built to handle. Wouldn't be the least bit surprised if you've burned out a valve or two."

The woman at the next table got up and walked quickly away. "Maybe," Kevin said. "What's hypothesis two?"

Raffa suddenly looked very old and tired. "That yes, you've got a snootful of Holy Spirit, but not from *us*."

"Ah."

"Quite. Because if it's not something left over from your old man's time, it means it's come from someone else. And I'm prepared to bet my pension it's not the Venturis."

Kevin could see his point. "Maybe it's from inside me. You know, runs in the family and all that."

Raffa looked at him. "No offence, Kevin, and you're a good kid, I've always said so, don't care who hears it. I used to say to your dad, boss, basically he's a good kid, you gotta make allowances. But the real hot stuff? I don't think so."

"Oh."

"On account of you were never in the family business. And even if you were, since when did you start doing miracles all over the place? It's not something that suddenly comes on, like acne or wisdom teeth. If you could do that kind of stuff, you'd have done it before. Trust me, it's not that."

"All right," Kevin said, slightly nettled. "So if it's not in the blood, where's it coming from?"

Raffa looked thoughtful. "I'm still going with hypothesis one."

"Fine. But for the sake of argument, if I'm not crazy and it is the Holy Spirit, where am I getting it from?"

"Beats me. Still, it could be worse."

"It could?"

"Sure. You could be diving in and out of phone boxes and wearing your shorts outside your trousers. Awkward these days, with everybody having mobile phones. There aren't the boxes about like there used to be."

Uncle Raffa and his pop culture references. He tried so hard. "Please don't take this the wrong way," Kevin said gently, "but I think you're wrong. I think this is what I've been waiting for all my life. I think this is Dad's will, sending me down here—"

"He didn't exactly send you. You slipped out the back way, leaving a note."

"Sending me down here *obliquely*," Kevin said, "so I could be his witness and lead his people away from the Venturi and back to the True Path. Free will, right?"

"Kevin—"

"The way I see it," Kevin went on, "there never used to be a genuine choice. There was Dad or nothing at all, just bleak nihilism and Richard Dawkins. No real options, you see. But now there is. You can believe in the Venturis and what they stand for, or you can believe in Dad and his way—right and wrong, compassion, forgiveness, being nice to each other, all that. It's a whole different ball game now, you see. There used to be this great big problem about existing, but everyone knows the Venturis exist, and if I go around doing miracles and it gets on social media, they'll know I exist too. Then it'll be a straight choice: them or me? Who's nicer? A straight choice between value systems. The marketplace or higher ethics. Screw your neighbour or love him. That's why I'm here, Uncle Raffa. I can feel it in my bones."

Uncle Raffa shook his head. "No, that's just wind. Comes from eating human food. Face it, son. You've done a couple of miracles, big deal. The fact is, you're allowed to stay here on sufferance. If you annoy the Venturis, sooner or later they'll have had enough, and then—"

"Like Jay annoyed the Romans, you mean."

"Kevin, this is *serious*. Forget about Jay. He had the ultimate safety net. He knew all along it was only temporary: they couldn't actually do anything to him, on the third day it'd all be fine, reset button, no harm done. But it's not like that now. If the Venturis kill you, you *die*."

Kevin gazed at him for a moment. "I can do that?"

"Yes."

"Gosh."

"Really die. As in not be here this time next week. Not be here *at all*."

"To die would be an awfully big adventure."

"It'd be *dumb*. Die, for this lot?" Raffa swept his arm in a semicircle. "Humans? Don't make me laugh. Son, they just ain't worth it. Bunch of uppity primates. What could they possibly ever do or say that'd be worth your life?"

"Uncle Raffa, I think you're kind of missing the point."

"And anyhow," Raffa went on, not even trying to keep

his voice down, "they won't kill you; they'll stick you in that Marshalsea place of theirs. Trust me, that'd be a whole lot worse. That'd be—"

"Hell?"

"Hell is fucking *Disneyland* compared with the Marshalsea. You think Jay would've risked winding up in there? Get real. He'd have run a mile."

"That's my brother you're talking about," Kevin said quietly.

"Yeah, and he's not stupid. Which you'd have to be, to take that sort of a risk." Uncle Raffa gave him a long, exasperated look. "I don't think you get the whole Jay thing," he said. "I don't think you understand what that was all about. Jay coming down to Earth . . ." He closed his eyes, trying to find the right analogy. "Jay coming down was Bob Hope singing to the troops. He drives to the front line in a Jeep. He does his bit. Twenty-four hours later he's safe in a plush hotel somewhere. Bob Hope never grabbed a rifle and cowered in a foxhole with the shells going over his head."

"Jay *died*."

"Yeah, but he got better real soon. Of course he didn't *die*. He's still alive, ain't he? And I've always reckoned not being alive is what death is all about. As you'll find out," he added viciously, "if you insist on pissing off the Venturis."

"You said they'd put me in the Marshalsea."

"Kevin." Uncle Raffa looked him in the eye. "Grow up. Just take it from me, the Chosen One you ain't. Don't even think about it. I'm real fond of you, you know that. If you try and do this, you'll only get it wrong. You're just not cut out for the family business. I'd hate for you to be remembered as the boy who put the mess in Messiah."

Kevin had known Uncle Raffa all his life—a bit of a

paradox, since Uncle had been created, and therefore wasn't around at the Beginning, but let that pass. He'd always respected him, been a tiny bit afraid of him; he'd always seemed so wise, so sensible, so very much everything that Kevin wasn't. Was it possible—in a broad, bigger-rock-than-he-can-lift sense—that Uncle Raffa could be *wrong*? Surely not, because Raffa and Gabe and Mike, and even Uncle Nick, were really just externalised manifestations of the will of Dad. And Dad couldn't be wrong, in the same way that water finds it hard to be dry. Except . . .

"Sorry," Kevin said. "Really I am. But this is something I've got to do. And if it means the Marshalsea . . ." He shrugged. "The humans have a saying: no great loss. It's not like anybody needs me for anything. Anything else," he amended. "No, listen," he added as Raffa started making angry gestures. "Think about it, will you? If not this, what am I *for*? Jay was for the redemption of Mankind—"

"A stunt," Raffa grunted. "A gesture. A public relations exercise."

"Maybe, but a very important one. And that's why Dad had a son, for the gesture. But he had two sons, and all my life I've wondered, *why*? And now I think I know. And that's a good feeling, Uncle Raffa, you've got no idea how good it is. Please don't spoil it for me, because I'm going to do this. Really."

Raffa was gazing at him with a strange expression, a blend of despair and admiration. "Kevin," he said, "you're an idiot."

"Yes, Uncle Raffa."

"No good will come of it."

"No, Uncle Raffa."

"You'll be sorry. There'll be tears before bedtime."

"Anything you say, Uncle Raffa."

"You'll be on your own. Gabe and me, we won't be helping you no more."

"Fair enough."

"Ah well. In that case ..." The old angel stood up, stretched out his arms and patted Kevin's cheeks. "Go for it, kid. Give it your best shot. We'll be rooting for you, Gabe and me."

"Thanks, Uncle."

"You know what? You remind me of your old man when he was your age."

"Gee, Uncle."

"Only you're stupid and he was smart. Apart from that, though, there's a definite resemblance. Take care, kid." Suddenly he grinned. "I was about to say, God be with you, but he's on Sinteraan, so you can forget that. You're on your own now."

"Yes, Uncle."

"You're still an idiot."

"Yes, Uncle."

"Be seeing ya." There was the tiniest ever flash of lightning, little more than a twinkle, and he was gone. Kevin stared blankly at the space where he'd been, then finished his coffee, got up and looked around for someone to pay. On my own, he thought. No Dad, no Jay, no blessed choir of uncles, alone in a world ruled by the Venturi brothers, whose regime he was about to challenge and maybe even overthrow. Oh boy.

"Dad," he said aloud, "if you're listening, take this bitter cup from me."

No reply. Instead, the waiter handed him the bill. The waiter had bunions. Kevin cured them, picked up his flight bag and headed back to the airport. He'd gone about twenty yards when a window opened in thin air and a fresh-faced young man in a baseball cap stepped out of it.

"Did you just cure that man's feet?"

Kevin nodded. "What about it?"

"Are you medically qualified?"

"No."

The young man nodded. "Practising medicine without a licence, one million U.S. dollars. Cash, cheque, or— Thank you, that'll do nicely." He stuck Kevin's card in his reader and handed him the number pad. "Have a really great day."

"Bless you, my child."

The young man peered at him. "You're weird," he said and vanished.

37

They're not allowed to talk about it to outsiders, on pain of penalties that would make the most hardened Freemason blanch with fear, but all members of the International Brotherhood of Postmen share a deadly secret. It happens like this. You apply for the job, you get it, they issue you with your uniform, give you a rudimentary form of training, warn you about the dogs, all that stuff. Then, when you're feeling pretty relaxed and happy with your choice of career, they spring it on you. There's this room, they tell you, in the sorting office, into which you *must not go*. If you do, they tell you, it won't just mean a disciplinary tribunal or even the sack. What do you mean? you ask. Then they look at you and say, What's the worst thing you could possibly imagine happening to you? And before you can answer, they say, This would be worse.

So you assume it's a wind-up, industrial humour, like the legendary left-handed screwdriver, and put it out of your mind. From time to time you pass the locked door that was pointed out to you, and you idly wonder what really goes on in there. Maybe you ask a few of the old-timers, but they look away and change the subject, and all that means is that they're in on the leg-pull, big deal.

Probably it's just a broom cupboard or where the supervisor puts his bike.

And then, assuming you stick it out that long, November slides into December and the first letters to Santa start to turn up in the daily collections. And you ask, What do we do with these? And they tell you, Just put them in this sack here or that pigeonhole there, don't worry about it. And you don't, until one day you happen to see someone, probably the supervisor or some grandee of equivalent rank, unlocking the forbidden door and sidling through it clutching a big fistful of envelopes. By this stage you're pretty sick of the joke because you're not a newbie any more. You were rather hoping you'd become One of Us, so you don't give them the satisfaction of asking again, you just pretend you haven't seen anything. But now the supervisor's going in and out of the secret room four or five times every shift, always hugging a fat wad of envelopes, and gradually it dawns on you that what he's putting in there is the Dear Santa letters, and when he comes out again he carefully locks the door after him, using four enormous keys. Also, the door is solid steel and easily an inch thick, and there comes a time, probably early morning, when you walk past the door and you're not sure, but you think you can hear this strange scrabbling noise on the other side, not quite chalk-on-blackboard but equally disturbing, as though something with claws was trying to get through.

Sooner or later someone will tell you about it, even though they're not supposed to on pain of death, disembowelment and loss of seniority. What it's all about, they hoarsely whisper, is this. We don't deliver Santa's mail. The elves come and collect it.

You smile. Sure, you say, and I suppose they come down the chimney. Yes, as a matter of fact they do. I bet, you say,

272 • TOM HOLT

and they park the sleigh on the roof too, don't they? And then they look at you with an expression in their eyes that you've got to be a postman to understand, and suddenly the joke isn't quite so funny any more. And either you believe or you don't, but either way wild horses wouldn't drag you into the forbidden room with the steel door and the four thirty-six-lever mortice locks. And sometimes, in your dreams, when you've eaten hot, spicy food just before going to bed, you find yourself standing in front of that door, and it slowly swings open, and you look past it, just a little peek, and your screaming wakes you up, and the rest of the household as well . . .

Which is just a roundabout way of saying that all those letters to Santa do get delivered, and one of them was noticed by a keen-eyed elf in Sorting and passed through expedited channels, and the Red Lord picked it up, frowned at it and sent for his house guest.

"Letter for you," he said.

Jersey's eyes weren't accustomed to the light any more, so it took him some time to read what was written on the envelope. "But that's crazy," he said. "Nobody knows I'm here."

"Just a wild shot in the dark," the Red Lord said, "and shoot me down in flames if you think I'm being silly, but how would it be if you opened it? And then we'd know."

After he'd read it, Jersey handed it over. "Who's this Bernie?" the Red Lord asked.

"I met him in Hell," Jersey said. "He works there. Actually, I think he more or less runs the place, like a sort of infernal Radar O'Reilly. He got me the job there."

"And you told him all about me."

"I may have mentioned you, yes."

"Thank you ever so much." The Red Lord narrowed his eyes. "Do you think he's on the level?"

Jersey shrugged. "He struck me as a nice enough person. Went out of his way to be helpful because he was sorry for me."

"I didn't ask if he was an idiot. Do you believe him?"

"On the other hand, he's very, what's the word, corporate. A no-I-in-team sort of guy. A true believer."

"That's not necessarily a bad thing. It all depends what you truly believe in."

"I think he believes in Hell. As a vibrant business concern and a nice place to work."

"Ah." The Red Lord flared his nostrils. "He's in the right place then."

"He thinks so."

"Information that would help get rid of the Venturi." The Red Lord picked a stray thread from the sleeve of his gown. "I don't know. It stands to reason Snib Venturi must've done some pretty unwholesome things over the years. On the other hand, who could possibly give him a hard time about it?"

"The Tribunal. You said."

"Them." The Red Lord scowled. "Mind you, it's not like we're looking to get him arrested and thrown in jail. All we need to do is embarrass him enough to pull out of a tiny corner of his empire."

Jersey grinned. "Now you're talking."

"You're only saying that because you saw my lips move. I don't know. It could work. If we caused a bit of a stir, knocked a cent or so off the share price ... That still doesn't explain how some clerk in Hell could've found out something Snib Venturi wouldn't want anyone to know. How would he have the opportunity? It's not like their paths would ever cross."

"We won't know if we don't try and find out."

The Red Lord sighed. "There's another way of looking

at this letter. We could regard it as a twenty-foot sign spelling out T-R-A-P in bright blue neon letters. But I don't suppose that would bother you."

Jersey thought for a moment. "Not really, no. Over the years I've been in more traps than an elderly pony. There was one time in the Vatican Library—"

"Yes, fine. I've watched your career with interest over the years, and it's perfectly true you've been caught in obvious snares and you've escaped with remarkable ease. But there's a reason for that."

"Really?"

The Red Lord nodded. "All your enemies have been idiots. Snake-filled pits, garbage crushers and cellars slowly filling with water when a single bullet to the back of the head would've got the job done in seconds. The Venturis aren't like that. I guess it's because they're in this business to make money, not show how diabolically evil they are. Almost certainly at some point they had a team of time-and-motion people in to research the most cost-efficient method of execution. Or, overwhelmingly more likely, they'll throw you in the Marshalsea and leave you there for ever and ever." He yawned. "Which would get you out of my hair, granted, and there's ever such a lot to be said for a quiet life, but I feel it's my duty to point out the risks."

Jersey sighed like a slow puncture. "You're right," he said. "I'm being stupid. OK then, we'll forget about charging in and thinking of something when the time comes. What do you suggest instead?"

"Me?" The Red Lord pulled a face. "Oh for crying out loud. What on Earth makes you think I'm interested enough to make suggestions? This is all your idea, remember."

"You brought me here."

"I did, didn't I?" The Red Lord sighed himself. "All right, here's what you do. Yes, Cinders, you shall go to the ball. But not alone and not empty-handed." He made a fist and tapped himself on the forehead. "This is what comes of getting involved in the petty concerns of mortals," he said. "Which I promised myself I wasn't going to do. You should see my fridge door. It's covered in yellow stickies, DON'T CONCERN YOURSELF IN THE PETTY CONCERNS OF MORTALS. But do I listen? Of course not. It's all this joviality and ho-ho-hoing. After a while it rots your brain."

38

What do you do when you're probably the smartest businessperson who ever lived, anywhere in the Universe, regardless of gender, species or dimensional orientation, and you've got a kid brother who's an idiot? Answer: you do your best for him, because you love him and you and he are so close you couldn't squeeze a Higgs boson between you, and it doesn't matter that he's dumb because you're smart enough for the both of you. Even so.

"It's OK," Snib Venturi said for the fifteenth time. "There's nothing to worry about. Relax. It's all under control."

But Ab was still brandishing the front page of *Intergalactic Deity* under his nose. "It says here we've been wiped out. All the money's gone. We're broke."

"No, it hasn't," Snib said, "and no, we aren't. Trust me."

"But all our money was in the bank. And the bank's gone bust. It says so in the paper."

Me, give me strength, Snib said to himself. "I know it does," he said. "I told them to say that. We own the usdamn paper. But that doesn't mean it's *true*."

Ab blinked twice. "Huh?"

"It's a lie," Snib said.

In the beginning the Universe was without form and void, completely and utterly blank, but not as blank as Ab's face. "Why would we lie about a thing like that?"

Snib sighed. "Listen," he said. "It's really very simple. A while back I transferred the bulk of our uncommitted capital to the Bank of Ultimate Truth. Remember? You should do. You had to countersign the cheque."

Ab nodded. "I remember that, sure."

"OK, so far so good. Now then. Last week I suddenly withdrew all our money from the bank. Which, incidentally, we own."

"Do we?"

"Yup. Only nobody knows that because I've been buying up the stock gradually through shell companies and dummy corporations."

"OK," Ab said, as though that was the most natural thing in the world. "So, why take all our money out?"

"To start a run on the bank."

"Why?"

"To make sure the bank failed. Which it just did."

"Oh."

"Crashed and burned. No survivors. Ninety trillion dollars Andromedan we'll never see again."

"That's awful."

Snib sighed. "No, it isn't," he said. "You see, I had to own the bank so I could make sure they wouldn't tell anyone we got all our money out safely just before it went down."

"Um."

"So," Snib ground on, "it looks to everybody else in the Universe that Venturicorp just took a real heavy beating."

"Well, we did."

"No, we *didn't*. We just lost ninety trillion. That's nothing."

"No, it isn't."

"*Comparatively* nothing. So, what do you think happened then?"

"We lost ninety trillion dollars."

"Apart from that."

"Um."

"What happened," Snib said patiently, "is that Venturicorp stock plummeted on all the major exchanges right across the Firmament. Stock that was trading at thirty-six dollars is now worth two."

"That's terrible."

"No it *isn't*. Because I've secretly bought it all back, at cents on the dollar. Which means we—that's you and me, bro—we now own seventy zillion bucks' worth of Venturicorp stock for which we paid peanuts. Plus all our capital, which used to be in the Ultimate Truth, is safely squirrelled away elsewhere, and all it's cost us is a measly ninety trillion. Net profit is six plus a string of zeroes from here to Alpha Centauri bucks, all for a few minutes' work. Now I call that smart, don't you?"

Ab scratched his head. "I guess," he said. "But what about the economies of three galaxies? It's going to be awfully hard on all the little people."

"Sure. And where were they when we laid the foundations of the Earth? Screw them."

"Suppose someone finds out? We'd be ever so unpopular."

Snib smiled indulgently. "Nobody's going to find out. But you know all this. You think I'd do something like this without telling you? I told you."

"No, you didn't."

"I sent you a memo."

"Um."

Snib closed his eyes for a moment. Undoubtedly Ab had read the memo and entirely failed to understand it, and he should have known that. But it was hard, terribly hard, to admit to himself that his own brother, who he loved so much, was quite such a thicket. "Don't worry about it," he said. "You know now. And you aren't going to worry any more. Are you?"

Ab didn't say anything. He looked miserable.

Snib hated it when he looked like that. "For pity's sake," he said, "what's the matter now?"

"It just seems a bit . . ."

"Business," Snib said. "Strictly business."

"I know. Only, there's one thing I don't get."

Just one thing? "What?"

"What do we need all this money *for*?"

The sort of question a child might ask—utterly dumb, but you can't quite figure out how to explain it. A theologian's question: suppose God accumulated a bankroll so big that even he couldn't spend it. "In case," Snib said.

"In case what, bro?"

"In case," Snib replied, more sharply than he'd intended. "In case something goes wrong."

"Such as?"

"I don't know, do I? If I knew, I'd make darned sure it never happened. But one thing's for sure. You and me, we ain't never going to be poor again, not like we were in the old days, when we didn't have two cents, and you were walking around with no soles to your shoes. We're through with all that. I won't let that happen to you again, I promise."

And then something wonderful happened. Ab smiled at him. "Thanks, bro," he said.

"That's OK."

"I know you'll look after me. You always have."

"I said it's OK. Don't go on about it."

"I know, because you promised Pa—"

"Don't go on about it," Snib repeated, and if he wiped the corner of his eye, it was almost certainly just a bit of stray grit. "And Pa was a good man, Ab, a really good man. He cared about us. It's just he was no businessman, that's all. A really great guy but no good with money." Like you, he didn't add. "Guess I take after Ma."

Ab grinned. "She was real smart, wasn't she?"

"The smartest."

"She'd have been proud of you."

"Of both of us, Ab. Don't you ever doubt that for a minute."

Worth it, he told himself when Ab had gone back to his office, to do whatever it was he did in there. Worth all the stress and the worry, just to see his brother smile like he used to in the old days, when Snib came back in the evening with one or two coins he'd managed to scrounge or steal somewhere, and they knew they'd be eating that night. He really was the most wonderful person in the Universe, though it was a shame he was so dumb.

Never mind. Snib took a deep breath and scrolled down the screen of his LoganBerry. Nothing that needed his personal attention, he was relieved to see, except possibly this ridiculous stuff about that crazy hold-out leftover god somewhere up near the planet's magnetic pole. Those clowns in Security, they couldn't catch a cold. Presumably at some point he was going to have to take charge of the matter personally. He opened the file. Pressure had been brought (he liked that phrase) on the CEO of the planet's redundant Afterlife, who was suspected of harbouring the malcontent Thorpe. Arrangements were in hand to apprehend Thorpe using his contacts among the Afterlife's staff. Fine, Snib thought. Once we've got him, I'll deal with him personally, and that'll be one less thing to fret about. Also, Thorpe's girl was in the Marshalsea. He grinned. Catnip.

He knew these hero types. It was all so unnecessary, such a waste of his time, but if there was one thing he'd learned long ago, it was the crucial importance of taking care of details personally.

A phone rang. "It's him again, on line two."

"By *him* you mean?"

"That guy. The one who used to own this place."

Snib sighed. "Not again. What is it this time?"

"Says he's got to talk to you, urgently."

"For crying out loud. OK. I'll take the call. Yes, hello."

A crackle. Cosmically speaking, Sinteraan was just down the road, but the line was awful. "Mr. Venturi?"

"Speaking."

"I was wondering if you'd had a chance to consider my offer."

Snib put his palm over the mouthpiece and riffled through his in-tray. Got it. "You want to buy back the Earth."

"That's right."

"I'm sorry, but it's not for sale. Great little place you had here, by the way. You did a really grand job on the lesser crustaceans."

"Sorry, it's a bad connection. What did you—?"

"Really ace krill. But no, I'm not interested in selling right now, thank you for your interest."

"Even though you just lost all your money?"

Careful. "Ah. You know about that, do you?"

"Well, it's all over the papers."

Snib smiled. "You should be careful about believing everything you read, Mr ..." He hesitated. He was ashamed to admit it, but he'd never quite managed to figure out how to pronounce the guy's name. Who has a name with no vowels in it, anyway? "Reports of our demise have been somewhat exaggerated."

"So you're not selling."

"Not for a price you could afford."

He hadn't meant to be rude, but the unpronounceable guy was annoying him. There was a pause.

"Hello? You still there?"

"Yup."

"You'd be surprised what I can afford, Mr. Venturi. Name your price."

Over the millennia some of the best minds in the Universe have put a lot of time and energy into trying to find a form of words guaranteed to get them the attention of the supreme being. Remarkable that none of them had ever hit on those three little syllables. True, he hadn't considered selling, but a blank cheque ... To gain time he said, "While you're on the line, I got a bone to pick with you."

"Say what?"

"I said—" Snib took a deep breath "—when we were doing the deal I don't think you were entirely straight with me."

A surge of righteous indignation crackled across hyperspace and down the wire into Snib's ear. "Are you calling me a liar?"

"Let's say you didn't give me all the relevant facts."

"About what?"

"You told me," Snib said calmly—the more the other guy shouts, the calmer you reply—"I'd be getting vacant possession. No other gods but you. Except for one very minor anomaly, I think was how you put it."

Another silence. He let it hang. Eventually, Mr. No-Vowels said, "Well, that's perfectly true."

"I think we may have to beg to differ there," Snib said smoothly. "The way I see it, this minor anomaly of yours has the makings of a real bad headache."

"Only if you provoke him."

"Ah. That's not what you said."

"I'd have thought you'd have had more sense than to ...
What's been happening, then?"

So Snib gave him a concise and mostly accurate account
of the Christmas man problem, while his fingertips danced
on the calculator on his desk. Name your price, huh?
Them's fighting words. "No offence," he concluded, "but
in my scriptures that's more than a minor anomaly. Seems
to me that at any one time up to ten per cent of the population of the planet believe in this guy. Roughly the same
proportion," he added spitefully, "as believed in you. On
a good day."

"Kids," the voice on the line spluttered. "Who cares
what kids think?"

"I made a deal in good faith. That's my way of doing
things. I'm a regular straight shooter. And that's all I'm
saying, OK?"

The longest pause yet. Then, "I'm not saying that what
you allege is true. But *if* it is, hypothetically speaking—"

"Of course."

"—then there's a simple way of dealing with the problem.
In fact, I'm surprised you haven't thought of it yourself."

Snib raised an eyebrow. "Is that right?"

"Sure. Raise an army and flatten the son-of-a-reindeer."

"OK," Snib said cautiously. "And the reason you didn't
do that when you were in charge is ..."

"It'd be massively unpopular, and I wanted to be liked.
No disrespect, but I don't see that as a problem in your
case. After all, nobody likes you much anyway."

This guy, Snib said to himself, is starting to get on
my nerves. "I'm a businessman," he said, "not an exter-
minator. Also, armies cost money. And I shouldn't have
to lay out on stuff like that because there shouldn't be a
problem, because the contract was for vacant possession,

not sharing the planet ninety–ten with a fat man in a red bathrobe."

A long sigh that made Snib's ear hurt. "Fine," he said. "You raise your army and send me the bill. Let no one say I ever welched on a covenant. And then we can talk about your price."

"Maybe," Snib said. "Meanwhile, just to clarify, I send in the troops to wipe out this jingle-bells guy, and you pay the tab. Is that agreed?"

"I just said so, didn't I?"

"I like to get these things right," Snib said.

"Fine. I'll want receipts, of course."

"You'll get them."

"And you'll need to find the little creep first. He's darned elusive."

"It so happens I have a lead on that," Snib said happily. "Two leads, or two parts of the same lead. Sorry, just thinking aloud."

"And watch out for those pesky elves. They can give you a nasty nip if you're not careful."

But then, Snib thought as he put down the phone, logic never was one of their greatest strengths. Anyone with an ounce of respect for logic wouldn't agree to pay a large sum of money to enhance the value, and therefore the selling price, of an asset he was negotiating to acquire. A logical being—Snib Venturi, for example—would have conceded that the reindeer man was a significant unsolved problem and would have reduced his offer accordingly. But then, what could you expect of a deity who installed his dominant species prototypes in an apple orchard and told them not to eat the apples?

Sell up? Make a fast buck and move on? It was an intriguing idea and something of a novelty. The Venturi Corporation didn't sell planets, it bought them, skyfuls at a time. Some wiseacre in one of the trade papers had speculated that the Venturis wouldn't be satisfied until they had the complete set, and he wasn't being nearly as funny as he thought he was. On the other hand ... Snib leaned across his desk, switched on his screen, accessed the planetary CCTV and set the cameras on wide-angle pan. It was all right, he decided, as planets go, but it was nothing special. It had mountains, but so did Draconis Prime and Gamma Orionis IV, and theirs were translucent and glowed pale green. It had forests, but they were shrubberies compared to the vast *o'oolk* groves of Snoovask, and the trees just stood about all day looking feckless—a bit like the dominant species, come to think of it. The Earth had seasons—four, which was a good number—and oceans, nice big ones, but they were blue, which clashed with the deserts and showed the dirt awfully. It had parakeets, which was one of the best things about it, but it also had spiders and earwigs and centipedes and woodlice. The music was mostly poor, and the architecture was boring, and the people ... Well, quite. Early on in the first month they'd been here, he'd had Finance cost out a full-scale flood to get rid of the lot of them, start again with a clean slate. But it was prohibitively expensive—you could buy two uninhabited M-class planets for what a decent flood would cost—and besides, he'd always considered major restructuring of that kind as an admission of failure. The same went for ice ages and nuclear wars. Always better to start with a greenfield site, and in an infinite Universe the one thing there's no shortage of is real estate. No, if the people are no good, you might as well cut your losses and move on. Or, better still, find a mug who'll buy it off you, cut your profits and move on. And there was also the Grand Design to think of. If Venturicorp was seen to sell off a planet it had only just recently acquired, the market would jump to the obvious conclusion, the share price would fall still further, the big galactic financial institutions would be looking to dump Venturicorp stock at any price, and he could really clean up. Logic suggested, therefore . . .

He stood up, crossed to the window and focused the eyepiece of the big telescope. No need to adjust its position; it was permanently aligned to point at one thing only—Mars, the next planet on the block, that unsatisfactory ball of rock and red dust that had once been home.

They could never go back there, not after the unfortunate incident. It was a fact he had to face. It was ruined beyond reclamation, beyond terraforming. Nobody could ever live there again. Which was why he'd done the next best thing, the only thing, and bought the house next door. It wasn't the same, of course. Everything was the wrong colour, the gravity was different, the days were forty minutes shorter, there was only one moon and it was ridiculously big and bright, so you had to sleep with the curtains drawn or wake up moontanned. But a man could sit on a bench in his garden after sunset and look up at the sky and see roughly the same stars as he'd seen as a boy, when gazing up at the stars was his favourite thing of all.

No, damn it; not for any price some mom-pop-and-holy-spirit outfit could afford. Ab had asked him what all the money was for. And he'd replied honestly, because he could never lie to Ab. But apart from that he'd never indulged himself the way the other big players did when they'd made their pile. No mountaintop palaces with rainbow driveways for the Venturi boys, no chariots of fire, no cherubim and seraphim with nothing to do all day but stand around looking pretty. They lived much as they'd always done—good plain food, a few suits of good-quality clothes (because quality is made to last;

you save money in the long run), a few bits and pieces of really first-rate art because there's no better investment. But no conspicuous consumption, status symbols, comets with personalised plates, monograms picked out in flaring supernovas. Practically every cent they'd ever earned was safely in the bank, put aside for a rainy day. So, if he wanted this stupid little planet just for the view, why not? He'd worked hard; he'd earned it, and no hayseed trinity or semi-literate bush-league thunder god was going to take it away from him.

But that was no reason why the sucker shouldn't pay to clean up the mess he should've cleaned up before he put the planet on the market. Most of Snib Venturi's success had come from sheer hard work and determination, but not all of it. From time to time there had been brief flashes of joyful serendipity, and this was clearly one of them. He picked up the phone and pressed 1 for Security.

"Rocky," he said cheerfully. "Go buy me an army."

39

Jenny had asked for a transfer. According to her application, she felt drawn to the challenge of filing the monthly fuel consumption reports, which she believed would assist in her emotional and spiritual growth as a member of the admin team. Even when she was a little girl, she'd written on the form, she dreamed that one day she'd have her very own filing system, while fuel consumption had been her driving passion for as long as she could remember.

Well, you have to put stuff like that on application forms, but he could read between the lines. She didn't want to work with Bernie Lachuk any more, and who could blame her? Certainly not the guys in DR. They'd given her the transfer, double-expedited and effective immediately. Meanwhile, if Bernie wanted anything typed, he had a choice between the Pool and his right index finger.

Fine, he thought, because the secret mission he'd been entrusted with was not without a certain element of risk, to the same degree that a containerload of pistachios may contain traces of nuts. If he didn't come back, there wouldn't be a tear-stained face behind the back-office desk or a waste bin full of wet tissues. Just as well, really.

There's enough unhappiness in life as it is without making it worse.

He'd dictated a short note, to be opened in the event of—well, the event—and sent it down to the Pool. It had come back in an envelope marked *To Whom It May Conserve*. They have predictive text software in Hell; they also have the people who designed it.

He dropped by the quartermaster's office. "What I need," he said, "is some small, utterly deadly weapon I can conceal about my person, preferably contained in or indistinguishable from a harmless everyday object."

The quartermaster nodded. "Don't we all?"

"Have you got anything like that?"

The quartermaster thought for a moment, went away and came back with a seven-foot pitchfork. "It's an every-day object," he pointed out. "Or at least it was a couple of hundred years ago. Still is in remote parts of eastern Europe."

Bernie pushed it gently aside. "All right, then," he said. "How about a revolutionary new concept in body armour, absolutely proof against all known conventional weapons but so light and thin you hardly know it's there? Some kind of bulletproof sunblock cream, maybe."

"Great idea."

"Have you got anything like that?"

"No."

"Right. In that case, I guess I'll have to settle for a subcutaneous homing beacon that lets you know exactly where I am and what's happening to me, so that elite forces can go in and pull me out at a moment's notice."

The quartermaster thought for a moment, then beamed suddenly. "Stay right there," he said. "I'll be back."

And some time later back he came, lugging a small crate behind him. In it were two pigeons.

"That's George," he said, "and the other one's George W." He waited, then added, "Worth two in the bush? Oh well. Anyway, look after them. A handful of millet first thing in the morning and last thing at night, and plenty of fresh clean water."

"No thanks," Bernie said firmly. "And I'm guessing a rocket-powered backpack or a collapsible autogyro that folds down and goes in your wallet is out of the question."

"Good guess."

Bernie sighed. "It's like this," he said. "I'm going on an incredibly dangerous mission into the very heart of enemy territory. It's practically a done deal that I'll be captured and viciously interrogated at some point. I'll have no back-up and anything remotely resembling a weapon will be taken from me the moment I arrive. Now, have you got anything at all that might possibly come in useful?"

The quartermaster gazed at him for about ten seconds, then reached under the counter and produced a small pack of chewing gum. Bernie gave him a polite smile and left.

The most direct route from the quartermaster's office to the hellmouths doesn't actually go through central archives, but Bernie wasn't in a hurry. Jenny was at her desk, collating fuel requisitions by date order. She looked happy, then she saw him. "Oh, it's you."

"Yes."

"What do you want?"

"Nothing. I was just passing. On my way out."

"Oh."

"On my way," he said, "to undertake an appallingly dangerous mission on behalf of the senior management. Of course, I'm not allowed to talk about it."

"Mphm."

"And even if I was," Bernie ground on, "I wouldn't,

because I'd hate you to be worried sick about me, in case anything, you know, happened to me."

"I can set your mind at rest on that score."

"Ah. That's all right, then."

"My pleasure."

"Well, I'm going now. I can't stay any longer. My top secret method of transport's probably waiting for me at an undisclosed location."

She didn't look up from her work, but she waggled a couple of fingers. He left her and drifted slowly down to the main gate, where the sentry was playing a game on his LoganBerry.

"I'm going outside now," Bernie said. "I may be gone for some time."

"Right you are."

A car (a small green Toyota with one brake-light cover missing) was waiting to take him to the landing strip, where he boarded the helicopter. It was piloted by a large friendly middle-aged woman who told him about her aunt's medical problems all the way over the Greenland Sea.

"Here we are," she sang out as the helicopter touched down on a featureless plateau of ice. "This is where you get out."

"Is it?"

"Of course it is, silly."

"What time will you be picking me up?"

She put on her reading glasses and consulted her schedule. "Nothing here about that, dear. You'll have to ring the office."

Bernie looked out of the window and shivered. "Right. Thanks."

"My pleasure. Wrap up warm."

The helicopter roared away into the clear grey sky,

leaving Bernie alone on the ice. He looked around. No sign of anyone or anything anywhere. That didn't signify, of course. Venturicorp's spectral warriors would, naturally, materialise out of a window in thin air the moment the target showed his face. There was absolutely nothing to worry about. This was, after all, a trap. So what could possibly go wrong? He wished he'd accepted the quartermaster's chewing gum. It'd be something to do to pass the time.

"Bernie?"

He spun round. Directly in front of him was a short young man in a red robe with white trimmings and a fake white beard poking out from under the hood. "That's me. Is that you under all that cotton wool?"

He got no further. All around him the ice erupted into flying splinters the size of roof tiles. He ducked, and someone grabbed him. He opened his eyes. He was lying on his back, surrounded by goblins.

"Sorry, Bernie," Jersey said. "It's a trap, you see."

"Yes, I know, but . . . Oh. You mean for me."

" 'Fraid so. All right, lads, hit it."

The ice floe on which they were standing groaned horribly and sank like a freight elevator. A moment later it came back up again, completely bare and empty apart from a single sprig of holly. A moment after that several hundred windows opened in thin air. Stormtroopers in white plastic spilled out onto the ice, glanced around, scanned the holly with their thermal imagers and stood about in small groups, looking rather foolish.

40

Snib Venturi closed the CCTV portal on his screen, counted to ten and broke a pencil.

His line, he knew, was, *Why am I surrounded by idiots?* A devotee of action movies across five galaxies, he'd seen this scene more often than he could remember. It was just that he'd never cast himself in the role of Baffled Villain before, and it was annoying him unbearably.

The telemetry from the stormtroopers' scanners was coming in. They showed nothing: no life signs, heat signatures, EM resonances, nothing to suggest that there was anything under the ice except more ice and, eventually, rock. The squad leader respectfully suggested packing the site with high-yield explosives and blasting a great big hole, to see if that would help. Failing which, could he please have permission to withdraw his men because bits of them were starting to fall off.

Twelve hundred kilos of ultra-high explosive, at AND$2,999.99 a kilo. Still, he wasn't paying for it, was he? "Go ahead," he said. "Cook it up real good."

Which they did, bless them, and, sure enough, when the rocks had stopped falling out of the sky and it was safe to get a camera down there, it revealed a vein of ice ten yards deep and a hole in the ground rapidly filling with seawater. Outstanding.

Never mind. He still had the young female, and the same clichéd narrative trope that had just made him break a perfectly good pencil in baffled rage would unquestionably bring the young idiot bustling down here as soon as he found out about it, and on Venturi turf without the reindeer guy to back him up it would be a very different scene, written, produced and directed by Snib Venturi, who would most definitely not interrogate the prisoner while sipping fine wines and stroking a white cat.

The section leader was still on the line. "We could blow up a few glaciers while we're here," he said hopefully. "I mean, they could be under a glacier, couldn't they? It's where I'd be."

"I bet," Snib said. "Sure, go ahead. Why not?"

The section leader looked as though he couldn't believe his luck. "Really?"

"Really. Do a proper job. Blast right down to the magma layer if you have to."

A slow smile crept across the section leader's face. "We'll have to use triple charges."

It occurred to Snib Venturi that in all likelihood they'd be using BlastSure from Venturi Chemical Industries. Sales had been sluggish recently. "Go ahead," he said. "If a job's worth doing, it's worth doing properly. And even if it's not."

"Sir?"

"What are you using down there? BlastSure?"

"BlastSure XD1000 Pro. It costs a bit more but—"

"Go for it, Section Leader. And that's an order."

A thought struck him as he put the receiver down, and he went to a filing cabinet and pulled out the planetary insurance policy. It was good cover (should be—it had cost enough); they were insured against everything that could possibly happen to the planet, excluding only deliberate sabotage and Act of God.

"Get me that idiot back right now."

The section leader was a bit hard to understand, mostly because he had a length of fuse between his teeth. "We're getting on with it, sir. You should have telemetry in—"

"On second thoughts," Snib said, "don't use the XD1000. Stick to the conventional stuff."

"Oh. OK, sir. We've got some BlastMaster PPP Limited Edition, if that'd be better."

"No, definitely not. Just dynamite. Got that?"

The section leader looked sad but resigned. "That's a copy, sir. Telemetry in five."

41

It's a little-known fact that you can get blisters walking on water. True, there has to be a perfect storm of contributing factors: shoes just a bit too tight, especially where the backs bear on the Achilles tendon; waves just the right degree of choppiness, due to just the right level of wind; most of all, distance travelled and pace travelled at. But it can be done.

Kevin trudged up the beach at Ibiza, flopped down on the sand and took his shoes and socks off. He'd started out some time earlier from Alicante. It would be unfair to say nobody had taken any notice of him. Some kids in pedalos had waved as he set off; people in speedboats had yelled at him to get out of the way; some sardine fishermen in a small boat had crossed themselves and looked the other way. A passing yachtsman had glared at him, then ostentatiously poured the contents of his glass into the sea. Because of the time the crossing had taken, he'd arrived on the island at five in the morning, and there was nobody about. Face it, he told himself, as he wrapped strips of torn-up handkerchief around the soles of his feet, it hadn't worked

Why hadn't it worked? When Jay did it, he'd been a

sensation. Crowds had followed him home, instantan-
eously converted. Curious, that. Kevin had never quite
managed to figure out why being able to get across a lake
without a boat had convinced people that Jay's proposed
moral and ethical system was superior to anyone else's.
After all, boats aren't that expensive, and most people in
a fishing community would know someone who had one
that they could borrow, if they didn't own one themselves,
and the logical leap from *this guy doesn't have to worry about
caulking and teredo beetles* to *this guy must be right about
the immortality of the soul* struck him as tenuous. Still, Jay
had wowed them with it back in A.D. 30. Maybe that was
it: simpler times, simpler people, and if you saw someone striding confidently across the waves, you wouldn't
automatically assume he'd just bought the latest thing in
ultra-compact jet skis.

He looked around, and over to his right saw a vast
building, terraced like a hillside, reminding him somewhat
of the ziggurats of ancient Babylon, which in these parts
could only be a hotel. In an hour or so they'd probably be
serving breakfast. He tried to get his shoes back on his feet,
but they no longer seemed to fit.

The more obvious explanation was that Jay had been a
hit with walking on water because Jay was Jay, the elder
son of God, the Chosen One, not the one who was always
having to be shown how to do things three times and still
got them wrong. Why was that? Theologically speaking,
they were all part of the same essential being, consub-
stantial and co-eternal, so anything Jay could do, Kevin
ought to be able to do just as well. He'd given that question a lot of thought over the millennia and never come
up with a convincing explanation. True, Jay was an inch
taller, and he could wiggle his ears and was double-jointed.
Somehow, that wasn't really enough to account for the

discrepancy. Oh yes, and Jay was smarter. At least, that was the conclusion that everyone seemed to draw; nobody had ever said so in so many words, of course, let alone offered any real proof. But Jay could work the computer and understood the filing system and knew how to do the climate and the space–time continuum and the causality web and all that stuff. Now, here was a thought. Did Jay know how to do all that because Dad had taken the time and trouble to show him, slowly and patiently, until he'd got it right? Not three times, not seven times, not seventy-times-seven times, but as long as it took, and without sighs and sharp intakes of breath and clicks of the tongue, until eventually Jay had got the hang of it?

I can do this, Kevin said to himself. And what's more, I can do it on my own. Which I'm going to have to do, because nobody's going to help me or show me how. And the first step is going to have to be, stop doing what Jay did, because I'm not him. If I'm really serious about this, I'm going to have to find my own miracles, and they've got to be right for me.

Um. Such as?

So he thought about the Venturi. He lay on his back and contemplated the sky. The little bit of it he could see from here was just a tiny part of what the Venturi boys owned, and they'd started with nothing. Correction, they'd started with a business plan, which they'd converted into an ethical system. They believed that people could do anything they liked, provided they had the money to pay for it. All that really meant was cutting your coat according to your cloth, not transgressing beyond your means, reducing your expectations to meet your ability to pay. The concomitant benefits, peace and prosperity, had risen out of that basic premise quite organically; if people know what they can and can't do, they tend not to overstep the mark, and of course the whole thing was posited on universal belief, which was possible because the Venturi took pains to prove that they existed. Dad and Jay had never done that. They'd wanted to be believed in, to be loved, for their own sake. Maybe that had been asking a little too much from puny creatures of a day.

Right. Lesson one: I won't let anyone be in any doubt about it. I exist.

He stood up and shouted at the top of his voice, "I exist! I'm real!"

His words echoed back from the forest-covered slopes. They sounded really silly. He sat down again.

"Sure," said a voice to his left. He looked round. "So you're real. So what?"

The voice was coming from a seagull. Kevin looked hard at it. Not Uncle Gabe or Uncle Raffa or Uncle Mike, not one of the cherubim or seraphim, probably not a power or a dominion or a throne, though he couldn't put his hand on his heart and say he knew them all by sight. "Are you a seagull?"

"Yup."

"But you can talk."

"Yup."

"That's . . . unusual."

"Nope," said the seagull. "What's unusual is, you can hear me."

"Ah."

The seagull ate a crisp packet. Then it said, "You're him, aren't you?"

"Am I?"

"You're that guy. You know, whatsisname's kid."

"Oh, him. Yes, that's me. But probably not the one you're thinking of. There's two of us, you see, me and my elder brother."

"You're the younger one."

"That's right."

"Like I said," said the seagull. "You're him."

"How do you know that?"

"You can hear me. Only he can do that."

Kevin blinked. Out in the sun without a hat—Uncle Gabe had warned him about that. But it was still early, and the sun wasn't particularly fierce yet. "Tell me about him," he said.

"You're the younger chick of the Big Guy," the seagull said, "the one who's gonna redeem the Earth and build the Nest of God. Everybody knows that. We learn about you in the egg."

"Is that right?"

"Sure. Passed down from generation to generation."

"Of seagulls."

"Yup. Makes you something of a celebrity. When you come into your own, the world will be one vast beach flowing with sandwich crusts and cold French fries, and there will be no more death. That's what they tell us, anyhow."

Kevin rubbed his eyes, then stuck his finger in his ear and wiggled it about. Not earwax, then. "Do they say anything about how I bring all this about?"

"Sure."

Kevin waited, then he said, "For instance?"

"You just be yourself," the seagull said.

"That's it?"

"Yup."

"Just be myself, and everything suddenly turns wonderful?"

"Yup."

Kevin sighed. "There's got to be more to it than that."

"Maybe," the seagull replied. "You'd think so, wouldn't

you? I mean, no offence, but I gotta say, at first glance you're not that great."

"I just walked on the water."

"You don't say."

"All the way from Alicante."

"Cool. I just flew here from Malaga. Do you fly?"

"No."

"Mphm. How long did it take you?"

"Fifty-two hours."

"Took me ten, and Malaga's over twice as far. One of those aeroplanes could do it even quicker. I guess transit times aren't what's so special about you."

"I guess so."

The seagull looked at him thoughtfully. "So, what else do you do?"

"Let's see. I fed five thousand people."

"McDonald's feeds four million people a day."

"I turned water into beer."

"By adding malt, yeast and hops?"

"No."

"Then that was different," the seagull said. "Different ain't necessarily better. What else?"

"I cured a couple of sick people."

"OK."

"And got fined for practising medicine without a licence. I know, don't say it. Different but not necessarily better."

"I figure," the seagull said, "if you're out to to impress people, you should consider doing stuff they can't do for themselves."

Kevin thought for a while. "Jay raised the dead."

"Who?"

"Jay. My brother."

The seagull pecked at a ketchup sachet. "You might want to be careful there," he said. "Seems to me there's an awful lot of Homo sapienses on this planet, maybe more than's good for it. Could be, death is nature's way of keeping the numbers down."

"Yes, but—"

"Sure, I know. But you can't raise 'em all; it'd be standing room only. And if you raise some but not others, all you'll do is piss people off. Pardon my fowl language. They'll say, he raised so and so but not my Aunt Jemima; it's not fair. You'll annoy more people than you please, that's for sure."

"Good point," Kevin said sadly. "All right then, what should I do?"

"Don't ask me; I'm a bird."

"There must be something you can think of, surely."

The seagull put its head on one side. "What we're taught in the egg is, you'll be yourself. Try it. What harm can it do?"

"You'd be surprised."

Using the very tip of its beak and one claw, the seagull managed to get the ketchup sachet open. "You ain't listening. I didn't say, try and be what your dad and your big brother want you to be, or expect you to be. Don't try and be— What did you say his name was?"

"Jay."

"Sure. Don't be him. Be you. That's all I'm saying. Hey, this red stuff is really good."

"It's mostly sugar, salt and monosodium glutamate. You want to go easy on it."

"Thanks for the tip. You see? You care about people, even seagulls. That shows you're basically a nice guy."

"I suppose."

"Not like the bunch of crooks who made the ketchup, right? They put all kinds of stuff in it to make it taste nice, but it don't do you no good. Quite the opposite. You see what I'm saying?"

"Yes," Kevin said. "I should try to be wholesome and beneficial rather than just tasting nice. It's not actually very helpful."

"Honest too. Honesty is good."

"I think they also put eggs in ketchup."

The seagull spat hard. "Hey," it said. "You might have warned me."

"Chicken eggs."

"We're all part of the universal brotherhood of fowls." It wiped its beak on the sand. "But I don't hold it against you. It's not like you personally murder eggs. That said, when you found the Great Society, you might just bear it in mind."

"I'll see what I can do. Not that that's at all likely. The Great Society, I mean."

"Sure it is. It's been foretold."

"By seagulls."

"Yup," said the seagull. "And we're smart, trust me. I mean, could one of your peabrain Homo saps find his way across five thousand miles of trackless sea without any sort of landmark whatsoever, and pick out just one tiny little rocky island to lay his eggs on, year after year, for generations? Thought not."

"Homo sapiens wouldn't want to. Homo sapiens has more sense."

The seagull made a clucking noise. "See that building over there? It's a hotel full of tourists. Germans mostly, and Brits. You go in there and have a look around, and then you tell me which species making an annual migration to a tiny overcrowded seafront locale you think is superior." It preened a stray feather. "Listen, it's been great, but any minute now they'll be chucking out the used cooking fat. There's bound to be little crunchy black bits in it, and I'd hate to miss them. Think about what I told you. Ciao."

The seagull spread its wings and soared into the air. Kevin watched it until it turned into a tiny black dot and merged with the sky. Then he forced his feet back into his shoes and hobbled up the beach to the hotel, where they'd just started serving breakfast. A miracle, he thought. A *Kevin* miracle. He thought about that. Dad and Jay, and probably Uncle Mike as well, would define a Kevin miracle as Kevin actually doing something right for once. Well, that was as good a place to start as any.

He walked up onto the terrace. The first breakfast sitting were just taking their seats—Brits, as the seagull had said, and Germans, with a couple of Danes and a single morose-looking Swedish man. "Is this where you go for breakfast?" he asked.

Several voices assured him that it was. Is the food any good? No, they told him, it's horrible. Then why do you eat it? Because it's already paid for. Why don't you complain? Because it wouldn't do any good. Besides, added a sad-looking British woman, we're on holiday; it's what we expect.

"What," Kevin asked, "in your view, would constitute a really great breakfast?"

No shortage of suggestions on that score. The Brits were unanimously behind sausages, bacon, eggs (Kevin thought of the seagull but said nothing), fried bread and plenty of toast and jam. The Germans were equally categorical about ham, salami, hard cheese and sauerkraut. The Danes pointed out the merits of rye bread and *wienerbrod*, while the Swede closed his eyes and said, anything, anything at all, except Shredded Wheat. Fine, Kevin said, and I could do with a short stack of pancakes with maple syrup. Let's all have that, shall we?

They looked at him. A few of them sniggered. Then the kitchen door opened, and out came the waiters with little trolleys. And behold, it was exactly what everyone had asked for, and it was very good.

One of the Germans looked at him and said, "Did you do that?"

"Yes."

"How did you do that?"

Kevin shrugged. "Call it a miracle."

"Yes, but seriously."

"Why do miracles have to be serious? Why not a fun miracle? Mind you, any kind of fun is pretty miraculous with the Venturis in charge." He stood up. "Anyway, if you enjoyed this miracle, why not tell your family and friends? Just let them know," he added, "Kevin was here." Then, pausing only to banish a looming raincloud and lower all the prices on the bar tariff by 30 per cent, he strolled down to the bay and walked out to sea, trying his very best not to limp.

42

" I'm going to commit a crime," Jersey said. "Several of them, in fact."

Mr. Dao looked at him. "Is that right?"

"Yes, and they're going to be very expensive crimes, so I need a great deal of money."

Mr. Dao leaned forward and lowered his voice. "I thought you were barred from this establishment."

Jersey glanced over his shoulder. "I am," he said. "So let's make this snappy, before the manager comes back. Will you lend me a great deal of money?"

"And last I heard, you were up at the North Pole with the crazy man."

"I was. This is a flying visit." He wiped a speck of reindeer spittle off his sleeve. "In more senses than one. What about it?"

"Naturally you can offer security."

"No."

"A great deal, did you say?"

"A very great deal."

Mr. Dao pursed his lips. "The Venturis are after you. If they catch you, they'll put you in the Marshalsea and weld up the lock."

"Very likely."

Mr. Dao drew his abacus across the table and flicked a few beads. "Very well," he said, and from the flowing sleeves of his gown he produced a chequebook. "Do you know why the Bank of the Dead is the most successful financial institution in six galaxies?"

"No."

"Or how come we survived the big crash of '08, when all around us our competitors were crashing in flames?"

"No."

Mr. Dao lowered his voice to a whisper. "We've never ever made a bad investment. Do you know why?"

"No."

"I can see into the future. Or rather, I exist outside linear sequential time, so today is yesterday and yesterday is tomorrow, and as far as I'm concerned, you've already paid back the loan with ten per cent interest." He held out the chequebook but didn't actually let go of it. "Even so. I'll need a mortgage on your future earnings, a pound of your flesh closest to your heart, your first-born child and every asset owned by your ancestors back to the Stone Age. Purely a matter of form, you understand."

"Of course. Where do I sign?"

Mr. Dao produced a legal document. "Here," he said. "And here, and here, and here, and here, twice on this page, here, here, here, here, there on the dotted line and here. Oh, and here. I think that's everything. A pleasure doing business with you, Mr. Thorpe. Please accept this free pen as a token of our esteem."

"Thank you." He looked at it. It was jet black and in the shape of a human femur. "You can really see into the future?"

"Yes, and unless you leave now, the manager will throw

you out in a very undignified manner. Goodbye, Mr.
Thorpe. And please be careful."

"I will."

"You won't, you know. But never mind."

Jersey grinned, tripped over the leg of the table, stag-
gered and regained his balance just in time. "Told you,"
Mr. Dao said with a trace of a smile. "Go get 'em, tiger."

43

"That's the four of reindeer on your three, the nine of sleighbells on your seven, add forty-six above the line and an extra ten for his hooves, making eight hundred and forty-two to me and three to you. I win." Bernie smiled and gathered up the cards. "Which means you owe me four million three hundred thousand dollars and fourteen cents. Hypothetically."

The elf looked at him. "You're good at this game."

Bernie shrugged. "Beginner's luck. And it helps that the fall of cards appears to be controlled by an inverse numerical sequence based on intervals governed by multiples of pi."

"It does?"

"It helps me," Bernie said. "Double or quits?"

The elf counted on her fingers. "Eight million, six hundred thousand dollars if I lose?"

"And twenty-eight cents. Hypothetically. But if you win, you don't owe me anything."

An hour ago the elf had been teaching the human how to play the game. What a difference sixty minutes can make. "How would it be," she said, "if you told us how to access Venturicorp headquarters using the semi-derelict access tunnel leading from hellmouth 34A first, and then we played another game?"

Bernie frowned. "I'd rather not stop now, if it's all the same to you. I fancy I'm on a roll."

"OK. One more game, and then you'll tell us?"

Bernie smiled. "I know," he said. "Let's make it interesting. Double or quits, and I tell you how to find the access tunnel. How about it?"

"I dunno. Eight million hypothetical dollars. I could get into a lot of trouble."

"You do want to find the tunnel, don't you?"

So they played another game. It didn't take very long. When they'd finished, Bernie said, "You know, this isn't really how I imagined being interrogated was like."

"Is that so?"

"No. I thought it would mean lots of shouting and getting beaten up."

"There is that approach, certainly. Do you think it would work?"

Bernie shook his head. "I don't think so. You see, I don't actually know how you get from the hellmouth to the access tunnel."

"What?"

"In fact, I didn't even know there was a tunnel till you told me. A cheque will do fine, by the way. I'm not sure I could lift all that cash without a crane."

"You might have told me you don't know."

"I don't suppose you'd have believed me. But it's true."

The elf nodded. "All right," she said. "I'll tell the boss."

"Good idea. You can get him to sign my cheque while you're at it."

After that Bernie had a couple of hours to himself. Then the cell door opened, and a huge fat man in a red Santa suit came in. He was carrying a chessboard under his arm, and in his hand he held an envelope.

"Are you familiar," he said, "with all those stories where the hero plays chess with Death for the lives of his loved ones?"

"Yes."

"Good at chess, are you?"

"Not bad."

The Red Lord nodded, unfolded the board and turned it over. On the back was Snakes and Ladders. "We won't play chess, then. Here's the deal. If you win, you get this eight million dollar cheque and safe passage out of here, just as soon as you've told me how to find the access tunnel. If you lose, I cut you into small cubes and feed you to the reindeer. How does that sound?"

"I don't know where the access tunnel—"

The Red Lord shook his head. "Don't be naughty," he said, "be nice. You know precisely where it is because you had Maintenance get estimates for fixing it up, and when you got them they seemed awfully high, so you went and took a look at the site for yourself. That's the sort of guy you are. Painstaking. Thorough."

"How did you—?"

The Red Lord tapped the side of his nose with his forefinger. "You tend to go to bed around half-eleven and you're generally up by six-thirty, at which point you have a shower, a cup of decaffeinated coffee and two Weetabix. You put your socks on before your pants. You brush your teeth for exactly two minutes. Also, you're a terrible liar." He reached into his pocket and produced counters and dice. "I'll throw first," he said. "I'm feeling lucky."

Bernie could feel sweat oozing into his shoes. "Let's not play the game," he said. "I'll just tell you about the tunnel."

"You sure?"

"It's just this feeling I've got," Bernie said, "that any dice you roll always come up six."

"Funny you should mention that."

Bernie sighed. "It'd probably be easier," he said, "if I drew it for you."

The only paper available had jolly robins on one side, but the other side was blank. "To scale?"

Bernie looked offended. "Naturally."

"What's this? The sensor grid for the alarm system?"

"No, it's where the pen stopped working and I had to scribble a bit to get it going again."

"Fine. You've been very helpful."

Bernie smiled weakly. "You wouldn't actually have fed me to the reindeer, would you?"

The Red Lord smiled. "What are mince pies filled with?"

"Mincemeat."

"Which these days signifies a mixture of dried fruits and spices. But that's relatively recent." He took the cheque out of the envelope and tore it up. "I don't mind if people play games with my elves," he said, "as long as they don't mind playing games with me afterwards. Understood?"

Bernie nodded. "I'm sorry," he said.

The Red Lord shrugged. "It's all right," he said. "Actually, I admire your loyalty and resourcefulness, not to mention your mathematical ability. In fact, I could use someone like you, if ever you're interested."

Well, you can't help being flattered. "That's very nice of you," Bernie said. "But Mr. Lucifer would be lost without me."

"We'll see. Enjoy the rest of your stay. I've assigned you the VIP guest room."

"Wow."

"Not so wow, this is it. Still, it's all to do with status, isn't it? Sounds so much better than dungeon."

Bernie lay down with his back to the wall and tried to get some sleep. He'd just fallen into a light doze when the door opened. He opened his eyes. "Oh," he said. "It's you."

Jersey had the grace to look sheepish. "How have they been treating you?"

Bernie shrugged. "What bothers me is the thought of the mess they'll have got themselves into at work. It's always the same whenever I'm away from my desk for five minutes."

"They'll manage."

"No, they won't. Management is exactly what they're worst at."

Jersey sat down next to him. "I just got back from a mission behind enemy lines."

"Oh yes?"

"Yup. I was successful. As a reward, they've given me the Presidential Suite."

"Ah."

They sat in silence for a while. Then Bernie said, "You do realise the Venturis have got your girlfriend."

"Yes."

"Presumably that's why this lot wanted the plans of the access tunnel."

"Correct."

Bernie nodded. "Did they tell you the access tunnel comes out in the north side of the Venturicorps HQ's main septic tank?"

"No, they didn't."

"Well, it does."

"Right."

"I didn't go in there myself," Bernie said, "because that would've been trespassing, and Venturicorp do love their automated defence systems. But the reason we need to refurbish those tunnels is the smell."

"I see."

"It leaks out, you see, into the main Hell complex. You can smell it right across the campus."

"Fine."

"And the residents are starting to complain, and to be fair I can see their point. Eternal torment is one thing, but—"

"Thank you, yes."

"Like I said," Bernie went on, "I didn't go there myself, but one of the work demons inadvertently crossed the line into Venturi territory."

"Oh yes?"

"Yes. Luckily, he's immortal and indestructible. Even so, it took six hours and a gallon of superglue, and he's still bumping into things."

Jersey nodded. "You're suggesting I should be careful."

"It might help, yes. Of course, I expect you're used to that sort of stuff."

"Fairly used," Jersey said cautiously. "Um, you wouldn't have any more detailed hints, would you?"

"Don't go."

"Aside from that."

"No. Listen," Bernie said, sitting up and turning to face him. "You don't actually have to do this."

"Actually—"

"No, you *don't*. She's not your girlfriend; she doesn't like you any more. And once the Venturis have crushed Santa, they'll let her go. And they're not really so bad, are they? I mean, yes, the world isn't exactly a cheerful place these days, but there's no crime and everybody's got a job. Maybe cheerfulness comes at too high a price."

"You're from Hell. Maybe your perspective is slightly skewed."

"Maybe. But honestly, do you really believe you stand

a chance against the most powerful organisation in the Universe? Think about it. And if it counts for anything—"

"Yes?"

"You can have your old job back any time you like. I mean it. It'll be there waiting for you. You might even get promoted to head of coleslaw."

"Thank you," Jersey said with a slight catch in is voice. "I appreciate that."

"But you're still going?"

"I think so, yes."

"You do realise the Venturi know all about that access tunnel? In which case, it's almost certainly a—"

"Trap, yes." Jersey gave him a lopsided grin. "Bernie, it's *always* a trap. All human life is a trap. Good and evil are hereby abolished was a trap, to get you to sin more than you can afford. Eat of the fruit of any tree in the garden but not this one was a trap, sure as God made little green apples. There is absolutely no circumstance on this Earth that isn't a trap in some form or another. Every time a newborn baby opens its eyes for the first time, there's an angel hovering overhead whispering 'Gotcha!' So long as you realise that, it's fine. You take precautions. You don't go blundering into the carefully laid snare and then say, goodness me, I never expected that. No, you look around, you weigh up the tactical situation, you say to yourself, if I was a trap, where would I be? And you always have a little something in reserve, just in case."

Bernie nodded sadly. "I asked our quartermaster for one of those," he said. "He offered me a pitchfork and a packet of chewing gum."

"Good choices. At close quarters a pitchfork makes a devastating weapon. And when it comes to plugging the hole through which seawater is flooding into your sealed underground tunnel, five sticks of spearmint can mean the difference between life and death. But presumably the elves took them off you when you got captured."

The door opened, and an elf stuck its head in. "It's time," it said. "They're waiting for you."

Jersey stood up. "Ah well. It is a far, far better thing that I do now."

"Is it?"

"It bloody well ought to be. See you around."

The elves escorted him to Sleighpad Six, where Donner and Blitzen were busily crunching their way through a large pail of bones. "The controls are set on autopilot," the elves told him. "Good luck."

"What? Aren't any of you coming with me?"

"Not likely. It's almost certainly a trap."

The usual smooth lift-off was followed by the usual gut-wrenching acceleration to—what? The last time he'd flown on the sleigh, his watch had grown a fourth hand. It felt incredibly fast, but when you screwed up enough courage to peer over the handrail, there was no ground below to gauge your speed by, and no sky overhead either. Everything was just plain white, as though the sleigh was a cardboard cut-out on a blank sheet of paper, but the smell of the reindeer—raw meat and bones didn't seem to agree with them—was very real indeed. He tightened his grip on the rail and closed his eyes.

A slight bump told him they'd landed. In front of him was a brick chimney stack, a trifle incongruous on a flat concrete roof. The rail gave him a leg-up and he crawled up the brick-red cowls and braced his feet against the rim while he unwound the rope from around his waist. A single self-securing crampon into the mortar, and down we go.

If the chimney was only the illusion of a chimney, nevertheless it came equipped with plenty of illusory soot, which he wiped out of his eyes with the back of his hand.

The rough texture of the illusory bricks ripped his coat and took the skin off his shoulders as he edged downwards a few inches at a time. Eventually his feet bottomed out on something solid, and he reluctantly let go of the rope and let his weight rest on the soles of his boots. Brushing away the illusory cobweb festooned across his face, he backed out of the grate and looked about.

Hellmouth 34A was a disused siding just beyond the northbound platform of the Ginza station of the Tokyo metro. He left the rope dangling, hoping very much he'd see it again, and switched on his flashlight. The section of collapsed wall was exactly where it had been marked on the plans. He heaved a few bricks out of the way, got down on his hands and knees and started to crawl. The Venturi sensor net ended 12.526 metres from the inside face of the wall. The detectors for the automated defence system were 0.688 metres further on from that. In the gap between these two perimeters—far enough in to be detected, not quite far enough to be zapped into subatomic gravel—he stopped, slouched against the wall and settled down to wait.

A blinding light shone in his eyes. "You, out of there," barked a voice.

"Sure," Jersey replied. "Please don't shoot, I'll come quietly."

Four security goons in the familiar white plastic armour grabbed him by the ankles and dragged him out into a sunken tiled area. It was spotlessly clean and smelled refreshingly of pine needles.

"I thought this was a cesspit."

"Drained it," said a guard, "in your honour. On your feet."

They bound his hands behind his back with cable ties and put a bag over his head. He dropped to his knees and started to scream. A few kicks didn't stop him, so they took the bag off his head. "What?"

"Excuse me, but is that bag polyester?"

"I don't know, do I? Now shut it, or I'll smash your face in."

"Only," Jersey said, "I'm highly allergic to man-made fibres in contact with my skin. They bring me out in big red welts. It's very uncomfortable."

"Tough," said the guard. "So what am I supposed to do about it?"

"In the left pocket of my coat," Jersey said, "is a bag. It's made of one hundred per cent organically produced hessian. I carry it about with me at all times for just this sort of situation. If you wouldn't mind?"

The guard took a step back. "You carry your own blindfolding sack?"

"Always. Otherwise it's such a nuisance, me kicking and screaming every step of the way, and the guards having to carry me up all those stairs."

The guard thought about it. "And if we use your bag, you'll come quietly?"

"As a little lamb."

The guard shrugged. "Get the bag from his pocket," he snapped. "Come on, move it. They'll be refilling the tank in four minutes."

Another guard pulled out the sack, unfolded it and handed it to his chief, who opened it. "There's something in here."

"Is there?"

"Don't get smart with me." The guard reached inside and drew out a small box wrapped in Christmas paper. "What's this?"

"Your present."

"What?"

"A small thank you," Jersey said, "for letting me use my own bag."

The guard took a scanning device from his belt and ran it over the outside of the box. "Socks?"

"Yes. A bit boring, I know."

"I like socks," the guard said. "Here, hold this." He handed his blaster to one of his colleagues, then tore open the wrapping paper. "My wife always gives me iPads and windsurfing gear and motorbikes, but you can't say anything, can you?" He opened the box.

"Hope you like them," Jersey said.

Out of the box jumped three dozen elves covered in chainmail and wielding axes. You couldn't call what happened next a fight. More of a foregone conclusion lovingly brought about by people who cared passionately about their work. "Thanks, guys," Jersey said, picking up a discarded blaster. "Right, follow me."

"Not on your life," said an elf. "We're going back. We'll wait for you in the sleigh."

"Hey—"

"No way we're going any further. It's bound to be a trap."

"No," Jersey said patiently. "*This* was a trap. We set it up, remember?"

"A different one," the goblin said. "Don't take any wooden nickels."

Before Jersey could protest further, the elves scuttled back down the dark tunnel, leaving him alone with four peacefully sleeping stormtroopers. Bother, he thought, or a monosyllable to that effect. Never mind. The show must go on, and all that.

A window opened in thin air, and a young man stepped out. He saw the stunned stormtroopers and took a step back. "Hi," he said in a slightly shaky voice. "That's four counts of resisting arrest and actual bodily harm."

Jersey took a folded cheque from his top pocket. "That ought to cover it."

"We don't actually take cheques."

"You'll take this one."

"Bank of the— Yes, fair enough. Um, it's actually for a hundred thousand dollars too much."

"Is it? Oh, right." Jersey swung back his fist and punched the young man on the jaw. "Better?"

The young man got up and spat out a tooth. "Ee still owe oo ive dollars and irty cents."

"Keep the change."

An excruciatingly weary, awkward half-hour later, he slithered feet first up to the grille at the end of a long, smelly ventilation shaft, bent his knees and kicked hard. The grille popped out and clattered on to a concrete floor. He cleared his throat. "Hello?"

On a bed in the room below a young woman was asleep. She opened her eyes and looked at him. "Oh," she said. "It's you."

"Yes. Look, I don't think they've detected me yet, so if we're quick . . ."

She yawned. "What do you want?"

"What do you think? You're being rescued."

"Oh. Have I got to be?"

"What?"

She sighed. "It's really sweet of you, and I expect you've been to a lot of trouble, and it was very clever of you to have got this far and please don't think I don't appreciate it, but I'd rather not be rescued just now if that's all right."

"*What?*"

"I'd rather stay here. It's quiet and peaceful and they bring you your meals on a tray."

"Have you gone mad or something?"

"I'm perfectly sane, thank you," she said, "which is why I don't want to be rescued, or at least not by you. I don't mean that in a nasty way," she added quickly. "It's just that your way of doing things is all explosions and fist fights and crawling along tunnels and ticking clocks and falling through trapdoors and dodging booby traps, which is absolutely fine for you because you're good at it, but I get out of breath walking up two flights of stairs. Also, I think the Venturi are in a different league from the sort of idiots you're used to dealing with, so you'll have your work cut out escaping on your own, let alone with me trailing along behind you. Also, this whole Father Christmas thing is doomed to failure. You really don't stand a chance, and pretty soon it'll all blow over and then they'll have no more use for me and let me go, and I won't be a hunted fugitive any more. I can get another job and carry on living a normal life without being worried sick all the time. Also, I quite like you but not at all in that way, and being rescued by someone sort of raises expectations, doesn't it, and I know for a fact you wouldn't be here if I was fifty-five and wore a size twenty, so let's not kid ourselves, shall we? Look, I know it's not really your fault that they grabbed me and put me in here. If anything's to blame it's deeply ingrained cultural stereotypes, but honestly all this action-adventure stuff is only going to make things worse, and I could get badly injured or possibly even killed, and that'd be just plain stupid, now wouldn't it?"

Jersey stared at her for a moment. Then he said, "So you don't want me to rescue you?"

"No."

"You're not coming."

"No."

"Fine." Jersey wiggled his left foot, which had gone to sleep. "You really think you'd be better off staying here than coming with me?"

"I'm convinced of it," she said.

"Right." He tried shuffling back, but his shoulders were stuck against the shaft wall. "That's that, then."

"I hope you're not terribly disappointed."

"Mind out." He shuffled forward until his lower half was through the hole in the wall, then dropped to the floor. His foot hurt terribly because of the pins and needles. "It's all right," he said. "I'm not stopping. I couldn't turn round in there—it was too tight."

"I quite understand, Would you like a glass of water or anything?"

"No, thank you."

"Do you need to use the bathroom before you go back? There's one just through there, en suite."

"I'll be fine, thank you."

He turned, jumped up and hung by his fingertips from the hole where the grille had been. With a tremendous effort he tried to pull himself up, but couldn't quite make it.

"Would it be easier if you stood on a chair? I've got one here."

"Thank you."

Standing on the chair, he was able to stuff his torso through the hole, but his hips got stuck and there was nothing to grab on to and pull himself along. He wriggled out backwards again. "Sorry about this," he said.

"It's perfectly all right. You take all the time you need."

This time he bent his knees and sort of sprang off the chair into the hole, which nearly made the difference but not quite. He tore his jacket squirming back out again, and fell off the chair on the way down.

"I hate to rush you," she said, "but they'll be bringing my lunch in about half an hour. It's probably sort of fish stew. Made with real sort of fish."

He took his jacket off, screwed it into a ball and stuffed

it into the hole. Then he got back on the chair and bent his knees.

"Just a moment."

Ah, he thought. "What?"

"Before you go," she said, "it's just occurred to me, I came across something that might come in handy for you. You wouldn't have a bit of paper and a pen, would you?"

He scowled at her, then fished his jacket out of the ventilation shaft. "Here," he said. "What are you talking about?"

"It's a bit complicated, so I'd better write it down." She did so. "There. Give that to Santa; he might find it interesting. Right then, off you go."

He shoved his jacket back into the hole, clambered up on the chair, then looked round. "You're sure you don't want to—?"

"Absolutely."

"See you then." He bent his knees and dived into the hole, banging his head and skinning his elbows, but found he had just enough traction to get his feet in. He squirmed a few yards, then stopped to catch his breath. Behind him he could hear the grille being jammed back in place.

It was a long, painful crawl to the junction but he was too preoccupied to notice. By the time he tumbled out of the long, sloping tube that led back to the air duct that led to the freight elevator shaft, he was so thoroughly cocooned in rage and misery that he didn't see the ten stormtroopers in white plastic armour sitting waiting for him until it was much too late. They gave him a sympathetic grin and helped him to his feet.

"Women, eh?" one of them said.

"You what?"

"We got her cell wired for sound," the stormtrooper explained. "Sort of like a trap, if you follow me."

"Ah."

The stormtrooper shook his head. "If you want my opinion," he said, "you're better off without. A girl like that, she'd only make your life a misery."

"Well—"

"Talk about ungrateful," another stormtrooper said, gently twisting his arm behind his back. "A bloke goes out of his way to come and save her, and it's, Not now, it's meatloaf on Thursdays."

"Sort of fish stew," the other stormtrooper corrected him. "Sort of meatloaf is Wednesdays."

"Whatever. All I'm saying is, you can do better than that."

"She's nothing special to look at, anyhow," the first stormtrooper said.

"Could do with losing a few pounds, that's for sure," a third stormtrooper put in as he looped a cable tie round Jersey's wrists. "Just as well she didn't come down the tunnel with you, she'd have got stuck like a cork."

"And attitude."

"Makes you feel like rubbish. I couldn't be doing with that."

"You forget about her, chum," the first stormtrooper said, clouting Jersey between the shoulder blades with a plastic-gauntleted fist. "And even if she didn't want to be rescued, there was no call to be so snotty about it. A bloke's got feelings, after all. Nah, you're better off, definitely."

"You're probably right," Jersey said sadly. "OK, so what now?"

"We take you up to the surface and shoot you," the stormtrooper said cheerfully. "That'll show her, eh? Bet you she'll feel a right fool."

They climbed a spiral staircase and came out into a small courtyard, where they chained him to a wall.

Then they lined up and took aim. "Well," said the first stormtrooper, "nice meeting you. Chin up. At least it's not raining."

The stormtroopers switched on their optical sights and peered through them. Their fingers tightened on the fire buttons of their blasters. Then there was a bright flash, and they all fell over.

"I don't know if that was the stun setting or not," said a female voice. "It's not marked in words; there's just these stupid little pictures which could mean anything."

It took Jersey's eyes about five seconds to recover from the flash. When he could see again, what he saw was Lucy, with a blaster resting on her shoulder and bits of dust and cobweb in her hair. "Guess what," she said. "You've been rescued."

He opened his mouth, but all that came out was a high-pitched squeak. She stepped over a fallen stormtrooper, knelt and retrieved a key from his belt. "Just after you'd gone I noticed this little microphone thing," she said. "It got dislodged when you kicked the grille out. And I thought, I bet they've been listening in, and now they'll know he's here and they'll catch him. So I thought, sod it. It's not very nice in those ventilation shafts, is it? Though I did not get stuck." She glared at a fallen stormtrooper, then undid the lock that secured the chain to the wall. "Well, come on," she said. "I'm guessing the other side of that wall is the south elevation of the main building, but I've got a lousy sense of direction."

"I thought you said you were going to stay. I thought you said being rescued was pointless."

"I'm rescuing you," she said. "That's different. Is there a first aid kit on Santa's sleigh? I took all the skin off my ankle getting through that stupid vent."

"Thank you."

She shrugged. "You're welcome. Now come *on*, will you? Where's this sleigh of yours parked?"

Her sense of direction was better than she'd given herself credit for. Not long afterwards they were standing on the edge of the septic tank, which was now a quarter full. "You'll be all right," she said cheerfully. "I don't think it'll come up much above your chin."

She turned to go. "You aren't coming with me?"

She shook her head. "Not likely. I explained all that."

"But—"

"If I'm quick about it and I don't waste time standing around chatting, I can probably get back to my cell before they know I've been gone. Take care of that piece of paper I gave you. Bye."

He took a long stride after her. She turned and shoved him in the chest. He stumbled back, tripped over his feet and toppled into the septic tank. Fortunately, its contents were just buoyant enough to break his fall.

44

From Almeria, Kevin took a bus to the French border and then a train to Lyon. He'd just come out of the main station concourse and was looking for somewhere to sit down and have a cup of coffee when the Devil swooped down, caught him up and carried him off to a high mountaintop.

"Hi, Uncle Nick."

"Hi, Kevin." Uncle Nick put him down, materialised two deckchairs, a thermal jacket and an oxygen mask, and sat down. "How've you been keeping?"

"Oh, fine. You?"

"Not so bad."

"I expect you miss the old man."

"Yup. And Jay too, of course."

Uncle Nick took a packet of sandwiches and a flask from the inside pocket of his cape. "You OK with the air up here?"

"Fine, thanks."

"Warm enough?"

"It's fine." Kevin looked around. "Say," he said, "from here you can see all the kingdoms of the Earth."

Uncle Nick poured a cup of coffee. "Not quite," he said.

"Burundi's over that way somewhere, and Nepal's under that big bank of cloud there."

"Isn't Nepal a republic now?"

"Constitutional monarchy." Nick grinned. "Not nearly as many kingdoms as there were last time I was here. I guess you could call that progress."

Kevin shrugged. "You could say it's now all just one big empire. The United States of Venturicorp. Is that your idea of progress?"

"Your dad once gave me a good piece of advice," Nick said. "Never discuss politics with family. I got some salt tablets, if you need any."

"I think they're for deserts."

"You're probably right." He offered Kevin a mug of coffee. "So, is that what all this is about? You want all of this lot?"

"The geography? No, not particularly." Kevin frowned. "Uncle Nick, I made a decision that maybe you should know about. I'm not just going to repeat all the stuff Jay did. So the whole temptation bit isn't really necessary."

"Jay's a great kid," Nick said, "don't get me wrong. But it wasn't like Jay was ever going to say yes. With him it was just a formality. And a media circus and a prophecy opportunity. I remember, this whole mountain was crawling with seraphim, setting up microphones, fooling around with lights and reflectors. We had to do the jump-down-and-be-saved-by-angels bit five times before they reckoned it had come out right. You hungry?"

Kevin sighed. "No," he said, "and if I was, I wouldn't turn a stone into bread."

"These are Danish salami on rye, and these ones are egg and watercress."

"Oh, go on then." Kevin took a salami sandwich. "How are things Flipside, anyhow?"

"Fine," Nick said, then he frowned. "Not so great right

now," he said. "There's this kid works for me, Bernie Lachuk. Truth is, he's the one who really runs the place, not me. Anyhow, the Venturis sort of leaned on me to send him on some stunt to trap that idiot who's been trying to find the jolly fat man, and he's been gone a long time and I think that maybe he got caught or something. And meanwhile, nobody knows what to do or where to find anything, the Dukes are at each others' throats all day long, and there's some girl in Archives who does nothing all day but cry her eyes out. To be honest with you, I'm glad to be out of there for a few hours."

"This is great salami."

"There's this amazing little deli in Copenhagen." Nick pointed. "Just about there. Do yourself a favour next time you're out that way."

"You needn't worry about Bernie," Kevin said. "He's fine. Right now he's playing cards with a bunch of elves. They owe him a considerable sum of money."

Nick beamed. "That's all right, then," he said. "I'd hate it if anything happened to the kid. He's bright, that boy. He's kind of the son I never had, you know?"

Kevin nodded slowly. "And family's important," he said. "But there's other things that matter even more, Uncle Nick. Was all this the Venturis' idea?"

For a moment Nick looked as though he'd been slapped. "I guess I deserved that," he said. "But when you're out playing golf somewhere and suddenly you've got Snib Venturi on the line saying things like violation of contract terms and aiding and abetting subversive elements, you panic. I panicked," he corrected. "Kevin, I don't know whether I've done anything wrong or not, according to the treaty, I mean. But I do know that Snib Venturi could make my life very awkward indeed if he wanted to. And the fat jolly man's nobody's friend, right?"

"I seem to remember you quite liked him."

Nick grinned. "Yeah, I guess I did. Mostly because he's a rule-breaker, and professionally speaking I was right behind all that kind of thing. Also he did wonders for gluttony, greed and covetousness in late summer and autumn. And, let's face it, much as I admire your old man—and Jay too, of course—I won't pretend I didn't get a bit of a kick out of seeing him winding them up the way he did. I don't know, things were a bit more fun when he was around." He wiped the smile off his face. "But that's one thing, and getting my charter revoked is another. We definitely do not approve of the fat jolly man. Do we?"

Kevin shrugged. "I hear what you say," he said, "and I can understand where you're coming from. I'm not sure I agree though. I don't actually like the Venturis very much, and I don't think they're the right people to run this world."

Nick sighed. "It's all right for you," he said. "I know, rocking the boat's not an issue when you can walk on water. Me, I like a quiet life. And I've got billions of souls to think about as well. What's going to happen to them if Snib Venturi closes us down? Where are they going to go? Who's going to look after them?"

Kevin raised an eyebrow. "You know, I never really thought of what you do as looking-after. Interesting perspective."

"I have responsibilities, is what I'm saying. I have people depending on me. My claws are tied." He glanced over his shoulder and lowered his voice. "This goes no further, right?"

"Of course."

"Then sure, yes, I can't stand those damn Venturis. They make me sick. All they're interested in is money. And you know what your old man thought about that. Money is the root of all evil."

"Actually, it's love of money is the—"

"I'd like nothing better than for the Venturis to piss off back to Andromeda or wherever they came from, and for your dad and Jay to come back, and for everything to be like it was. But that's not going to happen. So . . ."

"Better the Devil you know?"

"So we sit tight, keep our noses clean, and most of all we *do not* get involved with dissidents and subversives. OK, Kevin, I know you mean well, but—"

"Paved with good intentions?"

"You're not your brother. You're not your old man. They never wanted you in the family business, and I agree with them. You're just not cut out for it, that's all."

Kevin had gone very pale. "I see," he said. "You think I'm too stupid?"

"Stupid?" Nick looked blank. "Heck, no. You're a bright kid, Kevin: you're imaginative and smart and you got your head screwed on." He paused then said, "You think that's why the old man never wanted you in the business?"

"Well, yes. Wasn't it?"

Nick shook his head. "He knows you're not dumb, and so does Jay."

"So why wouldn't they ever teach me how to do things?"

Nick sighed. "It's not because they thought you were stupid," he said. "Far from it."

"Then why, for crying out loud?"

"It's a question of temperament," Nick said slowly. "They feel, and I agree with them, you're too soft-hearted. You care about people. You're too much of a nice guy. They reckoned you'd never be able to keep the necessary degree of distance between you and the little people. You'd let yourself get involved, and that's a bad thing in our line of business, son, a very bad thing. I mean, look at you and this Thorpe guy and his girl. You saw they were in trouble, you rushed in to help. You didn't stop and think, what are the bigger issues here? Running a world is no job for a bleeding-heart sentimentalist, Kevin. You got to have a ruthless streak. You need to be prepared to smite the cities of the plain, send the flood, cast the goats into the darkness and gnash teeth. You can't go soft on the livestock, or they'll never respect you."

"But I like them," Kevin said. "I like them a lot."

Nick shook his head. "It won't do, son. Take it from me. How'd it be if I ran my department that way? There's loads of people under my care who are really great guys when you get to know them, but do I allow myself to go soft on them? Listen, I got half the great poets and all the great musicians; I got all the charismatic politicians; I got all the best speechmakers and movers and shakers. Given half the chance, I'd take them out for dinner instead of boiling them in molten pitch. But I don't let myself think that way. You've got to be detached, Kevin. You've got to be *professional*."

But Kevin shook his head. "I don't know," he said. "Maybe that's the whole problem." He stood up. "I'm not saying I've got all the answers, Uncle Nick. I don't even know if I've got some of the questions. All I know is, I've got to try."

Nick gave him a sad look. "This isn't the way your old man would do things," he said.

"Sure," Kevin replied. "But I'm not my dad. I'm me."

45

When they were kids, growing like weeds between the paving stones of the mean streets of Z'vworpp City, Ab and Snib Venturi built themselves a galaxy. They had to do the best they could with what they could find—in dustbins, mostly, or litter retrieved from corners and gutters—thus, their first stars were little balls of silver foil from *gnuup* packets, their nebulas handfuls of cellophane wrapping, their planets pebbles, their comets stale *pjii* nuts with trailing beards of cotton wool, and the whole lot lived in a plastic carrier bag. But every evening they'd empty it out on some quiet corner of the pavement and arrange it all, just so, and in their hearts and minds the balled-up newspaper *was* the vast and infinitely mysterious galactic Core.

They knew their constellations as thoroughly as any professor of astonomy, and measured out the interstellar distances with serious precision, using their fingers as dividers. A faceted blue and white pebble was Gnoth, the home planet of the galaxy's most advanced species. Wrapping-paper rings encircled the grim ill-omened pebble of Snooi, home to the dreaded Bolons. Ninety-seven pebbles orbiting twelve shining stars made up the

Proob Confederacy, aloof guardians of ancient wisdom, whose space extended from the Core to the broken rubber gasket that represented the Uboth Anomaly. Squatting on the pavement in the crushing warmth of the summer evening sun, they were lords of infinite space, distant but fascinated spectators of the joys and sorrows of innumerable tiny lives, any of which they could change utterly or sweep away with a flick of the fingers. It was a good game. Without it they would never have survived.

And then one day Ab asked Snib where the bag was, and Snib said he'd thrown it away. The game was kids' stuff, he said, and they weren't kids any more. But it's all right, he said as his brother's eyes filled with tears, some day we'll have a real galaxy, dozens of real galaxies. *I promise you*, he said with that quiet, fierce intensity that scared Ab sometimes, who couldn't quite bring himself to say that he didn't want a real galaxy to rule, the cardboard and tinfoil one was just fine, and what was wrong with being poor and hungry and cold sometimes, as long as they were together?

Snib Venturi had made good on his promise, and the territory they controlled was so vast that if you stood back and looked at it from a distance, you could actually see the curvature of the Universe, where the gravitational pull of Time warps infinity into a perfect sphere. But Ab Venturi's most treasured possession, which his brother knew nothing about, was a suitcase. In it was a galaxy set. It wasn't much like the old one they'd made out of trash. The suns were crafted from genuine neutronium, the nebulas were priceless wisps of *znui* gossamer, the planets were gemstones and the black holes really were tiny miniature portals to alternate realities, which made packing them up again a bit awkward. Every evening when Snib had gone to bed, he'd retreat to his room and

set out the galaxy, painstakingly measuring the interstellar distances with fingers that were thicker now but
still accurate enough as they paced the luxurious deep-
pile *gveep*-wool carpet. It was his greatest pleasure, but
it wasn't the same when it was just him. On one point,
though, he was absolutely determined. Snib must never
know. He'd think it was childish, and get angry because
he'd think that Ab wasn't grateful for everything Snib
had done for him.

Snib was sitting up late tonight with a big pile of papers,
business stuff. It happened sometimes, when there was a
lot going on, and Snib was perfectly capable of working
round the clock if he had to. When that happened, Ab
didn't play the game, just in case Snib wanted something
and came looking for him. But this particular spell of
being-busy had lasted three days and three nights, and it
was a long time since Ab had gone three nights without
playing the game. It was calling to him; the suns and
planets and the little people on the planets needed him.
He could almost hear their voices in his head: *Our god,
our god, why have you forsaken us?* It wouldn't hurt, surely.
Three days and Snib hadn't come charging in at three in
the morning. He decided to risk it. He pulled the suitcase
out from under the bed, snapped the catches and swung
back the lid.

He was in the middle of calculating the trajectory of
a multiphasic ion storm through the asteroid belt of Fni
when the door opened, hitting him in the back. "Ab, I need
you to sign this. Hey, bro, what you got there?"

Ab couldn't speak. His hearts had stopped beating.
Slowly Snib knelt down and picked up a yellow giant.

"Hey," he said. "Cool."

"It's neutronium," Ab whispered.

"It's great. Where'd you get it?"

And then a sudden and quite unexpected inspiration struck Ab like a thunderbolt, and all the black clouds of despair lifted and the sun shone gloriously. "I got it for you," he said. "It's a present."

Snib looked at him. Incredibly, he smiled. "Aw, Ab. You shouldn't have."

"It's to remind you of the old days. You know, when we were kids."

Snib beamed at him. "That old galaxy set we made. I'd forgotten about that."

"We had so much fun."

"Didn't we ever." Snib was grinning. "They were hard times, bro, but in a way they were good times too. We *made* them good times, didn't we?"

"We did that."

Snib picked up a planet and rested it on the palm of his hand. Around it, three tiny moons buzzed in slow elipses. "Amazing detail," he said. "The moons actually move."

"It's got real gravity and everything. Look." With the blades of his fingernails Ab picked up a tiny asteroid and held it close to Snib's planet. It leaped a whole centimetre through the air and was drawn into geosynchronous orbit.

Snib laughed for pure joy. "This must have cost plenty."

"Well—"

"Worth every cent. Hey, bro, that's great. Thank you."

Ab smiled broadly, but his heart twisted inside him because Snib would take the game away and put it in a cupboard somewhere, along with the few other bits of cool stuff he'd acquired and never played with. "That's all right, Snib. You do so much for me."

"Tell you what," Snib said. "We'll put this on the table in the living room. Permanently. After all, this is our place: we live here. We don't need to pack our stuff away every night any more."

There is more joy in Heaven. "Sure," Ab said. "I'd like that."

"The only thing that's wrong," Snib said, "is the Core." He picked it up. Sinteraani *glerq*smiths, the finest in the galaxy, had wrought it out of the purest *kprz'wweebi*, but Ab knew what Snib meant. It wasn't quite right somehow. "We'll have to get a better one. Say, remember that old screwed-up sheet of paper? That made a great Core. I wonder what happened to that old galaxy set."

Ab took a deep breath. "I don't know, Snib. I guess I must've lost it somewhere."

"Doesn't matter. This one ..." He stopped and grinned. "This one's almost as good." He turned and sat down. It was so long since Ab could remember seeing Snib sit on a floor.

"There was something you wanted me to sign."

"What? Oh, yes, right. Doesn't matter, it can wait."

"You've been awful busy these last few days. I've hardly seen you."

Snib sighed. "It's this damn insurgency thing," he said. "I kidded Whatsisname, the guy we bought this place from, into paying for an army to take out the fat man." He closed his eyes and massaged his forehead with his fingers. "You just can't get good mercenaries these days. I've been on to Xxxplui and Freem and Gamma Orionis Four, but they're all booked up till Galactic New Year. And the trash they've been offering me—"

"Couldn't the Security guys handle it?"

"You know what Mum always used to say, if you want something done ..." Snib sighed and picked up a lesser Magellanic Cloud. "You're right," he said. "Let them do it. That's what I pay them for. You know what, bro? I feel tired a lot of the time these days."

"You work too hard. You always have."

"No such thing as working too hard," Snib said, then grinned. Mom had said that a lot too. "Well, maybe. But this stupid insurgency is getting on my nerves. We didn't have all this on Beta Coriolis Six."

"It's just one guy and some old leftover thunder god."

"The thing is, it always starts with just one guy. Then, before you know it, you've got Doubt. I gotta stomp on it, Ab, or it'll get out of hand. We got five galaxies watching us, bro, every little thing we do. The first tiny sign of weakness, they'll be on to us like snakes."

A great wave of sorrow swept through Ab Venturi. For a moment there his brother had been happy; now he wasn't, and it was all this damn Christmas man's fault. "You get him, Snib. Get him real good."

"I intend to." For a split second he looked really scary. Then his face fell, and he just looked very, very tired. "As soon as I can find him. And then . . ."

"Yes?"

"He'd better watch out, is all."

46

The Red Lord wasn't happy. "He's back?"

"Yes, boss."

"He didn't get captured?"

"No, boss."

"But it was a trap." The Red Lord scowled. "Fetch him here. Now."

"Yes, boss."

The Red Lord poured himself a big drink of milk and scattered nutmeg sprinkles on the top with a silver spoon. For a cup he used the jewel-encrusted skull of . . . Actually, he couldn't remember the guy's name; it had all been so long ago—some minor vegetation god or river spirit who'd tried to muscle in on his turf back in the old days, when stuff like that had actually mattered. He could sort of remember himself standing over the poor fool's twitching corpse and roaring, "I will drink my milk from your skull for the rest of eternity," or some such garbage, but what the quarrel had been about or how he'd overcome him he had no idea. And, ever since, the elves had been washing up the skull and putting it out for him every morning, and it was just the way things had been, were now and probably ever would be. A nice glass, which held more and didn't chafe your fingers, was probably out of the question.

Jersey limped in. His clothes were torn and his face was covered in bruises, and he didn't smell very nice. "Oh," the Red Lord said. "It's you."

Jersey slumped down in a chair. "Yup."

"You got away."

"Barely. The girl," he said bitterly, "rescued me."

"Shouldn't that be the other . . . ?"

Jersey shook his head. "Apparently not."

"So where is she?"

"She's still there. Didn't want to leave."

"Ah." The Red Lord cheered up a little. "You mean she's betrayed us?"

"Nope. Just didn't want to be rescued by *me*, that's all."

The Red Lord could see her point. Even so. "You clown," he said.

"Excuse me?"

"Clown," the Red Lord repeated deliberately. "You're useless."

"Yes," Jersey said wearily, "I think I probably am. Thank you so much for confirming it."

The Red Lord drank his milk. "You don't get it, do you?"

"Probably not. I'm not very bright. Apparently."

The Red Lord was annoyed but not entirely incapable of sympathy. "You really thought she liked you."

"Yup. Wrong about that too."

"Ah well. Look at it this way. Would you really want to form a meaningful and lasting relationship with someone so shallow and lacking in character that she'd willingly reduce herself to the level of sidekick? Fine now, but imagine what it'd be like in ten, twenty years' time. This dumb, oxlike creature following you around all the time and needing to be rescued every ten minutes. You're better off."

"That's what the stormtroopers said."

"Well, then." The Red Lord sighed. "Meanwhile, you've screwed up all my plans."

"Have I? How like me."

"The idea was," the Red Lord explained patiently, "that you'd be captured and forced to reveal the location of my secret fortress—that means this place here—whereupon Snib Venturi and all his goons would be here like a shot to get me."

Jersey nodded. "And that would be a good thing. I see."

"Yes," said the Red Lord, "because my elves are good enough lads in their way, but there's not nearly enough of them to risk a pitched battle in the open, whereas they can hold this place against a besieging army pretty well indefinitely."

"Which is what you want?"

"Yes," the Red Lord said, "because after a week, at most, Snib Venturi will be terrified that the market analysts across half the known Universe will be saying the Venturi boys can't even put down a little local rebellion, they must be losing their touch, and after the shellacking they took over the Bank of Ultimate Truth—"

"The what?"

"Doesn't matter. The point is, it'd look bad, and the Venturis could lose a lot of money. So they'll give up, make some plausible excuse about restructuring and go away. It was the only way we could win. And you—"

"I blew it."

The Red Lord nodded. "One simple thing. But never mind. I'll just have to think of something else."

Jersey was looking at the sole of his shoe. The Red Lord clicked his tongue. "Sorry," he said. "Am I boring you?"

"Maybe I didn't screw up after all." With the back of the Red Lord's teaspoon he picked something out of his shoe.

"Oh look," the Red Lord said. "It's a tiny little electronic tracking device."

Jersey looked stunned. Then he grinned. "I didn't escape. I wasn't rescued. They let me go."

"Presumably. Why are you smiling?"

"It means I wasn't rescued by some dumb girl."

The Red Lord smiled sadly. "They may have let you go," he said, "but if you ask me, yes, you had a lucky escape. And even more so," he added kindly, "did she. Now, piss off and get some weapons from the armoury." A warm red smile lit up his face, and Jersey backed away nervously. "You know what?"

"What?"

The Red Lord rubbed his hands together. "Snib Venturi is coming to town."

47

"Jay," hissed his father, "cut it out. People are staring."

It had been a long ride on the red-eye trans-dimensional conduit from Sinteraan, stopping at all the little planets along the way to deliver sacks of mail and crates of chickens. The nearest to Earth the conduit had taken them was Proxima Centauri. From there they'd hitched a lift from a saucer of bug-eyed monsters who were going to a poetry reading on Ganymede. The rest of the way they'd walked. Jay's feet hurt as a result, so he was resting them by hovering six inches off the ground. He'd hoped nobody would notice. "Sorry," he whispered back, lowering himself until his blisters rested on the hard asphalt.

"The last thing we want to do is draw attention to ourselves," Dad said. "We're not supposed to be here, remember."

"Can we stop and rest for a bit? I'm bushed."

They weren't supposed to be there because the contract with the Venturis specifically forbade them to visit Earth without six weeks' notice and written consent. To begin with, Jay had found the idea of doing something he wasn't allowed to strangely alluring—his first time, after all—but the thrill had worn off long ago, along with most of the soles of his shoes.

To his surprise Dad said, "Sure, why not?" So they sat down outside a cafe and ordered coffee.

"This was a mistake," Jay said, gingerly prising his shoes off his feet and flexing his toes. "We shouldn't have come, We should've stayed on Sinteraan and done the deal from there."

Dad winced. Jay contradicting him was something he was having trouble getting used to. "I don't think so," he said. "I think we need to be here, on the spot, seeing what's going on for ourselves. And then, when we get our planet back—"

"If we get our planet back."

"*When* we get it back, we can get started straight away on putting things right." He sighed. "I admit it, son: you were right and I was wrong. We should never have sold out to the Venturi boys."

Jay didn't say anything, and the waiter brought them their coffee. After he'd gone Jay leaned across and whispered, "Dad, did you bring any Earth money?"

"What? No. Did you?"

"We might find it a bit difficult paying for the coffee in that case."

Dad grunted. "Appeal to the waiter's better nature," he said. "You're good at that stuff."

"I'll text Gabe. He'll lend us the money."

Gabe didn't seem particularly happy to see them again. "Boss," he said, "what are you doing here? You know you're not supposed to—"

Dad silenced him with a wave of his hand. "Lend us five dollars."

Gabe put a coin down on the table. Dad picked it up and eyed it with distaste. On each side was a portrait;

Snib on one side, Ab on the other. "So what are you doing here?"

Before Dad could speak, Jay said, "Have you heard from Kevin lately? How's he doing?"

Gabe hesitated. Dad said, "Don't tell me. He's got himself in trouble."

"No," Gabe said quickly. "Not yet."

"But he's about to?"

Gabe shrugged and told them about the miracles, and how Nick had tried to talk to the boy but he wouldn't listen, and how the miracles were trending on social media like nothing else on Earth. When he'd finished, Dad gave him a sour look and said, "I thought I told you two to look after him."

"We tried," Gabe said. "But what could we do? His heart's set on doing this stuff. Lucky for him, Snib Venturi's all preoccupied with the tinsel-and-presents guy. Otherwise . . ."

Dad and Jay exchanged glances. "Looks like we got here just in time," Dad said. "All right, where is he?"

"Last I heard, he was in Tromso. That's a city in—"

"Thanks, I can remember where Tromso is," Dad snapped. "What's he doing there?"

Gabe looked down at his shoes. "He, um, filled the main tank at the city aquarium with doughnuts. People loved it. It cheered them up," he added defensively, "and he made sure all the fish and stuff were OK. No rare species were harmed during the making of this—"

"Cheered them up," Dad repeated.

Gabe nodded. "That seems to be his thing. He does stuff to cheer people up. The way he figures it, if people are happy, they don't need no laws or on-the-spot fines to keep them from doing bad things."

Dad was silent for a long time. Then Jay said, "Doughnuts?"

"Other times it's flowers or fireworks. Cheerful things."

Gabe took a deep breath. "Boss, I know you told him, stay out of the family business, but maybe you should cut the kid some slack, let him work this out for himself. And you know what, it's not such a bad idea at that. Redemption through joy. Not just the pursuit of happiness but actually catching the bugger. Far as I know, it's never been tried before. Why not let him give it a go?"

Dad leaned across the table. "Because when Snib Venturi gets hold of him, he'll lock my son up in one of his debtors' prisons," he hissed furiously, "and take it from me, that's too high a price to pay for the salvation of a bunch of semi-evolved monkeys. Also—" he leaned back in his chair "—what good is being happy going to do them? People don't learn anything from being happy. They learn from making mistakes and being punished for them. No, this is your fault, yours and Raffa's. I want you to find him and bring him here. Got that?"

Gabe sat perfectly still.

"Did you hear me?"

"Yes, boss."

"You're still here."

"Yes, boss."

Dad breathed out heavily through his nose. "Fine," he said. "I'll deal with you later. Come on, son."

Jay stayed where he was. "Where are we going, Dad?"

"Tromso. Where do you think?"

"Maybe we should talk about this some more."

For a moment Jay was afraid his father would explode or maybe have a stroke. But he sat down. "Sure, son," he said. "What do you want to talk about?"

Jay turned to Gabe. "Thanks for coming so quickly," he said. "We'll make sure you get the money back. I think you'd better go now."

"OK, Jay. Nice seeing you again."

"You too, Gabe. Give my best to Raffa."

Gabe hurried off and Dad said, "I asked you a question. What do you want to talk about?"

"About Kevin," Jay replied, "I guess."

"Good idea, let's do that. Son, do you really think Kevin ought to be allowed to make a fool of himself and then get himself locked up?"

It was a while before Jay answered. But eventually he said, "Dad, is that what you're worried about, that he might fail? Or is it more that he might succeed?"

Dad barked out a laugh. "Not much chance of that."

"Do you really think so?"

Dad drank some cold coffee and pulled a face. "Never could for the life of me see why humans like this stuff," he said. "Come on. Time's a-wasting."

"Dad," said Jay. "I thought we came here to do the deal with the Venturis."

"That'll have to wait. First order of business is to save your brother."

"Dad—"

Dad gave Jay a stern look. "When it was you down here," he said, "I made darned sure I was there to pull you out before it got nasty. I didn't leave you with those barbarians while I went and got on with something else. Are you saying I shouldn't do the same for your brother?"

Jay hesitated, then nodded. "OK, Dad," he said. "Whatever you think is right."

"I should hope so."

Jay put the coin in the middle of the table where the waiter would see it and followed his father. His feet were still hurting, and it occurred to him to wonder when the people of Earth, made in Dad's own image and for whom he'd endured severe though temporary discomfort on top of a green hill far away, had become *a bunch of semi-evolved monkeys* and *those barbarians*. But he dismissed the thought. Dad was just being Dad, and sometimes, for his own ineffable reasons, he chose to move in mysterious ways and pass all understanding. Jay just hoped this was one of those times, that was all.

48

Veltor is a small orange and grey planet in the Merionis cluster. Its dominant species originally evolved from small fast-moving rodents; the closest terrestrial parallel would be rats. From their ancestors the Veltrons have inherited cunning, ferocity, resourcefulness, courage when cornered, whiskers, ironclad digestive systems and small sharp teeth. They're bigger now—between two and a half and three metres, on average—and their burrows run deep under the barren surface of their planet, which their early experiments with nuclear fusion have rendered uninhabitable. Since they have long since eaten every last worm, grub and snail in the Veltron subsoil, they're entirely dependent on imports, and since they make nothing worth having, the only commodity they have to trade is their labour. Their special field of expertise is warfare. They're very good at it, although prospective employers are reluctant to hire them because of the collateral damage. Once they've been somewhere for any length of time (measured in hours rather than days) the place is fit for nothing, and won't be for some considerable time.

Security had hired 100,000 Veltrons. Sorry, they

explained, but they were all we could get. Snib Venturi sighed and said, all right then, but keep them safely in orbit till the last moment and then teleport them directly to the North Pole. It was a good idea, but the Veltrons gnawed the insulation off all the power cables in the teleport chamber, so they had to be ferried down to the surface in shuttles. By the time they landed, the vinyl seat-covers were in shreds and all the plastic trim had been nibbled off the navigation consoles. Security immediately ordered an emergency airdrop of 12,000 tons of cheese. By the time it arrived, the Veltrons had eaten their body armour and the synthetic stocks of their blasters and were noisily freezing to death.

Monitoring all this on his CCTV screens, the Red Lord was observed to frown. "What's the matter, boss?" asked a particularly brave and loyal elf, who'd been with him since the good old thunder-and-lightning days. "They're just a bunch of overgrown mice. The lads'll have 'em for breakfast."

"Better not," the Red Lord replied. "You don't know where they've been. You know the one thing I was slightly concerned about?"

"I dunno, boss. Neutron bombs?"

"Sappers," the Red Lord replied. "Nasty, determined little men digging tunnels under the walls." He stood aside from the screen so the elf could see. "Like that," he added.

Pyramids of granulated ice were forming on the frozen plateau. "What're they up to?"

"Burrowing. Funny, really. I was expecting earth-moving equipment, heavy plant and machinery. I never expected them to use their teeth. I think we may have to fall back on Plan C."

"You mean Plan B."

"No. Plan B was to take out the big yellow diggers with low-level strafing runs from the sleigh. Plan C . . ."

The elf gazed eagerly at him. "Yes, boss?"

"Is to make it up as we go along. Think you can do that?"

The elf was, above all, a realist. "No, boss."

"Me neither. Right then. Plan D."

The elf looked at him in wonder. "There's a Plan D?"

"There is now." The Red Lord stood up and hefted a thunderbolt in his right hand. It had been a long time since he'd had occasion to use one, and it was a moment before he remembered where to look for the point of balance, which is always further back than you think. He armed it, and it started to glow an alarming shade of light blue. "Fall in A and B Companies," he said. "C Company to the ramparts, D and E in reserve. Oh, and I'll be needing the sleigh."

The elf was mesmerised by the sight of the glowing thunderbolt, and the Red Lord could see his point. Mankind had developed a theory to account for the effects of the last time he'd used one, called tectonic shift. It was ingenious and completely wrong. "Just like the old days, eh, boss?"

"I bloody well hope not," the Red Lord said. "I've only just got used to Australia being an island."

"But you're going to blast them, aren't you?" the elf said hopefully. "Real good?"

"Depends on whether Plan D works."

The elf dashed off to his duty station while the Red Lord took a last look at the TV monitors. A shadow fell across the screen. He turned and saw Jersey, who was staring at the thunderbolt.

"Is that what I think it is?"

"Yup."

"As a legendary warrior of my own people once said, do you think that's wise, sir?"

"Certainly not. Trouble is, when I did my godhead training, you had to specialise at the end of First Year. You could do wisdom or you could do thunder and lightning. I couldn't stand the wisdom tutor, and there was this water nymph I was quite keen on doing Theory of Thunder. Was there something?"

"What? Oh yes. I forgot all about it until I found it in my trouser pocket."

The Red Lord raised an eyebrow. "It being?"

"This." Jersey held out a crumpled sheet of paper. "Lucy gave it to me. She said you might find it useful."

The Red Lord took it with his free hand, glanced at it and whistled. "That young woman," he said, "is so much too good for you. When this is all over, I'm definitely going to offer her a job."

"What sort of a job?"

"Mine, probably. She'd be ever so much better at it than me." He folded the paper and stuffed it his pocket. "Now go away and make yourself useful. You know what? Things are looking up."

He got out the piece of paper again and reread it, just to make sure. When he looked up, Jersey was still there. He pointed this out.

"Make myself useful in what way?"

"Don't ask me. You could sharpen something or patrol a corridor. Or there's always mountains of washing-up in the canteen."

Jersey scowled at him. "When I was in Hell," he said, "I met the boss of the Bank of the Dead. He said one day there'd be statues of me. There'd be a place called Thorpe City."

The Red Lord pursed his lips. "Irresponsible," he said.

"There's rules about that sort of thing. Nobody takes any notice of them, but there are rules."

"The point being," Jersey said, "clearly at some stage I do something that makes all the difference and saves the day."

"Arguably. Of course, it's possible that History gets it all completely wrong. It does that sometimes. I mean, look at King Arthur. And Oliver Winchester didn't invent the Winchester rifle, he just bought up the patent when the inventor went bust. I wouldn't worry about it if I were you."

"Clearly," Jersey said grimly, "I do something really heroic, and I haven't done it yet. Logically, it seems to me, the most likely time for me to do something heroic is in the big battle. Destiny is ringing my doorbell. But I probably won't hear it if I'm stuck in the kitchen washing glasses."

"And Jackie Dao said all that, did he? A statue?"

"Statues, plural. And a whole city."

"Silly bugger. Oh well. In that case you'd better take command of the army."

Jersey's mouth dropped open. "Me?"

"I suppose so. Manifest destiny and all that, and Jackie Dao's usually right about these things. Never ever play Ludo with that man. Well, don't just stand there. Go and get yourself some nice shiny armour and a helmet with a plume on it."

"All right," Jersey said. "I'll do that. Right away."

When he'd gone, the Red Lord read the bit of paper a third time, then folded it neatly and tucked it into the top of his boot. "Thorpe City, for crying out loud," he muttered. Then he wrapped a hanky around the thunderbolt and set off for the war.

*

The Veltrons had hit solid rock. It was slowing them down a bit, but not so you'd notice. The only real difference was that the spoil heaps were a dirty grey instead of white. Snib Venturi watched the heaps grow from the window of his trailer and turned up the heating. The cold didn't agree with him, and neither did the white glare of the ice. White, for pity's sake! What kind of a colour was that? Hurts your eyes and shows the dirt. Once all this nonsense was over, there'd be some changes made to this planet, and damn the expense.

The door flew open. Knocking first was one of Ab's blind spots, like when to put in apostrophes and which knife and fork to use for which course. "He's here."

"Who's here, bro?"

"Him. The jolly fat man. The reindeer guy."

"Shoot him."

"Tried that. Didn't work. And he's got a thunderbolt, and he says if we fire any more rockets at him he'll be seriously annoyed. You'd better come."

A thunderbolt didn't sound good. Certain levels of collateral damage were only to be expected, but there are limits. Snib thought about the insurance policy and stood up. "Who let that lunatic past the checkpoint with a thunderbolt?" he said. "And tell the rat people to knock it off for now. It's time we settled this."

As soon as Snib got outside he realised that he'd done Security an injustice. In the middle of the dreary ice plain stood a chimney stack at least a thousand feet tall. "It just appeared out of nowhere," Ab whispered in his ear. "We hit it with laser pulse cannon, but they just bounced off. So we tried interphasic torpedoes—"

Snib shook his head. Any form of conventional munitions would be a waste of time and money because of course the chimney wasn't really there, except in the eye of the beholder, where it mattered most. Which is why discerning gods throughout the ages have always opted for belief-based ordnance systems. If you believe your armour will stop the bullet, and so does the firer, the actual capabilities of the weapon are irrelevant. Faith, as Fidelicorp Weapons Systems put it in all their advertising material, it's not just for moving mountains any more.

Ab was clinging to his arm. "Shall I call the rat people?"

Snib shook him off gently and shook his head. "He's just a jerk," he said. "I ain't afraid of him."

"Wait for me. I'm coming too."

"No, Ab, you stay here. This won't take long."

"I'm coming too."

Snib felt his temper rise to breaking point, then ebb away. "Sure, bro," he said. "We'll do this together. Like old times."

"Just like old times."

Thus it was that the Venturi boys advanced alone across the frozen waste, Snib striding purposefully, Ab squarely behind him but keeping pace. When they were a dozen yards from the foot of the chimney a red shape reared up out of the grate and said, "That's far enough."

Snib looked at the thunderbolt in the Red Lord's hand. "You can put that thing down for a start. Or else no parley."

The Red Lord shrugged and laid the thunderbolt down. A cloud of steam hissed up around him. He blew it away. "Sorry," he said. "I didn't know it would bother you so much."

Snib glared at him. "You just proved my point," he said. "Anybody who'd even consider using one of those things inside an atmosphere isn't fit to own a planet."

"Valid point," the Red Lord said. The thunderbolt

stopped glowing. "I really only wanted to get your attention."

"You got it."

"Splendid. Now I suggest we talk about this like rational creatures."

Snib shrugged. "I'm listening."

The Red Lord took a deep breath. "Splendid. Here goes then. You obviously don't like me. I can't say I'm crazy about you. I was quite happy to carry on the same as I've been doing ever since the last lot took over, but I gather you don't like that idea."

"You're a nuisance," Snib said.

"Thank you."

"And an anomaly. People believe in you, even though they know I'm real and I'm in control. It confuses the issue. That's why you've got to go."

The Red Lord smiled. "I can see where you're coming from. On the other hand, I don't much like the idea of being wiped off the face of the Earth. That's immortality for you. Habit-forming."

"Funny man. But I'm a reasonable guy, Mr. Claus. You pack up your elves and your sleigh and your tinsel and get the Hell off my planet, and everything will be just dandy. You have one hour."

"I don't think so," the Red Lord said. "Suppose I do just that. Suppose I find another planet somewhere just entering its early Jurassic phase. I know exactly what'll happen. I'll just be settled in nicely when you'll turn up on the doorstep and throw me out, and the same thing, over and over again. Sorry, no. I like it here. I think I'll stay. You can stay too if you like, but leave me alone."

"I can't do that," Snib said.

The Red Lord sighed. "No," he said, "I don't suppose you can; it's not in your nature. All right, here's the schedule for today. For the next hour or so we have one doozy of a battle. You wipe out all my elves, whereupon I nuke your rat people with my thunderbolt and start a new Ice Age in the process. Or we settle this sensibly like grown-ups. What do you say?"

Snib stared at him for five seconds. Then he shrugged. "The rat people are mercenaries," he said. "You nuke them, I don't have to pay them. And Ice Ages aren't so bad."

"You really want to fight?"

"Of course not. But the alternative is you continuing to exist."

The Red Lord smiled. "Well, I don't want to fight," he said. "Fighting is silly. So I think I'll give in quietly and withdraw."

Ab made a funny squeaking noise. Snib ignored him. "You do that."

"And then I can spend the rest of eternity telling people how it was me who brought down Venturicorp and sent Ab and Snib Venturi back to snuffling for scraps in dustbins, where they belong."

Snib went bright red, and jets of steam shot up from under the soles of his feet. "Don't you *ever*—"

"Even as we speak," the Red Lord said pleasantly, "my sleigh is heading out of this solar system towards the offices of United Galactic Press on Delta Leonis Two. When it gets there, in about five minutes, unless he hears from me first, one of my elves will hand the editor a memo, in your handwriting, setting out the whole story behind the collapse of the Bank of Ultimate Truth. I don't think the editor likes you very much, so we can pretty much predict what tomorrow's lead headline is going to be. And after that, goodbye, Venturicorp. Of course, it'll mean economic disaster for five galaxies, but I can't help that. I didn't start this, after all."

For a long time Snib couldn't seem to make his tongue work. Then he said, "You're bullshitting. There's no such memo."

"Yes, there is. You sent it to your brother—hi there, Ab—and instead of eating it or setting fire to it the moment he'd read it, like any sensible being would've done, he left it lying on his desk for the first prisoner he interrogated to pick up and stuff down her blouse." He smiled. "She's smart, that girl. Probably now you'll have her killed, which is a waste. But I can't help that either."

"You'd do that?" Snib said. "You'd trash the economy of known space just to be able to say you beat me?"

"Let me see. Yes, I would, if you make me." The Red Lord cut out the grin. "But on balance I'd prefer not to."

Snib breathed out long and hard through his nose. "All right," he said, "let's hear it."

"Why don't we settle this in the spirit it deserves? Leave it to pure chance. Toss a coin."

"That's crazy," Snib exploded. "That's *stupid*."

"Not stupid," the Red Lord said. "Frivolous. There's a difference. It's a crucial one, and you'll never understand it as long as you live. Go on, Snib, what've you got to lose? Either way I'll call off my elf, Venturicorp won't crash and burn, and you'll have a straight fifty-fifty chance of winning. Or we can both lose, a lot of people will die, this planet will be wrecked and five galaxies will be sent back to the Dark Ages. Come on, Snib, be a sport. Where's your sense of fun?"

There was a silence that lasted for ever and ever, world without end. Then Snib said, "Fine. Let's do that."

"Excellent." The Red Lord stuck his hand in his pocket. "Now, it just so happens I have a coin with—"

Snib laughed. "I wasn't born yesterday. We use our coin."

The Red Lord glared at him. "All right, be like

that. And if you don't trust me, I don't trust you. Ab can toss the coin. You can manage that, can't you, little brother?"

Ab shot his brother an agonised glance. "Sure he can," Snib growled. "He's worth a million of you any day."

"It's a deal, then. Ab tosses, I call."

Ab fumbled in his pocket, spilled his keys and handkerchief out onto the ice, stooped and picked up a one-dollar coin. "Let him see it," Snib growled. "Satisfied?"

The Red Lord nodded. "One perfectly ordinary, genuine dollar bit," he said. "When you're ready, Mr. Venturi."

Ab balanced the coin on his trembling thumbnail and flicked it into the air. It soared and tumbled; Ab tried to catch it and knocked it flying across the ice; he jumped forward and put his foot over it. "Call," he said.

"Heads."

Ab lifted his foot. The Red Lord strolled over and looked down. "Heads it is. Isn't that right, Ab?"

Ab nodded. "He's right, bro. Sorry."

The Red Lord stooped, picked up the coin and dropped it in his pocket. "You won't begrudge me a souvenir," he said. "Right, I want you and your junk and your goons off this planet in three minutes. Which will leave me thirty seconds to call off my elf. Savvy?"

Snib gazed at him. "Savvy," he said quietly.

*

"That was Plan D?"

The Red Lord slumped into his throne and gave Jersey a weary scowl. "It worked, didn't it?"

On a TV screen a yard or so away Snib Venturi was telling the people of Earth about the change of management. He seemed very calm, almost relieved. "You know what?"

the Red Lord said. "I almost envy him. He's just got out of trying to keep order in this madhouse, and now that job's landed on me. Lucky bastard."

"You risked the fate of this planet on the toss of a coin. That's—"

"Shh. I want to listen to this bit."

Generosity in defeat, at least in public, is an old Martian tradition, and Snib Venturi was a very old Martian. "From now on," he was saying, "your planet will be under the watchful eye of someone who needs no introduction from me. You all know him as a fat man with a cotton-wool beard who comes down chimneys, but from now on he'll hold your destinies in the palm of his chubby hand. Yes, Virginia, there is a Santa Claus, and with immediate effect he's your lawfully constituted government. That's right, ladies and gentlemen of Earth, your new owner is Father Christmas. I kid you not. Goodnight, bless you all, and we now return you to your scheduled programme, *Miracle on 34th Street*."

The screen went black. There were little red spots in the middle of the Red Lord's otherwise milk-white cheeks, but he was smiling. "I call that quite gracious in the circumstances," he said. "Ah, sod it. I suppose I'd better go out there and talk to them before they start setting light to parked cars. You, stay here, mind the store. If anybody prays, take a message."

Jersey gazed levelly at him for a moment. "I still say it was a stupid, irresponsible risk."

The Red Lord sighed. "No, not really," he said. "It was a Venturi coin. Heads on both sides. Be good while I'm gone. If you ask the elves nicely, they'll probably find you someone to eat."

*

Outside on the ice there was already a media scrum twenty yards thick, through which, with great effort and violence, an angry old man and his red-faced son were forcing their way as the Red Lord walked out into a cordon of straining elves.

"You bastard!" the old man yelled.

"Language, Dad."

"You no-good, conniving, treacherous son of a bitch!"

"Dad," Jay hissed earnestly, "not in front of the humans, OK? There are people *filming us*."

The Red Lord stopped, grinned at the old man and threw back his hood. "Hello there," he said. "Long time no see. What are you doing here?"

"We were going to buy it back," the old man shouted. "We were in negotiations with the Venturi. Everything was going to be fine. And then you had to—"

"Save the day at extreme inconvenience and personal risk." The Red Lord frowned. "Which would never have been necessary if you hadn't sold out in the first place. And another thing. If you think Snib Venturi would've sold this lot back to you, you're delusional."

Jay grabbed the Red Lord's sleeve. "Don't you dare talk to my father like that."

An elf prised Jay's fingers open. The Red Lord gave him an it's-all-right nod, and the elf let Jay go. "Snib just wanted you to pay to have me killed," the Red Lord went on. "He would never have done a deal with you. And by the way, if you're happy humiliating yourself in front of the massed lenses of your former subjects, that's fine by me. An you hurt none, do what ye will, that's always been my motto."

The old man raised his hand as if to throw something, then apparently realised it was empty. "You ain't heard the last of this, reindeer boy," he said. "We'll be back."

The Red Lord shook his head. "In about five minutes," he said, "you're going to feel such a fool. Leave them be, fellas. They're harmless enough."

Elves gently but firmly pressed the old man and his son back into the crowd. The Red Lord moved on towards the small stack of packing crates the elves had put together for him to stand on. He climbed up, wobbled a bit, got his balance and held his hand up. Immediately the crowd fell silent. The Red Lord cleared his throat and began to speak.

"Hello there, boys and girls," he said in a voice that echoed off the firmament yet barely rose above a whisper. "Now I know all of you, and you all know me. Hi there, Luke, Karen, Steve, Jayden, Mark; say, haven't you grown? I think nearly all of you have seen me before, though you thought I thought you were asleep. You may all have forgotten about me, but I've been keeping my eye on you, every single one of you. I know who's naughty and who's nice." He stopped and turned his head slowly, and everyone in the crowd met his eye and looked down, flushing. "There's a nice line in the old scriptures, *to whom all desires are known and from whom no secrets are hid*. Well, I guess that's me. And believe me, the desires are not a problem as far as I'm concerned, and the secrets are no big deal. By and large, you're an OK bunch of bipeds. You're decent enough people, given half the chance. I think we'll get along nicely.

"Now you tried the old way, laws and rules and the rule of law, and I think we can all agree it was a mistake. No law or rule ever stopped anyone from doing bad stuff until it was too late, and I reckon the concept of punishment sucks, so we won't be doing that any more. You tried the Venturi way—unfettered capitalism and the free flow of market forces—and it was an improvement, but there was no fun any more, no joy, and I think there's a bit more to life than economic necessity. I never was much of a one for political theory, and in my view ethics is just an eastern county in England pronounced with a lisp. I like to keep things simple. That way we all know where we stand.

"From now on it's presents at Christmas for everybody, not just kids. Now I think you all know I make a list, and in that list there are two categories, the good N and the bad N. And I know when you're sleeping, and I know when you're awake, so if you want your heart's desire in your stocking on Christmas Eve, you know what you've got to do, and if you want coal, you know how to go about that too. Simple as that. You can have everything you really and truly want, or not; the choice is yours. Just don't for one second believe that anything you do or say or think will go undetected, because it won't. I'll know, and you can be sure about that."

The Red Lord paused and looked around again, and once again nobody could meet his eye for more than a moment. Then he grinned and continued: "Unfortunately it's not quite that simple, because there's times when, with the best will in the world, we don't know what the right thing is, and that's why I want to introduce you to a young man who I think will be able to help you." He raised his hands, and two elves came forward with a large sack. They opened it, and Kevin fell out.

"This," the Red Lord said, "is Kevin. Now Kevin is a good egg, but all I ever gave him was a cowboy hat, so he's due a whole lot of back presents. So, to put things right, I'm going to give him the Earth and all that therein is." He smiled. "Say thank you, Kevin."

Kevin struggled to his feet and blinked twice. "Thank you," he said.

"You're welcome. Now I'm giving this planet and the

whole lot of you to Kevin here because I know he'll take care of it, and you. I strongly suggest you get to know him. He'll be visiting your neighbourhood some time very soon. Kevin isn't going to tell you what to do, and he's not going to smite you with a thunderbolt if you don't do it; that's not his way. He doesn't want your money, and he's not going to look down his nose at you if you want to be different from the people next door. But once you've got to know him, if ever you're in two minds about what the right course of action might be, or whether you're being naughty or nice, you just ask yourself what would Kevin do? That's it," the Red Lord said. "That's all there is to it, the law and the prophets. And if you can't figure it out for yourself, then just ask him, and he'll be happy to tell you. Short of assembling flat-pack furniture or reinstalling Windows, he's the go-to guy for the difficult questions. Him, remember, not me. I've got far too much on my plate as it is."

There was dead silence. Kevin smiled feebly, lifted his hand and waved, and three rows back Dad turned to Jay and whispered, "That's my boy."

*

Since nobody seemed to want him for anything, Jersey liberated one of the Veltron skimmers and flew to the nearest hellmouth, then walked down to the Hole in the Wall. He found Mr. Dao flicking beads along the strings of his abacus. "You lied to me."

Mr. Dao looked up. "No," he said.

"Yes, you did. You said there'd be statues of me, and Thorpe City. But I didn't do anything."

Mr. Dao smiled. "Sit down and have a cup of tea. That's an order."

Jersey felt as though his legs had been kicked out from

under him by an invisible boot. "I was just a bit player," he said. "A sidekick."

"Hardly even that," Mr. Dao said gently. "But I told you the truth. There will be statues, lots of them. They'll represent the crucial turning point in human history, the moment when the Blessed Lucy gave Jersey Thorpe the Venturi memo. People will come from miles around to gaze at them and remember how one act of intelligence and courage—"

"Yes, all right," Jersey snapped. "But what about Thorpe City? They don't call towns after sidekicks."

Mr. Dao patted the back of his hand. "In most Western cultures they have a strange tradition, which I have to say I've never understood, but who am I to pass judgement? In your society it's the custom that when a woman gets married, she takes her husband's name. Hence," he added, "Thorpe City." He poured some more tea and sipped it. "Actually, there is a Jersey City," he said. "You may have heard of it. It's not called after you, of course, but you can pretend it is, if it makes you feel better."

Jersey was staring at him as if he had diamonds dribbling from his nose. "Husband?"

"She likes you," Mr. Dao said, "but not when you're being an arsehole. Come to think of it, she's sitting at that table in the corner over there, eating caramel shortcake. You might do worse than go and talk to her."

"I—"

"Only do try not to be a jerk," Mr. Dao said. "I know it's hard, but sometimes we have to do the difficult things if we want to get our heart's desire. Even if we don't deserve it."

Jersey peeped over Mr. Dao's shoulder and saw her. She saw him too and waved.

"I think I might just go and say hello," Jersey said.

"And sorry," Mr. Dao said. "Mustn't forget that. *I*

promise not to be a pain in the bum ever again probably wouldn't hurt either. But far be it from me to interfere."

"Look," Jersey said. "About the money you lent me. I thought I'd be able to get it back from Santa, but when I asked he pretended he couldn't hear me. So . . ."

Mr. Dao sighed and flicked a bead across a wire. "Forget about the money," he said. "I just shorted Venturicorp at two dollars seventy-seven. Didn't Santa mention it? Money will never be a problem for anyone on this planet, ever again."

"Ah. Well, in that case . . ."

Mr. Dao pressed his palms together in formal salutation. "Go in peace, little brother. Remember what I said about not being a—"

"Yes. Thank you."

As he walked across the cafe, Jersey tried to think of the right words, but they didn't seem to be at home. As he took the last step, and she looked up from the book she was reading, a voice in his head said, *What would Kevin say?* And so he sat down beside her and said, "Hello."

"Hi."

"I'm really sorry for being a pig."

"Good."

"I don't deserve you."

She smiled at him. "What on Earth has deserving got to do with anything?"

He thought about that. "I don't know."

"You've been talking to Mr. Dao."

"Yes."

"He told you. About Thorpe City."

"He told you?"

She nodded. "Do you mind?"

He shook his head. "No."

"Go on. You do mind. Just a bit."

"Well, yes, just a bit. But only because I'd assumed—"

She smiled at him. "We don't do assuming any more. We think with our brains instead."

He nodded. "That would be better, yes."

And then she kissed him.

49

Snib Venturi woke up with a start, out of a dream of shimmering nebulas. He'd always been a light sleeper. On the streets where he'd grown up you had to be if you wanted your shoes to still be there in the morning.

There was, or had been, someone else in the room. He reached under his pillow and his fingers closed on the butt of his blaster. Then he found the light switch with his other hand.

Nobody there. But, at the end of the bed, a big red stocking. There were giants on the fifth planet of the ninth sun of the Leonis cluster whose feet would have filled it, but they mostly wore sandals. Snib thumbed the intercom and called his new chief of Security.

"Bernie?"

"Here, Mr. V."

"Get a team with scanners in here right now. I think someone may have left me a bomb."

So the security team came and scanned the stocking, and there were lots of bleeps and clicks and high-pitched whistles. But no bomb. "It's safe," the team leader said, "whatever the Hell it is."

"There's something inside it."

So the security people got a remote-controlled robot, which opened the stocking with its hydraulic arm and pulled out a square box. It was wrapped in paper decorated with holly wreaths and jolly robins, and there was a big red bow and a tag which read, HAPPY MARTIAN WINTER SOLSTICE.

"Thanks, boys," Snib said. "Now get lost."

Snib opened the box, and inside it was the most beautiful thing he'd ever seen: a gold and silver model galactic Core, exquisitely reproduced in folded metallic tissue, like a rose. Well, more like a cauliflower, but stunningly lovely nevertheless, and in the very heart of the swirling folds was a single teardrop-shaped diamond—which is, after all, just a form of coal that's been under enormous pressure for some time and then finally gets its chance to shine. A bit like Snib Venturi.

He stared at it for a long time. Then he grinned. "Ab!" he yelled at the top of his voice. "Get in here. You gotta see this!"

extras

orbit

meet the author

© Charlie Hopkinson   Tom Holt

Tom Holt was born in London in 1961. At Oxford he studied bar billiards, ancient Greek agriculture and the care and feeding of small, temperamental Japanese motorcycle engines; interests which led him, perhaps inevitably, to qualify as a solicitor and emigrate to Somerset, where he specialised in death and taxes for seven years before going straight in 1995. Now a full-time writer, he lives in Chard, Somerset, with his wife, one daughter and the unmistakable scent of blood, wafting in on the breeze from the local meat-packing plant.

if you enjoyed
THE MANAGEMENT STYLE OF THE SUPREME BEINGS

look out for

KINGS OF THE WYLD

The Band: Book One

by

Nicholas Eames

GLORY NEVER GETS OLD.

Clay Cooper and his band were once the best of the best, the most feared and renowned crew of mercenaries this side of the Heartwyld.

Their glory days long past, the mercs have grown apart and grown old, fat, drunk, or a combination of the three. Then an ex-bandmate turns up at Clay's door with a plea for help—the kind of mission that only the very brave or the very stupid would sign up for.

It's time to get the band back together.

Chapter One

A Ghost on the Road

You'd have guessed from the size of his shadow that Clay Cooper was a bigger man than he was. He was certainly bigger than most, with broad shoulders and a chest like an iron-strapped keg. His hands were so large that most mugs looked like teacups when he held them, and the jaw beneath his shaggy brown beard was wide and sharp as a shovel blade. But his shadow, drawn out by the setting sun, skulked behind him like a dogged reminder of the man he used to be: great and dark and more than a little monstrous.

Finished with work for the day, Clay slogged down the beaten track that passed for a thoroughfare in Coverdale, sharing smiles and nods with those hustling home before dark. He wore a Watchmen's green tabard over a shabby leather jerkin, and a weathered sword in a rough old scabbard on his hip. His shield—chipped and scored and scratched through the years by axes and arrows and raking claws—was slung across his back, and his helmet...well, Clay had lost the one the Sergeant had given him last week, just as he'd misplaced the one given to him the month before, and every few months since the day he'd signed on to the Watch almost ten years ago now.

A helmet restricted your vision, all but negated your hearing, and more often than not made you look stupid as hell. Clay Cooper didn't do helmets, and that was that.

"Clay! Hey, Clay!" Pip trotted over. The lad wore the Watchmen's green as well, his own ridiculous head-pan tucked in the crook of one arm. "Just got off duty at the south gate," he said cheerily. "You?"

"North."

"Nice." The boy grinned and nodded as though Clay had said something exceptionally interesting instead of having just mumbled the word *north*. "Anything exciting out there?"

Clay shrugged. "Mountains."

"Ha! 'Mountains,' he says. Classic. Hey, you hear Ryk Yarsson saw a centaur out by Tassel's farm?"

"It was probably a moose."

The boy gave him a skeptical look, as if Ryk spotting a moose instead of a centaur was highly improbable. "Anyway. Come to the King's Head for a few?"

"I shouldn't," said Clay. "Ginny's expecting me home, and…" He paused, having no other excuse near to hand.

"C'mon," Pip goaded. "Just one, then. One drink."

Clay grunted, squinting into the sun and measuring the prospect of Ginny's wrath against the bitter bite of ale washing down his throat. "Fine," he relented. "One."

Because it was hard work looking north all day, after all.

The King's Head was already crowded, its long tables crammed with people who came as much to gab and gossip as they did to drink. Pip slinked toward the bar while Clay found a seat at a table as far from the stage as possible.

The talk around him was the usual sort: weather and war, and neither topic too promising. There'd been a great battle fought out west in Endland, and by the murmurings it hadn't gone off well. A Republic army of twenty thousand, bolstered by several hundred mercenary bands, had been slaughtered by a Heartwyld Horde. Those few who'd survived had retreated to the city of Castia and were now under siege, forced to endure sickness and starvation while the enemy gorged themselves on the dead outside their walls. That, and there'd been a touch of frost on the ground this morning, which didn't seem fair this early into autumn, did it?

Pip returned with two pints and two friends Clay didn't recognize, whose names he forgot just as soon as they told him. They seemed like nice enough fellows, mind you. Clay was just bad with names.

"So you were in a band?" one asked. He had lanky red hair, and his face was a postpubescent mess of freckles and swollen pimples.

Clay took a long pull from his tankard before setting it down and looking over at Pip, who at least had the grace to look ashamed. Then he nodded.

The two stole a glance at each other, and then Freckles leaned in across the table. "Pip says you guys held Coldfire Pass for three days against a thousand walking dead."

"I only counted nine hundred and ninety-nine," Clay corrected. "But pretty much, yeah."

"He says you slew Akatung the Dread," said the other, whose attempt to grow a beard had produced a wisp of hair most grandmothers would scoff at.

Clay took another drink and shook his head. "We only injured him. I hear he died back at his lair, though. Peacefully. In his sleep."

They looked disappointed, but then Pip nudged one with his elbow. "Ask him about the Siege of Hollow Hill."

"Hollow Hill?" murmured Wispy, then his eyes went round as courtmark coins. "Wait, the Siege of Hollow Hill? So the band you were in..."

"*Saga*," Freckles finished, clearly awestruck. "You were in *Saga*."

"It's been a while," said Clay, picking at a knot in the warped wood of the table before him. "The name sounds familiar, though."

"Wow," sighed Freckles.

"You gotta be kidding me," Wispy uttered.

"Just...wow," said Freckles again.

"You *gotta* be kidding me," Wispy repeated, not one to be outdone when it came re-expressing disbelief.

Clay said nothing in response, only sipped his beer and shrugged.

"So you know Golden Gabe?" Freckles asked.

Another shrug. "I know Gabriel, yeah."

"Gabriel!" trilled Pip, sloshing his drink as he raised his hands in wonderment. "'*Gabriel*,' he says! Classic."

"And Ganelon?" Wispy asked. "And Arcandius Moog? And Matrick Skulldrummer?"

"Oh, and..." Freckles screwed up his face as he racked his brain—which didn't do the poor bastard any favours, Clay decided. He was ugly as a rain cloud on a wedding day, that one. "Who are we forgetting?"

"Clay Cooper."

Wispy stroked the fine hairs on his chin as he pondered this. "Clay Cooper...oh," he said, looking abashed. "Right."

It took Freckles another moment to piece it together, but then he palmed his pale forehead and laughed. "Gods, I'm stupid."

The gods already know, thought Clay.

Sensing the awkwardness at hand, Pip chimed in. "Tell us a tale, will ya, Clay? About when you did for that necromancer up in Oddsford. Or when you rescued that princess from... that place...remember?"

Which one? Clay wondered. They'd rescued several princesses, in fact, and if he'd killed one necromancer he'd killed a dozen. Who kept track of shit like that? Didn't matter anyway, since he wasn't in the mood for storytelling. Or to go digging up what he'd worked so hard to bury, and then harder still to forget where he'd dug the hole in the first place.

"Sorry, kid," he told Pip, draining what remained of his beer. "That's one."

He excused himself, handing Pip a few coppers for the drink and bidding what he hoped was a last farewell to Freckles and Wispy. He shouldered his way to the door and gave a long sigh when he emerged into the cool quiet outside. His back hurt from slumping over that table, so he stretched it out, craning his neck and gazing up at the first stars of the evening.

He remembered how small the night sky used to make him feel. How *insignificant*. And so he'd gone and made a big deal of himself, figuring that someday he might look up at the vast sprawl of stars and feel undaunted by its splendour. It hadn't worked. After a while Clay tore his eyes from the darkening sky and struck out down the road toward home.

He exchanged pleasantries with the Watchmen at the west gate. Had he heard about the centaur spotting over by Tassel's farm? they wondered. How about the battle out west, and those poor bastards holed up in Castia? Rotten, rotten business.

Clay followed the track, careful to keep from turning an ankle in a rut. Crickets were chirping in the tall grass to either side, the wind in the trees above him sighing like the ocean surf. He stopped by the roadside shrine to the Summer Lord and threw a dull copper at the statue's feet. After a few steps and a moment's hesitation he went back and tossed another. Away from town it was darker still, and Clay resisted the urge to look up again.

Best keep your eyes on the ground, he told himself, *and leave the past where it belongs. You've got what you've got, Cooper, and it's just what you wanted, right? A kid, a wife, a simple life.* It was an honest living. It was comfortable.

He could almost hear Gabriel scoff at that. *Honest? Honest is boring*, his old friend might have said. *Comfortable is dull.* Then again, Gabriel had got himself married long before Clay. Had a little girl of his own, even—a woman grown by now.

And yet there was Gabe's spectre just the same, young and fierce and glorious, smirking in the shadowed corner of Clay's mind. "We were *giants*, once," he said. "Bigger than life. And now..."

"Now we are tired old men," Clay muttered, to no one but the night. And what was so wrong with that? He'd met plenty of *actual* giants in his day, and most of them were assholes.

Despite Clay's reasoning, the ghost of Gabriel continued to haunt his walk home, gliding past him on the road with a sly wink, waving from his perch on the neighbour's fence, crouched like a beggar on the stoop of Clay's front door. Only this last Gabriel wasn't young at all. Or particularly fierce looking. Or any more glorious than an old board with a rusty nail in it. In fact, he looked pretty fucking terrible. When he saw Clay coming he stood, and smiled. Clay had never seen a man look so sad in all the years of his life.

The apparition spoke his name, which sounded to Clay as real as the crickets buzzing, as the wind moaning through the trees along the road. And then that brittle smile broke, and Gabriel—really, truly Gabriel, and not a ghost after all—was sagging into Clay's arms, sobbing into his shoulder, clutching at his back like a child afraid of the dark.

"Clay," he said. "Please...I need your help."

Chapter Two

Rose

Once Gabriel recovered himself they went inside. Ginny turned from the stove and her jaw clamped tight. Griff came bounding over, stubby tail wagging. He gave Clay a cursory sniff and then set to smelling Gabe's leg as though it were a piss-drenched tree, which wasn't actually too far off the mark.

His old friend was in a sorry state, no mistake. His hair and beard were a tangled mess, his clothes little more than soiled rags. There were holes in his boots, toes peeking out from the ruined leather like grubby urchins. His hands were busy fidgeting, wringing each other or tugging absentmindedly at the hem of his tunic. Worst of all, though, were his eyes. They were sunk deep in his haggard face, hard and haunted, as though everywhere he looked was something he wished he hadn't seen.

"Griff, lay off," said Clay. The dog, wet eyes and a lolling pink tongue in a black fur face, perked up at the sound of his name. Griff wasn't the noblest-looking creature, and he didn't have many uses besides licking food off a plate. He couldn't herd sheep or flush a grouse from cover, and if anyone ever broke in to the house he was more likely to fetch them slippers than scare 'em off. But it made Clay smile to look at him (that's how godsdamn adorable he was) and that was worth more than nothing.

"Gabriel." Ginny finally found her voice, though she stayed right where she was. Didn't smile. Didn't cross to hug him. She'd never much cared for Gabriel. Clay thought she probably blamed his old bandmate for all the bad habits (gambling, fighting, drinking to excess) that she'd spent the last ten years disabusing him of, and all the other bad habits (chewing with his mouth open, forgetting to wash his hands, occasionally throttling people) she was still struggling to purge.

Heaped upon that were the handful of times Gabe had come calling in the years since his own wife left him. Every time he appeared it was hand in hand with some grand scheme to reunite the old band and strike out once again in search of fame, fortune, and decidedly reckless adventure. There was a town down south needed rescue from a ravaging drake, or a den of walking wolves to be cleared out of the Wailing Forest, or an old lady in some far-flung corner of the realm needed help bringing laundry off the line and only Saga themselves could rise to her aid!

It wasn't as though Clay needed Ginny breathing down his neck to refuse, to see that Gabriel longed for something unrecoverable, like an old man clinging to memories of his golden youth. *Exactly* like that, actually. But life, Clay knew, didn't work that way. It wasn't a circle; you didn't go round and round again. It was an arc, its course as inexorable as the sun's trek across the sky, destined at its highest, brightest moment to begin its fall.

Clay blinked, having lost himself in his own head. He did that sometimes, and could have wished he was better at putting his thoughts into words. He'd sound a right clever bastard then, wouldn't he?

Instead, he'd stood there dumbly as the silence between Ginny and Gabriel lengthened uncomfortably.

"You look hungry," she said finally.

Gabriel nodded, his hands fidgeting nervously.

Ginny sighed, and then his wife—his kind, lovely, magnificent wife—forced a tight grin and reclaimed her spoon from the pot she'd been tending earlier. "Sit down then," she said over her shoulder. "I'll feed you. I made Clay's favourite: rabbit stew with mushrooms."

Gabriel blinked. "Clay hates mushrooms."

Seeing Ginny's back stiffen, Clay spoke up. "Used to," he said brightly, before his wife—his quick-tempered, sharp-tongued, utterly terrifying wife—could turn around and crack his skull with that wooden spoon. "Ginny does something to them, though. Makes them taste"—*Not so fucking awful,* was what first jumped to mind—"really pretty good," he finished lamely. "What is it you do to 'em, hun?"

"I stew them," she said in the most menacing way a woman could string those three words together.

Something very much like a smile tugged at the corner of Gabe's mouth.

He always did love to watch me squirm, Clay remembered. He took a chair and Gabriel followed suit. Griff trundled over to his mat and gave his balls a few good licks before promptly falling asleep. Clay fought down a surge of envy, seeing that. "Tally home?" he asked.

"Out," said Ginny. "Somewhere."

Somewhere close, he hoped. There were coyotes in the woods nearby. Wolves in the hills. Hell, Ryk Yarsson had seen a centaur out by Tassel's farm. Or a moose. Either of which might kill a young girl if caught by surprise. "She should've been home before dark," he said.

His wife scoffed at that. "So should you have, Clay Cooper. You putting in extra hours on the wall, or is that the King's Piss I smell on ya?" *King's Piss* was her name for the beer they served at the pub. It was a fair assessment, and Clay had laughed the first time she'd said it. Didn't seem as funny at the moment, however.

Not to Clay, anyway, though Gabriel's mood seemed to be lightening a bit. His old friend was smirking like a boy watching his brother take heat for a crime he didn't commit.

"She's just down in the marsh," Ginny said, fishing two ceramic bowls from the cupboard. "Be glad it's only frogs she'll bring home with her. It'll be boys soon enough, and you'll have plenty cause to worry then."

"Won't be me needs to worry," Clay mumbled.

Ginny scoffed at that, too, and he might have asked why had she not set a steaming bowl of stew in front of him. The wafting scent drew a ravenous growl from his stomach, even if there were mushrooms in it.

His wife took her cloak off the peg by the door. "I'll go and be sure Tally's all right," she said. "Might be she needs help carrying those frogs." She came over and kissed Clay on the top of his head, smoothing his hair down afterward. "You boys have fun catching up."

She got as far as opening the door before hesitating, looking back. First at Gabriel, already scooping at his bowl as if it were the first meal he'd had in a long while, and then at Clay, and it wasn't until a few days after (a hard choice and too many miles away already) that he understood what he'd seen in her eyes just then. A kind of sorrow, thoughtful and resigned, as though she already knew—his loving, beautiful, remarkably *astute* wife— what was coming, inevitable as winter, or a river's winding course to the sea.

A chill wind blew in from outside. Ginny shivered despite her cloak, then she left.

"It's Rose."

They had finished eating, set their bowls aside. He should have put them in the basin, Clay knew, got them soaking so they wouldn't be such a chore to clean later, but it suddenly seemed like he couldn't leave the table just now. Gabriel had come in the night, from a long way off, to say something. Best to let him say it and be done.

"Your daughter?" Clay prompted.

Gabe nodded slowly. His hands were both flat on the table. His eyes were fixed, unfocused, somewhere between them. "She is ... *willful*," he said finally. "Impetuous. I wish I could say she gets it from her mother, but ..." That smile again, just barely. "You remember I was teaching her to use a sword?"

"I remember telling you that was a bad idea," said Clay.

A shrug from Gabriel. "I just wanted her to be able to protect herself. You know, stick 'em with the pointy end and all that. But she wanted more. She wanted to be ..." he paused, searching for the word, "... great."

"Like her father?"

Gabriel's expression turned sour. "Just so. She heard too many stories, I think. Got her head filled with all this nonsense about being a hero, fighting in a band."

And from whom could she have heard all that? Clay wondered.

"I know," said Gabriel, perceiving his thoughts. "Partly my fault, I won't deny it. But it wasn't just me. Kids these days ... they're obsessed with these mercenaries, Clay. They worship them. It's unhealthy. And most of these mercs aren't even in real bands! They just hire a bunch of nameless goons to do their fighting while they paint their faces and parade around with shiny swords and fancy armour. There's even one guy—I shit you not—who rides a manticore into battle!"

"A manticore?" asked Clay, incredulous.

Gabe laughed bitterly. "I know, right? Who the fuck *rides* a manticore? Those things are dangerous! Well, I don't need to tell you."

He didn't, of course. Clay had a nasty-looking puncture scar on his right thigh, testament to the hazards of tangling with such monsters. A manticore was nobody's pet, and it certainly wasn't fit to ride. As if slapping wings and a poison-barbed tail on a lion made it somehow a *fine* idea to climb on its back!

"They worshipped us, too," Clay pointed out. "Well *you*, anyway. And Ganelon. They tell the stories, even still. They sing the songs."

The stories were exaggerated, naturally. The songs, for the most part, were wildly inaccurate. But they persisted. Had lasted long after the men themselves had outlived who (or what) they'd been.

We were giants once.

"It's not the same," Gabriel persisted. "You should see the crowds gather when these bands come to town, Clay. People screaming, women crying in the streets."

"That sounds horrible," said Clay, meaning it.

Gabriel ignored him, pressing on. "Anyhow, Rose wanted to learn the sword, so I indulged her. I figured she'd get bored of it sooner or later, and that if she was going to learn, it might as well be from me. And also it made her mother mad as hell."

It would have, Clay knew. Her mother, Valery, despised violence and weapons of any kind, along with those who used either toward any end whatsoever. It was partly because of Valery that Saga had dissolved all those years ago.

"Problem was," said Gabriel, "she was good. Really good, and that's not just a father's boasts. She started out sparring against kids her age, but when they gave up getting their asses whooped she went out looking for street fights, or wormed her way into sponsored matches."

"The daughter of Golden Gabe himself," Clay mused. "Must've been quite the draw."

"I guess so," his friend agreed. "But then one day Val saw the bruises. Lost her mind. Blamed me, of course, for everything.

She put her foot down—you know how she gets—and for a while Rose stopped fighting, but…" He trailed off, and Clay saw his jaw clamp down on something bitter. "After her mother left, Rosie and I…didn't get along so well, either. She started going out again. Sometimes she wouldn't come home for days. There were more bruises, and a few nastier scrapes besides. She chopped her hair off—thank the Holy Tetrea her mother was gone by then, or mine would've been next. And then came the cyclops."

"Cyclops?"

Gabriel looked at him askance. "Big bastards, one huge eye right here on their head?"

Clay leveled a glare of his own. "I know what a cyclops is, asshole."

"Then why did you ask?"

"I didn't…" Clay faltered. "Never mind. What *about* the cyclops?"

Gabriel sighed. "Well, one settled down in that old fort north of Ottersbrook. Stole some cattle, some goats, a dog, and then killed the folks that went looking for 'em. The courtsmen had their hands full, so they were looking for someone to clear the beast out for them. Only there weren't any mercs around at the time—or none with the chops to take on a cyclops, anyway. Somehow my name got tossed into the pot. They even sent someone round to ask if I would, but I told them no. Hell, I don't even own a sword anymore!"

Clay cut in again, aghast. "What? What about *Vellichor*?"

Gabriel's eyes were downcast. "I…uh…sold it."

"I'm sorry?" Clay asked, but before his friend could repeat himself he put his own hands flat on the table, for fear they would ball into fists, or snatch one of the bowls nearby and smash it over Gabriel's head. He said, as calmly as he could manage, "For a second there I thought you said that *you sold Vellichor*. As in the sword entrusted to you by the Archon himself as he lay dying? The sword he used to carve a fucking doorway from his world to ours. *That* sword? You sold *that sword?*"

Gabriel, who had slumped deeper into his chair with every word, nodded. "I had debts to pay, and Valery wanted it out of the house after she found out I taught Rose to fight," he said meekly. "She said it was dangerous."

"She—" Clay stopped himself. He leaned back in his chair, kneading his eyes with the palms of his hands. He groaned, and Griff, sensing his frustration, groaned himself from his mat in the corner. "Finish your story," he said at last.

Gabriel continued. "Well, needless to say, I refused to go after the cyclops, and for the next few weeks it caused a fair bit of havoc. And then suddenly word got around that someone had gone out and killed it." He smiled, wistful and sad. "All by herself."

"Rose," Clay said. Didn't make it a question. Didn't need to.

Gabriel's nod confirmed it. "She was a celebrity overnight. Bloody Rose, they called her. A pretty good name, actually."

It is, Clay agreed, but didn't bother saying so. He was still fuming about the sword. The sooner Gabe said whatever it was he'd come here to say, the sooner Clay could tell his oldest, dearest friend to get the hell out of his house and never come back.

"She even got her own band going," Gabe went on. "They managed to clear out a few nests around town: giant spiders, some old carrion wyrm down in the sewer that everyone forgot was still alive. But I hoped—" he bit his lip "—I still hoped, even then, that she might choose another path. A better path. Instead of following mine." He looked up. "Until the summons came from the Republic of Castia, asking every able sword to march against the Heartwyld Horde."

For a heartbeat Clay wondered at the significance of that. Until he remembered the news he'd heard earlier that evening. An army of twenty thousand, routed by a vastly more numerous host; the survivors surrounded in Castia, doubtless wishing they had died on the battlefield rather than endure the atrocities of a city under siege.

Which meant that Gabriel's daughter was dead. Or she would be, when the city fell.

Clay opened his mouth to speak, to try to keep the heartbreak from his voice as he did so. "Gabe, I—"

"I'm going after her, Clay. And I need you with me." Gabriel leaned forward in his chair, the flame of a father's fear and anger alight in his eyes. "It's time to get the band back together."